Designs of Darkness to Appall

Don Michael LaGrone, MD

Cover Design by Ben LaGrone

Editing by Matt Walker

This is a work of fiction. Names, characters, places, brands, media, and incidents are either the product of the author's imagination or are used fictitiously. Any resemblance to similarly named places or to persons living or deceased is unintentional.

The growing problem of PTSD in the military and how the military and the VA treat it are represented by true circumstances. The military has known the cause of PTSD and how to prevent it since 1943.

Library of Congress Control Number: 2016904541

This book is dedicated to Betty and Douglas Duffy,
whose warmth, love and intellect are in my heart.

Every gun that is made, every warship launched, every rocket fired signifies,
In the final sense, a theft from those who hunger and are not fed, those who
are cold and not clothed.
This world in arms is not spending money alone. It is spending the sweat of its
laborers, the genius of its scientists, the hopes of its children… This is not a way
of life in its true sense. Under the cloud of threatening war, it is humanity
hanging from a cross of iron.

Dwight D. Eisenhower

Part I:
Camp Valkyrie

Chapter 1

IT IS A STORY without end.

A young lieutenant deep in the heart of the jungle, leads his platoon wading forward through the mud and rain of the monsoon season. He hears the click beneath his feet. His last thought, his pregnant wife and the child she carries. In a moment the air is thick with charred palm leaves and bloody flesh. Men close to him are dead or dying. Crying, moaning. Body bags, always close at hand appear and bodies are quickly bagged, at least all of the body the medics could find and the lucky wounded are air evacuated. It makes widows and orphans and bereaved parents. It means pension machinery cranking up, and it makes the hearts of some swear pacifism and in the hearts of others, lasting hatred.

Ripples in a pond.

A soldier out of the kill area sees the carnage the blast has created, and shoots himself in the head. Another soldier, one who had been standing nearby just minutes before, will thereafter believe in Jesus or a rabbit's foot. Another man sees the remains of his best friend's skull, and the image will haunt him all the way to an asylum the rest of his days. The children will feel the father's trauma, which will be passed to his children's children...

Ripples of blood passing through generations.

* * *

It was a cold October morning in 1971, and Lieutenant Thomas Williams was dead.

The sound of the bugle woke Mike from his reverie. Never the morning person, he wiped the sleep from his eyes and shifted awkwardly. The leaves in the cemetery were still wet with dew. Before the grave was a casket draped in the stars-and-stripes. It was flanked by two members of the honor guard, their gloved hands raised in salute. Inside the casket was Tommy's left foot. At least, what remained of it.

Mike felt the pressure gripping his palm. It was the mother of the deceased, and he gave it a reassuring squeeze. As Tommy's best friend, Mike had grown up beneath Mrs. Williams's watchful eye. Now the two stood, silent, staring at a hole in the earth.

Tommy's father lingered near the back of the crowd. It was the first time Mike had seen the old man in a suit, he had to admit. He still could smell the cigars and whisky from a mile away. Mrs. Williams tightened her grip, and he realized the ring was gone from her finger. "So," he mused, "she never forgave him after all."

To the right of Mike was Tommy's widow. She had long blonde hair with a face smeared with powder to hide the tears. She sobbed throughout the ceremony, the mascara streaming down her cheeks onto her pregnant belly. Mike recognized several of his high school buddies, but he could think of nothing to say. The words dried on his tongue. Tommy was gone.

"What a difference a night makes," thought Mike. Just a few hours earlier he had ascended the podium to receive his medical degree. It was the proudest moment of his life. Medical school was tough—not just the long hours of reading and memorizing, but the arrogant hazing of the professors who loved to kick ass. After years of sacrifice he could finally call himself "Doctor" Michael Pike. Mostly he felt relief. All evening he had basked in the pride of family and friends alike. Now, here he was, hung over at his best friend's funeral. Tommy was gone, exterminated, blown to oblivion by a land mine quite possibly made in the USA where it is a big business protected by political graft and corruption.

*   *   *

"At the very least, the military gave him a proper send-off," offered Mike. He picked at the crumbs on his napkin. "Two servicemen to fold the flag. A bugler, even. I hear some families are lucky to get a letter and a recording of 'Taps.'"

It was a weak attempt at consolation, and he knew it. The reception was drawing to a close. The catering staff was already clearing the trays. Still, Mike felt the need to say something, anything, to the grieving mother.

The elderly Mrs. Williams had been silent all morning. She stared listlessly now at the tablecloth as she spoke. "A 'proper send-off.' Do you know what the officer said when he came to my door, Michael?"

She paused to pour another cup of coffee.

"He told me my son was leading the squadron when he stepped on a mine. He said it like he was reading a script. No emotion. No feeling at all."

Mike waited patiently as she stirred the cream and sugar. Her hands were trembling.

"I suppose I was in shock. I didn't know what to say," she continued, "but when he told me 'Ma'am, your son died for his country,' I don't know what came over me. I lost it."

"Mrs. Williams!" cried Mike, "we've known each other a long time. A *long* time. And I've never seen you…"

"I just lost it, Michael. I snapped. The dam inside me burst. All the anger and grief came flooding out."

"What did you…I mean, how did you…"

"I told the bastard to go straight to hell in a hand basket, that's what I did. I told that empty suit that my son died for nothing. For no reason at all!"

"Mrs. Williams!"

"I told that bastard. And I don't regret a word of it, not a word. It's a damned holocaust! They took my boy. They'll be coming for you next, Michael."

The surge of anger that possessed her now subsided. For the first time, there were tears on her face.

"Aw, Mrs. Williams, I can take care of myself. Besides, they can't draft me! Not during my internship at least."

Mike drew a hand through his dirty blonde curls. He smiled bashfully. Mrs. Williams's gaze made him feel like a little boy, and the thought was unsettling. He struggled for the words to show his maturity. There were none.

"Don't let them take you next, Michael. Do you hear me? Don't let it happen."

*　*　*

Mike leaned back and propped his feet on the desk. It was midnight, and he was wide awake, again. The study was littered with stacks of old papers and books. There was a hole in his sock, and he wiggled a toe through it. He sighed. There was still so much to take care of. The internship was only a week away! Yet here he was. Exhausted, but unable to sleep.

"Poor Tommy," thought Mike. It had been an unlikely friendship. Tommy, the rebel, and pudgy little Mikey. The boys had been inseparable since freshman year. Tommy had always been the adventurous one, the bigger and louder of the two, with little Mikey tagging close behind.

Mike remembered riding the bench together on the football team. Even now, the thought made him grin. The two had swapped stories for hours on those long bus trips. They both had big plans for the future back then. Mike always dreamed of becoming a doctor or scientist. He was obsessed with it. Tommy, on the other hand, had a restless imagination. For weeks he would collect minerals and read every book on geology. The next month it would be something different. Marine biology, veterinary medicine, heck, he even wanted to be a test pilot at some point. Anything to get away from his old man.

Mike sighed. It just didn't seem fair. Kids like Tommy didn't have a chance. Mike knew he had had it easy. He had a family that did not discourage his ambitions too much and took care of tuition. Tommy came from the other side of the tracks. Old Man Williams worked long hours at the refinery and ruled his house with an iron fist. If he could make a living without a degree, he used to say, any son of his could do the same.

Then Vietnam came along, and for boys like Tommy, it was only a matter of time. The draft board preyed on young men like him, young men whose fathers worked in refineries and factories. One by one, the boys in Tommy's neighborhood began to disappear. Many would never return.

There was no glory in a soldier's life. Everyone knew it by now. Those who returned from duty were welcomed home as "baby killers," or worse. Fortunately, Mike's good grades had let him defer the draft for a time, but the threat of conscription remained a constant fear. The draft board was a predator; always watching, always waiting. Struggle in a class, fall behind the other students, and the dogs of war were on you like a wounded lamb.

Tommy experienced that pressure tenfold. If he wasn't studying, he was working odd jobs for tuition. There were always professors eager to fail their students, to "separate the men from the boys," and provide the lamb for the slaughter. Classes filled quickly for professors with good reputations. Students at the back of the line were out of luck. Poor, overworked Tommy registered late for Organic Chemistry, the most important class required for pre-med. His fate was sealed.

Mike closed his eyes. He could vividly recall the last time he'd seen Tommy's cockeyed smile. It was a few nights before basic training. Mike could tell his friend was struggling to put on a brave front. "I'm glad it happened, Mikey," he'd said, downing a beer and a shot in quick succession. "At least my old man'll be happy for once. Besides, I was never meant to be a doctor like you. I can come home and finish school on the G.I. bill. Law school or something. I figure Uncle Sam owes me that much?" Tommy had laughed then, his spirits buoyed by the liquor and company, but there was a bitter edge in his voice. Mike knew Tommy better than anyone. His friend was angry. He was scared.

"Poor Tommy," thought Mike, as he closed the photo album. He slowly paced the room. There had to be some obscure place to tuck away their book of memories. Somewhere behind the stained volumes, old journals, and pizza boxes, out of sight. Some dusty corner of his mind to store away his grief. Sentimentality was not a luxury he could afford, not now. Only a tough internship stood between him and the front lines.

"I'm safe. I just have to do well. I just have to work hard, and I'm safe," Mike reassured himself. He readjusted his glasses and pulled the pencil from his ear. Headache or not, he had to press forward. For his sake. For Tommy. "Work your ass off, and they can't touch you. Not for three or four years. They can't touch you." And work he did.

Chapter 2

IT WAS A FRIGID winter afternoon in 1972, and the draft board office was as cold and sterile as Mike had imagined.

He shivered in his woolen jacket. His chubby cheeks were red and swollen. The place could be a hospital," he thought, rubbing his hands to keep warm, "and no one would know the difference." On the wall hung a portrait of Nixon framed in gold leaf. A large clock ticked off the seconds.

The minutes.

The hours.

Mike coughed audibly. How long were they going to leave him waiting? He'd spent the last hour just staring down the dusty corridor. The rattle and hum of the radiator burrowed into his brain. President Nixon wouldn't stop staring from across the room. "Got you, son," he seemed to say. "No one gets past Tricky Dick!"

The secretary stared at Mike with a forlorn look. She was working the gum in her mouth like a cow on the pasture. She looked as though the life had been dried out of her, like a raisin in the sun.

"As I've informed you, Mr. Pike, the chairwoman is a busy lady. Perhaps if you'd made your appointment at three…"

"I was fifteen minutes late. Fifteen!" Mike rolled his eyes. The long wait had steeled his resolve. "And that's with a traffic pile-up in poor weather. I'm not leaving until I meet with Mrs. Pope."

"Mr. Pike, we cannot be held responsible for…"

"Fifteen minutes! It's what…a quarter-to-five now?" Mike started towards the marble counter, eager to plead his case. He fished around in his pockets. "This isn't supposed to be my problem! I have an internship. See? I have the papers right here."

"Mr. Pike. There is no need to raise your voice. As I said, the chairwoman is a busy lady, and furthermore…"

"Mrs. Anderson! Is this young man causing trouble?"

The interruption took them aback. To the left, at the entry to the hallway was a towering woman. Mike's throat ran dry. She was taller by at least a foot, with the bulk of a tackle and frizzy white hair lit up by the light behind her. The lines on her face looked as though they'd been etched in granite.

"Y-yes, Mrs. Pope. This is a Mr. Michael Pike. Your three o'clock. As I've been telling him you're very busy…"

"I was just fifteen minutes… I won't take up much of your time, I swear."

Mrs. Pope limped forward on to inspect the documents. Mike considered her cane with some interest. It was impressive craftsmanship, a silver shaft with the golden head of a lion.

"Not only are you *late*, Mr. Pike, but your papers are a crumpled mess. Could you please inform me as to why I should give you any of my time at *all*?"

Mike's mind raced. He could feel sweat beading on his neck. He had to think of something. Anything.

"B-because I could save you time later," he managed to stammer, "I have an internship, you see, and I'm not eligible for the draft."

The color seemed to drain from Mrs. Pope's face. She stared at Mike with a look of contempt.

"Not eligible, hm? Well, we'll see about that. If you'll follow me, Mr. Pike."

* * *

"Let's get down to brass tacks, Mr. Pike. Why should I give you a deferment? What, pray tell, is so special about *you*?"

Mike took a moment to collect his thoughts. He'd gotten this far, and the evidence on his side. All he had to do was turn on the charm.

"Well, Mrs. Pope, I recently completed medical school."

He waited a moment to gauge the reaction. There was none.

"I graduated with excellent grades, and as my letters here show, I have an internship that exempts me from the draft. So I figured I'd stop by to sort this all out."

"So you came to sort this all out. How kind of you. Do tell me, Mr. Pike, what year of Our Lord is this."

"Ma'am?"

"The year, Mr. Pike," she repeated, tapping the calendar with her cane.

"Uh, 1972?"

"January 30th, 1972, to be precise. You're an intellectual, Mr. Pike. I'm sure you know the significance of that date?"

"I'm afraid I'm a bit confused, ma'am."

Mike shifted awkwardly in his seat. He hadn't anticipated the cross-examination.

"If you were a patriot, Mr. Pike, you'd realize this is the fourth anniversary of the Tet Offensive. That means for four years I've had scores of young men come through my office. I've had a lot of hippies, commies, cowards, and so-called intellectuals, and every one with a new sob story. They make me sick."

Mrs. Pope was in her element. The vein on her temple was throbbing. The florescent lights lit her bouffant like a halo. Her cane, the glittering scepter of justice.

"That means, Mr. Pike, that you've already enjoyed a four-year deferment. Now, had you been a graduate student, you'd have some defense. Medical school, however..."

"But!" Mike interjected desperately, "medical school IS graduate school."

"It most certainly *is not*! There is nothing on file about medical school. As far as I'm concerned, the only difference between you and the other boys on my list is that you seem to expect special favors."

"No ma'am! Absolutely not!"

"I believe this conversation is over," Mrs. Pope replied curtly. She began shuffling the papers on her desk, as though he'd already left. "I'll pass your case to the board for deliberation. You will be notified as to our decision. That is all."

Mike trudged through the snow towards his old Volkswagen. The windows were caked with frost. As he sat waiting for the engine to heat up, Mike had never felt so frustrated and alone.

* * *

The following week was a blur of activity. Mike contacted his superior, who contacted his dean, who went to the local congressman to contest the legitimacy of Mrs. Pope's claims. In a matter of days, Mike was stunned to receive a call from his congressman.

"It's all a misunderstanding, son, a matter of red tape," he was assured, "but go in for the physical anyway."

The danger passed, but Mike's anxieties remained. The memory of Mrs. Pope and her silver cane would haunt him over the following months. Having shed his naiveté, Mike took steps to ensure the completion of his internship. He enlisted in the reserves and signed up for the "Berry Plan," which offered a deferral to all doctors taking their residency. There were a few agonizing days of waiting, for the "plan" was set up as a lottery system. Applicants were awarded a one, two, or three year deferment plan. As luck would have it, Mike was granted the full three years his residency required and then he would go on active duty.

The U.S. government, meanwhile, faced mounting pressure from the American public. Support for the war hit rock bottom. By August, 1973, the Nixon administration had been forced to withdraw all military forces from Vietnam, Laos, and Cambodia. America's ill-fated crusade for democracy was at an end. Just two years later, the NVA would claim victory with the fall of Saigon. The war, it would seem, was at an end.

Mike was about to learn how wrong that was.

Chapter 3

IT WAS A CHILLY morning in the spring of 1974, and Major Michael Pike was reporting for duty.

He checked his watch as he pulled into the administration parking lot. Five minutes until 0800 hours. Thank God! Once more, he had escaped falling victim to his own sloppy planning. It was a miracle his old relic of a Volkswagen even survived the journey. Camp Valkyrie was a remote location, a base surrounded by prairie as far as the eye could see. What if the engine had stalled? How long would he have been marooned on that old country road rarely travelled? He shuddered to think of a thirty mile walk.

Mike signed in and received his uniform. As he dressed, the realization hit home. This wasn't the reserves. He was now an active duty Air Force Major, a staff physician at one of the military's largest regional hospitals. Mike looked at the official-looking stranger staring back through the mirror. He gave a salute. It all felt so surreal. He placed his medical insignia in its proper place and he noticed there were other pins to choose from. "What are those pins with the wings?" he asked the clerk.

"Those are for the flight surgeons—not for regular doctors like you."

"What do flight surgeons do?"

"They go to a special school and take care of the pilots, mostly," said the clerk.

"I don't think I'll be here that long," said Mike.

The clerk shrugged his shoulders to show his indifference.

For its location, the sheer size of Camp Valkyrie was an overwhelming surprise. Mike wandered the hospital for almost an hour in search of the department chief. The deafening roar of the jets doing touch and goes outside was disorienting. He finally located the office with the help of a kindly nurse.

*   *   *

"Well, if it isn't the last of our young Berry Planners! Come, have a seat Major Pike. Meet some of your new associates!"

Mike winced. The smell of cologne and sweat hit him instantly. The Colonel Lowe was a middle-aged man, short and balding. He offered an oily handshake.

"Allow me to make the introductions. Major Pike, meet Major Daniels and Major Kennedy. To your left is Major Edward Moon. Moon is in his second year of service at our fine institution."

As they shook, Mike was struck by the contrast between the two. The colonel's mannerisms seemed too exaggerated, too theatrical. Mike could feel his beady little eyes inspect every button on his uniform. Moon, on the other hand, sat slouched in his chair. He was unshaven, and it looked to Mike as though he'd just rolled out of bed. Even now he seemed barely awake.

"That's right, boys." Moon yawned. He gave a mock-salute and a wink. "Colonel Lowe is always pleased to get a fresh crop of Berry Planners. You need something, you knock on my door. You dig?"

The colonel's cheeks flushed. Mike could feel the tension between the two men. To his credit, Lowe recovered quickly, with a grin that exposed the silver on his molars. A stack of folders was passed around the room.

"Thank you, Major Moon, but let's get down to business. Gentlemen."

The colonel cleared his throat to continue.

"Key words. They're our bread and butter here. Your folder will contain a full list of officially sanctioned key words. Study them. Commit them to memory. If you do not, I assure you, you will struggle here at Camp Valkyrie."

He paused for dramatic effect. Mike and the recruits were already skimming their folders.

"Key words, gentlemen. Don't think I'm kidding. The board in San Antonio sifts through each report with a fine-tooth comb. Your patients won't get a dime's worth of disability compensation unless those reports meet spec."

"The man speaks the truth," added Moon. "Think of that folder as the gospel, the board as the Father Almighty. It decides who stays and who goes, who gets discharged and who gets reassigned. It's the money faucet. The goose that lays them golden eggs."

Mike's mind began to wander. It all seemed so absurd. Key words? Years of medical school, just to fill in the blanks? There was a wooden bird on the colonel's desk, and he watched its head dip over and over in a bowl of water. So this was the life of a military psychiatrist. Following the manual to fix a broken toy.

"Excuse me, sir, I don't mean to interrupt."

"Yes, Major Daniels?"

"Maybe I missed something, sir, but where exactly do we come in? I mean, it sounds to me like any grease monkey could do our job. Why do you need us?"

Colonel Lowe's brow furrowed. He mopped the sweat from his forehead and grinned.

"Why, major! We still need you to make the diagnosis! I don't see an issue with that. Your folder is meant to advise you on administrative matters. The Air Force needs to run like a finely tuned machine."

"So the illness comes from the top down!" Mike exclaimed. "The system defines the dysfunction, the patient conforms to the system's definition. How is anyone supposed to get better?"

"No, no, you misunderstand."

The colonel's patience, it appeared, was wearing thin.

"The illness remains the same! Only the descriptive words, the modifiers, the degrees of illness are dictated by the board. It allows us to input the data in standardized form."

Moon stifled a yawn.

"Just wait till he shows you his bulletin board. It's something else, all right."

"Quite right, Major Moon. Now if you'll follow me, gentlemen."

*   *   *

Colonel Lowe led the four to a much larger office. Behind the desk sat a thin and withered figure hammering at a typewriter. On the wall was an enormous board, and upon it a maze of color-coded columns. The sight almost made Mike dizzy.

"Gentlemen. Meet Sergeant Slimm."

The sergeant greeted them with a grimace. He fed another sheet into the roller.

"Sergeant Slimm is the Non-Commissioned Officer in Charge. The guardian of the board, if you will. Sergeant, would you be so kind as to explain?"

"Thank you, sir."

The sergeant rose slowly. He let out a long hacking cough into his handkerchief.

"This here is the brains of our operation, see? It lists every patient, where they can be located, and their current status."

After another fit of wheezing, Slimm hobbled to a jar of colored magnets.

"Ahem, excuse me, as I was saying, we have a variety of magnetic letters we use for each patient. 'S,' for instance, stands for schizophrenia. 'C' for character disorder. 'D' for depression…"

It felt to Mike as though he were in one of those war movies he'd watched as a child. He was among the generals, examining the battlefield. Colonel Lowe stood proudly, his arms folded like a chunky Napoleon. It was obvious he took great pride in his board. The sergeant's speech ended in a coughing fit, and Lowe mercifully reclaimed the stage.

"Now do you understand?"

"So let me get this straight," voiced Daniels. "Are you saying this is something akin to a giant insurance company? Your reason for existing is to indemnify our patients?"

Moon burst out laughing and shook his head. The whole room turned towards him as he doubled over.

"Hoo boy, I never thought of it that way. Gotta hand it to the rookie, boss, he got ya there!"

The colonel's face went white.

"Or not, Major Daniels," he answered curtly, "and perhaps you should say 'our' reason for existing. You have been assigned here to do your duty. I would advise you to rethink your perspective. I run a tight ship, and I have no room for mavericks."

"B-but we're here to practice medicine…aren't we?"

All eyes turned to Kennedy, who had until now been silent.

"Oh, you can do that too," Moon chuckled. "So long as you finish your work first."

Chapter 4

MIKE PLACED THE BOX on his desk. So this was his office. The walls were a hideous avocado green, and the paint was warped and peeling. His chair pivoted on a rusty hinge. The air smelled faintly of mildew. On the wall was a poster of Uncle Sam with the slogan, "Your Doctor is Watching You!"

Mike sighed. At least he brought his own supplies. The Air Force, it appeared, had only thought to issue him a typewriter and an ash tray. There was a timid rap at the door.

"Come in!"

Mike recognized the timid redhead instantly. Kennedy stood in the doorway, smiling awkwardly.

"Sorry to bother you! But Moon and the other second-years are here, if you'd like to join us in the lounge."

"Thanks Kennedy, I'll be right there," said Mike, rearranging the pictures on his desk.

Kennedy started to leave, but turned back once more.

"Nice office, by the way! Sure looks nicer than mine!"

* * *

The lounge was a sparsely decorated room. It was thick with the smell of cigarette ash. A pot of coffee percolated on the counter. For the most part, the second-years stood around the couch cracking jokes. Mike and his companions, meanwhile, sat awkwardly around the conference table. He was offered a brownie. It looked as though it had petrified.

Minutes passed and Mike's lungs began to burn. He hated secondhand smoke. Small talk with Kennedy and Daniels seemed to be going nowhere. He was about to shove off when he heard a sound like nails on a chalk board. Moon had pulled up a chair.

"Hey boys! Sorry about the fellas. But you know how it is, you get in a routine, you get used to the same people, all that jazz. But we're happy to have ya!"

He pulled out a Marlboro and offered the pack.

"Any of you boys play tennis?"

The three stared at him blankly.

"Okay then, golf? Don't tell me you fellas don't play golf?"

"I like golf," offered Kennedy.

"Sure," Mike chimed in, "I like both, actually."

"There you go! Don't let the drab accommodations get you down. The buildings may be a little old, but the place is like a self-contained Disneyland. We've got theaters, bowling alleys, clubs, and card games going all the time. The Base Exchange can find anything your heart desires for cents on the dollar. It's a fine gig, all right."

"That all sounds well and good," said Daniels, "But where do we get our supplies? I only have three pencils in my office and no paper clips. I need paper clips. They do give us paperclips don't they?"

Moon chuckled and toyed with his lighter.

"That'd be ol' Slimm's department. Slimm takes care of supplies."

"Well I also need light bulbs, stationary, and pens."

"Slimm."

"And they will have paper clips, right?"

"What'd I just say?"

Daniels was obviously annoyed. With his crew-cut black hair and insistence on detail, he seemed like a neurotic ass. It appeared he and Moon would not get on well.

"You know, Major Moon, I have to say I'm a tad disappointed. I expected something different from the military. Instead, all we get is a folder, a quick orientation, and a guide that doesn't seem to give a damn."

"Easy there, Major Killjoy."

"With all due respect, I'm surprised the colonel doesn't adjust your attitude," spat Daniels, standing in disgust.

"Just look at your uniform. Your pins aren't even straight."

Moon folded his arms behind his head and smiled serenely.

"You think I give a damn? Hell, I'll wear em on my underwear. What are they gonna do, court martial my ass? Heaven forbid! I'd have to go back to being a *real* doctor."

Daniels face contorted in anger. His words were laced with acid.

"Well, I'm just trying to do my job. Good afternoon, Major Moon."

"Sure, sure. Don't let the door hit your tight ass on the way out." Moon shrugged, as the door slammed shut behind them.

"Takes all kinds, I suppose. Takes all kinds."

* * *

Mike folded his legs on the bench and stared at the sky. Finally, a relief from the noise and smoke of the lounge. He drank in the cold country air like water. The stars glittered like the crystals of a geode, and Mike squinted to make out each constellation. The big dipper, the Pleiades, Orion's belt. His father pointed them out so long ago.

"Nice view, eh! Can you believe it?"

The crunch of boots on the gravel broke his concentration. Moon was sauntering towards him

"I'm a city boy, so when I saw the stars out here, man, that just blew me away! Real poetical n' shit. Mind if I join ya?"

Moon took a seat and drew a cigarette from his pocket. Mike groaned inwardly. So much for the clean air.

"So, that was orientation, right? When does our training start?"

Moon raised an eyebrow.

"Training?"

"I assume there's a training period, right?"

"Nope. Not anymore at least. The hospital commander, Colonel Creaser, decided to cancel OBMT after last year."

"OB—what?"

"OBMT. Officer's Basic Military Training," Moon continued. "Our performance was so poor last year, and I guess he just didn't want to suffer the embarrassment again."

"Is he sensitive or something?"

"Well, poor Creaser happens to have a cousin working at base ops."

Moon smirked. He took a long draw off his Marlboro.

"One of the higher-ups?"

"Exactly. From what I've heard, he's been a pain in Creaser's rear long as anyone can remember. Could be jealousy, psychosis, who knows."

Moon tossed the filter and crushed it under his heel.

"What I do know is the guy is mental. He hates all doctors. Calls us Commies. Believes it, too. After last year's OBMT he had the stones to accuse Creaser's whole staff of mutiny. Can you believe it?"

"Mutiny? Isn't that the Navy?"

"The military in general. The crackpot claimed we'd performed poorly on purpose, like it was some grand conspiracy."

"This is all a lot to process," Mike replied, chuckling nervously.

"I've been here one day, and I've seen arguments, been fed key words, and now a conspiracy…"

Moon smiled.

"Kid, you don't know the half of what goes on behind the scenes here. When these turkeys get together they're worse than a sewing circle. Just do like I do. Show 'em you're a model soldier and they'll eat out of your hand. They all seem to fear the honest officer."

"But that's just it! I don't understand how to be an officer! I have no background, no military training."

"Let's see."

Moon sat pensively for a moment. He rubbed the stubble on his chin.

"Are you wearing the uniform, Major Pike?"

"Well, yes. I mean, of course."

"Then you, sir, are an officer."

Chapter 5

THE WORDS ECHOED in Mike's head for days. Sure, you had to take Moon with a grain of salt, but the idea was an appealing one. "Could it really be that simple?" Mike pondered, as he stared at the ceiling on those long and lonely nights. "Do the clothes make the officer?"

Mike thought back to his childhood. He recalled the days when he was King Arthur, Robin Hood, Zorro, any hero he pleased. When he donned the robe and wore the crown he *became* those figures. For weeks he had coveted his cousin's Prince Valiant suit. That plastic armor and sword had made him sick with envy. Now he had a costume of his own, a finely tailored uniform. Who was to say he was not an officer?

Try as he might, Mike could do nothing to convince himself. He played the part. He learned the protocols and went through the motions, but time failed to ease his doubts. After a week, his mind was made up. He resolved to learn the role he had been called to play. After all, he reasoned, he owed that much to the soldiers in his care.

His initial efforts yielded little result. Sergeant Slimm greeted the request for training materials with a vacant stare. No one, Mike was informed, had ever asked. He was directed to Colonel Lowe, who, after digging through the archives, came up with a dusty old volume. The title was written in gold letters, *The Officers Handbook: Rules of Conduct Befitting an Officer of the United States Air Force*. It had been published nearly a decade ago. The book became Mike's constant companion on his rounds. He studied each page with care.

*   *   *

The golden opportunity came only a month later. Moon's invitation had come as a shock to Mike and Kennedy. New arrivals were rarely welcome at the Officers' Club. One was expected to 'know the traditions', at the very least.

Even then, most doctors had a tendency to avoid the club. The base commander's deputy, a popular patron, considered doctors no worse than Communists. They were often harassed or ignored. "Still," Mike thought with excitement, "what better place to learn what makes an officer, than an Officers' Club?"

People either loved or hated Moon, Mike learned, and the major had forged many a friendship at Camp Valkyrie. He had a charisma that was slicker than oil on salt water. The invitation was extended by two administrators serving as line officers. Guests, Moon had been informed, were welcome.

It was a Friday night, and the club was packed. It took several minutes of elbowing to locate a table. The drinks came fast and cheap, far cheaper than in any bar Mike had ever been. He remembered the handbook.

Ch. 4. Sec. A. Part I. An officer may consume liquor, but he must do so responsibly.

Moon slung his arm over Mike's shoulder. He wore a sloppy grin and smelled of whiskey.

"A toast, my friends, to Major Ricks and Captain Lu! Two of the finest officers in our proud Air Force! Cheers!"

Ricks was from Chicago, and he and Moon were downing shots one after the other. The two were laughing like hyenas. Lu, an administrator from Korea, sat idly stirring his cocktail. He turned to Mike.

"So, Major Pike. Have you enjoyed your stay at Camp Valkyrie?"

"It's all right, I suppose."

"It must be good for your family I imagine."

Mike felt his blood turn to ice water. He felt the muscles in his face contract. His hands began to tremble, and he hid them beneath the table.

"My… family?"

"Yes! Yes, as I recall from your file, you have a wife? Surely, I hope she feels welcome. Do you have children?"

"Look! The waitress!" Mike yelled hollowly. "Next one's on me! The next round's on me!" He left a wad of bills on the table and stumbled towards the safety of the restroom. He tasted blood and realized he'd been biting his lip. "It's none of his business," Mike thought. He gritted his teeth and splashed cold water over his face. "It's none of his business at all."

* * *

Moon and Ricks had befriended a group of female officers. They were just being introduced as Mike returned.

"Everyone's married! 'Cept Ricks and Kennedy here!" declared Moon. "Though ol' Ricks may as well be! The ol' dog!"

The noise in the club seemed to escalate over time. A man and woman nearby began arguing loudly. Mike heard the tinkling of broken glass. In a corner of the room, an officer stood on his table and sung with an Irish brogue. Others joined in.

Ohh...!
At the air show last December
A day I'll long remember
I flew up in the clouds with foolish pride!

"Damn it all," slurred Moon. "Damn drunkards! We'll have to shout to talk!"

Ricks hiccupped and slapped him on the back. "Ahh, it's why we all drink! To deal with the bastards." He stood on his chair and took up the refrain.

When my flaps began to flutter
And I lost my rear tail rudder
I fell back to the earth and surely died!
Ohh...!

One of the girls pinched Mike's cheek and giggled. "This one's the cutest! He's got a baby face! Look Connie, hasn't he got a baby face?"

Mike blushed. He was both annoyed and flattered. Moon wrapped his arms around the girl.

"Aw, c'mon honey! You want a real man, not a boy! Piss and vinegar, not milk and cookies! We're a dying breed these days!"

Moon was incensed now, and he raised his glass in the air.

"To Vietnam! The biggest fuck-up in military history!"

All eyes turned to their table. Mike winced inwardly. It was too late now.

"And to the assholes that put us there, by God! May they die the death of a thousand cuts!"

For the first time that night, the room was silent. The song broke off at the chorus.

"What'd he say?" a voice called from the back.

"He said to go fuck yourself!"

"Well... I'll be God Damned... I'll be damned if I'll take that!"

Mike saw a drunken colonel lurching towards their table. He was stumbling wildly through the crowd with a broken bottle. Ricks and Lu did their best to restrain Moon, who was furiously attempting to wriggle free. Mike caught a glimpse of Kennedy. He looked like a deer in the headlights.

The room crowded around the two combatants. The fight seemed inevitable. Moon tore free of Ricks. His elbow struck Mike full force in the jaw and sent him reeling. The colonel had almost reached his adversary when he lost his balance. He fell, his own momentum propelling him forward, and his head struck a table with a sickening crack.

A pool of blood began to form. A woman screamed. The spell was broken and the crowd surged forward. The limp form of the colonel was hoisted by two captains. Moon was still shouting as they carried out the body.

"That's no way to end a fight, you bastard! You get back here and face me like a man!" Moon weaved awkwardly as he tried to step forward. He slumped back into his chair with a grunt.

"That's enough, Moon," hissed Kennedy. He took Lu by the arm. "Please just take him out to the car. If he struggles I'll get Ricks to help."

Moon was in no state to protest as he was led out. Mike was still gingerly clutching the side of his face. The blow must have cracked a tooth, at least. He tried to tune out the noise around him as he wrapped a handful of ice in a napkin. The cold compress did little to ease the pain. Some patrons had filtered outside to watch the colonel stretchered onto an ambulance.

The confusion of the spectators quickly subsided as people returned to their tables. In a few minutes it seemed all was forgotten. Spirits were high once more.

> *My blood began to bubble*
> *And I saw St. Peter at those pearly gates!*
> *Ohh…!*

Kennedy collapsed in his chair by Mike. He was out of breath and panting.
"Um, Mike, I'm not sure if you wanted to stay, but…"
He trailed off in midsentence. Mike was already putting on his coat.

*   *   *

Kennedy offered to drive, and the two said their goodbyes to Lu and Ricks. Moon lay sprawled in the bed of his pickup. He was snoring heavily.

"Do you think he knew that colonel?"

Mike turned to Kennedy.

"Nah, and if I know Moon he won't remember a thing tomorrow."

"But what happens to him tomorrow? Do you think they'll lock him in the brig? Do you think the hospital will notify the colonel's friends and family?"

"Suppose the medics will take care of everything."

Mike closed his eyes. It hurt to talk. The remainder of the drive was spent in blessed silence.

Chapter 6

MIKE GROANED. He tried tucking his head beneath the covers, but there was no relief. He looked at the clock. Only a quarter past six. The sun was already streaming through the blinds. Mike took a moment to will his limbs out of entropy. He sat on the edge of the mattress, his eyes still bleary with sleep and his jaw still ached. This had better be good.

The walk to the hospital lifted Mike's spirits considerably. It was his favorite weather, chilly and bright, and the wind from the prairies carried the bittersweet smell of cedar and diesel oil. Life at Valkyrie was rarely so peaceful. Mike felt as though he were strolling through suburbia, as he passed the rows of houses with manicured lawns. When he arrived, a pot of coffee was percolating in the break room. Thank heaven for small blessings.

* * *

As expected, Colonel Lowe was waiting in the clinic. The portly officer wheezed with exhaustion as he waddled forward. It was only morning, and already the sweat was soaking through his shirt.

"Last night! Air Evacuation. No time!" Lowe huffed. "Patients. Lots of patients! Most of 'em fresh outta 'Nam."

The news took Mike aback. Air Evacs were a frequent enough occurrence. In only a month he'd seen veterans all the way from Guam, the Philippines, and Japan. But Vietnam?

"But sir! Didn't the war…"

"End a year ago? In case you didn't notice, Major, the North and South are still fightin' like rats in a trap. It's not over yet. Not for us, neither."

So America was still in Vietnam. The war raged on after all. The thought made Mike sick to his stomach.

"Is there a problem, Major Pike?"

"No, sir."

"Good, because you're gonna have one helluva day."

*   *   *

Unit Two South was a curious place. Mike had never seen a ward quite like it. At the entrance were doors of reinforced steel, the doors of a bank vault, and yet they remained open. It felt at first as though he had wandered into limbo. Everything was white—from the paint on the walls to the nurses' uniforms—a dull eggshell white. The halls were thin and windowless, and lined with steel doors. Dust motes danced beneath fluorescent lights.

Mike truly sympathized with his patients. He didn't know how they could stand it; the cold, suffocating monotony of life in a military psych ward. He often found them drifting through the halls in their blue-striped pajamas and robes. Those cogent enough were forever reading and re-reading magazines, or staring through the bars at the television. Everyso often, from deep in the heart of Two South, came sounds that would make Mike shiver.

As much as he loathed his surroundings, Mike couldn't help but admire the staff. A small army of nurses and technicians kept close tabs on each patient. The chief tech and head nurse kept Two South running like clock-work. Right on schedule, as he entered, there were three nurses running a full inspection. From the condition of the lavatory, to the amount of soap dispensed, each detail was recorded with care.

Much to his chagrin, Mike had been appointed command of Two South almost upon arrival. Both the chief tech and head nurse reported to him directly. It was his first taste of leadership, and he found the experience thoroughly miserable. The staff—many of whom were his senior—resented his position, and took pains to make their displeasure known.

The demands of running a unit were exhausting, but bearable enough. What Mike could not accustom himself to—try as he might—were the for-malities attached to his rank. Each morning the head nurse would call the orderlies to attention, and he would be forced to walk the long gauntlet to his station. On his first day, the staff had stood over a minute before he remembered the magic words.

"At ease!"

* * *

By now, Mike's initial embarrassments were a month behind him. With each day his stammering decreased. He felt more sure of himself; more confident. Still, his shyness would often get the better of him. He took comfort in one his few friends in the unit, Head Nurse Judith, who was an old hand at Camp Valkyrie. She was waiting today at the nurses' station.

"Still not used to the call to attention, sir?" she smiled fondly as she scanned her charts. "You're blushing like a schoolboy."

Mike bit his lower lip.

"It's ridiculous. It's a hospital not a regiment. I'm not General Patton. I'd rather just come in and get to business."

"Well, sir, I'm glad you're ready to work. We have a priority patient in need of your immediate attention."

Mike had heard stories about these "priority" patients. They were always high-profile individuals, their cases supposedly "confidential." From secret operatives to psychotic generals, however, one fact was constant. If the patient wasn't a danger to himself, you could be damn sure he was a danger to others.

"I've… never had a priority patient."

"I have, Major Pike, and I have to warn you. Be on your guard. Things can get very ugly if you're not careful."

* * *

Judith continued her briefing as she led the way. Unit Two was a hive of activity, as nurses and techs struggled to accommodate the flood of new patients. Perhaps it was the caffeine, or the adrenaline rush of having to dodge gurneys and wheelchairs, but Mike couldn't help feeling more annoyed than anxious. He quickened his pace to keep up.

"Even if she is a priority case, don't you think the circumstances are extreme? I should be processing these new patients. These people need care. They need it now!"

"Your first priority now, sir, is the general's daughter. You need to focus."

"But the others…"

"They're well cared for. You just need to assess her needs and condition first. You'll have the whole rest of the day to—oof!—make the rounds."

The nurse tripped over a cable and regained her balance. Finally, they reached a room secluded from the others. The interior was at least twice the size of a standard cell. Its small luxuries—a window, a few plants, even a television—signaled the status of its occupant. On the bed lay a blonde girl dressed in civilian clothes. Her face was pale and contorted.

"Once again sir, the patient is Miss Rosenthal, daughter of General Rosenthal. Patient is suffering hallucinations and fits of psychosis. Her behavior is combative, and she may pose a threat to both herself and others."

Mike considered the young woman carefully. There was something very different about her. Her features soft—almost delicate—and her curly blonde hair hung down to her shoulders.

"She's a soldier?"

"Peace Corps. Building mud huts in Thailand, or whatever they do."

Mike walked to the side of the bed and examined her closely.

"Nurse, is the patient sedated?!"

"They administered Thorazine on the Air Evac. She was babbling nonsensically. Something about dead children in the village. Dying children."

"That's it? They sedated her for that?"

"Pilots get nervous with patients like that on board," Judith shrugged. "They get doctors to write up prescriptions so the techs can administer them in-flight."

Bending over the bed, Mike carefully checked her vitals. Her jaw hung slack, and a few bubbles of saliva had collected at the corner of her mouth. Her fists were clenched.

"Sir, Colonel Klinlivin instructed us to continue administering sedatives. If you let us know what we should give her now, we can take care of her for the time being."

Mike winced inwardly at Klinlivin's name. Not again! What was the point of running the unit when Commander-In-Chief of Nursing made all his decisions? Something within him snapped. This time he was going to handle the case his way.

"What we're going to give her is a chance to wake up and gather her bearings."

"But Colonel Klinlivin…"

"I heard you," Mike fired back, "but hold that order for now."

Judith nodded in assent, and quietly motioned in the techs to clean the patient.

"Trust me on this one Judith. I want to hear what she has to say, first."

Chapter 7

MIKE FINISHED HIS ROUNDS before checking the priority patient. She was still asleep, and he sat in a chair at the foot of the bed with a heavy sigh. He could certainly use a nap after a day like today. At least the techs had cleaned her up nicely. The color had returned to the patient's cheeks, and she lay with her hands folded over the covers. Relief from the sedatives had returned her to the living.

The major was about to leave when he noticed a movement in the sheets. The young woman groaned softly. Her eyes fluttered open, and with great effort she propped herself up on the pillow.

"Good afternoon, Miss Rosenthal. Are you feeling all right? Can I..."

"Water?"

"To your right, ma'am"

She took a long, cool drink from the glass at her bedside. There was a slight tremor in her hand. She returned the doctor's gaze with a wan smile.

"God, I feel like I've been sleeping for days. Where is this? I mean, where... where am I?"

"You're at Camp Valkyrie, ma'am. You arrived via Air Evac last night. Here let me get you a refill."

Mike rose to take the empty glass. When his eyes returned to the patient, he noticed a change in her demeanor. She was anxious now, apprehensive.

"Before you say anything else there's something I need to know."

"What's that?"

"Do you work for my father? Tell me the truth. Do you work for my father?"

"I-I've never met your father, ma'am," Mike answered awkwardly. "I'm Major Pike. I'm a doctor in the Air Force. You're in an Air Force hospital."

The concern written on the girl's face seemed to dissolve. She smiled and took a drink, as Mike pulled up a chair.

"Oh God, don't call me ma'am! We're practically the same age! Name's Cassandra. Cassie for short."

"Well, nice to meet you, Cassie. Name's Mike."

"Well, Mike, you may not have met my father, but you don't seem like his type. And anyone who ain't his type is a friend of mine."

"Is your father in the Air Force?" Mike took his clipboard from the   bed. Anything he learned now could be critical.

"My father thinks he *is* the Air Force. He thinks the world is his Air Force, and every person in it a subordinate to command. He's a tough sonofabitch, let me tell ya."

"Does he scare you?"

"Hell yes, he scares me!" Cassie laughed. "Why the hell you think I left for Thailand? To get away from that asshole. He and my mother, who he's got right under his thumb!"

"Can you tell me what happened in Thailand, Cassie?"

The question appeared to trigger a response. In an instant, her relaxed posture went rigid, her muscles taut. She stared towards Mike with a look devoid of warmth.

"You seem like a good man, Major Pike. I know we just met, but I've always been able to sense this kind of thing. And right now, I really need your help."

"My help?"

"Do you really want to know what happened?"

"I do."

"The babies. In the village. The babies were dying. Every day, more and more..." Cassie broke down, her body wracked with sobs. "They would come in the night and take them. Each night. They would carry their tiny bodies in baskets. I followed the procession one night to the outskirts of town. And... and... Oh God..."

She was crying too heavily to continue. True or not, she told her tale in earnest, and Mike felt touched by her sorrow.

"Do you want to continue later...Cassie? We can talk more tomorrow if you like."

"No, I-I'm all right." She swept her hair from her face and dabbed at her eyes.

"What happened next?"

"It was horrible. There was a clearing in the forest and it was littered with the dead. It was like a mass grave. Some had been there so long that only the bones were left. The tiny skulls of children grinning back at me in the moonlight. Tiny limbs picked clean."

Mike shuddered inwardly at the description. It couldn't be true, it was so disturbing, and yet the details were so vivid. He swallowed the lump in his throat.

"So what did you do? And how can I help you?"

"I know it's hard to believe. I tried, I really did." Cassie's voice was softer now and trembling. Her eyes began to well with tears. "I tried, but they wouldn't let me help them. They told me it was me. I was killing them. They chased me into the forest. I must have walked for days before the boss found me."

"The boss?"

"My boss, over in Bangkok. His people found me deep in the jungle. That's what he told me. I was unconscious and dehydrated. I tried to get back! I told him. The children are still dying! They know it's not me now. You have to let me go back!"

Mike finished scribbling in his notes and looked up.
"Cassie, you're not going to be much help in your current state. "

"But the children…"

"You need to recover, first of all, then you'll be free to go."

"But he won't let me! I know he won't," Cassie sighed.

"Who?"

"My father. He won't let me out of his sight. Now more than ever. He'll lock me up again in that house."

Mike set the clipboard on a tray. He was now genuinely concerned for the safety of the patient, but for reasons unexpected. This was abuse.

"Has he… Has General Rosenthal ever locked you up before? Against your will?"

The silence between them was answer enough.

"You don't have to worry, Cassie; you're safe here. We can protect you. I can protect you."

Cassie chuckled and laid her head back on the pillow. She spoke softly now. She was tiring, but the bitterness in her voice was unmistakable.

"Seems like there's always some man who wants to protect me. The military is just full of men who know what a girl needs."

Chapter 8

"**I WOULD ASK YOU** to keep your voice down, Major Pike," warned Lowe. "These office walls are paper thin. What we are discussing is confidential."

"But if it's communicable, sir! There's no telling what tropical virus she's contracted, but its effects are lethal," Mike protested. "She needs to be placed in quarantine, at least! Everyone on that Air Evac needs to be evaluated. The patients, the techs…"

"The techs have gone back for more. I appreciate your concern, Major, but we follow orders. We'll receive another Air Evac tomorrow."

"And my priority patient?"

"We hold her as long as her daddy sees fit."

"On what authority?!"

"Chain of command, Major." The colonel drew a box from his desk and lit up a cigar. Mike declined the offer. "General Rosenthal works in D.C. and his authority comes from the top, and if you think…"

He puffed at the Cuban, and the acrid blue smoke curled in the air.

"…if you think, for one second, I'm getting between the general and his baby girl, you're out of your damn mind!"

* * *

Mike was fuming as he returned to his quarters. It wasn't his first time to be stonewalled by the colonel. Lowe would always bob his head vigorously, like the bobbing bird on his desk, always with the same condescending grin stamped on his face, smoking his cigars. Nothing changed. Mike was beginning to think things never would.

Lowe's mishandling of the priority patient had come as no surprise. It was just the latest in a series of sloppy, opportunistic, and downright unethical decisions by the Valkyrie brass. Just that day, a twenty-year old sergeant with schizophrenia and alcoholism had been cleared for service. It was nothing, Mike was told, another case of "Battle Fatigue." It was a common occurrence. Veterans suffering from recurrent nightmares, involuntary muscle spasms, panic attacks, depression, and a host of other symptoms were processed and often shipped back to their deployment. The diagnosis was always the same: "Battle Fatigue," "Shell Shock." In the mind of Colonel Lowe, the hospital resources were better spent on the "real" patients.

Mike sighed. He felt helpless. After re-reading the Officer's Manual, he'd taken to repeating the instructions in his head. Focusing on particular instructions. They had become for him a mantra, a calming mechanism. Today, he focused on one rule in particular.

Ch. 2. Sec. B. Part II. An officer maintains an attitude of confidence and optimism.

The words echoed hollowly in his brain. Try as he might, Mike could not fathom how the strongest military in the world could treat its own with such wanton disregard.

*   *   *

Mike was still swallowing a mouthful of hash browns as he raced after Nurse Judith. Of all the times for a crisis, he groaned inwardly, it had to happen on his lunch break. Judith's voice was hoarse and breathless.

"We were concerned this would happen, sir. The patient hasn't been sleeping. She's become increasingly violent and delusional!"

"I don't blame her," said Mike, choking down his food. "She may as well have been kidnapped, the way she was locked away and drugged up before getting here."

"We need you to calm her down, Doctor. She's trashed the room. She refuses to let anyone in besides you."

"Judith, listen carefully. Did she give any indication as to what set her off?"

"All I said was that the general was on his way! After that..."

*   *   *

Mike slowly turned the knob. The last thing he wanted was to provoke a distressed patient. He peered into the room cautiously.

"Cassie? Are you all right?"

The room was a disaster. The potted fern had been uprooted, and soil had been smeared across the linoleum floor. The glass from the bedside table lay shattered on the ground. Cassie was sitting Indian-style in the center of the room. She had wrapped herself in bed sheets, and brandished a large shard of glass like a knife.

"Cassie, I need you to.."

"I've been waiting for you," she interrupted. "I need to leave. Now!"

Mike approached slowly, careful not to make a sudden movement. Cassie's hair was wet and matted. Her face was caked with dirt. There was a feral look in her eyes.

"Why do you need to leave now, Cassie?"

"My father is coming. They told me he's coming today. I don't want to see him!"

"You need to take deep breaths and stay calm. It's going to be all right."

"You don't understand!" wailed Cassie, "he makes me crazy! I'm already crazy enough. I hear the voices, they are getting stronger. It feels like they're swallowing me whole! My teeth are giving me a bitch of a pain."

Mike placed an arm around Cassie as she began to sob. With a little effort, he managed to pry the jagged weapon from her fingers. Her hand was soaked with blood.

"Talk to me, Cassie. What do they tell you, the voices?"

"They tell me to go. I am called."

"And if you stay?"

"If I stay, I can bend over and kiss my sweet ass goodbye," she moaned. "They're taking over. It's only a matter of time…"

*   *   *

A small audience of personnel had assembled, as Mike emerged from the room. Pure exhaustion and frustration had banished his usual shyness. Red-faced, he turned on the crowd in a rage."

"What is this to you?! A show?! Some sort of game?! Get back to work, so we can keep pretending this place works like a real hospital!"

He turned to Judith, who was wide-eyed with shock.

"I need the patient placed under twenty-four hour suicide watch. I want an eye on her at all times, understood?"

"So we can hold her for her father?"

"No!" Mike exclaimed. "Because she's fucking suicidal!"

Chapter 9

WITH THE CONSTANT interruption of Air Evacuations and patient incidents, there was little that surprised the staff of Two South. Even the arrival of a priority patient made hardly a ripple in the pond. The story of Cassie's breakdown made the usual rounds. By the next morning it was all but forgotten. The day of the general's arrival was no different. Just another day at Camp Valkyrie.

Mike wet his finger as he thumbed through the morning priorities. The days seemed to melt together now in a blur of patient reports and interviews. The results were always the same. Some would be returned to active duty; those he knew he'd see again. Others would be discharged without benefits, doomed to a life of disability and poverty. Mike sighed. It was just another day at Camp Valkyrie.

* * *

The first patient of the morning was Airman White. Twenty-four years old. He could have been twice that age, thought Mike, judging from the graying hair and sunken features. According to the report, his Captain had been a high-profile pilot at a Midwestern base. By the airman's account, he suffered a severe case of vertigo midway through an air show, causing the C-131 transport plane he was navigating to careen towards earth. It was only by sheer luck the metal behemoth had missed the review stand.

"Yeah, it was one hell of a time to go blank," mused the airman. "That was a big show, too, the congressman, the brass, everyone was there. They were shaking down the political big-wigs for funding. Of course they were gonna need a scapegoat."

"But your pilot's report says…"

"I know what it says. The guy's a grade-A bastard. I don't drink. Anyone who knows me knows I don't drink! Even my blood test showed negative!"

"So, you're saying you've suffered from vertigo before?"

"Six months now." Airman White bit his lip. His eyes roamed nervously around the room. "The base doctor can't find the cause."

Mike studied the report again, pouring over every detail. Everything was there, all right: negative blood alcohol, chemistries, an MRI of the brain. Putting on his reading glasses, he looked closer.

In a moment he saw it. Clear as day.

Mike flipped to a second MRI from just six-months prior. That confirmed it. There was definitely an opacity in the mastoid area behind the left ear. A sinister growth that had calcified over time. Mike shook his head in frustration. How could they have missed it? It wasn't mentioned anywhere in the patient's chart, and yet there it was. Another comparison of the MRIs confirmed his fear. Whatever it was, it was growing.

"Did they tell you about this?" Mike asked, indicating the marks on the scan. The airman shook his head. "Well, it's growing, and whatever it is, it's been the cause of your vertigo for sure."

"Does that mean I'll be able to stay in the service?"

"Honestly, I don't know what it means, but I would be prepared for the worst. If only the doctors back at your base had been more thorough, maybe something could have been done, but at this stage…"

"But can I stay in the service?"

Mike's footsteps felt heavy as he left the room. He felt what was becoming a familiar sensation creeping along his spine. A paralyzing sense of hopelessness. Again he was too late. Another victim of military indifference. Mike didn't have the heart to break the news to the young airman. He would wait for the neurosurgeon to return the inevitable verdict. Just another day at Camp Valkyrie.

*   *   *

The second patient of the day was Airman Williams, a grizzled old veteran on the verge of retirement. He served in Hawaii as an officer's aide and, according to his report, his skills as a barber had made him a legend in the barracks. "They wouldn't let me retire!" He laughed, as a grin spread across his wizened face. "I'm just too good with those clippers!"

The airman's grin faded as Mike read the report aloud. He had apparently lost his touch. It had reached the point where he couldn't even cut in a straight line. For months the staff had chalked up his mistakes to age or exhaustion, but their concerns only mounted. After he cut large gaps in the general's hair, however, the problem became impossible to ignore.

"They say it's my old anxiety that's come back, but it's a load of bull," exclaimed the airman. "I'm not crazy, and I'm not off my rocker, I swear!"

"But you have a history of anxiety attacks and, let's call it 'disruptive' behavior?" Mike furrowed his brow.

"It's different this time! I know when that happens, and it hasn't happened in years. Now it's different. I get these wild jerks in my bones. Like, Snap! Like a rubber band." The airman motioned violently with his elbow. "Once they start, I can't control them."

"Are you taking any medicines? Anything at all?" asked Mike. The airman pondered for a moment.

"Same ol' thing I've taken for years, Doc. Thorazine for the anxiety. Hell, even at my worst, I wouldn't scalp the general on purpose." The airman's voice dropped to almost a whisper. "I do believe the Devil's got me, Doc. Do you think that's possible?"

Mike couldn't help but chuckle as he scribbled out a prescription. "I think the Devil may have bigger issues on his plate, Airman Williams, I'm fairly certain those violent spasms are a side effect of heavy Thorazine use." He ripped the paper from his pad and handed it over with a smile. "We'll add a small dose of Cogentin, cut your Thorazine dosage in half, and that ought to fix you up."

The relief shone in the old barber's face, as though a weight had been lifted. "That sure is a wonder, Doc; it sure is. Thank God, because I don't know what I'd do if they put me out of the service."

Mike stopped making notes. The airman's response had piqued his curiosity. "Haven't you ever thought of retiring, Airman Williams? I mean, don't you have a family? Why not settle down?" From the look on the man's face, he immediately regretted asking.

"I do. A daughter." Airman Williams stared down at his lap. For the first time since Mike saw him, he looked like an old man, broken and alone. "We never did see eye-to-eye. I haven't seen her in thirty years." His voice wavered and trailed off. He raised his head and attempted to regain his spirits. "But then, you know how it is, in a military family."

Mike knew. He was seeing it more and more.

It was just another day at Camp Valkyrie.

Chapter 10

GENERAL ROSENTHAL never arrived that day. Some business or other always seemed to demand his attention. It was late on a rainy Friday when Mike was finally summoned to meet the general's entourage. "I know it's improper procedure," Judith apologized, as Mike made his way to the conference room, "but the man is a general! I had to let him on the unit. He just marched right past me!"

"You could at least have asked them to wipe their boots," he remarked, as they followed the trail of muddy prints.

The mood in the room was tense. At the head of the table sat General Edward "Butch" Rosenthal in full regalia. His medals and decorations glittered in the florescent light. The man was every bit as intimidating as Cassie described. Age seemed only to have sharpened his features, which appeared to have been carved out of granite. He stared intensely into Mike's eyes.

"At ease, Major. Now, let's get down to brass tacks, shall we?" the general announced in a deep, baritone voice. "Gentlemen, Major Pike is here to report on the status and condition of my daughter. Following this report, you will follow the procedure for a swift air evacuation." Rosenthal grunted; he paused to ask Judith for a glass of water. "Major Pike, if you will?"

Mike swallowed the lump in his throat. All eyes turned toward him, as he fought to organize his thoughts. If only they had given him time to rehearse! Now, having been rushed to this meeting without a moment's notice, he felt woefully unprepared.

"Major Pike, if you will, please!"

"W-well, Sir, Miss Cassandra Rosenthal, th-the patient in question, is seriously ill." The general leaned towards him, as if scanning the words for some hidden import. "She's very sick," Mike continued, as he found his voice. "Some exotic disease or infection we believe. Possibly typhus."

"So it's a fever is it? Carried by rats? My God! A daughter of mine infected by rat fleas." The general had since broken eye contact. He was already thumbing through his planner.

"She's psychotic, and I believe possibly suicidal. I recommend keeping her under quarantine. She'll be able to rest, and we'll have more time to address the—"

"It's a fever. So that explains the psychosis." General Rosenthal snapped the leather booklet shut, as if to emphasize his point. "Thank you, Major, that will be all."

"But sir!" Mike protested, "We can't be certain yet! We have to run more tests, confirm the organism!"

"That will be ALL, Major. I won't have my daughter locked up in a psych ward. These gentlemen will airlift her to Johns Hopkins where she belongs. I can keep tabs on her there from the Pentagon. "

"Sir, I can't allow the patient to be moved."

"Excuse me, Major?" The officers around the table, many of whom had risen to leave, now paused. Mike gritted his teeth. He could feel the cold sweat dripping down his back.

"Sir, the patient can't be moved. It's too dangerous. The patient needs a stable environment. An air evac could prove disastrous."

Blood rushed to the general's face. His lips curled in a snarl of contempt. "*Allow*?! Let me make this clear, Major Pike. You do not *allow* me to do anything. I give the orders. You follow them. Do I make myself clear?" From across the room, the words stung like a slap to the face. Mike looked helplessly around the table for support. There was none to be found. Even as they left, the men seemed to back away from the hapless physician.

"I'll expect the patient ready for transport at 0400 hours. Major Pike, you will report to Colonel Lowe, who will be informed of your insubordinate behavior. That is all."

Mike could feel his eyes burning with tears. His lip trembled, as he struggled to maintain his composure. It was as though an iron grip had pulled him back to his childhood. Here he stood facing the principal's wrath. Helpless and alone.

* * *

"Respectfully, sir, I was obligated to speak on behalf of the patient. You realize the general plans to fly her to Johns Hopkins?"

Colonel Lowe tore a bite from a hoagie as he listened. He ate slowly and methodically, like a cow chewing its cud. Every time he was here, Mike thought, the office looked more and more like a pig sty. Letters were scattered across the Colonel's desk, many of them caked with stains. In truth, the man himself seemed more preoccupied with his meal than with the Major's point.

"So what's the problem?" Lowe belched and wiped the corners of his mouth. A few traces of mustard lingered behind. "You're angry about being disciplined, I get that. General Rosenthal has a stick up his ass. But what are you gonna do? He's Pentagon. Just get the patient in shape and ship her on out. Case closed."

The colonel leaned back in his chair. His belly strained the buttons on his jacket, as he lit up a cigar. Mike, however, was undeterred. Over the past few hours, his humiliation had fermented into a bitter sense of rage.

"Sir, it's not a handful of demerits that concerns me. I have a duty to my patient. The risk of exposing her to others like this, in her condition, could be catastrophic. And that's not even considering the stress it would place on the patient, and in her state—"

Lowe waved him off in midsentence. He stared at the young major with mild annoyance. There was always one, he thought to himself with a sigh. Every few months there would always be that one jackass who had to make life difficult; had to play the damn martyr. Still, he had to give the man credit. The bedraggled major looked as though he hadn't slept in days. Patches of blonde stubble had grown on his face like weeds in a vacant lot. Lowe smirked. The boy would break sooner or later. You can't beat the system.

"Look, Major, I appreciate your concern, I do, but your first duty is to your country—to the United States Military—and in the military we respect the chain of command. So just pack her up, ship her out, and make this easier on all of us."

Mike had heard enough. His arms shook as his lifted himself from the chair. The colonel's voice followed behind him as he took his leave.

"And for God's sake, Major Pike, try to take it easy!"

Lowe cursed as the ash dropped from his cigar. He swept the cinders to the ground, but they left a long smear across the page of his report. There's always one, he thought to himself, as he closed his eyes to nap.

Chapter 11

"CASSIE? I WISH you'd look at me. Cassie?"

Mike coaxed as gently as he could. Two nights of little sleep took their toll on the major, and he fought to conceal his irritation. It was as though he were talking to a child. Cassie's fever had made her as stubborn and intractable as ever. She refused to eat now, and a tray sat untouched on the bedside table.

"I'm not here to take you anywhere. It's just me, Mike. Your friend! I just came to check on you."

Cassie's head peeked from beneath the covers. She stared at Mike with bloodshot eyes. The fever was getting worse. Her face and neck were drenched with sweat, and her body shivered under the blanket. She spoke like one in a trance, her voice distant and monotone.

"He's coming. He is coming for me. Can't. You said…"

She trailed off as her eyes became cloudy and unfocused. A stream of blood began dripping from her nose. Mike used a tissue to stem the flow. The nosebleeds hadn't been an issue until yesterday. According to her chart, it had been added to a list of symptoms including diarrhea, constipation, dehydration, tremors, hallucinations, and a rash.

Cassie's head fell back on the pillow. Mike stroked her hair and helped her with a glass of water. He tried to offer what little comfort he could. After all, he had grown fond of the patient over the last few days. It wasn't fair what she had to go through, nor that she was powerless to stop it.

"Just relax, that's it. It's just me. You're going to be feeling much better soon," he told her with a smile, "we don't have the blood cultures back yet, but we'll be able to get your fever down and I'm starting an antibiotic."

Cassie smiled back weakly and closed her eyes. Mike crept out of the room as quietly as he could. She needed her rest more than ever now. Judith was outside the door, and he handed her the patient's chart. "Give her aspirin and an ice bath to get her temperature down," Mike instructed, "then start an IV with doxycycline. And whatever happens, don't let them take her anywhere until it's done."

Judith took down the notes with a skeptical expression and shook her head. Mike knew she was thinking the same thing he was. Moving the patient, in her state, was asking for trouble. It was a disaster just waiting to happen.

*   *   *

General Rosenthal and his four-man crew arrived just as Mike left the ward. They marched past without even an acknowledgment. Following them from behind, Mike caught up just as the general finished barking directions. His men disappeared with gurney in tow.

"Save your breath, Major," the general remarked curtly. "I have an ambulance waiting outside, and she'll be no worse off than she is on this goddamn psych ward."

"But General, sir, she has to have the antibiotic by the IV bag! At least let us get her fever down before you take her outside!"

Mike pursed his lips. He knew his pleas were futile. The general, it seemed, was impervious to reason. In desperation, Mike sifted through the papers at the nursing station and returned with a folder and a pen. He still had one card left to play.

"Sir, I need you to sign this release," said Mike, as he thrust the packet forward. "This states that I have informed you of the severity of your actions, and that you take responsibility for any consequences that may occur as result."

For the first time since his arrival, Rosenthal looked generally shocked. In a moment, his lip curled back in that familiar snarl. It was a look of pure contempt. He tossed the papers in a nearby wastebasket.

"I'm not signing anything. Do you understand me, Major?" spoke the general in a low, menacing tone. "And if you interfere with this, I swear to you, you will wish you hadn't."

*   *   *

Giving up on the general, Mike ran to Cassie's room. He arrived just as the air evac team was shifting Cassie onto their stretcher. Fortunately, Judith had started the IV, and the patient appeared in stable condition. The cold   bath had lowered her temperature. She moved slowly and mechanically under the men's guidance.

"Cassie," Mike offered, "I tried everything I could. I can't stop your father." Cassie stared at him, her eyes wide with confusion. Mike looked away. "These men will take care of you though, they'll make sure you get the care you need."

The general's men were friendly enough, and they followed Mike's instructions carefully. All four agreed to change into the sterile masks and gowns provided by Judith. They scrubbed their hands raw before pulling on rubber gloves. Fear motivated their compliance, and the men were eager to complete the task as safely and quickly as possible.

"Thanks, Doc," muttered the crew leader, as he zipped up his gown. "We weren't told anything about this."

Furious at his men's pace, General Rosenthal stormed into the room just as the crew was adjusting their masks. He was livid.

"What the hell are you men doing!" the general bellowed, "and why the *hell* are you dressing like women!"

Mike had had enough. He would not be bullied now, not with everyone's health on the line. "It's required, sir," he stated, as matter-of-factly as possible. "Otherwise you are endangering the mission, and it is my duty to stop you."

The general glared at the major, his stare burning with anger, but he fell silent. It was as though the words Mike quoted from the manual had turned a switch inside him.

Ch. 1. Sec. C. Part II. It is an officer's duty to relieve his commander, should that commanding officer's judgment endanger the mission.

Rosenthal turned to his men. "Give the staff time to prepare her for transport," he ordered gruffly. With what little time they had, Mike and Judith worked quickly under the general's impatient eye. In a matter of minutes, the air evac team was rolling her out to the elevator.

"Damn," said Judith, still panting from exertion. "I'm glad that's over!"

Chapter 12

MIKE LOCKED THE DOOR to his office. It was rare that he lost his temper, but when he did it frightened him. Adrenaline coursed through his body like a drug. His blood boiled and frothed below the surface. His heart pounded like a hammer in his chest.

He could remember the last time the darkness had consumed him; when it had swallowed him whole. It was just a few years ago. He arrived home that evening same as any other. It had been immediately obvious that something was wrong. The front door hanging open in the breeze. One of the windows had been shattered. The kitchen tiles were covered with shattered glass and pottery. A pot on the stove had long since boiled over, leaving a bubbling mess.

The living room.

It was as though the living room had been converted into a butcher shop. The carpet and sofa were soaked with blood. The place had been ransacked. He could still remember that sound in the corner. That gurgling moan…

Mike shuddered. He tasted bile in his throat. In an attempt to calm down, he closed his eyes and breathed deeply. The nausea passed. The last thing Mike wanted was to dredge up memories from the past. "If you hit the field angry, you've already lost," he remembered his high school coach telling him, "you can't make the right decisions when you're pissed off." Hardly poetic words, Mike thought, but they stuck with him. Until that damn general was off the base, he had to keep his wits about him.

* * *

Fifteen minutes later, a banging stirred Mike from his slumber. He raised himself unsteadily from his desk. At the door were two air policemen. Both were attempting to catch their breath. Mike wiped the sleep from his eyelids and stared.

"Major," said the first man, having gained his composure. "We are in urgent need of Colonel Lowe, can you tell us where he is?"

"He's in his office," Mike answered irritably. "At least he oughta be. I saw him heading that way when I left the unit."

"We checked his office. We checked everywhere we could. This is an emergency, sir. We need a psychiatrist, immediately!"

Mike turned from one man to the other. The urgency in their voice roused him considerably.

"I'm a psychiatrist. What's going on?"

"Then you need to come with us. There's a patient on the ninth-floor ledge threatening to jump. The hospital commander sent us here to find help!"

Mike had already donned his coat. A disturbing realization had already dawned on him. As he rushed after the two men, he desperately hoped he was wrong.

*   *   *

The elevator ride seemed to last an eternity. To help, the younger of the two officers told Mike the story. The subject was a patient; a young woman, short, with curly blond hair.

Mike cringed inwardly and clenched his fists. It was definitely Cassie.

She seemed docile enough, the man recalled, when they unlatched her from the gurney. When her father took hold of her, though, she just snapped. She sunk her teeth in the general's arm and broke free. From there, she had run headlong into the building. The men had almost caught her in the stairwell, but she somehow eluded their grasp. She made it as far as the roof, only to stop, as if frozen, at the ledge.

If anyone came any closer, she had warned, she would jump.

*   *   *

Mike was struck by the crowd on the roof. A large group of hospital staffers, at least sixty-strong, had gathered to watch. It wasn't the size of the crowd that surprised him, but the atmosphere. A human life was on the line, and here they were, chatting and giggling as if it were a company picnic. It was surreal.

Mike stopped for a moment. Everything seemed so relaxed! But any hopes he may have had, however, disappeared when he was shoved beyond the crowd. There, just a few yards away, sat Cassie on the tin ledge of the roof, her legs dangling over the side. Suddenly, a force yanked him back by the collar. He turned to find himself inches from General Rosenthal's glare.

"There is no way this goddamn shrink is talking to my girl!" Mike recoiled as the saliva spattered his cheek. The hot breath seared his face. When he felt the grip on him slacken, Mike sprung into action. Years of training seemed to kick in. He was operating on instinct.

"Officers, I want the general restrained, immediately!" Mike motioned over the two policemen, who seemed hesitant to approach. "General Rosenthal, I have been ordered by the hospital commander to help your daughter. You are interfering with that order. I am therefore placing you under arrest."

There was a moment of uncertainty. The attention of the crowd turned to the new source of conflict, and they spoke rapidly in hushed tones. To Mike's relief, the officers restrained the general's arms on either side. Rosenthal himself seemed as stunned as the crowd. He gave no resistance as he was escorted from the scene.

*   *   *

Mike walked forward. The murmur of the crowd seemed to evaporate in the wind. He could hear the birds perched nearby; feel the gravel crunch beneath his feet. If Cassie could hear him, she gave no sign. She continued to sit, motionless, staring into space. The breeze whipped her hair across her face. When he was close enough, Mike noticed her fingers curled around the ledge. She was crying softly.

"Cassie!" hissed Mike, his voice barely above a whisper. "Cassie, what the heck are you doing?"

Cassie turned, and Mike stopped in his tracks. He cursed himself inwardly. The words he'd used seemed awkward and accusatory. Still, what else could he say? Standing here, at the edge of the precipice, his mind drew a blank.

"That selfish bastard. And you. I trusted you!" Cassie's face was streaked with tears. She rocked back and forth perilously. "I might as well die now than go home with him. The blood of the children is on my hands. The blood is on all of your hands."

Mike still inched forward slowly. He could see the ground, far below, and the view made him dizzy. There was a red dot down at the front of the building, a fire truck. Another large crowd had gathered on the ground. The police were driving up with lights flashing.

"Cassie, I can't hear you. Can I get closer?"

Her eyes narrowed with distrust, but she nodded in assent. As Mike inched forward, her head lolled to the side. Her eyes rolled back. To Mike, she looked as though she would pass out any second.

"Cassie, you're really scaring me..."

With one last step, Mike lunged forward. Cassie shrieked as his arms wrapped tight around her waist. With all his strength, Mike wrenched her backward, and the two figures collapsed onto the dusty roof. A group of physicians rushed to help, and Cassie fought as best she could to resist. Both she and Mike were exhausted by the time they were finally separated.

"You bastard!" Cassie spat, as Mike wiped the blood from his mouth. It took three men to hold her down. After a few moments she went limp. A stretcher was brought to carry her back to the ambulance.

"You're a real bastard," remarked General Rosenthal, as Mike limped past him over the roof. "A real son of a bitch."

* * *

The show was over and the crowd dispersed. Mike followed close behind the nursing staff and air police, as they whisked Cassie back to the safety of the ward. She was sedated now, and under close supervision. Tragedy had been averted.

In the quiet of the room, Mike sat watching Cassie sleep. At one point, an officer poked his head in to report.

"Major, I'm sorry to trouble you, but we have some paperwork we need you to fill out. And, well, there's the business with the General..."

"You may as well release him," Mike sighed. "I doubt any time in the brig is going to make the man a better father."

After a half-hour, when he was sure the patient was stable, the tired major shuffled back to his quarters. His eyes were heavy now, and he felt beaten and drained. He collapsed on the bed and fell into a dark, dreamless sleep.

Chapter 13

MIKE PASSED THROUGH the following week in a fog. He heard nothing from Cassie, nor General Rosenthal or Colonel Lowe for that matter. Life went on at Camp Valkyrie as if nothing had happened. Everything seemed surreal to Mike, as though something within him had snapped. The days melted together, and he went through his rounds feeling like a ghost in the shell.

A break in the routine came, that weekend, with an unexpected visitor. Mike groaned and rubbed his eyes, the rap at the door dragging him back to the land of the living. He looked at his clock and groaned again. Two in the afternoon already? He never slept in this late, not even on a Saturday. He lumbered to the door in a daze.

"Hey there buddy, you still sleepin'?"

Mike shielded his eyes as the light poured in. On the doorstep was Moon; unshaven as usual, with that familiar cockeyed grin.

"Just thought I'd check on you. Man, you just, well, you haven't been yourself." Moon was not one to wait for an invitation. He strolled past Mike's slumped form and surveyed the room. The smile on his face dissolved into a look of concern. "Jesus, Mike, are you all right?"

"Yeah, I've been fine," Mike responded curtly. He plopped onto his mattress and ran a hand through his hair. It was true, the state of his room betrayed his apathy. The floor was strewn with dirty clothes, papers, and take-out containers. "Things have just felt weird since... you know... the incident."

Moon frowned. He hunched over, leaning his elbows on the kitchen counter. "I hear that, brother, but you got to talk about it. You been isolating yourself from everyone lately. No one's seen you in the lounge or the mess hall—not anywhere, really—besides the ward."

Mike opened his mouth, but no response came. He shrugged instead.

"It's not healthy, man." Moon stood for a moment stroking his stubble. In a moment, his high spirits returned, and he grinned. "I might know what you need, man. That's why I came by."

"And what's that?"

"Meet me outside the lounge building at seven tonight and you'll see."

* * *

It seemed to Mike like forever since he'd last left Camp Valkyrie. He hadn't realized until that night just how long it had been. The cab had taken the two men to a barbecue joint in town, a place Moon swore by, and the smell of smoked brisket alone began to ease Mike's tensions. After months of cafeteria fare, he'd almost forgotten the taste of real food.

It wasn't long before the two were talking like old friends. For the first time in days, Mike allowed himself to relax. It was as though a dam within him had burst. The warm relief of companionship and pecan pie a-la-mode seeped into his tired limbs.

After a heavy meal, Moon led Mike to a little bar across the street. It was a little hole-in-the-wall establishment; dark and cozy, with a dusty pool table and a jukebox in the corner. Whisky gradually loosened the men's tongues, and for the first time that evening, Moon cut to the matter weighing on both of their minds.

"Pretty weird, eh? How no one talks about stuff on the base? Like the incident you had with that crazy girl up on the roof."

Mike squirmed on the stool. He had known it was only a matter of time.

"Yeah, man, it's just messed up. She... Cassie... I should have seen things coming. Now it's as if the whole thing never happened. Like people could just disappear off the face of the earth, and no one would notice."

Moon flicked his lighter and lit another cigarette. "Yeah, it's a messed up system they got running, but I have a feeling there's something else you're not tellin' me, bud."

"Something I'm not telling? Like what?"

"Jesus, Mike, you were sweet on the girl! You know it. Don't blame you. That was one groovy babe. Curves in all the right places."

Now was Mike's turn to laugh. He blushed in spite of himself. Moon elbowed him playfully. "Yeah, yeah, man, you think I didn't know? Damn! First time I saw you give her those puppy-dog eyes, I knew you were hooked."

"Nah, well, maybe a little." Mike paused to drain the rest of his glass. "It's just… she reminded me of someone I used to know."

"Old girlfriend?"

"Wife."

Moon's eyes were as wide as saucers. He motioned the bartender for another round.

"Whoa, Mike! I always pegged you as a bit of a mama's boy, but damn, I didn't know you had an old lady!"

"I still have one, in fact," Mike bit his lip. He stared down at the counter. "She looked — looks — so much like Cassie, too; same blonde curls, same eyes, even the same smile if you can believe it."

"Even the same… you know…" Moon cupped his hands just below his chest, as if hefting two pendulous breasts. Mike rolled his eyes. "So what are you down about? You got a bangin' hot broad at home, man, I'm jealous, I don't mind tellin' ya!"

"Don't be."

"Why, she a ball-buster? She crazy like that other one?"

"No. Cassie has a chance. My wife is lying almost brain-dead in a hospital. That's why."

Moon's face drew taut and serious. It was the first time Mike had seen him without his playful veneer. "I came home from work and the place was broken into. I found her by following the trail of blood. I don't know how she managed to crawl even that far."

He took another drink to steady his voice.

"She'd been shot in the head. It must have been point-blank, considering the massive damage to her skull. There were bits of her flesh and bone on the floor around her, and she… she just lay there… twitching…"

Moon draped his arm around Mike. "I had no idea. Jesus, Mike, I'm really sorry."

Mike nodded, and wiped the tears from his eyes.

"It's okay. It's just… it's troubling you know? I hate feeling helpless all the time. Like I can't protect the people I care for."

"Hey! You can't do this to yourself man. It's not your fault," Moon offered. "Besides, everything'll work out, you just got to give it time."

The words felt hollow, and he knew it.

"You know what would help… right nowww…?" Mike slurred.

"What's that, brother?"

"Another round."

Chapter 14

MIKE SIGHED AS HE READ the schedule. It was the third night this month Moon had begged him to cover as "Medical Officer of the Day." He groaned and rubbed his forehead. With a friend like that, he thought to himself, who needed enemies? It was times like this that he wished he were not so much of a pushover. Well, it couldn't be helped now.

The weather that month had been violent, even for tornado season. The clouds would swallow the sky for days, and storms would drown the prairies in a stream of constant rain. Mike knew it would to be one of those nights. He could tell from the thunder. The first patients trickling in only confirmed it. It was more than another storm, said one local, as he shivered in a blanket, it was a Texas Blue Norther. The fields were flooding, and the sides of the road were littered with dead animals and cars half-sunk in mud. A woman cradling a screaming child warned of disaster on the horizon. Great pillars of clouds were funneling towards the earth. It was only a matter of time, she announced, before they would arrive; crushing everything in their path.

Mike knew well the carnage a twister could wreak. He had seen the aftermath himself: barns crushed to pieces; vehicles overturned; the brick and mortar debris of houses thrown piecemeal by the wind. All he could do, he knew, was remain calm and focus on one patient at a time.

From across the base, a siren blared from one of the towers. It was a familiar sound by now, and it meant only one thing: Air Traffic had a tornado on the radar. In a moment, the other sirens on base followed suit, and a horrible doomsday wail echoed across Valkyrie Base.

The hospital was always busy during tornado warnings. The first few times, nearly half the base—even the locals—would flock to the relative shelter of the ward. As time wore on, and the alarms became more frequent, Mike noticed a disturbing change. Children were being temporarily housed on Two South until the storm blew over. This ward, that usually held adult patients, had transformed into a daycare overnight. Each of these young

patients suffered the same symptoms: insomnia; night terrors; and gen-
eralized anxiety. More often than not, Mike was instructed, it was best to
prescribe valium. It was not an issue worth troubling the base commander.

*   *   *

The ER was packed; as usual, it was woefully understaffed. The hours passed
for Mike in a flurry of activity. There were so many cases to address, and
always so little time. In one room, a young wife was suffering a panic attack;
in another, twin boys clung to each other and sobbed. A drunk airman,
whose car had stalled when he tried driving through a flooded underpass,
had come within seconds of drowning. Two others stumbled in from the
Officers' Club across the street. The inebriated were given an IV and served
coffee. No one was to step foot outside that night.

By the early hours of the morning, the storm finally began to wane.
Gradually, the patients trickled out, until a lull settled on the ward. The quiet
came as a relief to Mike. When he was content the staff had the unit under
control, he poured himself a cup of coffee and retreated to the waiting room.
He singled out the comfiest looking chair and collapsed.

The foyer of Two South offered Spartan accommodations. It was a drafty
room; small and sparsely decorated. Two lounge chairs and a ratty-looking
couch sat facing a coffee table, upon which was splayed a collection of old
magazines. They were all months old, and the pages were frayed and yellow at
the edge. At least the place offered silence and sanctuary, and that was enough
for Mike. All he could hear was the steady patter of rain against the windows.

"Hey!"

The voice startled Mike, who was surprised and a little annoyed to have
company. A man in military fatigues had been sitting on the adjacent couch.
He was a young, heavyset man, with a brutal looking scar across his cheek.
His face seemed creased and weathered by the elements.

"Uh, hello," Mike answered flatly. Every fiber of his body ached from the
long shift, and he was hardly in the mood to chat. "You know, if you ring the
bell we can get you checked in." He motioned weakly towards the counter.

"Oh, that's all right, really. I just came to wait out the storm."

"The worst of it passed a couple hours ago."

Mike eyed the officer curiously. Something wasn't quite right, he felt,
and experience had taught him to trust his instinct. The man's hands shook

intermittently. As he spoke, his eyes scanned the room, as if anticipating an ambush at any moment.

"Yes, I guess I knew that," the officer said, as his smile disappeared. "It's still going on in my head though."

"What do you mean?"

"The noise—the thunder, the sirens, the rain—it just sets me off. I try to find some quiet space and sit until it passes.

"Until what passes?" Mike took a slow sip of his coffee. He savored its warmth. The officer fell silent. His face twitched; his eyes welled with tears. As he leaned forward, Mike noticed that the man—perhaps a foot taller, and as muscular as a marine—appeared as helpless as a child.

"Major, I... I don't know if I can talk about it." The soldier wiped a tear away roughly with the back of his sleeve. "I need some answers, though. I can't live like this. I know it. I'm not sure how much more I can take."

Despite himself, Mike sighed as he rose from his chair. It took a supreme act of will, but he fought the urge to melt back into the comfort of the cushions. He stretched his limbs turned to the officer.

"I'll be right back. Do you take milk or sugar?"

*   *   *

The rain had stopped, and the airman and the doctor sat together in the courtyard outside. Mike had figured they could both benefit from a little fresh air. The privacy didn't hurt either. It was a small courtyard, enclosed by walls of glass and brick. Few people spent any time there—aside from Mike—and it had gone neglected as long as he could remember. The lawn was a patchwork of weeds and wild grass now. At the center of the courtyard sat the ruins of an old fountain.

The two sat for a moment, listening to the birds and watching the water drip from the windows. The airman swore suddenly, and Mike saw the man had spilled steaming liquid down his collar. His hands were shaking hard now; too hard even to drink. He rose violently and spat in frustration.

"It's this shit all the damn time. Goddamn it."

"Calm down. Here, take these," said Mike, offering a handful of napkins from his pocket. The man snatched the tissues and pressed them against his chest.

"Can you describe how it feels when you're... umm... triggered...like this?" asked Mike. "Is your heartbeat racing? Do you feel...dizzy?"

The airman returned to his seat. His eyes were smoldering, and he stared forward, grinding his teeth.

"Yes, goddammit! I feel panicked, like I need to run; need to find   cover. I feel...terrified." He pulled out a cigarette and struggled with the lighter. Mike offered a hand, but the airman recoiled. When it was finally lit, he took a long, slow drag.

"Terrified."

Mike was listening intently now. His feelings oscillated between clinical fascination and human empathy, a combination he found distinctly unsettling.

"How long have you been suffering from these symptoms?"

"About six months after I got back from 'Nam. I go over all the things I—we—did. I replay them in my mind over and over. I don't even remember what it's like to not feel wracked with guilt all the time."

"What happened, exactly?"

"I think about my friends there. We were brothers. Through all the shit that went down over there, we had each other's back, you know?" The airman kept staring vacantly into space. He crushed the cigarette beneath his boot. "We flew at least two hundred sorties without an incident. It was the last fucking mission too. We lost two men. I circled back around to see what happened and they were gone. There was just a cloud of smoke and ashes falling from the sky."

The airman's voice cracked and he dropped his head in his hands. Mike picked at the moss and the damp cracks in the stone. He wished he knew the right words to say.

"You know, all the times we flew over those tiny encampments and vil-lages," the airman continued, "we'd see those little clouds of smoke down on the surface. I never thought about it then. I think them now. All the time."

"But you're home now." Mike smiled weakly, and, uncertain how to react, gave the airman a pat on the back. The man wiped his face and stared back at the ground. His cheeks were puffy and red. "You're safe now, you have a family that supports you. And the military—"

Mike broke off as the soldier lifted his head and laughed. He laughed so hard his body shook, and Mike began to wonder if the man really was off his rocker. It took a few moments for the airman to compose himself. He was still wheezing and coughing as he wiped the tears from his eyes.

"Oh the military, yeah, they've been a real help. A few shots, dental, a physical. You know how easy it would have been for me to put on   civilian clothes and go to a normal hospital, where it wouldn't ruin my career to say: 'I can't sleep without nightmares. My children are afraid of me. My wife tells me she doesn't love me anymore. How do I deal with this'?"

"How do you deal with things now?"

"I drink. I have these attacks. Then I drink some more."

The two sat in silence. It was not the man's story that upset Mike, so much as how often he'd heard it. Every day, it was a different variation of the same tale, which had been told over and over until it became familiar; almost commonplace. The airman had all the symptoms, too: the mood swings, the paranoia, the feelings of alienation from all that was once familiar, or even loved.

Those who came forward with the condition—"battle fatigue," they called it—were forever marked. It was a fact Mike had learned early on. He had seen words like "cowardice" and "unbalanced" marked on the files in red ink. "What had become of the real, red-blooded American men?" Col. Lowe had lamented once, in the board room. "That's the one thing you can say about war. It separates the men from the boys."

The doctor and the airman sat in silence for a while longer. Both knew there was nothing left to say. The airman thanked Mike for the company and shook his hand. As he sat alone a while longer, watching the sun rise, a realization dawned on Mike, and he felt ashamed.

He didn't even know the man's name.

Chapter 15

IT WAS EARLY MORNING when Mike finally left the hospital. Already the first signs of life had begun to stir at Camp Valkyrie, as he shuffled to the barracks for a welcome rest. The frosty winds from the prairie chilled him to the bone. Finally, he collapsed into bed, letting the sweet comfort of sleep overtake him.

Mike awoke late that evening with an aching head. He groaned and rolled over in the covers. Just beyond his bedroom wall, he could hear the muffled sounds of an argument. Neither voice was recognizable to Mike, nor could he discern—not that he cared—what the disagreement was about. As the exchange became more heated, he could make out bits and pieces of the conversation. It was something about money. Of that he was certain.

Now wide awake, Mike sat up in bed with a groan, rubbing the sleep from his eyes. It was obvious he wouldn't be getting any more rest. He was just considering a shower when he heard the sounds of a scuffle outside. A dull thud. Cursing. Something serious was going on, and his curiosity was piqued.

In the hallway, Mike stared wide-eyed at the scene. One man, a tech he recognized from a nearby ward, was holding a young captain by the collar. He released the man, and the two stared back at Mike, who felt awkward in his underclothes.

"Can I help you?" Mike asked, nervously.

Neither man answered immediately. The captain smoothed out the creases in his shirt and gave a half-hearted salute. The tech, meanwhile, stared back, shuffling his feet sullenly. If he recognized Mike's rank, he certainly didn't show it.

"Oh, um, Hello Major," the captain finally stammered. "I apologize for the disturbance. We can…go elsewhere."

"Just a private argument, sir," added the tech, his lip curled in a smirk. As the two men turned and moved down the hall, he turned back and gave Mike a wink. "And if you heard anything, well, I was never here. Remember that."

*   *   *

The memory of the encounter was still fresh in Mike's mind after a long, luxurious shower. He had recognized the tech; he was one of the few who worked the forensic unit, a locked ward for patients facing criminal charges. What he was doing in the officer's quarters—arguing about money and roughing up a captain, no less—he could not figure out. Those final words of warning echoed in his head. This was obviously a man unafraid of authority.

In an effort to distract himself, Mike tried to focus on the paperwork that had mounted on his desk. It was no use. The throbbing in his head made concentration impossible. Just as he had begun to make headway, a loud pounding on the door shocked him from his concentration. He could tell who it was from the laugh outside.

"It's unlocked, Moon. Come on in."

Moon strolled in with his usual swagger, but Mike noted a definite change in his friend's appearance. For once, Moon's clothes were neatly pressed and he was clean-shaven. His well-coiffed hair was slick with oil. From across the room, Mike could already smell a heady mix of cologne and after-shave.

"Mike, I want you to meet someone," Moon announced, gesturing behind him. "This is my friend, my charming companion, the lovely Miss Flapjack."

Mike recognized the face. She was a new addition; a lieutenant assigned to one of Camp Valkyrie's bureaucratic offices. She comically rolled her eyes and shook his hand with a vice-like grip.

"Ugh, would you listen to that Lothario? I feel like I'm dating a game show host!" Flapjack laughed. She brushed back the bangs that hung over her eyes. Her appearance put Mike more in mind of a tomboy than a pencil-pusher, in her worn jeans and combat boots. Only the large coke-bottle glasses seemed to give her away.

Mike smiled ruefully as he reached for his jacket. As usual, Moon had failed to inform him there would be company. Despite his annoyance, there was something about this stranger that intrigued him.

"So Flapjack, huh?" he said, in an attempt to be sociable. "That's an... unusual name!"

"Thanks. My parents gave it to me!"

"Because you like pancakes?"

"Because I liked the name," she replied, as though it were the most obvious answer on earth. "And no one else has it. That's the best part. It's all mine."

"Like Einstein?"

"Well, yeah," Flapjack shrugged. "I guess all the unique traditional names had been taken. I'm just glad they didn't call me Buffy, or Cici, or Khaki, or Bunny, or whatever. Just Flapjack. It's pretty much the best name."

"I can't argue with that." Mike grinned. Everything Flapjack said seemed to carry a sense of conviction, of finality. She could have told them anything, he realized; they were powerless to refute it.

*   *   *

"Hm, yeah, I know the guy." Moon turned down the radio. It had begun to storm, yet again, and he strained to see through the rain on the windshield. "I think they call him Cocky, or Cochran. Something like that. Why?"

Mike craned his neck forward from the backseat. "He was in the barracks earlier arguing with a captain. It was about money or something. I think he threatened me." He turned to Flapjack in the passenger seat, who stared back with bemused interest.

"Yeah, he's quite the entrepreneur." Moon bit his lip and continued. "Now, you didn't hear it from me, but he's known in some circles as a bit of a bookie; takes bets on sports games: football, basketball, stuff like that— maybe a drug business on the side."

"But," Flapjack chuckled, "You didn't hear it from him!"

"Isn't that a problem though?" asked Mike, "being in the military and all?"

"I don't use his services man. It beats me," answered Moon. "I guess he just hasn't been caught yet."

"Ricks is on that unit," offered Flapjack. "Doesn't mean he would know the guy, but you could always ask." She groaned in mock annoyance and leaned her head against the window. "I've been here a week and this stuff is old news. Are you boys really that much out of the loop?"

*   *   *

It took them a while to find the restaurant. After all, Flapjack, who'd recommended the place, hadn't been there for years, and the town had changed since then. Her father would sometimes bring her along when he had business at the base. Finally they found the ramshackle building next to the courthouse on the town square. A rusty sign hung near the entrance, the name almost illegible. They had arrived at Judy's.

Mike coughed and surveyed the interior. It was a small dining room, and the mesquite smoke made his eyes water. On the greasy wall hung a number of hunting trophies, the heads staring back through glass eyes. Flapjack had already skipped over to the jukebox in the corner. An old country song blared through the speakers.

"Well, bless my stars, if it ain't l'il Flapjack!"

Coming towards Mike was a massive woman, a grease-stained apron wrapped tight around her girth. Pinned to her chest was a tag so old that the name had almost worn off. A cigarette dangled from the corner of her mouth.

"My eyes told me you was here, but honey, you been gone so long I almost couldn't believe it mah-self! How yo' folks been? They ever gon' come visit ol' Judy?"

Flapjack flashed a wry grin. "And what if mom and dad did come by? It'd break their hearts to see you smoking again!"

"Now don't you start, child! I've known you since you was knee-high to a billy goat. You oughta know by now ol' Judy too tough for the cancer!" She ruffled Flapjacks hair, and beamed at her companions. "And how about you boys, now? You ready for the best home cookin' ya'll ever had?"

Before Mike could respond, Judy had already shepherded them into an empty booth and was on her way back to the kitchen. A waiter took their drink orders.

"Isn't she going to come back with menus?" asked Mike. "We haven't even ordered yet."

"Judy doesn't have menus!" laughed Flapjack. Dinner is always a full plate of the best barbecue you ever tasted."

"What kind of meat, though? Beef?"

"You can't tell! The sauce is so good nobody cares!"

*　*　*

Mike leaned back in the booth with a full belly. Flapjack was right. He could honestly not have guessed what animals he'd consumed. Every other patron seemed to recognize Flapjack, and she greeted them with unflagging enthusiasm. Each one, it seemed, had a story to tell. They had known her since she was a girl when her dad and sometimes she and her mother with him would fly to Valkyrie for 'business'.

"Well, much as I've loved the free drinks and great food," said Moon, stifling a belch, "we had better turn in soon. We have 'Race Relations' first thing in the morning, and they'll do something nasty to me if I miss that again."

"Yeah, I've heard of that," said Mike, "but I still don't really know what it is."

"It's a program to lower racial tensions in the military," Moon answered, "Probably a good thing when it started, too. They lecture mostly about drugs and alcohol now."

"We're required to turn in pot-smokers, too," Flapjack giggled, elbowing Moon in the side. She winked at Mike.

"Have you ever turned anyone in?"

The question made Flapjack hesitate. She rolled a toothpick from one side of her mouth to the other thoughtfully.

"Well, I've known my share of women before I came here with drug problems that I tried to get into rehab," she sighed, "but no, I wouldn't report anyone to their commander. That goes nowhere but trouble for everyone involved."

"They all drink pretty heavily, too," added Moon. "It's a forbidden subject to address, even at staff meetings. We all have to adhere to the rule of silence."

"And what about gambling, or whatever that Cochran fellow was up to?"

Mike turned from one friend to the other. A pall seemed to have fallen on their good spirits. Moon looked at Mike grimly.

"There are some things that go on at the base that it's best to stay out of. Really shady stuff."

"So you don't think I should report it?" asked Mike.

"Suit yourself," Moon shrugged, "but I wouldn't. Remember, snitches get stitches."

'Snitches get stitches.' Hmm. Mike had not heard that since elementary school.

Chapter 16

THE SOCIAL ACTIONS building was packed the next morning. Staff meetings, Mike had noticed, were never this well-attended. "Race Relations" was a rarely held seminar, and as if to compensate, the base had brought in an outside speaker. Attendance was mandatory.

"Mike, hey! I brought you some snacks, brother!"

Moon plopped down in the adjacent chair and handed him a donut. Wow, thought Mike, they'd even brought food, the surest sign of a special event at Valkyrie. Moon leaned in towards him and whispered in his ear.

"Don't look now, but you got a stalker mad-doggin' you at eight o'clock."

Mike turned behind him to his left. Sure enough, he was being watched, and he recognized the man instantly. Cochran sat staring back at him, dead-eyed and arms folded. The unblinking eye contact, the contemptuous sneer on his face, all combined to make Mike queasy. The tech noticed him looking back and smiled, exposing tobacco-stained teeth, looking for all the world like a giant rat. Mike shuddered.

"Just ignore him, Cochran's too yellow to mess with you face-to-face, besides," continued Moon, "I think they're about to start. Dig that speaker, eh? He looks like a homeless vet..."

A hush suddenly fell over the crowd as a grizzled-looking man ascended the podium. He wore a tye-dye shirt with a bandana around his head. He appeared to have not shaved in weeks.

"Hey you cats, the name's Mongoe, and I used to be a homeless vet."

Moon stifled a giggle, as Mike elbowed him in the ribs.

"But you know what? The Good Lord came into my life five years ago, and he got me back on my feet, clean and sober."

There were a few half-hearted claps from the audience before he continued.

"But y'all ought to know some figures. On any given base, it's estimated that up to 80% of the personnel use drugs in some form or other. And that's not all." Mongoe cleared his throat. "You know 10% of career officers are alcoholics? And another 25% are problem drinkers? How y'all supposed to be healthy and raise a family with them monkeys on your back?"

"Are they going to shut us down?"

All eyes in the room turned to the back of the audience. It was a colonel that had asked, and his face turned red from the attention.

"You're wondering why the base runs an officers' club and sells booze?"

"N-no…" stammered the colonel. "Just wanted to know if they're… making changes is all."

"The answer is no," said Mongoe. "The Pentagon requires that the base commanders make a profit, and that won't change. Y'all just need to turn your troubles over to Jesus. Do that, and we'll see those numbers go down. Can I get an amen?"

*   *   *

"Can you believe that speaker? Where'd they dig up that old fossil?" Moon laughed at his own joke from the back seat. Mike turned to Flapjack, who seemed far more irritated with Moon this morning than the night before.

"Oh hush," she admonished, turning a corner towards the barracks. "Try to look past appearances. The man's an alcoholic. He's gone from being homeless to actually trying to make a difference. He's talking to fellow soldiers."

"It means he's a loon," Moon retorted.

"No, it means he's sincere."

Moon giggled in the back seat, as Flapjack frowned in annoyance. Mike was meanwhile lost in thought. It was one of the strangest meetings he'd ever attended. For a talk entitled "Race Relations," Mongoe had not raised a single racial issue. The presentation itself was short and perfunctory. An inspirational pep talk, a request to turn over any drug abusers on base, and an educational film on the 'Danger of Marijuana'. To say the least, he found the experience underwhelming.

"I noticed Cocky was giving you the evil eye."

Mike turned to Flapjack, who was smiling at him softly. She turned her eyes to the road as she spoke.

"I know what you're thinking—you want to do something—but believe me, he'd love nothing more. I know his type. He's an opportunist just waiting for you to react."

"Is there any way this guy can hurt me?" asked Mike. "The look he was giving me, it was pure evil!"

"Just stay out of his way," said Flapjack. You have to understand that a military base is more than what it appears. It's—how to put this—it's like a city-within-a-city, you know? There's a whole 'nother world lurking beneath the veneer of honor and respectability."

Flapjack must have noticed the confusion in Mike's face, and she laughed playfully, touching his shoulder.

"You might be naïve, Mike, but you're a good guy. You're gonna do fine."

"I tell you what I'd do," said Moon. "I'd pop him one real good. Pow! Right in the kisser."

Flapjack rolled her eyes and drove on in silence.

When he arrived home, Mike found a message on his answering machine.

*   *   *

The white walls of the room had yellowed with age, Mike noticed. In places, the wallpaper had torn, leaving patches of exposed clay. Across the table sat Lowe and Ricks, their looks were grim. Cochran sneered at him from the far end.

"Now relax, Major, I don't want you to think of this as a formal repri-mand," Colonel Lowe began. "Just a warning. We take mistreatment of our personnel seriously."

Mike shuffled nervously in his chair. How could he possibly relax? In this windowless cell, under the heat of the fluorescent lights, it felt like an interrogation room.

"Now, my technician, Mr. Cochran, has brought to my attention that you intimidated him at the officer's barracks, is that correct?"

Mike's jaw dropped. He couldn't swallow. His throat felt like cotton. Surely they couldn't be serious.

"Now, Colonel Lowe has told me you're something of a rebel, Major, so I'll make something clear," said Major Ricks, his voice measured and firm. "You're free to protest how we do things here, if you must, but you will not bully my staff members, is that clear?"

"But it's a lie! How can you believe that! There's no proof!"

Mike gripped the edge of the table, digging in his nails. He was practi-cally trembling with rage.

"Please restrain yourself, Major," said Ricks, his tone unaffected. "We have eyewitnesses. Two from the barracks."

This could not be happening, thought Mike. Two "witnesses," and from his own barracks, too. These were his own colleagues and neighbors, the people he trusted! He had never felt so betrayed. Cochran, meanwhile, was nodding his head, a look of serenity on his face. He was soaking in the victory.

"So I would warn you, Major," ordered Colonel Lowe, "to tread   lightly. Understood? "

"Colonel, in the first place, he and a captain were arguing in the barracks just outside my door. When I opened it, he was threatening the Captain. In the second place, what was he even doing in the officer's quarters? I actually said nothing to him, but he had no reason to be there. Ricks, you have no business accusing me of anything. Why would you be protecting this…this… person? This makes no sense to me. You're making a mistake, Colonel Lowe."

Lowe looked flustered. He was disciplining one of his doctors—a thing he loved to do. Power and control were not familiar to him. It was exotic, almost erotic. And now, Mike had reframed it into a 'mistake', like a prostitute rebuffing him. He suddenly had the urge to go pee. "Let's just all behave. This is the goddamn US Air Force, after all." He shoved away from his desk and made for the bathroom. Damn Creaser, he thought. He had a bathroom in his office and Lowe had to run for it.

The three men sat looking at each other. "Ricks, I don't understand your part in this. He's got something on you, doesn't he? You owe him money?"

"You'd better be careful," said Cochran.

"I'm not the one with the enterprise. I don't have to be careful. Look, Cochran, I don't give a damn if you're a bookie, as long as it doesn't interfere with my patient's care or me or the 'mission' whatever that may be. So leave me alone!"said Mike. "And you, Ricks, how can we work together if I don't trust you?"

"Lowe's on my side."

"Bullshit! That poor guy would believe anything. Who's gonna save your ass, Ricks? This little rat or Lowe? Or will it be Moon and me and Kennedy and the rest? You'd better think about it. Lowe's not back so I think this meeting is over." Mike got up and walked out. He would not forget that he had an enemy now.

Chapter 17

FOR ONCE, THE BURDEN of the work was a blessing for Mike. The wound to his pride began to wane with the hours. By midnight, it was merely a dull ache in his mind. All that was left was to retreat to the barracks and sleep off the rest.

As Mike pulled out of the parking lot, something in the rear-view caught his eye. The building was closed, and yet there was a white van creeping around the far end of the lot. He tried to take down the license, but the van was unmarked. Whatever their intentions, the occupants had no interest in being identified.

Mike's gut instincts kicked in. He felt an urge to get away, to remove himself from the premise as quickly as possible. He wanted no more interaction with Lowe. Yet, much to his dismay, Mike found himself tailing the van from a distance. He had to know what was going on. It was the only way he'd get any sleep.

The van reached the gate and pulled out onto the empty road. To Mike's relief, he only had to tail them for a handful of miles. The mysterious vehicle parked next to the hospital and began to flash its lights intermittently. From three stories up, they were answered by the beam of a flashlight. The message had been received.

Mike swore inwardly as the van swerved into the alley. It was on its way to the back of the building. Against his better judgment, Mike parked and began to creep quietly in their direction. From the cover of a few trash bins he could make out the sound of muffled voices.

In the moonlight, Mike could make out two figures, both in white uniforms worn by technicians. They had backed-up the vehicle and were motioning towards someone inside. Slowly, the storage doors of the building began to open. Several figures in blue robes began to emerge. One-by-one, they would scurry into the van, only to return moments later. The scene was perplexing to Mike, and more than a little disturbing. These were clearly patients, and whatever they were getting, it was clearly illicit.

When he was sure the van was gone, Mike returned to his car and wiped the mud from his pants. The best course of action, he felt, would be to report the incident at once. Besides, the security offices were on the way to the barracks, so it was no inconvenience. If anyone knew what to do, it would be them.

Mike had never been to the security office. What he found came as a shock. There was only a single officer on duty; a fat, slovenly man, his shoes propped on the desk. A magazine on his chest rose and fell with each snore. Mike rang the bell once, twice, and a third time before the man finally began to stir.

"Ugh. Can I help you?" The officer grunted and rubbed his eyes. He made no attempt to hide his displeasure. Mike looked down at a half-eaten donut in disgust.

"Well, I think so. I just saw a white van pull up behind the hospital and give something to a lot of patients."

"And?"

"And… well, that's it.

The officer scrawled something down on a notepad and belched.

"Well, that's unusual," he mused. "I'll make sure to report that to the captain, yessir. We can't have that."

Mike left the security officer feeling more disgruntled than before. It felt as though he were living in the twilight zone; as though everyone knew something he didn't. It was all a big joke at his expense. Flapjack's words echoed in his mind. She was right, he decided, as he drifted to sleep. Nothing here is ever as it appears.

* * *

Strange occurrences were nothing new at Two South. In a military hospital, Mike had learned to expect the unexpected. Still, the scene that morning, just days after the incident with the van, had him dumbfounded.

Mike had been drawn by the sounds of an argument. He could tell the first voice was Judith's, but the other was unfamiliar; it was a thick, husky timbre, with a rich accent. In the front, by the large double-doors, he found the source. The absurdity of the scene made him laugh out loud.

Judith and the patient were staring at him now, but he couldn't help it. Judith was a diminutive woman, and the sight of her arguing with a man twice her size was too much to bear. To make matters worse, the staff had dressed the patient in a robe three-sizes too small. The fabric was wrapped skin-tight around his massive bulk.

"If you're quite finished, Doctor," snapped Judith, "perhaps you can talk to Airman Anque. He arrived in on the air evac last night and is demanding to leave at once."

The airman lumbered towards Mike. He was a Native American, at least seven-feet tall, with a bone-crushing handshake. Outwardly, Mike remained calm and professional. He was a doctor, he reminded himself, merely reasoning with a patient. However, feelings of amusement had turned to genuine fear. Before him was a man like the Rock of Gibraltar; a man practically shaking with rage.

It took some negotiating, but the patient gradually began to calm down. The airman and Mike made a compromise. He would return to his room, so long as he would be allowed to state his case. Having been placated, a transformation had come over Airman Anque. The raging bull was now gentle as a lamb. He began chatting with Mike as though the two were old friends, only pausing to throw back his long, dark hair in laughter. The manic behavior was unsettling to Mike. The man could turn on him at a moment's notice.

"Doctor," began the airman, when the two were both seated, "You must understand that I cannot stay here. This place is not my home."

Mike kept one eye on the door as he listened. He cursed himself for not leaving it open. Now, if things turned ugly, as they very well could, he would have to fend for himself. He choked down a lump in his throat.

"Well let's see what can be done," Mike offered. "You'll have to tell me how you got here in the first place."

"They say I'm crazy, but it's a mistake, my friend." The airman leaned forward. He spoke softly now, as though imparting a secret. "I have been in your Air Force for three months. I am of the Kiowa people. We are a dying tribe."

"I'm sorry to hear."

"I speak not of sickness and hunger, Doctor, though such conditions are familiar on our reservations. I speak of our traditions. Our beliefs. The thing we hold sacred that are trampled underfoot!" The airman's voice had begun to rise now. It broke with emotion.

"I can't begin to understand what you've been through," said Mike, in an effort to ease the tension.

"Many of our tribe have forgotten the legend of the ghost dancers; the prophecy that foretold a savior, the one who will bring back the buffalo and the old ways."

There was a moment of awkward silence. Despite Mike's uneasiness, the story had stirred his curiosity.

"I am sure you are wondering, what has this to do with me?" the airman continued. "I am that savior. I realized this in a dream. The tribal elders turned their backs on me, but their pockets are lined with corporate blood money. When I spoke against the oil companies my family abandoned me. My friends told me I was delusional. I lived alone on the streets for many months."

"And that's when you enlisted?"

"That's when I saw the sign. The one with the bearded old man. He pointed down at me saying 'I want you!' It was a message from beyond. The man at the recruiting station confirmed it! He could see that I was strong and powerful indeed; that the ghost dancers had chosen me. These men offered me clothes, food, shelter, and companions. It was a place, they said, where I could realize my dream."

"So they roped you in, huh?" Mike shook his head. He knew recruiters were trying new tactics, but this? It was sickening.

"That is when they sent me here. I spread my message. I tried to unite my new followers, and they refused to hear. I was sent to a doctor. He told me I would be let out if I came here. And now, fate has brought us to this room."

Mike sighed. The man was mentally ill, that much was plain, and the way he had been treated was appalling. It was as though the service took no responsibility for the lost and the vulnerable among them.

"I'll tell you what, Airman Anque," said Mike. "I'll take your request to the commander, that much I can promise. It's not up to me to make these decisions. In the meantime, you have to stay here and cooperate."

"Doctor, you are a noble man, and I shall respect your request," answered the airman, extending a thick and calloused paw. "But I warn you, I cannot be caged for long. I cannot be contained."

Chapter 18

MIKE LEFT THE WARD feeling frustrated and concerned. He worried for the safety of his staff, yet he couldn't help empathizing with the airman's pain. Here was a man cast aside by society; abandoned by the system. There was no place in this world, it seemed, for the mentally ill.

After some thought, Mike decided to consult Colonel Creaser. He had long since given up on Colonel Lowe. Unfortunately, Creaser was at the golf course, and he was left instead with the deputy. Colonel "Bulldog" Mack was a short, squat caricature of the base commander. Moon had compared his grimace to a bulldog chewing a lemon, and the nickname had stuck ever since.

"So what's the problem, Major?" shrugged Bulldog, "It's not that unusual a story. It'll take a week or two for them to process his case in San Antonio. Just babysit till then."

"I have to emphasize, sir, that this man is psychotic, paranoid, and has the potential to be very dangerous."

Nonplussed, the colonel shuffled through the papers on his desk. He still had yet to make eye contact.

"Look, Major, this is what we pay you for. If he's a problem, tranquilize the sonofabitch or something, and another thing," Bulldog continued, finally peering up from his notes, "you really should have gone through Colonel Lowe. You know how it is."

"Chain of command," sighed Mike.

"Precisely!"

*　*　*

"Ah Major Pike," groaned Colonel Lowe, as though greeting a hernia. "To what do I owe the pleasure?"

"Look, I know we haven't seen eye-to-eye on other matters, but we have a serious problem on Two South. A mentally unstable, seven-foot, muscle-bound problem. This man is psychotic, and what's more he's angry—rightly so—for being tricked into enlisting. Something has to be done." Mike bit his lip. The quicker he could end their meeting the better. Though he had little expectation of support, the ornery colonel was his last resort. Lowe rolled his eyes.

"He'll be processed like anyone else, Major. I don't see a problem. If you have an incident, just use a sedative. Tell your nurse to call the Air Police."

"Don't we have some form of security in the hospital?" asked Mike. "I'd really hate to involve the police."

"We don't have that kind of money to waste here," grunted Lowe. "If you can't handle your ward like a man, then call the police. That's what they're here for."

As usual, Mike left the colonel's office more frustrated than before. As he closed the door, Lowe's nasal voice trailed behind.

"And really, Major, if you can't use a needle, I'm surely not doing it."

*   *   *

Mike trudged back to the ward the next day with a heavy heart. He felt personally responsible, as though he had somehow failed in his duty. When he saw Airman Anque sitting in the lobby, in the same ridiculously small robe, Mike envied men like Kennedy and Khrushchev. At least they could do their dirty business by telephone.

"Airman Andrew Anque," he began, taking a chart from Judith. "I spoke with the commanders, and they've assured me you'll be given a discharge."

"Good. I would like to leave right now."

"That's the problem," Mike continued. "It's going to take a few days to take care of."

In an instant, Airman Anque was on his feet. His face contorted with anger. "I knew it! They want to keep me here because they know who I am! They want to keep my people in filth and darkness!" Despite his terror, Mike felt rooted to the spot. All eyes in the room had turned upon them.

"Andrew, th-think about this," he stammered. "A-are they really smart enough to know who you are..." Mike was interrupted by an almost inhuman roar. He heard the sickening crunch of drywall and fiberglass. A thin white dust hung where the airman had punched a hole in the wall.

"No! None of you do! You all think I'm crazy, just like the elders!"

From the corner of his eye, Mike saw Judith dart for the telephone. He dove for the relative shelter of the nursing station. As the staff watched, the airman's eyes scanned for a suitable target. He took hold of a cart and hurled it across the room.

"I will not be imprisoned! You cannot contain me!" he yelled, as two members of the Air Police burst in. Mike saw them reach for their weapons. He braced for the inevitable.

"Wait!"

The sound and force of the exclamation brought life to a halt. Everyone, even the wild-eyed patient, had turned to its source. Mike peered over the countertop to see Judith easing towards the fray. Her voice, at first commanding and maternal, had turned gentle. She kept her eyes locked with Airman Anque's.

"Andy, listen to me," she coaxed, motioning back the police. "These people do not understand, but I do."

Judith came closer and placed a hand on his arm. A nearby nurse gasped. The furious warrior was now docile as a puppy. He hung his head.

"They think I'm crazy…" he muttered, as she stroked his hair.

"They do not understand your wisdom, and you must keep it locked in your heart," said Judith, "if you are silent, they will not fear your words, and you will gain freedom."

As the airman slumped in a nearby chair, the room breathed a sigh of relief. Judith smiled and patted his head affectionately. The police left after a few words. Slowly but surely, the staff returned to work. Order was restored.

Wide-eyed, Mike approached Judith. He was speechless.

"What, you think you're the only hero around here?" she laughed. "When you've been around as long as I have, you learn a thing or two."

"That was… wow… I've never seen anything like it!"

"You'll get used to it, Doctor Pike." Judith shrugged and turned towards the door. "And now, if you don't mind, I'll take my lunch break."

Chapter 19

MIKE NEVER QUITE KNEW what to expect on the ward anymore.   In a matter of hours, the crisis was all but forgotten. The ward was a hive of activity once more. Mike's itinerary for the afternoon covered almost two pages. At least, he consoled himself, it was no longer than usual.

The first case on the agenda was a familiar one: a twenty-four year-old mother of two. She was in bad shape, with two black eyes and a patchwork of bruises on her neck and arms. Mike shook his head. He'd met several of the wives on Valkyrie this way. Many in much worse condition. Each new occurrence made him sick to his stomach.

"Hello, Natalie. I'm Doctor Pike. Could you tell me what happened?"

The mother twitched nervously. Her eyes turned from the pink bundle nursing at her breast. She stared back at Mike, her eyes wide and frightened.

"Are these sessions confidential?"

Mike took a seat. He knew the answer to his next question before he even asked.

"That depends. Does it involve your husband?"

"Yes."

"Then it may not be confidential. I'm afraid his commander has full access to the records."

"I don't want to get him in trouble." Natalie looked down to her infant. She spoke softly now, her voice tinged with shame. "He's a good man. He means well. It's just… we have a baby now… and it's getting worse."

"What do you mean?"

"He just came home a different man, Doctor," she answered, her eyes welling with tears. "He talks about death all the time now. He can't sleep. He has these… these fits… and he can't control himself. I could handle it when he took it out on me. But yesterday he picked up the baby and started shaking her! I was terrified."

Mike nodded. He wanted to hold her; to put his arm around her and tell her everything would be all right. Despite this, he kept his 'clinical distance' from the patient. He hated himself for it.

"What did your husband do in 'Nam?"

"He was a pilot and sometimes would volunteer for an air evacuation team. Sometimes he would enter the combat areas to retrieve the wounded and the dead. He lost friends. He says he still sees their hollow, sightless eyes when he dreams. He can still smell the burning flesh and napalm. It all haunts him."

Mike bit his lip. He had heard variations of the same story; some more graphic than others. The tales of men who had seen too much and been gone too long.

"He needs some help. If he were to-"

"I've asked him to go to the clinic," she interrupted. "He just says they'll kick him out. And this life is all he has."

"I think you need to stay with someone—your parents, maybe—just for a little while," said Mike, after a moment of deliberation.

"They live in New Mexico," she answered. "I can take the bus. It's just, I don't know what to do about him."

In that moment, a question struck Mike; a question so simple he kicked himself for not asking it sooner. It was something that never crossed his mind.

"What do the other wives do?"

Natalie wiped her eyes and looked at him curiously. It was an odd question, Mike knew. A woman's life on a military base was her own affair. The lives of men and women were governed by unwritten rules. A wife never meddled in her husband's affairs. She was the guardian of the home and the family. Her problems, and those of her friends and neighbors, were to be kept private.

"Well, I can't speak for the others..." she began, tentatively. "But I've been told there are meetings with counselors. They tell us to report to the commanders."

"But you came here?"

"Some of the wives—the older ones, usually—warn us not to. We're reminded that we have a duty to our husbands; that we need to be strong and tough it out." She reached into her purse and pulled out a worn photograph. It was worn and weathered with age.

"This is how he used to look." She smiled weakly as Mike took it from her grasp. "That's the man I lost. Things were so different then, before his first tour. He used to be so happy and full of life."

Mike's hands began to shake. He looked closer. It took him a moment to recognize the man in the picture. He looked like a ghost of his former self now. Staring back from the photo was the man he had sat with in the courtyard.

*   *   *

Mike met the young mother once more for a follow-up. She had decided to leave for Albuquerque with her children. After a great deal of thought, she had called her husband's commander to report his behavior. If that didn't get him into the clinic, she thought, then nothing would.

News travels fast on a military base. Almost a week later, the story had spread throughout Valkyrie like wildfire. A commander had arrived at an officer's door with two air police in tow. He berated the man in full view of his neighbors, calling him a coward and a wife-beater, telling him he was under arrest. The surprise and humiliation triggered a panic attack in the young officer. He saw only the Viet Cong surrounding him. Before the police could act, the man had drawn his weapon and fired multiple shots. One police officer died at the scene; the other officer and the commander were in critical condition. The young captain fled but was found only hours later. He had shot himself in the head.

News of the event shocked Mike to the core. It was all so senseless. The victim was a veteran who had survived the horrors of war in enemy territory, only to die at the hand of his own service weapon. He tried not to think of how Natalie would react to the news. How society would blame her for her "betrayal." He tried not to think of the infant who had lost her father.

It is a story without an end, thought Mike.

Ripples passing through generations.

It was this event that caused Mike to begin to think of the trauma to the unborn and even generations beyond. There was an attempt to understand this question by those seeking some reconciliation for survivors who suffered the Holocaust and the rest of the world. It was becoming clear that subsequent generations had problems and that the problems could be inherited — not just psychologically but genetically. A young lawyer in New York was referring to it as transgenerational stress disorder. The idea, as far as Mike knew, had not been applied to military children, but why not? Their parents often go through horrific events which change them and their children forever. What happens to them? Do they have depressions or attacks of rage or are they like everyone else?

Mike called the attorney and asked about the research he had been citing. The attorney told Mike the effect of trauma was the same for everyone. Everyone had their breaking point. The Holocaust was a crime against humanity, perhaps changing the world forever. No one knew what would happen to the children of the Holocaust and their children—or what they would become. It was as if evil had injected itself into the human lineage.

Some observations were being made by social scientists of what happens to traumatized children when they grow up. Some early observation seemed to recognize a pattern. The children would band together in gangs when they became a little older. It wasn't the Boy Scouts either- their gangs were delinquent- stealing, fighting, destroying—as if imitating their abusers—doing what was done to them.

There had been several suicides on the base and the base commander ordered them to be closed cases. No one was to talk about them. Mike was shocked at this and couldn't understand it at the time. He would later, however. The 'chain of command' controlled everything—information about sexual abuse of women, child abuse, spousal abuse, even fights between neighbors in the base housing. It was an Iron Curtain to seal the military from the rest of the world. Even internally, people didn't talk. If you had a problem with your neighbor, you told your commander who talked with your neighbor's commander. To talk with a doctor was the same. Your commander could read your clinical files.

Part II:
The Refugees

Chapter 20

IT WAS MARCH, 1975, and the winter frost had begun to melt on the prairie. Life at Camp Valkyrie was quiet. Too quiet.

Word of seismic events from abroad was splashed all over the papers. Officers and airmen alike discussed them in hushed tones. Mike wished he could relax and enjoy the lull. Moon seemed to be making the most of his time, at least. In some respects, Mike envied his friend's oblivious nature. News from Saigon had been increasingly grim. It was obvious, at least to him, it was the calm before the storm.

* * *

The stories were initially brushed aside. The Viet Cong had captured the airfield at Song Be in January. It was no cause for alarm, Colonel Lowe had said; this was only a setback. It was in the aftermath that the gravity of defeat sunk in. The South Vietnamese had suffered a casualty rate of nearly 85%. Over 27,000 civilians were taken into custody. Each and every captured official faced summary execution. President Nixon had resigned in 1972, and with him had gone his promise of protection.

Few could have imagined what happened next.

Emboldened by American inaction, the North Vietnamese began a campaign of carnage. In March, President Thieu abandoned the Central Highlands and the ARVN defenses crumbled. Ho Chi Minh was at the gates of Saigon by late-April. The war was over.

But Camp Valkyrie's struggles were just beginning.

Refugees had begun pouring from the country en masse. Homes and possessions were sold for pennies. The price of passports skyrocketed. In early-April, President Ford authorized "Operation Babylift" to fly more than 2,600 orphans out of danger. The first plane crashed, killing more than half its passengers. By mid-April, over 6,000 government officials had been evacuated. Those left behind faced certain death at the hands of the NVA. Twenty C-141s and twenty C-131 airplanes were flying day and night to remote outposts in the Pacific. By mid-May, over 50,000 refugees had been crowded onto the shores of Guam.

It was only a matter of time before Mike would find himself swept up by the largest evacuation in American history. It was an operation that would eventually relocate 130,000 refugees to the United States. Little did he know he would soon find himself on a distant shore; a stranger in a strange land.

* * *

By the end of March, chaos descended on Camp Valkyrie. The air police were on constant patrol with their German shepherds. The base commander issued a general alert. All leaves and TDYs were cancelled. The huge SAC bombers were in the air. Even Colonel Lowe was bustling from meeting to meeting with renewed vigor.

For Mike, the constant demands came as somewhat of relief. He finally had something to which to apply himself. Lately, he had been growing more paranoid of Cochran and his gang. The officer's suicide a few months before still weighed heavily on his mind. Work provided an escape from such troubling thoughts.

The call came at the end of the month. It was a message delivered by Colonel Creaser's secretary himself. Mike had been selected as part of a "Patch up Team," a group of six doctors, nurses, and liaison personnel chosen to take part in the evacuation. The message was short and concise. Following a short briefing, they would be transported to a remote base in the Pacific. The location was top secret.

Mike was pleasantly surprised at the briefing. Both Moon and Flapjack had been selected as well. He also recognized Major Ricks, the man Moon identified as Cochran's boss. He had never met the other members of the team before—a surgeon named Castro and a nurse named Sybil—but he was assured they were two of the best.

No one was surprised to see Flapjack. In little over a year, she had distinguished herself as a hard worker and master negotiator. Her handling of the Airman Anque situation, in particular, had earned her Mike's admiration. It had taken several weeks to discharge the airman, who sat on the same couch, day after day, staring into space. Mike had only to mention his frustrations to Flapjack in passing. The next day, and every day after, she would come to visit the patient and offer reassurance. In less than a week, she had finalized arrangements with an Oklahoma congressman's office securing his release. When faced with resistance from the board in San Antonio, she called the Bureau of Indian Affairs and the National Council of Indian Tribes to speak on his behalf. One way or another, she got the job done, and Airman Anque could not thank her enough. Mike could still remember their tearful farewell. The airman had embraced Flapjack in a crushing bear hug. He even asked her to accompany him on his spiritual journey. Flapjack had that effect on people.

The selection of Moon—or himself, for that matter—was a mystery to Mike. Neither of them was particularly well-known, nor had they endeared themselves to the Camp Valkyrie brass. If anything, they were recognized as trouble-makers who challenged the status quo. Perhaps Moon's relationship with Flapjack had merited his inclusion, thought Mike. But what about himself? What was it the colonel saw in him?

It was a question he would have little time to ponder.

*   *   *

The call came only a day later. It was the midnight of April 1st when the team was roused and hastily boarded on a C-141 aircraft. They were welcomed aboard by the co-pilot shortly after take-off. Apparently, he informed them, even the Air Force hadn't picked a destination yet. Moon's suggestion of the Philippines was quickly shot down. President Marcos was no longer allowing refugees to land at the Clark Air Force Base. He feared the threat of being "overwhelmed" by refugees—not to mention the Viet Cong and Korean agents mixed with them—was too much of a risk.

The first stop on their journey was California. There they were joined by at least two-dozen patch-up team members from San Antonio. It wasn't long before they were airborne once more. They were over the Pacific by dawn.

Chapter 21

"WHERE ARE WE GOING?"

The question came from a San Antonio member in the back corner.

"They won't tell us," answered Castro. "The captain will probably tell us when he gets the order."

"Has anyone heard from home?" asked Flapjack. Mike had never heard her sound so anxious. She had always seemed so sure of herself. "They wouldn't let us use the phone back in California."

Everyone on board appeared tense and uneasy. The deafening whine of the jets made sleep impossible. A few admitted it was their first experience with air travel. Two had already vomited in the trash compartment, and an acrid smell permeated the hold.

"If you can't contact anyone, how should we be able to?" snapped a bleary-eyed Ricks.

"It's been that way since we left Texas," another voice chimed in. "We haven't been allowed to use a phone or a radio transmitter. Hell, we aren't even allowed to write letters!"

Mike crawled to Flapjack's side and put his arm around her. She looked petrified. "We should know soon," he told her softly. "It'll probably be somewhere like Guam or some other American outpost; somewhere relatively safe." She smiled weakly.

To the left of Flapjack, Moon rolled his eyes. Lack of sleep had left him irritable in the extreme. He shook his head and groaned. "Refugees from Valkyrie flying to meet refugees from Saigon, he chuckled. "I hope the fat cats in charge know what they're doing, because I sure as hell don't!"

*   *   *

The hours passed in silence. The roar of the jets seemed to taper off by nightfall. Mike awoke in darkness. It took a few moments for his eyes to adjust. Everyone around him still slumbered. Rubbing his eyes, he turned to a window and looked out on the ocean. The moon was full and low in the sky, bathing the water in gold. To Mike, all felt calm. The scene was strangely peaceful. He wondered if he would ever feel a moment like this again.

Chapter 22

THE TEAM AWOKE early that morning. The pilot had come to brief them over a meager breakfast. Finally, they were told, a destination had been confirmed. They would be landing in Guam. The initial target had been the Philippines, as Moon had predicted, but plans were altered when President Marcos got cold feet.

"I've been hearing some bad shit over the radio," he told them over coffee. "You guys may see some of it when you get there."

"Like what?" asked a nurse.

"There's a lot of physical and mental trauma," said the pilot. "The poor bastards have been through a long war already. These folks are leaving their homeland; leaving behind their friends, relatives, and everything familiar. It's a tough situation. There's no telling what they might do."

A murmur passed through the huddled group. Nearby, Mike could hear voices of sympathy, confusion, and anger. These refugees had been abandoned by their government and betrayed by their allies. President Ford played golf while Saigon burned. Congress refused to fund the Defense Assistance Vietnam program and other security guarantees. Mike felt a knot in the pit of his stomach.

"You feel it too, don't you?" a voice whispered.

There was a hand on his shoulder. It was Flapjack.

"Feel what?" he asked.

"The shame."

* * *

After breakfast, the crew broke off into groups. The Camp Valkyrie members found themselves huddled in a circle near the tail-end of the plane.   There was little to do besides talk. Sybil, the nurse, seemed particularly anxious. Her blonde hair was a mess, and her blue eyes were heavy with sleep.

"What exactly are we getting into here? What is a 'Patch-Up Team' anyway?" She asked, brushing her bangs from her eyes once more. "I'd feel a lot better if only I knew what was expected of us, or at least that there was some plan in motion."

"You don't have to be afraid," said Flapjack. She smiled warmly to Sybil. "We have each other for support, you know."

"We have to. That's what makes the military work." All eyes turned to Mike. He cleared his throat. "Well, at least part of it. What Flapjack said about supporting one another."

Moon groaned loudly. "Don't tell me you buy into that bullshit, Mike."

"No it's true," he continued. "Teamwork is everything. Without it, do you really think the higher-ups have our backs? I can't tell you how many cases of domestic abuse I've seen swept under the rug."

"I know," said Flapjack, grimly. "Commanders always decide not to prosecute." Her eyes locked with Sybil's. The two nodded. "The women on the base look out for one another. We have to. We're told that abuse, rape, and violence are, well—"

"Occupational hazards," finished Sybil.

"Exactly."

Moon's eyes widened with disbelief. He let out a long, low whistle. "Damn, that's cold."

"Tell me about it," added Ricks. He looked as surprised as the others. "I always knew there was a whole world beneath the surface of Camp Valkyrie, but wow… I can't imagine being in that situation. Having to share a foxhole with your own rapist!"

"I'll tell you what I would do," said Sybil, quietly. "I would cut off his balls and stuff them in his gasping mouth."

Everyone looked at Sybil in disbelief. It was surreal to hear such rage from a person so small.

"All right!" Moon pumped a fist in the air. "Let's hear it for big Sybil!"

Slowly, Flapjack put a hand on Moon's arm until he put it down. She led Sybil over to a corner, where the two sat holding hands. As Sybil lay her head on Flapjack's shoulder, she began to stroke her hair. Moon looked at Mike curiously.

"Was it something I said?"

* * *

Mike was awoken suddenly that night. Someone was shaking him. It was their second night in the air, and the rest of the crew lay asleep in the darkness. Mike grumbled and turned over. In his ear he heard a voice, soft but insistent.

"Hey, wake up! You're gonna want to see this."

There was a blinding flash of light in his eyes. He squinted and sat up. Before him sat a grinning Flapjack. Behind her stood the co-pilot with a flashlight.

"If you guys want to watch the landing you have to come now. We can only take two of you," he whispered insistently.

Flapjack pulled at Mike's sleeve. The two were ushered into the cockpit, where the first colors of dawn hung over the Pacific. As the two strapped themselves in, an older pilot introduced himself. He and his partner always liked to invite a passenger or two to watch the descent.

"Guam should be visible any second now," remarked the younger co-pilot. "We'll be touching down at Andersen Air Force Base on the eastern side of the island."

"This is foxtrot zebra niner niner zero to base," barked the captain. "Come in base."

The radio crackled to life.

"Roger, niner-niner-zero," a voice replied. "Come in."

"Permission to land?"

"Okay for landing."

The captain slowed the engines and deployed the landing gear. As if in response, the plane shuddered and pitched forward. The clouds dispersed. In the distance, Mike could see the small kidney-shape of the island growing larger and larger. It wasn't long before they were gliding over the cliffs and the fishing boats on the beach. There was a rush of air on the hull as the wheels touched the concrete runway. The impact was sudden and jarring. Had they not been buckled in, it would have thrown them from their seats.

As the plane rolled gently into the terminal, the co-pilot looked back at the two passengers. Mike was gripping the armrest with white knuckles, while Flapjack was grinning like a schoolgirl.

"Welcome to Guam!"

Chapter 23

THE REST OF THE CREW had little time to acclimate to their surroundings. In a matter of minutes they were whisked off the tarmac by two VW buses. Mike was surprised to find the captain and co-pilot among the other passengers.

"Our plane was enlisted in the evacuation!" the pilot laughed, as if in response to Mike's curiosity. "That includes us too. We'll ride over to the quarters with you folks to spend the night."

The bus was packed and humid, and Mike and his colleagues found themselves crushed against one another on the bumpy ride. As if things couldn't get worse, a few of the patch-up members in the back had joined in a rousing chorus of the Air Force song.

> *Off we gooo, into the wild blue yonder!*
> *Climbing hiiiigh, into the sun!*

Mike looked over to Flapjack. She seemed visibly awkward and uncomfortable. Moon was sweating through his shirt. Both of them looked about to snap.

> *Here they come, zooming to meet our thunder,*
> *At 'em boys, give 'er the gun,*
> *Give 'er the gun now!*

"God damn, it's great to be back in the saddle," exclaimed the captain. The co-pilot smiled curtly in response.

"Yeah? You've seen some action ol' timer?" remarked Moon, in a tone of apparent disinterest.

"Son, I was here for three tours. I made my bones hauling troops and sup-plies across enemy lines. By my second tour I was trained to fly the fighters, and I had my very own phantom."

"Phantom?" asked Sybil. She, and a few other passengers, had turned to listen.

"The F4 Phantom. God, that baby was sweet," continued the pilot. "I almost lost count of my kill rate back then. It was something like 280 by '73."

"By yourself?" asked Flapjack.

"By the whole group," said the captain.

"But how many did you… kill?

"I don't know, really. Maybe two or three, I suppose."

The co-pilot groaned. "I don't know why he's being modest now. He's always bragging about that record of his. Four kills in one sortie. Five when he's drunk."

The group had all turned around to the captain. Even after moving to give the man some space, Mike could still smell his sweat and cheap cologne.

"Come on now," chuckled the pilot, shooting his colleague a mortified look. "We don't go telling all our secrets! These folks could even be against the war."

"No, no," said Moon, eager for more details. "I admire your bravery. I've had enough with the damn pencil-pushers and desk jockeys at Valkyrie."

Sybil pouted and bit her lip. "Well I don't care for it. There were human beings in those other planes. They probably had families they loved and cared for."

"Don't get me wrong," added Mike, "I'm not saying you didn't have to do it. But I don't know how you can be so calm about killing people."

"Hell, I wasn't talking about the people!" the captain exclaimed. "I was talking about the plane! If you're going to fly into danger, the Phantom's the one for the job. It was so powerful. Honestly, you feel like a god!"

Sybil shook her head. "That's exactly my point. Why do you want to be a god? What's wrong with peace?"

"Look, I know my buddy likes to talk big, but he's no 'baby killer,' and neither am I."

Attention turned now to the co-pilot. Until now he had kept mostly silent, but now he spoke passionately in his friend's defense.

"I mean, when I first started, they put a rifle in my hands and told me what to do," he continued. "I went to flight school after a tour on the ground and flew cargo plans for a while. We both know that war is hell. Don't you think we know that?"

There was an awkward silence among the passengers, a lull broken by the sounds of the rocks and potholes on the road. All eyes turned back to the pilot. He shrugged sheepishly.

*   *   *

It took almost an hour to reach the base camp. The weary travelers found relief in the warm showers and the stark but comfy barracks afforded them. There was a hot meal waiting, and they spent the afternoon relaxing in the tropical warmth. No one wanted to think about the grueling work that lay ahead.

Mike was lounging in a hammock when he saw two figures leaning over him. The first he recognized instantly as Moon. He had to squint in the sunlight to make out the second. It was the co-pilot.

"Care for a smoke, doctor?" said the co-pilot, extending a pack of Lucky Strikes his way. Mike shook his head. "Fair enough—more for me then."

"Mike, meet Charles," said Moon. "Man, from what he said on the bus, I bet this cat has some stories to tell."

The man lit his cigarette and inhaled deeply. He was much shorter than Moon, but he looked stronger and more self-aware. There was a tired look in his eyes. He chuckled hoarsely.

"Just call me Charlie."

"Hey Charlie," said Moon, "tell Mike what you were telling me about the Air Force!"

Charlie sighed. "Like I said, it's no big thing. Moon said you guys got a raw deal, I just told him the Air Force ain't so bad. It got me a degree in aerospace engineering and a steady paycheck. It's sort of like being a good cop patrolling the bad side of town, you know?"

Mike squinted at the co-pilot above him. Even in this relaxed atmosphere, the man seemed to be standing at attention. "But you were on the ground in 'Nam, right Charlie?" he asked. "You didn't see anything that made you question your mission?"

Charlie tossed the cigarette aside and drew another. Moon offered a light. "People ask me that all the time. Yeah, I saw some combat, and yeah, I fired my weapon. Truth is, I still don't know if I ever hit a damn thing." He took a long draught and smiled grimly. "You'd be surprised how often I saw men firing at the sky or the trees. Firing at anything other than the enemy right in front of 'em. They say the same thing happened at D-Day, you know. Some soldiers never fired at all."

"Mike works with a lot of the wounded," said Moon. "He says a lot of 'em come back a little crazy in the coconut."

Mike cringed. "I wouldn't say that. I just tend to see a lot of mental trauma, is all. A lot of these men have trouble coping back home."

"Bunch of cowards if you ask me," Charlie announced angrily, grinding his ash underfoot. "At least they got to go home. I worked with a number of our Vietnamese allies. Brave souls. I'd risk my life for 'em any day. It's a shame they've likely been slaughtered by the NVA. Anyway, we sure as hell won't be seeing 'em here."

"Why not?" asked Mike. Moon just grinned sardonically and shook his head. Apparently, he already knew.

"Because money talks, kid," said Charlie without a trace of emotion. "The wealthy ones will be at the front of the line. The diplomats, the politicians, the generals and their families."

Mike sat up, his eyes wide with surprise. Moon broke into laughter. "I knew that would get him," said Moon, holding his gut with both hands. "Mike's our warrior for justice at Valkyrie. I just knew he'd be stunned."

"You're telling me we're only here to save the rich?" asked Mike. He still couldn't believe it.

Charlie shrugged. "Do you think the U.S. wants the poor and illiterate? If they want to escape, they have a hell of a long swim."

"See Mike?" said Moon, as his laughter subsided. He wiped the water from his eyes and put a hand on Mike's shoulder. "Looks like the military has a heart after all. A heart of gold!"

Chapter 24

THE FIRST MEETING on Guam passed in a blur. Mike and his fellow workers were provided with maps outlining the "tent city," a makeshift camp designed to shelter refugees. Their jobs, they were told, were to man the processing stations. Interpreters were available when necessary. Moon, Ricks, Flapjack and Mike were all assigned to do mental health evaluations when requested. "Make sure not to go overboard," the commander had warned. "We don't need a stress disorder diagnosis on every refugee bound for America!"

Mike had grown used to the officer's condescension. It was nothing he hadn't experienced at Valkyrie. It seemed to him that the Air Force had no high opinion of his profession. He was at least pleased to learn he would be working closely with Flapjack, who had been placed in charge of social evaluations. Most refugees would not have birth certificates, but would likely have some form of identification. It was up to her to weed out those with forged or stolen documents.

Work was to begin immediately. The commander informed them that the tents would be up by morning. Processing would begin at 0600 hours sharp. While they were warned of the danger of suicide bombers, the commander assured them that metal detectors and bomb-sniffing dogs would be at every station. The reassurance did little to ease Mike's anxieties.

* * *

It was evening when the size and scope of the operation finally sunk in. Mike lay awake in his cot, listening to the rustling of the palms and the buzzing of tropical insects. This was where it would all go down. Guam. The epicenter. Without the Philippines, there was no other safe haven to be found. Even the United Nations had turned their backs. It was America's decision to intervene in Vietnam, and, according to the U.N. Secretary General, it was America's burden to bear. How could such a small team of medical workers process over a hundred-thousand fugitives, Mike wondered; how could they possibly provide the throngs with proper sanitation, or fresh food and water? In such a densely-populated area, the danger of contagion was overwhelming.

Any hope of sleep was dashed after midnight, when the C-141s began rumbling in and out of the airport at regular intervals. The noise, combined with jet lag and anticipation, had given Mike a terrible headache. When it began to subside at two in the morning, he decided to take the short walk to central command. They would have to report there in three hours anyway, he reasoned, and perhaps he would find some company.

Mike soon realized he was not alone in his concern. Several other members of the patch-up team—Moon and Flapjack included—had already arrived. With their bloodshot eyes and the worn expressions on their faces, they looked every bit as tired as he felt.

"Hey brother, pull up a chair!" exclaimed Moon. "We've got a regular party going on in here!"

Mike looked over to Flapjack. He was pleased to see the look of relief on her face. She was an eternal optimist, Mike had learned, or rather "another doe-eyed hippie," as Moon put it after the break-up. The two remained friends, but Mike could tell her patience tonight was growing thin. They both knew Moon was prone to chain-smoking and complaining when stressed. He shot her a weak smile.

"Meet some new friends of ours!" Moon continued, "Art, from Tacoma, and Brenda, from San Antonio. And Art's in the same head-shrinking business as you, Mike."

Art was an older man, with salt-and-pepper hair and a pasty complexion. He raised an eyebrow, adjusting his gold-rimmed glasses. "I hear you've had the same issues as we have," he told Mike. "All my patients from the war have already been packed off to the VA or discharged."

"But... they might still get help at the VA, right?" asked Flapjack hopefully. Moon rolled his eyes.

"Not likely," Art replied. "I've made a few contacts there over the years. From what they've told me, the Veteran's Affairs office has been dismissing cases of battle fatigue and Agent Orange exposure at an ever-increasing rate."

Brenda sighed loudly. "They don't even mention Vietnam on our base anymore. If they're that eager to whitewash history, I can only imagine what life will be like for these poor Vietnamese in America. They'll be a constant living reminder of our nation's stupidity!"

Mike looked from Art to Brenda. The two looked like an elderly couple. With her silver bangs and earrings, and the regal way she held her cigarette, she appeared to Mike like an old matriarch.

"I've been wondering myself," Mike admitted. "Will there be enough civilian sponsors to handle the migrant flood? Will the refugees have any access to medical care? And what kind of fate is in store for them? Will they be herded on to reservations or internment camps? Or exploited like so many other minority groups have been? It's not like our country has the best track record for hospitality!"

Mike's voice cracked as it began to rise. When he finished, his throat felt parched and sore. Everyone at the table, aside from Flapjack, was staring at him with bemused expressions. They think I'm naïve, thought Mike, just because I think things need to change; just because I'm expressing what everyone would rather ignore! It seemed that only Flapjack had taken him seriously. The look in her soft, blue eyes was warm and understanding. It provided some comfort to his wounded pride.

Moon broke the silence with a chuckle. Art, in turn, gave Mike a patronizing smile. "Well it's not our job to worry about those issues," said Brenda, knocking the ash from a Marlboro. "The politicians got us into this mess, the politicians will just have to get us out."

"Besides," added Moon, "The President should have thought about this before he invited the whole damn jungle in."

Chapter 25

RICKS AND CASTRO arrived just in time for breakfast that morning. Both appeared to have somehow enjoyed a good night's sleep, a realization that made Mike almost sick with jealousy. After choking down a meal of burned toast and eggs, the team boarded the military bus, eager to see the new "tent city" and its inhabitants. The refugees were coming in on big C-141 cargo planes from Subic Bay and Tan Son Naht airport, the commander announced, and unloading at Andersen on an almost hourly basis. The first groups to arrive had been orphans. Thousands of children had already been processed by the San Antonio team and were on their way to America.

It only took a few minutes for the bus to arrive. The "Tent City" had been established on the ruins of a Japanese airstrip near Orote Point. Mike stared across the expanse in amazement. Exactly 3,200 tents were spread as far as the eye could see. In just twelve hours, two-thousand marines had constructed a camp with 300 showers and 191 toilets! It was almost impossible to believe.

The team was met with a barrage of orders and instructions almost the moment they disembarked. A group of Australian nurses and Canadian officers had arrived on an earlier bus, and they were already desperate for reinforcements. A representative from the Canadians requested that all French-speaking refugees be referred to their headquarters immediately. The Canadian government would take refugees, he explained, but faced pressure from the French-Canadian community.

As quickly as he arrived, the officer was gone. The commander's sergeant took his place and began barking orders and organizing each individual station. Administrators were shown their processing tent where INS would provide documents to eligible refugees. Those refugees would then be assigned to one of four camps located in different states. Some would lack documentation, they were told, but it was no large concern. Many of the

Vietnamese would be familiar enough with one another to verify identities. Mike, along with the other doctors and nurses, was led to the medical tents, where they would provide treatment to almost 90,000 in the coming months.

Mike and the other experienced physicians quickly took over the tents and secured their medical supplies. No one had brought so much as a stethoscope, but they had been provided with all the medicine and instruments they would need. One tent was set up as a triage station, and another for emergency care. One was for pediatrics and the other for adults. The rest would house six patients apiece on standard military-issue cots.

The speed and efficiency of the patch-up team made Mike dizzy. These were the best of the best. Overnight, this tiny island had become a small city-state, with the most well-staffed hospital in the military!

Suddenly, a harsh noise interrupted their efficiency. The workers paused and listened to the telltale roar of a C-141 nearby. A new batch of patients had arrived. Now came the real test. Mike felt a shot of adrenaline course through his veins.

This was it.

* * *

The rest of the day passed in a blur. For Mike, instinct took over. This was what he had been trained for. The first few hundred posed no large problem. Most were fluent in English, and there were interpreters for those who did not. These were the South Vietnamese elite; the diplomats, civil employees, and military personnel. Their homeland had nothing to offer them now but a death sentence. Then came the doctors, lawyers, teachers, and scholars. Many were of ethnic Chinese descent, Mike noted, and he was staggered at the sheer number of doctors among them. He was told that night that the South would lose the majority of their best doctors. Unfortunately, many of the most educated among them spoke French, and were lost to the Canadian delegation.

Mike worked late into the night, propelled by a constant stream of caffeine and sugar. His dreams were haunted by the children he saw. Many had run barefoot across broken glass in the embassy. Others suffered severe burns on their limbs. The Australian and American nurses had done their best to comfort them. Castro stitched them up, and they were given tetanus shots and antibiotics as needed. Still, many remained in shock, while others cried inconsolably. They were terrified by these strangers in starch-white uniforms.

The adults fared little better. They too suffered the effects of shock. Injuries ranged from broken bones to gunshot wounds. At one point, on a particularly busy day, Mike had even joined Castro in suturing patients. Necessity made him a quick learner. Each member of the patch-up team had had to adapt.

For Mike, the days were spent tending to the minds and spirits of his patients. It was a particularly thankless job here on Guam. Just as on Valkyrie, his kind was mocked by the surgeons and administrators. For them, in the rush to process and release refugees from the camp, his role was considered unnecessary. Flapjack, Castro, Moon, and Ricks, it seemed, were his only friends in Tent City.

When would others realize, Mike often wondered, that the deepest wounds aren't always shown on the body? Several of the older adults lacked their maintenance medications and suffered from withdrawal. Young and old alike were grief stricken by the loss of their loved ones. Some had such serious medical conditions as diabetes, heart failure, epilepsy, and hypertension, and required intensive care. Depression and anxiety spread through the camp like a sickness.

Still, for all the problems they faced, Mike found that first week the most rewarding of his life. The resiliency of the Vietnamese migrants inspired him. They had developed a makeshift society to support one another. The eagerness of the Americans to court these educated professionals was obvious, as they were kept well-fed—at roughly $64,000 a day—and encouraged to eat to their heart's content. The residents of Guam even pitched in and invited some refugees to dinner each evening. In that summer of 1975, over 90,000 people would learn the strength of the human spirit in the face of war and destruction.

Hope had been found in the ashes of tragedy.

Chapter 26

THE WORKLOAD TOOK its toll over the first few days. There was enough physical trauma to keep the surgeons working around the clock. A friend of Castro's even suffered a nervous breakdown. Each member of the patch-up team had been pushed to the limit of their abilities. It was times like these Mike realized the value of friendship. Moon's stubborn perseverance and Flapjack's ebullience gave him the strength to go on. If they could do it, he owed it to them to continue.

The refugees of Tent City did what they could to ease the burden. They had organized their own system to get their paperwork and documentation in order. A sense of order prevailed, and the use of toilets and showers followed a strict schedule. Only one central conflict, it seemed, stood to divide the denizens of Tent City. A growing faction had begun to express a desire to return to their homeland. This small minority had clashed with the other refugees on multiple occasions. At one point, the situation even came to blows.

At first, Mike thought little of the conflict. It was natural to feel homesick. It was no surprise, either, that some in the military felt the desire to fight for their country, or that families would worry about those left behind. As far as he knew, there were only a handful of malcontents, with no sense of unity or leadership. It was in his third week that he learned just how far things had escalated.

* * *

It was a particularly scorching day on the island. Even in shelter, Mike could feel the heat baking his cracked and sunburned skin. Tempers ran high during these dry spells, he knew, and he tried to stay wary as he worked.

It was mid afternoon when he heard the shouting. It came from nearby, in the direction of the INS tents. That was where Flapjack was working! Mike excused himself and hurried to provide some assistance. Workers had been attacked more than once in Tent City. Most incidents had been peacefully resolved, he knew, but he was taking no chances. Anything could happen.

Chapter 27

MIKE'S CONCERNS WERE well-founded. In less than a week, Colonel Tru had gained a degree of notoriety among the Tent City staff. There were rumors that he had formed his own militia. Several of Mike's patients sympathized with the colonel's desire to return to his homeland. Flapjack confirmed these suspicions. She had close contact with the brass, and had heard that hundreds—even thousands—of refugees had banded together under a common cause. They longed to return.

The tensions in the camp brought a new level of complexity to Mike's work. Now, in addition to shock and post-traumatic stress, he found himself treating those affected by the present conflict. The debate over whether to stay or leave had divided families against one another. One such case, Mike would discover, involved a particularly high-profile refugee.

The man had come in near the end of the day, when much of the staff had already turned in. Mike had a habit of putting in overtime. It allowed him to finish his paperwork, and he enjoyed talking with the patients in their tents. Something about this particular stranger, however, set Mike on edge. He entered the medical tent in a state of agitation, his posture slumped, his face haggard and unshaven. To Mike, he looked like a man who had not slept in days; a man who had given up.

"Can I... help you sir?" asked Mike, uncertain whether to call for security.

The man collapsed on a nearby cot. He ran a hand through his shaggy hair and groaned. "They told me not to trouble you, Doctor, but they tell me you are a man who understands women."

"I'm not sure about that!" said Mike, blushing, "but I can see what I can do."

"My name is Tien Nguyen, and my wife, Doctor, you must help her," he continued. "an evil spirit has possessed her. She talks of joining the others and returning to Vietnam. It is madness."

Mike raised an eyebrow. "But how do you want me to help?"

"I believe she needs the medicines, Doctor," replied Tien. "She knows I worked undercover with the CIA. To even think of going back… it is suicide!"

"I'll need to meet your wife first," said Mike, after a moment of thought. "I can keep the clinic open a little longer if you can bring Mrs. Nguyen over now."

Tien bolted upright at Mike's offer. He sat on the edge of the cot now, his eyes wide with concern. "I-if you believe it will help, I will fetch her," he stammered reluctantly, "but I must warn you, Doctor, she is not of sound mind. The devil has her."

Mike sighed and rubbed his temples as the man shuffled out of the tent. There was obviously more to this story than met the eye. Whatever was going on, he was determined to get to the bottom of the matter.

* * *

Mike's suspicions were confirmed when he met Mrs. Nguyen. Things just didn't add up. Unlike her husband, she carried herself with the grace and poise of an aristocrat. There was a healthy blush on her cheeks. With her delicate features and porcelain skin, she shared nothing in common with the wretched creature beside her. It was as though she had just come from a ballroom, while her husband had crawled out from under a bridge.

Mrs. Nguyen met Mike courteously. With the flick of a wrist, she dismissed her husband, who scurried from the tent like a mouse. Before he could offer her a seat, she had already settled on a nearby stool, her hands folded neatly in her lap. She tossed her long, dark hair behind her in one fluid motion.

"I believe," she began, "that my husband has fed you some story about my being some devil-in-heels. Well, that would be just like him."

Mike shrugged. "Pretty much," he replied. "He told me you wanted to return home, where he'd face summary execution."

A peal of laughter rang through the tent like a bell. Mrs. Nguyen doubled over, her arms wrapped around her sides. It took her a moment to regain her composure. "Oh, I want to return, just not with that idiot," she chuckled, rubbing a tear from her eye. "I don't suppose my loving husband explained how he brought his mistress along with us. No, I'm sure he must have left that out of his little story. Hah!"

"No," said Mike, furrowing his brow. "No, he most certainly did not."

Mrs. Nguyen leaned back and crossed her legs. "Oh, it was bad enough he thought I didn't know about his little affair back in Saigon," she continued, placing her hands behind her head. "Now he expects us to live together as a little family. The lord of the manor, his obedient wife, and that cheap harlot, living together in America. Isn't that just precious?" She spat on the ground in disgust.

Mike chewed on the end of his pencil as he considered the situation. After a moment, he struck on an idea. "Tell me, Mrs. Nguyen—"

"Oh, just call me Hue," she interjected, "I've come to detest my husband's surname."

"All right, Mrs... Hue," said Mike, quickly correcting himself. "There's certainly nothing wrong with you, of course. Your anger is justified. But do you really think that returning home is the wisest course of action? The southern nobility—male and female alike—face the gravest danger from the Viet Cong."

Hue bit her lip. She leaned over towards Mike now, a look of concern on her face. "But my home is all I know, Doctor—"

"Just call me Mike," he interrupted, as he flipped through the pages of a notebook and began writing. "Tell me, Hue, you speak English fluently and articulately, do you have any relatives at all overseas? Any connections abroad?"

Hue took a moment to ponder. "I think I have a cousin in San Francisco," she thought aloud, "my sister is in the camp, and I'll ask her. She would know."

"That would be the ideal thing to do," said Mike. "For now, at least. You don't have to stay in America, but you can at least find support there for now. Let me know what you learn from your sister."

"I'll let my dear husband know it's okay to return," said Hue, as she stood to leave. "I'm sure you'd like a few words with that... what do you call him in America? Dan Wanh?"

"Don Juan!" laughed Mike. "And yes, I most certainly would!"

Chapter 28

"WELL, I HAVE GOOD NEWS and bad news, Mr. Nguyen."

Mike couldn't help the disdain in his voice. Tien sat hunched over on the cot, a pale, withered shell of a man. He must think he's some sort of martyr, Mike thought to himself, with all those secrets eating him from the inside out. If he didn't know better, he could have pitied him.

"I'll take the good news first, Doctor," said Tien, "will my wife be all right? The burdens of war are not meant for such delicate flowers."

Mike shifted uncomfortably. "Well, the good news is that your wife isn't crazy. That, and she's not interested in dragging you back to Vietnam."

"Ah, I suppose she told you what happened between us," groaned Tien, shaking his head. "I should have broken things off, but I had to take her along. My mistress has a baby. The Communists would have killed them both because of our relationship."

"Did your mistress work for the CIA too?" asked Mike.

"No, but she knows too much. She's met the director, Mr. Colbert, and she's learned a great deal as my secretary."

"That brings us to the bad news," Mike continued. "Your marriage is likely over. From what you've told me, your career at the CIA is finished. It seems to me like your only option is to start a new life in America with your mistress."

Tien stroked his chin thoughtfully and nodded. "This is true, doctor. I am not a perfect man. I feel responsible for this young woman I have seduced. She depends on me for protection, both for her and the child."

"There's one more thing," added Mike, just as Tien had risen to leave. "I'd like to speak with your former secretary if I may. It's important she understands the gravity of the situation."

* * *

Mike looked at his watch. His frustrations were mounting. It had been an hour since Tien left to fetch his mistress. The pains of hunger clawed at his belly. He had already missed dinner to deal with this melodrama. Just as he made up his mind to turn in, they arrived at the door.

"I apologize for the delay, doctor," mumbled Tien. He shuffled his feet awkwardly at the entrance. "This is darling, Tina Vu. I shall leave you to counsel her."

Mike couldn't help but raise an eyebrow. As much as he had come to dislike Tien, he had to admire his taste in women. Compared to the stately Mrs. Nguyen, Tina was no more than a girl, a tomboy with the lithe, compact figure of one accustomed to hard work. She grinned artlessly at Mike and shook his hand with a firm grip.

"Why don't you have a seat," offered Mike, "and tell me about yourself. I hear you have a child?"

Tina grinned. "I do. She is with Mr. Nguyen now. Would you like to see picture?" Before Mike could respond, she had already thrust an old photo towards him. It was worn and frayed at the edges. "She just turn six months. Her name is Tum Vu, but I call her Mary. She will need American name, you know. Fit in."

"She's very beautiful," said Mike, handing the picture back. He couldn't fathom how such a charming young woman could be attracted to a man like Tien. He had to be at least twenty-years her senior. "I just want to make sure you're careful, you know," he continued. "Traveling with your lover's wife has a lot of risks. You must be aware of the anger and jealousy she must be feeling."

To Mike's surprise, Tina broke into a fit of giggles. She covered her mouth with her hands in embarrassment. For a moment, he wondered if she fully understood her situation.

"Oh, that hen has nothing to worry," she laughed. "I do not want that crusty old man. I want to go to America."

"Are you sure?" asked Mike. "It seems like he cares about you and Mary."
"Well, I care of him not at all. He is ticket out of Saigon," Tina replied, with an air of finality. "My husband is killed working for him. I have nothing. No relative. So, I decide, I will go to America."

"Is there anywhere in particular you'd like to go?" asked Mike.

"Le bon ton roulette."

"You speak French?"

"I do."

Mike picked up the phone. "So tell me Tina," he asked, as he dialed an extension, "have you ever considered Canada? Because I know someone who'd like to speak with you!"

Chapter 29

WHILE THE REFUGEES and workers made the best of their circumstances, tensions began to run high in both camps. Long hours and cramped conditions began to wear down even the most disciplined officers. With disturbing frequency, Mike found himself treating the patch-up team members themselves, many of whom suffered the effects of stress, anxiety, and depression. The conflict among the refugees only made things worse.

It was during his second week on Guam that Mike learned how far things had deteriorated. It had been a particularly difficult weekend throughout the camp. A new group of refugees had arrived—many in critical condition—and the surgeons were kept working for days without sleep. In his medical tent, Mike had allowed them to rest on the three emergency cots between procedures, but the demand was too high. Some took their breaks curled up on the floor, or collapsed in a nearby chair. Mike's rule was simple: first come, first served.

It was during the third day of intensive care that tensions boiled over. Castro had arrived at the tent after a long procedure, and, for the fourth straight time, all the cots were accounted for. He looked to Mike beseechingly, hoping, perhaps, to appeal to their Valkyrie connection. Mike shrugged sadly. He sympathized, but it wouldn't be fair to play favorites, he knew. The San Antonio surgeons needed rest too.

Castro spat in the dust. He shambled to a nearby cot and jabbed the occupant with his boot. The exhausted man simply groaned and rolled over. "Damn this place," snarled Castro. Before Mike could stop him, he shoved his foot once more into the man's side. "You need to get up," he ordered, as the surgeon looked up angrily. "I haven't slept in forty-eight hours. It's my turn."

"Screw you, buddy," the man groaned, rubbing his eyes. "I have a critical patient in the next tent over. I got here first."

With a sudden shove, Castro toppled the man to the ground, taking his place on the cot.

"What the hell is wrong with you?" cried the surgeon.

"Just get out of here," Castro snapped. "Go find somewhere else."

Mike got between them just before the man attacked. "Whoa, you two, calm down, I can get the tech to find another cot."

"I don't want another one!" said the surgeon indignantly. "I want this one. I got it fair-and-square." He kicked the cot angrily. Castro shot up with his fists raised, ready to strike.

"God damn it, both of you, that's enough!" said Mike. The two men ignored him. Their eyes were locked on one another, sizing each other up.

"Look, I have to head to work now," said a nearby voice. A surgeon in the corner of the room had just awoken. He rose, wiping the dirt from his scrubs. "You can have mine if you want."

"I don't want yours, I want the one I had," whined the San Antonio surgeon. "I was there first."

"Captain, I'm giving you a direct order to back off," said Mike. "Another cot is available. You can sleep on that."

"You can't give me an order, you're just a Doctor."

"As chief medical officer of this tent, I can, and I have," Mike replied, looking him square in the eye, "and if you want to risk an Article 15, then by all means carry on."

It was not often that Mike raised his voice. When he did, however, it was with conviction, and the surgeon knew it. He backed down, cursing under his breath, and settled on the other cot. In a few moments he was fast asleep.

* * *

"You should have let me fight him."

Mike looked up warily from his chart. Castro lay on his side, watching him with bloodshot eyes.

"You shouldn't have intervened," he continued. "I needed to fight that guy."

Mike rolled his eyes. "How would that go over with the other refugees, who've already been traumatized? You're a doctor, not some high   school punk."

"Is that what you think of me?" said Castro, angrily. He stumbled to his feet. "I'm some sort of punk?"

"Look, why don't you go back to the barracks?' said Mike, wearily. "I can stay and watch your patient, and we can send for you if necessary."

Castro raised his fist. "You want to go, huh? You want a piece of me?" he asked. His arms shook unsteadily.

"Jesus, Castro," said Mike. He rose from his chair, making his way to the entrance. He wanted as much distance as possible. "You're cracking up, man!"

"Everyone else might be, but not me," Castro grunted. "Now be a man and fight."

"You need someone to whip your ass?" asked Mike. He projected his voice as loudly as possible. If he were lucky, the security officer outside might hear. He sized Castro up. Even in his bedraggled state, the surgeon had the height and weight advantage. "You know that's labor, and I charge for that," Mike continued, "a thousand bucks per ass-whipping, plus tax."

He had no sooner spoken than two air policemen entered the tent. To his fortune, someone outside must have heard. They looked from Mike, to Castro, to one another, assessing the situation. "Dr. Castro needs a little help getting back to the barracks," said Mike.

"What seems to be the problem?"

"He's exhausted. He just needs some rest."

Castro's eyes went wide. His face twisted into a grimace of frustration. Still, he did not resist as he was escorted from the tent. One of the policemen returned later with instructions for Castro's patient. It was almost dawn when Mike finally collapsed on the cot. He sunk into a deep, restless slumber.

*   *   *

It took Mike all his strength to will himself awake. He checked his watch and groaned. It was only two hours later, and already he could hear the constant babble of morning voices outside the tent. After a quick breakfast, he went to check on Castro's patient just a few tents from his own. It appeared that the procedure had been a successful one. The patient was awake and in high spirits. When Mike introduced himself, he broke into a wide grin.

"Well, any friend of Dr. Castro's is a friend of mine," he said, beaming. "That man is a miracle-worker. I've never met a man so concerned and attentive."

"Yes," Mike agreed. "We're lucky to have him."

The patient nodded vigorously. "I'll say. If the rest of you Americans are like him, I believe we're in good hands. Yes sir!"

Chapter 30

FOR ALL ITS HARDSHIPS, life at Tent City seemed to have yielded some unexpected benefits for Mike. He had initially had reservations against working with Ricks. After all, the man was Cochran's commander, and Cochran had been a thorn in his side for months back on Valkyrie. However, he was pleasantly surprised by Ricks's easygoing nature. He was neither as cantankerous as Moon, nor as disturbingly optimistic as Flapjack, and he provided Mike occasional relief from his constant companions. The two had become friends almost overnight.

Moon and Ricks worked closely together. Both had been stationed in the medicine clinic to help those with diabetes, cardiovascular problems, and other chronic conditions. Mike had met several of these patients when he stopped by to visit. They saw mental patients too, Ricks told him, but those with schizophrenia and depression rarely came forward. In their culture, it was taboo, a mark of weakness.

Moon disagreed. Sure, some were ashamed, he reasoned, but most were just too terrified or shell-shocked to come forward. Theirs was a society that had been at war for over forty years. Self-sufficiency and independence were their highest virtues. In Vietnam, according to their Buddhist traditions, you work hard, you support your extended family, and you suffer in silence. To rely on foreign medicines for a malady of the spirit, well, it was a terrifying prospect; incomprehensible even!

It was three weeks later, however, that Mike began to have his suspicions. Something seemed to lurk behind Ricks's charismatic façade. Flapjack had noticed it first. He was always talking behind others' backs, she told him, always scoping out weaknesses, always watching over his shoulder. She didn't have proof, she admitted, but she was sure he was the reason so many refugees avoided the medicine tent. Moon had laughed off the theory. At first, Mike didn't believe it himself. That would all change very soon.

* * *

It was a windy Thursday when Ricks first came to his medical tent. The visit surprised Mike for multiple reasons. Neither Ricks nor Moon ever wandered from their Tent City sector. They preferred to avoid the refugee settlements. It was up to Mike and Flapjack to make the long walk across camp. Yet in swaggered Ricks—on his day off, even—with his arm around an old refugee! It was a curious sight, to be sure.

Ricks's companion only heightened Mike's unease. He was a thin, wiry figure, with a pencil-thin mustache. In his oversized Gabardine suit, he looked like the caricature of a traveling huckster, although out of his element in the olive green tents. Ricks introduced him as only "a prominent businessman," a man with a proposition to be heard.

As soon as he had arrived, Ricks was gone from the tent, leaving Mike with his mysterious comrade. The stranger took a seat and wiped his forehead with an oily handkerchief. He motioned Mike to sit as well. When he leaned forward, Mike almost choked on the smell of aftershave. It brought tears to his eyes.

"I hear many a good thing of you. Yes. An honorable man." The creature nodded as he spoke, as if in agreement with his words. "I was a blessed man in my country. Night clubs. Pretty girls. Pretty boys, too. A powerful man. A man who is your friend. Your good fortune."

He spread his arms and grinned from ear-to-ear. Mike had never seen so many gold teeth in his life. The man dabbed his forehead again and continued. "You are a doctor? An honorable profession. I can make things happen. Organ transplant, medical supplies, drugs. Wholesale. For you, very cheap-"

"I'm sorry," Mike interrupted. "But I think you may be looking for someone else."

The man threw back his head and laughed loudly. He pulled a silver cigarette case from his pocket and offered a smoke. Mike declined, shifting uncomfortably in his chair. "Ah yes, I forget myself!" the man chuckled, waving his cigarette in the air. "An honorable man, yes. An ethical man. So I come to you with an ethical job. One of great honor."

"I appreciate it, but—"

"I was forced to sell my fortune to the wolves. All I have now I carry here, in this chest." The dusty briefcase landed on the desk with a thud. With a snap, he unhinged the latches and opened it. Curiosity got the better of Mike. Against his better judgment, he turned the contents towards him. He had to know what was inside.

What Mike saw left him speechless. It was as though he had stumbled upon a pirate's treasure. The case was stuffed with glittering jewels and precious metals. Scattered across small bars of gold were emeralds and dia-monds half the size of a child's fist. He stared at the glittering array of wealth before him, dumbstruck, before quickly slamming the case shut.

"A-a-are you insane?!" gasped Mike, fumbling with his words. "What are you doing with this? And why the hell are you showing me?"

The man chuckled and snatched the handle of the briefcase. He placed it at the side of his chair, patting it affectionately. "You see, fortune smiles upon us friend," said the businessman softly, leaning forward. "I tell only few of this fortune. But there are those men ruled by greed, you know. Dishonorable men. They would rob us of our fortunes. They would not see us live like kings in America!"

"Then do something with it!" Mike sputtered. He rose to his feet awk-wardly, slamming both palms on his desk. "There are authorities here that can transfer it safely for you. There's a bank on Guam, too! Take it there, for God's sake!"

The man shook his head. "It is not so simple, I am afraid," he sighed. "Doctor, you will fly on military plane to your base. You will carry this for me safely?"

"No," said Mike, making his way towards the entrance. "Absolutely not. I can't."

"Doctor, you do not understand," the man insisted. "I give you twen-ty-five percent for all this for carry!" He rose with his suitcase. Mike escorted him from the tent quickly.

"No, no," he said, as the stranger stomped off in a huff, dragging the suitcase beside him. "Take it to a bank! And good luck."

* * *

That night, at dinner, Mike slammed his tray on the table. Moon and Flapjack looked up in surprise. Ricks remained with his head down, slurping his soup.

"Who the hell were you trying to fix me up with, Ricks?!" Mike demanded. Ricks looked up and smiled nervously. He dabbed his mouth with a napkin.

"Oh, hey Mike."

"Who the hell was that?!"

"Oh, Mr. Dang?" answered Ricks nonchalantly. He shrugged. "I don't know him too well, he just told me he needed a fellow he could trust."

"What's going on?" asked Flapjack nervously.

"Oh nothing," said Mike angrily. "Only Ricks here introduced me to a fellow who took me for a smuggler, is all."

"A smuggler!" gasped Flapjack. Ricks's face fell.

"Whoa, now, Mike, I didn't know, honest!"

"I had someone make me a similar offer, actually," said Moon. "Don't bite, trust me. Those kinds of deals can be used against you as blackmail. They can accuse you of not handing over the full amount, and since you can't report it, they have you by the throat."

"Gosh, I'm sorry, Mike," said Ricks. He put a hand on Mike's arm. "I bet he is a damn Commie too. One of them red bastards."

Mike didn't reply. He eyed Ricks warily and returned to his meal.

"That's what you get for trustin' them gooks," Ricks continued. He smiled uneasily. "I suppose I learned my lesson, eh?"

*　*　*

The rest of the meal passed in relative silence. Mike excused himself as soon as he finished. On his way to the barracks, he heard footsteps catching up with him. It was Flapjack, and she placed a hand on his shoulder, breathing heavily.

"I'm sorry about Ricks," she panted. "It's like him to pull a stunt like that."

"I should have known," said Mike.

"Known what?"

"That Cochran would be working under a guy like that. Someone always looking to exploit the suffering of others for his own gain."

Mike felt Flapjack's hand touch his own as they walked. It felt warm, comforting even, and he held it in his own. It had been years since he had felt a woman's warmth. He had almost forgotten how much he had missed it.

"It's scary isn't it?" she said, as they approached Mike's tent. "The war has shaped these people to become survivors. Brought to do things they wouldn't have done before."

"It's also created a market for their skills," said Mike tiredly. He hugged Flapjack tightly and turned in for the night.

As he lay in his cot, a mixture of guilt and relief swept over Mike in waves. Flapjack's touch awakened something in him. Something he had held locked inside for years. Could he do it? He wondered. Could he start a new life? He thought of his wife lying in the hospital bed. Then he thought of how selfish he was being. After all, he was surrounded by refugees who had made hard choices of their own. They had been forced—at the point of death—to abandon their country, their culture, and their loved ones. And yet they persevered.

What is the price of loyalty? He thought silently. And what is the price of letting go?

Chapter 31

OVER THE NEXT WEEK, an orange haze enveloped Tent City. It was a bad omen to the Vietnamese. The Air Force meteorologist assured them that the radar was clear. The locals, however, knew better, and fortified and barricaded their homes. It was the first sign of typhoon season on Guam. Anxiety spread quickly throughout the encampment. The sky grew darker. The winds howled against the canvas of the tents. At any moment, it seemed, they were on the verge of collapse.

It was during that time Mike learned how the system worked. Corruption, he found, was as alive on Guam as it was back at Valkyrie. The wealthiest and most powerful refugees bought their passage the quickest. It was the other hard working diplomats, officers, and professionals who were forced to make the best of their situation. It must have seemed like purgatory for them, thought Mike, and yet most of them showed tremendous courage. They continued to support one another in the face of enormous uncertainty.

*   *   *

For Mike, each day brought new challenges. He tried to focus on his work as a general medical officer and help however he could. By now, he had become preoccupied with the mental trauma of the refugees. Many of his hours were spent taking notes and trying to understand the length of time from the point of trauma to their breakdown. Because there were usually multiple episodes of trauma, it was difficult work. If everyone is vulnerable to breakdowns, how many breakdowns do you get?

Back at Camp Valkyrie, Mike's research yielded mixed results. Much of the literature he found had been done at VA hospitals after WWII and the Korean War. They used the same pejorative terms he'd heard often before, such as "shell shock," and "battle fatigue." He had never read anything that could have prepared him for Guam. Here, half of Tent City seemed to suffer from some form of traumatic disorder. Few of them had ever seen combat, however. Many of them were just women and children! For Mike, it was as perplexing as it was overwhelming.

*   *   *

Mike collapsed in a hammock during a rare lull in the weather. The sand beneath him was damp, and the air was so thick he could taste the brine. As he closed his eyes, his thoughts drifted back to the curious case he had that morning. It seemed like he was always learning something new about the Vietnamese way of life. He found their culture fascinating. Still, on days like today, he had trouble understanding them.

It had all happened early that morning. A young man brought his aging father to the tent. The old man had stopped talking days ago, according to his son, and his eyes watered at night. Just last night he had been found wandering around the settlement in a daze. It was at that point that the family decided to consult a physician. Their pain could no longer remain secret.

Mike had been touched by the deference the son showed his father. He had never seen a relationship so intimate. As the young man watched, Mike gave the father a check-up and found he had elevated blood pressure. There were also mysterious red patches on the man's forehead and temples. He had no idea where they had come from.

As the man rested, Mike poured the son a cup of coffee, and the two sat down to talk. The young man told him how his parents had sent him to America for his education. He had worked as an attorney for years. They had been some of the lucky ones, he said. Unlike most refugees, his whole family had arrived in Guam safely, including his mother, his sister, and his wife and two children. The escape from Saigon had been a great source of grief for his mother and father in particular. Everything they owned had been invested in a chain of bakeries, into which they had poured their life's work. The children helped to make the noodles. Mike could still remember the smile on the man's face as he told how the noodles had educated him. It was as though the man had travelled back in time through his words. They took him back to a happier time.

Mike swatted a fly from his cheek. He shifted uncomfortably. It bothered him that he remembered each case less distinctly each day. The son, like so many before him, had echoed the same troubling sentiments; sentiments that Mike found hard to stomach. According to the refugees, they had deserved their hardships. They were being punished for mistakes made in another life. Therefore, they felt it their duty to suffer in silence.

It was all too familiar to Mike. Though it aggravated him, he had to admire their stoicism. It was something the young man had told him today, however, that had stuck in his mind. The Cambodians, he had said, had a word for torture—Tieru Na Kam—which was also the word for "Karma." Mike found it hard to believe there could be a culture more devoutly masochistic than the Vietnamese. Their whole life philosophy left them vulnerable to Communism!

The older patient's blood pressure remained elevated, so Mike admitted him to a hospital tent and began administering treatment. In a matter of hours, the man's confusion dissipated, and he was able to discuss his condition. He told Mike how the pains in his head brought tears to his eyes. His migraines were agonizing. They occurred daily, too, like clockwork. He spoke proudly of how he had resisted complaining. To do so would bring shame to his family.

It was later that afternoon that an elderly woman arrived at the tent. She introduced herself as the man's wife. When Mike asked about the red spots on his head, she told him that her husband had been consulting a traditional doctor; a practitioner who held great power and influence among the refugees. The red marks had been left by a procedure called "cupping," in which the doctor would heat tiny cups and place them on the patient's body. As the cups cooled, it would create a mild suction effect, which was believed to "draw out" the offending agent. The process always left marks on the skin. Mike was assured they were not permanent.

* * *

It was the traditional practices regarding children that disturbed Mike the most. During his first morning in the pediatric tent, a woman brought in her nine-year old son who had been suffering nightmares. He had not been himself lately, the mother had said, and he had refused to take care of his grandmother. He had even tried to run away several times. Such behavior, the woman lamented, had brought dishonor to their family.

When Mike examined the boy, what he found disturbed him. The boy had what appeared to be cigarette burns all over his arms and stomach. Some had already left prominent scars. When asked, the mother answered without hesitation that it was the result of discipline. The grandmother had often placed burning incense on the child to cure his evil ways. Fortunately, a Vietnamese nurse had overheard and seen the look of horror on Mike's face. She quickly intervened. After a brief, but heated exchange in their native tongue, the mother stormed from the tent in a huff. The boy trailed behind her reluctantly, staring at the ground.

"We see it fairly often, actually," the nurse had told Mike. "It's a traditional form of discipline in many regions."

"But it looks painful," said Mike. "In the States it won't be tolerated, especially in the schools. They could lose custody of their children."

The nurse shrugged. "We do what we can. We tell them that they will have to change their methods in America, but trust me," she said, smirking, "you'll probably see much worse."

*   *   *

The nurse had been right. Just a few days later, Mike was called to see a woman in her tent who was unable to move. The case itself had been relatively routine. The patient's fever and the pain in her lower abdomen clearly indicated appendicitis. It was what Mike saw as he was calling the medics that stopped him in midsentence.

In the back of the tent, lying curled under a cot, lay two children, their limbs bound tightly with twine. Mike called to them, but got no response. As the medical team arrived with a stretcher, Mike crept towards the two captives nervously. The last thing he wanted was to frighten them. When he received no answer again, he carefully pulled the bodies from their cramped quarters. One of the children, a little girl, had passed out from loss of circulation. The other was an older boy, whose white, tear-streaked face stared up at Mike in fear.

The children had been securely bound. It took Mike a few minutes to finally untie their knots. He would occasionally attempt conversation, but received no answer. The boy remained silent for over an hour. Sitting pensively next to his sister, he seemed almost oblivious to Mike's presence. Eventually his sister came-to.

Mike sat in the stale, humid air of the tent and waited. The children had crawled in a corner and eyed him with suspicion. Under their wide-eyed, curious stares, Mike felt as if he were some sort of freak; a specimen under a microscope. He wondered if this was how animals felt in the zoo.

It took over an hour before a man arrived at the tent. He was taken aback to see Mike, but his surprise quickly turned to anger. He stormed past Mike towards the children.

"You have no right to be here!" said the man gruffly, examining both the boy and girl. "And you have untied them! Why have you done such a thing?"

Mike cleared his throat. The man was obviously the children's father. He wore a sweat-stained, unbuttoned shirt, from which sprouted a thick crop of chest hair. He was a tall and imposing figure. Mike summed up his courage.

"Why would you tie them in the first place?" he replied. "It's dangerous. The girl had passed out, too. You can't do something like that!"

"And why not?"

"Because it's illegal! In the United States, I mean. That kind of thing is illegal."

The man's face fell. He sat on a cot and stroked the stubble on his chin. "I do not see the problem, sir," he said, with concern in his voice. "The children are simply being disciplined. They must learn the virtue of patience."

Mike shook his head. "You have to learn a different way," he said, leaning forward. "Do you understand? This is considered child abuse in America!"

"I apologize," said the man. His head was lowered in shame. "Our ways are different. It is tradition."

The incident profoundly impacted Mike. It took some insistence on his part, but eventually the pediatric ward printed out flyers for refugee parents. There needed to be no doubt, he had argued, about what was and was not acceptable child-rearing methods. A second pamphlet was printed on the risks of practicing traditional medicine in America. Such treatment often left bruises, red marks, and burns, which could be seen as signs of abuse.

Chapter 32

AS SHOCKING AS Mike's experiences were, he would not learn until many years later how much worse they could have been. This first wave of refugees had been the lucky ones. They were among the privileged class, and came in large family groups. Many had already sent their children to western schools. It was those who arrived longer after Mike had left that suffered the most. The Cambodians arrived in terrible condition. Families had been fractured and displaced. Their children had experienced the horrors of the concentration camps. Many arrived with no knowledge of American culture and little family support.

He heard most of the stories from Moon. Only Moon had volunteered to stay, even as conditions grew increasingly unsanitary. The tents were crowded beyond capacity, and epidemics would sweep through Tent City on a regular basis. Even among survivors, life was often nasty, brutish, and short. Moon admitted that he and the other staff members often lay awake at night. They had nightmares of their tents being overrun by the starving, desperate masses.

* * *

Moon didn't need to tell Mike how the women had suffered. He knew all too well. Even early in the evacuation, he was shocked to learn how female refugees had been treated. Women and girls of all ages had experienced rape and sexual abuse at the hands of their captors. The victims rarely came forward. Many patients blamed themselves for their rape, believing they had brought dishonor to their families. It was Karma, they said. It was the natural way of things.

Karma. Mike had heard the word enough times to make him sick. He often wondered if such fatalistic beliefs made the refugees easy targets. Almost all of their boats had been attacked en route to Guam by pirates, who were more than willing to act as Karma's rapists and assassins. Were the ideals that sustained them destroying them, too? There was no easy answer.

*   *   *

Mike would never learn how many Southeast Asians were killed during the evacuations. It took him over a decade just to find the shocking estimates. In 1975 alone, Mike had read, at least 155,000 were killed on the roads. In the NVA "re-education" camps, at least 200,000 had been executed, while an additional 165,000 died of torture, malnutrition, sickness, and exhaustion. From 1975 to 1987, an estimated 2.5 million had died from political violence. After a famine in 1988, the total death toll would rise to around 3 or 4 million people. All of them victims at the hands of the Communists. In Mike's opinion, much of the blame lay with the United States, as well. They had betrayed an old and trusted ally, and abandoned them to be slaughtered.

Of course, back in 1975, none of them had known the extent of the tragedy. Neither Mike nor his colleagues had ever experienced the horrors of war on such a massive scale. It was as though they were witness to a holocaust. In those first few weeks, even Moon admitted to having recurring nightmares. In the days before Mike would leave Guam, as conditions began to deteriorate, the refugees became increasingly eager to escape. There was a rumor that the NVA had planned an attack on the island. Water was being rationed and food had become scarce. The situation was becoming increasingly desperate.

It was only late in the evenings that Mike had a chance to relax. These were the hours when Flapjack was stationed in the medical tent, and the two often talked and comforted each other. Even she seemed worn out by the stress. One night, after the death of a patient she had grown close to, she finally snapped.

"I can't take it," she told Mike. "I feel numb, except for my stomach, which just feels sick. What is wrong with the world, that it brings so much pain and suffering to so many?"

"Good question," said Mike. "Three decades after WWII, you would think we would have learned something."

Flapjack collapsed on a cot. Mike had never seen her look so haggard and exhausted. "Why would Ford go back on Nixon's promise, anyway?" she asked. "It seems like the one time we could have intervened and done some good."

Mike sighed. "He said the public lost its will because the truth became public. There was Watergate. There was Daniel Ellsberg, too, and he was just acquitted last year. Remember that? The Pentagon knew the war couldn't be won years ago. Ellsberg gave the Pentagon Papers to the Times and there was this long legal battle over their publication."

"I remember," groaned Flapjack, rubbing her head. "My father was outraged."

"Then the Plumbers broke into Ellsberg's psychiatrist's office and were planning to discredit him. It was pretty ugly business, and Americans were fed up with Nixon and Johnson. It wasn't just the lies, it was the wanton killing of our troops in an unwinnable war."

"I don't think the military lost its will," said Flapjack. "I think we could have stopped this slaughter. Even the survivors will never be the same."

"I'm just glad I'm not the President," said Mike. "I couldn't live with so many skeletons in the closet."

Flapjack sat up angrily. Her face was flushed with emotion. "I don't feel any sympathy for that bastard," she cried. "I don't have sympathy for any of them! Not one!"

Chapter 33

FLAPJACK AND MIKE were not alone. After a month of constant pressure, day after day, many others had reached the end of their rope. Those without an outlet to de-stress would inevitably crack. Mike had seen it happen, and it wasn't pretty. The human spirit could only endure so much.

Mike would never forget the first time he'd seen one of the doctors break down. It was during the third week. Each night the helicopters would bring in more of the wounded. He would hear them flying low over the tents every few hours. On one night in particular, late after midnight, Mike was roused by a frantic voice from outside. A messenger had orders from the hospital commander himself. There was an emergency on the surgical floor and the commander couldn't contain it. As a last ditch effort, he decided to call for a psychiatrist.

Mike dressed quickly and jumped into a nearby jeep. A guard met him at the entrance to the air base hospital. "It's one of the doctors, sir," he said breathlessly. "He just won't work anymore! He just broke down crying!"

When he ran into the surgical suite, Mike found one of the surgeons outside the operating room bent over. He was sobbing into his sleeves. Leaning over his huddled body was the commander, whose voice had become hoarse from yelling. No matter how much he berated the man, however, the surgeon refused to rise. As he passed them and walked into the suite, what Mike saw made him feel nauseous. There was a man on the table—an American officer—who was covered in blood. His legs were gone. All that remained were two grotesque stumps. The patient was still being prepped for surgery, and the techs had stopped most of the bleeding. Still, Mike could tell that he was just clinging to life. A large pool of blood on the floor had already begun to coagulate.

"Major! Help us out here!" barked the commander. He sounded more like a drill sergeant than a doctor. Mike left the suite and faced the superior officer. "This sonofabitch needs to toughen up, goddamit!" He rasped hoarsely. The vein on his forehead was throbbing.

Mike tried his best to ignore the commander as he approached the surgeon. It was obvious the man's temper was only making things worse. He crouched at the surgeon's eye level and spoke slowly and calmly.

"Look at me," he said, and the man slowly peered from his arms. "Everything's going to be okay," Mike continued. "We're going to go to that conference room to your left and talk things over, all right?" The man nodded weakly.

The commander curled his lips in a snarl. "Like hell you will. You listen here, Major-."

"*Officer's Handbook*, sir. Chapter 2, Section B, Part 3," recited Mike, as he helped the surgeon to his feet. "An officer shall not be forced into duty if he is mentally unwell. He is to receive the proper and necessary treatment." Mike could hardly believe the words that were coming out of his mouth. How much had he actually memorized?

"Proper treatment, my ass," grumbled the commander, but he made no effort to stop them. Mike shut the door to the conference room, and the surgeon slumped in a nearby chair. Tears were still running down his face.

"I can't do it anymore," he said, wiping his eyes with a handkerchief. "They've placed land mines all around Saigon and they're blowing people to shit! He's the fifth one I've had tonight. The fifth! And none of them have legs. It's just a mess of shredded muscle, blood, and shattered bone."

Mike cringed inwardly. He wondered if he could have lasted as long. With the commander gone, the man seemed visibly relieved. Even though he was still shaking, he was beginning to regain his composure.

"No feet. No feet," the man repeated, staring down at the table. "Do you know how awful that is? They keep screaming about the pain, but there's nothing there. It's so fucked up."

"The world is a fucked up place," said Mike. He placed a hand on the man's shoulder. The surgeon drew his sleeve across his face and rose from the table. The two looked each other in the eye now. They seemed to share a common bond, Mike felt.

"I think I'm ready to head back out there, Doc," said the man grimly. "I just needed some time."

Mike shook his head. "I can appreciate the sentiment," he responded, "but right now I need you to return to the barracks. Get some rest and return."

"But the commander—"

"That's an order," Mike interrupted. He smiled gently and clapped the man on his shoulders. "You let me worry about the commander."

*   *   *

"That asshole better be behind you, Major!" snapped the commander. His eyes had widened in disbelief when Mike returned on his own. "We've got to move right now. Another flight's already on the way!"

Mike swallowed the lump in his throat. "I relieved the man for the night sir."

"You did what?!"

"I relieved the attending surgeon, sir," he repeated. "The man won't be effective in his current state. His nerves are shot."

The commander said nothing. It was as though Mike's words left him speechless. He paced a few steps, back and forth, fuming, until he found a suitable target. Mike drew his hands up instinctively as the man hurled a nearby chair. It clattered down the hall.

"Major, you get that man back here right now! Do you know how many lives your insubordination may have cost? Do you have any idea?!"

"But you're a qualified surgeon, too, aren't you sir?" Mike asked. "Couldn't you just take his place for a few hours?"

The commander was bent over now, wincing in pain. His tantrum had bruised his ankle badly. He looked up at Mike sourly as he rubbed his shin.

"Yes, Major, but-."

"You'll have to take it," said Mike, cutting him off. "That man is at the end of his rope. If he experiences further trauma tonight, we might lose him for good. It's our only option."

The commander ignored Mike's warnings. He called down the hall for a guard. "Go wake up Castro," he said, when the officer arrived. "Tell him to get his butt down here on the double!"

*   *   *

On his way back to the barracks, Mike decided to check in on the young surgeon. The man was still awake when he arrived. He rubbed his eyes sleepily and called Mike in.

"I didn't mean to let anyone down, Doc," he said weakly.

"You didn't, don't worry about that," Mike reassured him. "But if you can't sleep, I can walk you to the hospital room. They can make sure you get some rest."

The man shook his head. "I don't know, Doc. I don't know if I can sleep. Every time I close my eyes I see the images in my head."

With Mike's reassurance, however, the surgeon eventually relented. After finding him a bed, Mike instructed the nurse to give him 2 milligrams of Ativan IM and check on him periodically. It wasn't long before the man was fast asleep.

On his way back, Mike stopped by the operating room to make sure things were under control. In a far corner sat the commander with his legs crossed. He shot Mike a look of pure malice. Castro, meanwhile, was hacking the meat from a man's mangled stump. He wiped his hands on a sterile towel and gave Mike a bloody finger. Mike saluted and left.

Chapter 34

ONCE THE FLOODGATES opened, they never closed. Every day the small staff on the island faced a new wave of traumatized refugees. The C-141s were delivering an average 5,000 people a day. They were hit the hardest on May 7th, when three ships arrived with over 15,000 passengers. Two days later, they were followed by two more ships, which brought in an additional 8,000. Tent City was eventually forced to expand. Supplies were stretched to their limits.

The refugees themselves arrived in terrible condition. They were packed into the hold or on the decks of their ships like sardines, with no facilities to wash or relieve themselves. The smell in the harbor was putrid. Mike was at least fortunate that the naval base was on the other side of the island. The refugees were then packed onto school buses and taken to Tent City. They were often met on the outskirts by the residents of Guam, who were generous enough to take them in, clean them up, and offer their support.

New arrivals were met with little ceremony. There was the occasional joyous reunion, but for the most part they were politely acknowledged and quickly integrated into the community. Many were rushed to the medical tent suffering dehydration and exposure.

It was in the beginning of June when things finally came to a head. The doctors, surgeons, and nurses were understaffed and running low on supplies. When they learned that no reinforcements were coming, they tried to work more efficiently. A triage team of nurses was assigned to briefly assess new arrivals. Each patient was then assigned a priority level and provided the necessary level of care. Emergencies received immediate attention. This new system worked so well that the staff now had time to rest. After a month, they were even rewarded a day off!

*   *   *

A day off! Mike never thought the words could provide such a relief. He and his companions all knew how they would spend it. After all, there was not much to do on the island except go to the beach! Moon had learned the location of a perfect little cove from a resident. He was joined by Mike, Flapjack, Ricks, and a few of the Australian nurses he had grown chummy with. It was only a short trip by jeep, and the view when they arrived was breathtaking.

Mike had never seen a place so peaceful. Before them stretched the white sands of the shoreline, which gave way to the glistening, blue-green waves of the bay. As he looked out on the Pacific, he found it hard to fathom that such suffering and beauty could coexist on one tiny island. They were far away from the constant noise and crowded confines of Tent City. All was quiet, as the trade winds rustled the palms.

"It looks like we better enjoy the sun while it lasts," remarked Sybil, as they laid out their blankets and towels. "It looks like we're in for some rain."

Mike had seen the dark clouds on the horizon. Everyone had. Right now, no one seemed to care too much. Today was their day off. Nothing else mattered. They would de-stress and relax, even if it killed them!

"So what should we talk about?" asked Sybil. She was already lounging under an umbrella. In her sun hat and large aviator glasses, she looked like a co-ed on spring break. Moon took it upon himself to rub lotion on her back.

"Maybe we shouldn't talk at all," said Ricks. "Maybe we should just sleep."

Flapjack grinned. "Well, I have something," she laughed. "Did you know we're actually real close to the Mariana Trench."

"Huh? How did you know? Who told you where I got it?" Ricks, who had been half-asleep, sat up with a start. He stared at Flapjack in surprise."

"Got what?" asked Flapjack.

"You know. Come on."

"I have no clue…"

"The marijuana," answered Ricks reluctantly, rolling his eyes. "Come on. How did you find out I got the marijuana from the French?"

Mike burst out laughing. "That's… not what she said," he chuckled. Both Ricks and Flapjack stared at him curiously. "It's Marian… ah, nevermind."

"Wait a minute," said Moon. "Did you say you had the mary jane with you? That's pretty risky, don't you think? I told you to keep that stuff under wraps."

Ricks shrugged. "I dunno, I guess. It's not like the dogs can smell it. There's too many smells in that shantytown anyway. They're focused on the refugees."

"You're something else, you know that?" said Moon, shaking his head. "I knew you were using at Valkyrie, but this is a whole 'nother level!"

"Ah, hush. I'm gonna share. Puff 'n pass," said Ricks, as he licked the edges of a torn sheet of paper. He rolled a fat cigarette and handed it to a nurse. "Just puff 'n pass, sister. It's all groovy."

* * *

A light blue haze hung in the air around them. The joint had been passed around the party at least three times now. Moon took a long puff and doubled over coughing. He looked up at Mike with a glassy, unfocused expression, gazing through dilated pupils.

"Are you sure you don't want a hit, man?" wheezed Moon. "This is the way to relax, trust me."

Mike smiled thinly and shook his head. He and Flapjack were the only ones declining to partake. Ricks and an Australian nurse continued to eye them suspiciously. The constant scrutiny made him uneasy, as if he were being judged. Suddenly, he felt the soft weight of Flapjack's head resting against his shoulder. She leaned against him and yawned.

"So you were telling us about that, uh, what was it again?" asked Mike. His head felt slightly dizzy.

"The Mariana Trench," said Flapjack dreamily. "Just south of Guam, 36,000 feet deep. It's… it's pretty intense, you know? To imagine?"

"I heard about that in college? Yeah, it was college," said Moon, as if confirming the fact with himself.

"That's far out," mumbled an Australian nurse. She was staring at her hands intently. "That's like… that's like the center of the earth."

Flapjack laughed. When she spoke, she sounded to Mike as if she were deep in thought, detached from the group and pondering. "You can relax," she assured them. "The earth's center is like 4,000 miles away. The trench is only, like, 7 miles deep."

"Deep enough to dump all those evacuation helicopters, eh?" said the nurse. She passed the paper stub to Ricks, who burnt his finger. He cursed loudly.

"I wondered what they were going to do with all that stuff from the ARVN," said Sybil. "That must be the military solution."

"Wouldn't surprise me," snapped Moon. He spat in the sand and began rolling another joint. "Just in case you wondered if the U.S. was serious about ending the war."

*   *   *

It wasn't long before Mike and Flapjack were on their own. The Australian nurses had gone for a swim, while Ricks and Sybil had left to smoke further down the beach. Despite not smoking himself, Mike felt somehow light-headed and dizzy. It was difficult to put together his thoughts coherently. He felt a vague sense of annoyance at Ricks for exposing them all to a drug bust. The military showed a great deal of enthusiasm for hunting and prosecuting anyone involved in narcotics. Back at Valkyrie, trained dogs would be used to inspect nearly every vehicle arriving at the gates.

"Mike, are you okay?" Mike turned slowly to Flapjack and nodded. She laughed. "You poor thing. Your eyes are bloodshot! You're probably experiencing a contact high."

"It's… it's pretty wild when you think about it," said Mike.

"What's that?"

"You know, the hypocrisy of it all. They sold alcohol, and I mean, people—I mean, at Valkyrie—would go through the gates with toxic blood-alcohol levels, and no one would care."

"I know, right?" agreed Flapjack. "I envy you, Mike. You seem to always be able to make the right decisions. It's hard with all the corruption and the hypocrisy. And I mean… you've had to deal with your own problems…"

"Yeah, like my wife," said Mike absently. He regretted the words the moment he heard them.

"Oh no! Mike, I didn't mean…"

"It's okay," he continued, lying back on the beach towel. He stared up at the clouds above him. "It's something I think about a lot lately to be honest."

"It's… well, I can't even imagine what that must feel like for you," said Flapjack softly. Her voice was distant and sad. "But, I mean, you can't beat yourself up over it. Look at the refugees we work with."

"How's that?"

"Well, they've had to make those kinds of decisions too. Either leave the life you know—home, stability, the familiar—or suffer a fate worse than death. It's hardly a choice, really. Life pushes us forward."

Mike propped himself up on his elbows. He looked to Flapjack, who was staring off towards the sea. For some reason, he felt the urge to lash out, to take offence to the comparison, but he could think of nothing to say. Perhaps she was right, he thought. Perhaps he had more in common with his patients than he realized.

Chapter 35

"**MIKE! OH MY GOD,** guess who I found?"

Flapjack's cry roused Mike from his nap. It had not rained after all, but the sky was already beginning to darken, and the sun was turning orange. He and the Australian nurses turned to see Flapjack hugging one of the two men descending the cliffs towards them. Both were American dressed in civilian clothes.

"Everyone, this is my dad," said Flapjack happily. She had her arm around a tall, middle-aged man with sandy-blonde hair. He smiled sheepishly and extended his palm. "This is Mr. Colbert and my dad, David," she continued. "They both work for the government."

"Gee Flapjack," said one of the nurses. "I didn't know your dad was one of the big wigs!"

"Yeah, you always told me he was a paper shuffler!" The group turned to see Moon approaching the campsite. He was hauling a stack of firewood.

Mike shook hands with both men. David grinned and looked him straight in the eye. His grasp was firm and confident. Mr. Colbert was smaller and mousier than Flapjack's father, and he seemed to regard the strangers around him with distrust. He shook their hands warily and spoke very little.

"Well," said Moon, dumping the firewood on the ground with a sigh. "This is Guam, and I know why I'm here. But I'll be damned if I know what's brought you fellas to our little island!"

"Mr. Colbert... that name sounds familiar," said Mike. To his relief, his mind seemed to have returned to normal. "I believe one of the refugees told me he had worked with you." Mr. Colbert said nothing. He peered suspiciously at Mike through his thick-rimmed spectacles.

"You'll have to excuse my friend here," laughed David. He winked at Mike. "He's one of those strong-silent types, you know?"

"But dad, why are you here? Why didn't anyone tell me you were coming!" Flapjack almost stumbled over her words in her eagerness. To Mike, she sounded as giddy as a little girl. David beamed down at her.

"Well, honey, it came as a surprise to me too!" he laughed. "Mr. Colbert came to discuss how the evacuation was going, and, well, he brought me along for the ride!" Mr. Colbert cleared his throat and adjusted his glasses. He drew a cloth and began to clean them.

"I'm sorry to cut this short, gentlemen, ladies," he finally spoke, still wiping the lenses. "But I'll need to speak with Miss Flapjack in private, please. We have sensitive matters to discuss." Flapjack raised an eyebrow in surprise. She looked to Mike and shrugged. Clearly, whatever they were about to discuss, she knew as little as he did.

"You too, Mike," said David. There was a sudden change in his tone. He sounded serious now. Like a father addressing his child. He turned to the group and broke into a smile. "You don't mind if we borrow these kids for a while do you? They'll be back soon, so save 'em some s'mores!"

* * *

"All right," said Colbert, almost as soon as they were out of earshot. "I've been told you had an interaction with Colonel Tru. Is that correct?" Flapjack looked nervously up at her father. He nodded reassuringly.

"Yes, only briefly. And Mike helped me out."

"Can you tell us everything you know about him?"

"Well, most of what I've heard has come second-hand. Rumors, you know?"

"It's okay, Flapjack," said David calmly. He put his arm around her. "Anything you can tell us would help."

"Well," said Flapjack, "I know he's become an influential leader among the refugees. He wants to repatriate because his wife and children are still in Vietnam. I hear more and more people are wanting to join him."

"He's a damn fool," groaned Colbert. "The NVA will kill him. Or worse... they'll put him in one of those work camps. And that's a fate worse than death."

"Anything you want to add, Mike?" asked David. Mike shook his head.

"I've heard the same as Flapjack, really," he replied.

"Look," said David grimly, as they arrived at a clearing with a jeep. "We need to arrange a meeting with Colonel Tru without anyone knowing. Can either of you help arrange that?"

"I could manage that," said Flapjack, after a moment of thought. "When would you want to do it? Tomorrow?"

"Tonight, if possible. We have to leave early tomorrow morning." Flapjack looked crestfallen upon hearing the words. Her response didn't quite cover the hurt.

"Aw, Dad, but you just got here, I haven't seen you in months."

"I know, sweetheart," said David sadly. "But you'll be home soon. And we'll have plenty of time to catch up then. Right now, what we're dealing with is bigger than either of us. There are lives at stake."

"If… if I can help, I'd be happy to go with you, Flapjack," Mike offered. Colbert shook his head as he stuck the keys in the ignition.

"I don't believe that's necessary. After all, it's your day off. I'm sure your friends are waiting for you."

"Now, Colbert, we have an extra seat," said David, as he helped Flapjack into the vehicle. He winked at Mike and gestured him over. "If Mike wants to come, he's more than welcome. He's just going to have to miss out on those s'mores!"

*   *   *

Colbert rolled up the windows, but it was already too late. The stench in the jeep was overwhelming. Tears were streaming from their eyes. Even Colonel Tru, who sat stoically between Flapjack and Mike, showed visible discomfort.

"Goddammit, I should have known," cursed Colbert. He squinted to keep his eyes on the road. David looked back at his passengers. He tried to laugh, but coughed violently.

"The island is… being sprayed," he gasped between breaths. "We've been… scheduling malathion treatments for… mosquitoes. Just a precaution. We… can't have an epidemic." David choked and blew his nose in his handkerchief. Colonel Tru nodded, but said nothing. He appeared to be deep in thought.

After what seemed like forever, they arrived at the naval base on Orote Point. Mike, Flapjack, and even David burst out of the vehicle. Never had the fresh, Pacific air tasted so good. As if to maintain their military dignity, both Colbert and Colonel Tru made a slow and deliberate exit, as though nothing had fazed them. Still, Mike could see the relief plainly written on their faces.

On the outside, the base looked modest enough. It was a small naval outpost in the remote Pacific. On the inside, however, Colbert led them through a maze of offices and control rooms. It took a few minutes, and more than a few passcode-confirmations, before they finally reached their destination. David referred to it as a "confidential briefing room," but Mike knew as well as the rest where they were headed. The interrogation wing.

Mike had no idea what to expect. He'd only seen interrogation chambers in spy movies. The room they arrived at shared nothing in common with those dank, hopeless cells.

Here, oil paintings hung from the wall; an oriental rug lay spread below a mahogany conference table. All the colors were calm and muted. Colbert took a seat at the head of the table and beckoned them forward.

"Colbert," said the Colonel, after they were all seated. It was the first word he had spoken since they had found him in his tent. His voice was dry and emotionless. "It's... a pleasure to see you again." Colbert laughed and extended his arms.

"Tru, it's been too long, hasn't it?"

"Three years, I believe."

"Too long, too long! I do miss the old days!" Colbert's enthusiasm sounded hollow; his laughter forced. If he were attempting to put Tru at his ease, Mike thought, he was hardly succeeding.

"Colbert, David, I'm afraid I don't have much time—"

"Neither do we," David interrupted. "First of all, the President sends his regrets. We know you've suffered a great deal. However, we also know what you're planning, and I'm afraid it's completely unfeasible."

"Unfeasible?"

"Exactly. Impossible. There are other ways we can help extract your family."

"That's why we're here," added Colbert. "We want to help develop a plan to extract your family." Colonel Tru stared down at the table. He sighed deeply.

"I regret that my decision is made. I will be returning to the mainland. Only by giving myself up can I guarantee their safety."

"Listen, Tru," David insisted. "You can trust us. You think we haven't been doing our best? We've already located your wife and children at Phnom Penh. They'll be taking her to a 're-education' camp in a week or so. It's the perfect moment to strike."

"It's too deep for a ground operation," argued Tru. "And there's no way to fly over all that anti-aircraft fire."

"Not in an American craft," said Colbert wryly. "But I bet they wouldn't suspect a Soviet plane."

"You have one?"

"We do indeed," said David. "Well, at least, we will. It's in Thailand at the moment." Colonel Tru thought for a moment. Finally he sighed again, rubbing his goatee.

"It's not just about me, you understand," he replied, his eyes watering. "I am not the only one who has left loved ones behind. There are hundreds of us. And their voices call for our return."

"Colonel Tru!" cried Colbert loudly, slamming his palms on the table. "Do you not understand the consequences? You are leading your people like lambs to the slaughter—"

"Colbert, please!" said David. As he stared at his colleague, the fire in Colbert's eyes died out. He looked away and grumbled quietly. "Now Colonel, we can't stop you," David continued, turning his gaze to Tru. "We won't risk a rebellion at the refugee camp by standing in your way. If you want to go, then we can't stop you. All we ask is that you give us two weeks before your departure."

"Every day I stay, the odds of them killing my children increase," said Tru. "I know that. There are over 1,500 of my countrymen who feel the same."

"Two weeks," repeated David. "In return, we'll provide you with the ship and provisions. It is the best deal we can offer." The room was silent. Tru looked from David to Colbert, and then back to David. Finally, he hung his head in submission.

"Two weeks. But I assure you, nothing will change my plans."

* * *

Only Mike and Flapjack returned with David. Colbert and the colonel remained at the Orote base that night. According to David, the two had a lot to catch up on. "Don't let their icy demeanor fool you," he laughed, "those two share too much history to be enemies. They share more in common than you might think!"

Mike couldn't help feeling like a third wheel. Flapjack sat in the front seat next to her father, and the two spent the trip back chatting about old times. It had finally started to rain, and Mike leaned his head against the back window to rest.

"—And Flapjack tells me a lot about you, Major Pike!" Mike caught the end of the sentence as it was directed towards him. Flapjack giggled in response. "Now you better take care of my daughter while she's away," continued David. "I'm counting on you. She's going to need help acting as liaison between us and the colonel."

"I'll do what I can," said Mike, "but will we be here that long?"

"Yeah, Dad, will we?" asked Flapjack. "I keep hearing they'll be sending us Stateside in a matter of weeks." David chuckled.

"It'll be more than enough time. Trust me. It should only take us a week to accomplish our plan."

Chapter 36

MOON AND THE REST of the team arrived late the next morning. Mike didn't mind. He had been hoping for some time alone with Flapjack, and breakfast provided the perfect opportunity. There were still so many questions from the night before. He had to learn more.

"So did you know your dad was in the CIA?" he asked. Across from the table, Flapjack picked at her eggs. She seemed hesitant to answer. When she spoke, he got the impression that she chose her words carefully.

"Keep your voice down," she hissed, leaning forward. "And no... well, not really. And we don't even know if he's CIA."

"After last night, I can't see many other possibilities."

Flapjack nodded slowly. "All he ever told me was that he and mother worked for the government. I'd assumed he was just a paper shuffler—" She paused for a moment. "—Well that's not exactly true. I suppose on some level I knew there was something more. I just assumed he kept quiet for our own protection."

"You never wondered?"

"Of course I wondered. But I knew better than to ask questions." There was a hint of scorn in her voice, and Mike decided not to push the issue. After a few moments, however, her defenses relaxed. She smiled at him sheepishly. "I guess I'm not being fair," she said softly. "It's a sensitive subject for me. Dad would disappear to D.C. or a place I heard him call 'the Farm', for a week, a month, a whole summer. I used to think it was because of me, you know? Something I did wrong. Sometimes it felt like he would never come back."

Flapjack's eyes teared up, though she tried to hide it. Her hand began to shake. Mike reached across the table and touched her arm reassuringly. She looked at him with gratitude. They both knew how hard it was to think about home. In a refugee camp on a distant island, emotions were a luxury they could rarely afford.

"You must have been lonely."

Flapjack wiped a tear from her cheek. She smiled fondly. "Actually, I really wasn't. I had a whole herd of imaginary horses in my closet." She looked at Mike and smiled. "And I always felt Mom and Dad's love. I have memories of our vacations in the Adirondacks, trips to our cabin by the lake. Mom was strong, you know? A real frontier woman." Mike looked at her curiously. She chuckled. "A feminist, I mean. She didn't put up with any nonsense. I used to think she was strict. But now I understand. She was teaching us to be independent..." Flapjack trailed off. There was a faraway look in her eye. "But I'm sorry, Mike. I know I'm going on. It's just been so long since I've seen them, you know?"

Mike nodded. His grip on her arm tightened, just a little. He wanted to tell her he understood; that there was nothing to worry about. Still, the words seemed caught in his throat.

"No! It's... good!" he tried to reassure her. "I've been wanting to get to know you better!" She rolled her eyes.

"I appreciate it, Mike, but really..."

"So what does she think of your travels?" he blurted. The question seemed to take her by surprise.

"My travels?"

"Yeah, your mom, I mean. After all, you're way off in Guam, you know, the Gateway to the East!"

Flapjack pondered for a moment. "She likes the traveling part. She doesn't care for the military, though. It's her feminist side. She says the military wants to control women rather than empower them. But—" she added, "—I'm sure she'd approve of the company I keep."

As she spoke, Flapjack leaned in towards Mike. They were both blushing. He could feel the heat of her breath on his cheek. He leaned in towards her and closed his eyes.

"Someone mention feminism?"

The voice caught both of them by surprise. Moon had found them, and he seemed hardly aware of his intrusion. He tossed his tray on the table loudly and groaned. "I'm a feminist too, ya know. Equal rights for chicks, I can dig it."

"Is that right?" asked Mike. If Moon detected his sarcasm, he was too busy shoveling bacon into his mouth to care.

*   *   *

It was during Mike's last days on the island when signs of crises began to emerge. It was almost the end of April, and the evacuation had grown into a Biblical size exodus. The constantly fluctuating population of Tent City had risen to almost 40,000 refugees. Privacy was non-existent. Living space was hotly contested. The tents were packed with desperate men, women, and children, as rations began to diminish. Daily shipments of aid and supplies had little effect. The need was just too overwhelming.

As conditions declined, tensions rose. By now, Colonel Tru had amassed a substantial following among the refugees. The officials that once ignored him now feared his growing influence. Mike had heard all the rumors. Some said he was forming a militia. Others were convinced he was a Viet Cong agent. Each claim seemed more outlandish by the day.

Colonel Tru was a cunning tactician. He was content to remain a silent and enigmatic figure, neither confirming nor denying the rumors around him. None of the staff knew when or where he held court. Mike and Flapjack were the only foreigners he would consent to speak with. From those rare meetings, Mike learned that a ship had been prepared and a time scheduled for his departure. He would disappear in the night with his followers. They were bound for the homeland, and nothing could persuade him otherwise.

Like most of the camp's dissidents, the colonel lived at the far edge of Tent City. It was here, at the fringes of refugee society, that Mike began to develop an appreciation of the Vietnamese language. Here, the residents spoke almost exclusively in their native tongue. Their words seemed to flow together with a rhythm and cadence that seemed almost musical. He could hear them arguing or telling stories loudly outside the colonel's tent.

Nhin vao nhung nguoi my dien ban nghi rang no se giet chung toi!
Stinks thuc pham.
Ong da bi giet chet va vo bi ham hiep.

Once, Mike's curiosity got the better of him, and he asked the colonel to translate. Tru said nothing. He had only stared at the major with a mix of pity and amusement.

Chapter 37

MIKE HAD NEVER seen Flapjack so distressed. Day after day passed, and there was still no word from her father. When he finally did make contact—just two days before Tru's deadline—their meeting was a grim one. David had interviewed survivors, and it appeared the situation in Vietnam had grown worse. Brutality against the South continued to escalate. Those who were not executed were sent to the work camps, where rape, torture, and starvation took their toll. Several refugees had been disfigured by burns. Others had lost their ears, fingers, and even limbs to the machetes of the North Vietnamese. Mike could only imagine what lay in store for Colonel Tru.

Violence abroad was not David's only concern. Right now, he told them, it seemed the military's greatest enemy was the American people! Support for the war had hit rock bottom. Resettlement efforts had caused a public outcry, with one poll reporting a disapproval rating of 54%. The armed forces now faced pressures from both the domestic and global communities. Under such dire circumstances, an effort to rescue Tru's family had not been approved. The Pentagon was content with the knowledge that his wife and children were still alive, and, for the moment, out of imminent danger. Still, the situation was perilous.

Flapjack told her father of her meetings with Colonel Tru. There was a tone of deep disappointment in her voice as she relayed the news. David reassured her that she had done the best she could. The final decision ultimately lay with the colonel. If he was set on returning, the military would not stand in his way.

The communication with the mainland was a short one. Flapjack and her father barely had time for a few parting words before transmission was cut. When she turned to face him, Mike realized he had never seen her so completely demoralized. Lack of sleep had left dark rings around her eyes and her hair was disheveled. Her lip was trembling, as though she were about to cry, but no tears came. She collapsed on the couch in the communications office with her head in her hands. Mike sat down beside her.

"You did your best."

"Yeah, sure."

"No really," he insisted. "Do you think anyone could have gotten to him? Beating yourself up over this is like… like being mad that you can't part the Red Sea."

Flapjack shook her head. She leaned back, staring at the ceiling as she spoke. "It's just… not the ending I had hoped for you know? I really thought we could save him. Like I expected some fairy tale ending," she chuckled hollowly. "Pretty naïve, huh? But that's me."

"Come on now," said Mike. He placed a hand on her leg gently. She jerked it away. "You're too hard on yourself," he continued. "For what it's worth… I think you're really amazing. And really…"

"Why do you always do that?" interrupted Flapjack suddenly.

"Do what?"

"That. That nice-guy, I'm-so-pure-and-moral, I-need-to-fix-everything routine?"

Mike recoiled suddenly. He felt his blood turn to ice water. "What are you talking about, Flapjack?" he asked.

"Oh come on," she said, brushing the loose strands of hair from her face. "You never just listen, you always have to try and save me. It's so… so patronizing. Like I'm a little girl." Mike stared in shock as she rose to leave. He felt numb.

"And another thing," said Flapjack, biting her lower lip. "I'm not so dumb that I don't know what you're doing." Mike looked at her blankly. She sighed in exasperation. "Do I have to spell it out for you, Mike? You have a wife. You're committed to her. I'm not going to play the mistress."

"I…I didn't want you to," Mike stammered, stunned she would think that. "I don't know what to say."

"Look, I like you I really do, but you need to focus on yourself before you try to help others," said Flapjack, her voice softening. She turned to leave. "Mike, life can be what happens while you're waiting for moments that never come."

Chapter 38

NEWS CROSSED the Pacific slowly. The staff, refugees, and military personnel learned of developments sometimes weeks after the American public. Reports had begun to arrive from military headquarters indicating the scale of the evacuation. The numbers were staggering. On May 2nd, at least 24,000 refugees arrived in an Arkansas resettlement camp over 7,000 miles away. On May 4th, another 6,000 were flown to Florida, while a further 17,000 arrived in Pennsylvania on May 28th. Mike had grown close to many of his patients, and he read a great deal about their experiences through the press.

It hardly surprised Mike to read how large Chinatowns and Vietnamese communities had emerged in major cities. He had expected as much. It was only natural that people would want to live among others who shared their unique language and culture. He was surprised to find that the fate of the individuals varied widely. Often, it seemed as though success or failure were a matter of chance. The lucky ones found support, and were able to forge a life for themselves as leaders and professionals. Others, the young who became disenchanted with the "American Dream," had joined one of the many Asian gangs that emerged from obscurity. Life in the streets was often nasty, brutish, and short, but many young adults saw no alternative.

It was more than greed or power that motivated these gangs. Many had formed out of necessity. With anti-immigration sentiments high, these refugees faced a host of potential dangers in an already foreign land. In one case, Vietnamese fishermen in south Texas had to fight for an injunction against the Ku Klux Klan, who had openly threatened their business. Being part of a gang meant being part of a community. It meant protection.

Colonel Tru had returned to his home. There was a short delay, but on October 15th he and 1500 ex-ARVN officers boarded a ship to Vietnam. Mike and Flapjack had hardly spoken since their argument. Still, both were present to wish the colonel safe passage. They had become friends with him over time, which only made things harder. Tru shook both their hands. They exchanged the words he had taught them.

Cam o'n ban da co gang, toi se kong quen ban (Thank you).

Tam biet an toan (Take care of yourself).

The ship raised anchor. Flapjack and Mike watched as it sailed further and further towards the horizon. Their course had been set. They were on their way to a dangerous harbor, where an uncertain future lay waiting.

*   *   *

The colonel was no ordinary man, and the manner of his departure was extraordinary. Hundreds of refugees had congregated along the coastline. Some even wept. It was as though the whole event had been elaborately planned. A burial at sea, thought Mike grimly. He wondered if he would ever see that tall, stoic gentleman again. He would later say the Viet Cong made him wait offshore for days before allowing him to come into port. They couldn't believe anyone would want to return to a communist country with such cruel conditions.

Mike stayed long after the crowds had dispersed. The buses transported the refugees back to the tents. Saying farewell had left him feeling pensive, and he sat watching the waves lap against the rocks. When he finally turned to leave, a gleam of light caught the corner of his eyes. There, along the railing of the pier, lay a pair of coke-bottle spectacles. Mike could have recognized them anywhere.

So Flapjack had forgotten her glasses. As awkward as he felt, a strange thrill passed through him. The last few days had been the longest period of silence between them in months. It was during that time that Mike realized just how fondly he had grown towards her. She had become his best friend since their arrival on Guam. As angry as she may have been, he knew she felt the same. There was a curious understanding between them. It was as though they had both awaited this opportunity to present itself. And here it was, sitting on a pier at Orote Point.

Flapjack was absent from her quarters when Mike arrived. She missed dinner as well. Mike raised his concern in the mess hall. With a mouth full of mashed potatoes, Moon told him that she had most likely gone to visit Sybil. The two seemed to be spending a great deal of time together, added Ricks, but neither man knew why. Moon was his usual self, but something seemed off about Ricks. The blood seemed to drain from his face at the mention of Sybil. Mike noticed the man's pallor, but dismissed it from his mind. He had more pressing concerns to attend to.

The door to Sybil's room opened a crack. Flapjack peered at Mike curiously in the doorway. The room was dark and the shutters were closed. The lamplight bathed the room in an amber glow.

"Mike! What are you doing here," she hissed between her teeth.

"I… Uh… I found your glasses…" Mike stuttered awkwardly. He dangled them for her to inspect. Flapjack sighed.

"Who's that at the door?" a voice croaked from the back of the room. Flapjack rolled her eyes.

"It's no one. Uhm, well, I mean, it's Mike."

"Hi Mike!"

"Oh… uh, hey… Sybil?" Mike rubbed the back of his neck as he spoke. He looked at Flapjack sheepishly. She was biting her lip.

"Look Sybil," said Flapjack, turning her back to Mike, "are you sure you want to see anyone right now?"

"I can come back later," he offered.

"No, it's okay. Come on in Mike."

Flapjack was still watching him warily, but she opened the door further. She muttered a few words of thanks as she wiped the dust off each lens. Crouched in a ball by the side of the bed was Sybil. Two pillows cushioned her, as she rocked back and forth, her arms wrapped around her legs. Mascara was dripping from her cheeks. She looked like a mess.

"Jesus, what happened?" gasped Mike.

"Trust me, you don't want to know," said Flapjack. She sat cross-legged next to Sybil, and motioned Mike forward.

"He might as well know," whimpered Sybil. Mike passed her a tissue, and she rubbed her eyes. "I'm not going to keep this secret. Just… you tell it, Flap. When I think about it… his hands on me…" her voice began to choke in midsentence. Flapjack wrapped a blanket around her as she began to sob violently. Her body seemed wracked with anguish.

Mike sat and watched, as Flapjack spoke soothing words to their companion. In a few minutes, Sybil seemed to have exhausted herself. It took both their strength to move her from the floor to the bed. Flapjack tucked her in and spoke a few soothing words. Then, without a word, she walked past Mike and out the door to the courtyard.

"Come on," she said, beckoning softly. "I'll tell you the whole story on the way."

*   *   *

Mike's eyes adjusted slowly to the lights outside. He squinted and rubbed them. For the first time in days, he heard Flapjack laugh.

"You think that's bad? Imagine being cooped up in that cell for hours," she said, as her voice became somber. "Poor Sybil. We've been covering her shifts and bringing her food, but I'm not sure how much longer she can hide in there."

"Hide from what?" asked Mike.

"From the world, I suppose," she sighed. "You remember that night on the beach? When everyone split up and you met my dad?"

"Yeah."

"Well, Sybil was assaulted that night."

Mike winced. A wave of nausea washed over him. "Oh my God… Oh my God…" he repeated. "What happened? How… Is she okay?"

"Physically she's okay," said Flapjack. She was staring at the ground. "But mentally she's just a mess."

"But then when?"

"She won't say. She says she doesn't remember, if you believe that. She's afraid."

"But why now?"

Flapjack sighed and thought for a moment. "It beats me," she said, shaking her head sadly. "I guess she's just been holding it in all this time. Then just a day or two ago she snapped."

"What else do you know?" asked Mike. He held the door open as they entered the mess hall. As the smell of roast meat and vegetables hit them, Flapjack's eyes glazed over.

"Let's talk about it more after dinner. I haven't eaten all day," she answered, as she began walking ahead of him. "But remind me on our way back," she called over her shoulder, "I have a special favor to ask of you."

Chapter 39

IT WAS LATE that evening, and the base was quiet. Flapjack and Mike sat on an old couch in the lobby. For a few minutes, the two were silent, and they passed the time listening to the radio. Even at Orote Point, the signal was terrible. Flapjack switched it off. When she spoke, she sounded tired and relieved.

"Thanks, Mike."

"Thanks?"

"Yeah," she continued, as she collapsed in an armchair. "Sybil really likes you. If you hadn't talked her into it, I doubt I could have convinced her to get help."

"It was nothing," said Mike. He leaned back and propped his shoes on the coffee table.

"I guess I owe you a bit of an apology," said Flapjack finally. "I didn't mean to go off on you like that. You're a good guy. It's just... I was really upset. I was so worried about all those people."

"It's okay, I understand," Mike offered. He smiled weakly.

"No, it's not," she continued. "I don't know what came over me. I guess I just got tired of people always seeing me as a little girl. I wanted to make a difference this time. It's... it's hard being a woman in the service. Just look what happened to Sybil."

"How did it happen, anyway?"

"Well, from what she's told me, Moon was off getting trashed with two of the nurses. She and Ricks met up with a few of his friends further down the beach. After a bit of smoking, she took a nap, and woke up with a man on top of her, holding her down."

"Holy shit."

"Yeah, it sounds like he was trying to rape her," Flapjack continued. "I can't imagine what would have happened if she hadn't managed to scream and fight him off. It was Ricks who eventually managed to pull the guy off."

Mike whistled and shook his head. He had heard horror stories like this from military wives. Never had he thought female officers suffered the same abuse. "So Ricks was the hero, huh," he said finally. "So why didn't he report the incident?"

To Mike's surprise, Flapjack laughed. The sound was nothing like her familiar giggle. This laughter sounded dark and hollow, almost mocking. It made him shiver. "Occupational hazards," she said, shaking her head sadly. "Occupational hazards, Major Pike."

*   *   *

Mike and Flapjack visited Sybil the next day. Even in a hospital gown she looked better than before. Her eyes were still red and swollen, but she smiled and told them she was starting to feel better. The therapist on the base had spoken with her. For the first time in weeks, she felt safe.

"I really owe you two a lot," she told them. "Especially you, Flapjack. I couldn't have gotten through this without you."

Flapjack smiled and stroked her hair. "How are you feeling now?" she asked.

"Well, things are a bit better. I still wake up from the nightmares though. I keep dreaming about horrible things. I can't even describe them. It's hard to sleep. Most of the time I just lie awake for hours."

"Don't worry," Mike reassured her firmly. "We'll get to the bottom of this. Ricks is a bastard if he won't report this. I won't let it stand."

Sybil stared down at her blanket. Her corner of her mouth twitched as she spoke. "No, it's all right," she said softly. "I appreciate the concern though."

"Well, Flapjack and I won't let it stand."

"Um, Mike…" began Flapjack. When he faced her, she averted his gaze.

"I told Ricks not to report it, Mike."

"You did WHAT?!" he asked incredulously. Sybil picked at the dessert on her tray nervously.

"I told him not to report it," she answered, looking up to face him. "I've seen it before. I report this, my career is over, and besides… I shouldn't have dressed like that. I was being a tease."

"An occupational hazard, Mike," said Flapjack grimly. "That's what they call it. For a woman in the military, this is part of the job. An unspoken rule."

"Don't tell me you're in on this too," Mike groaned.

"I'm going to respect Sybil's wishes. Besides, I mean, technically she wasn't raped, so she escaped the worst of it." The way she spoke sounded robotic to Mike. It was as though she were reading from a script. Her complacency only inflamed his outrage. As he stormed out of the room, his mind was made up. Sybil deserved justice.

*   *   *

In the small, windowless cubicle, Mike began to sweat. The office of the base commander was even smaller than Colonel Lowe's back on Valkyrie. As he waited, he began to question his decision to schedule this appointment in the first place. Perhaps this is what Flapjack meant, he thought to himself nervously. Perhaps he shouldn't be interfering in problems that weren't his business.

"Ah, Major Pike, is it? Thank for your patience," said the commander, as he struggled in with a stack of papers. Mike came to his aid. "Ah, thank you," the man continued, breathing heavily. He wiped his palms and extended an arm. "So what can I do for you, Major?"

Mike shook the man's hand. "Well, Commander Stevens, I'm afraid I have some very troubling news to report?"

"Oh?" the commander searched his desk for a pen and paper.

"Yes. I need to report an attempted rape."

Commander Stevens bit his lip as he scribbled in his notebook. "An attempted rape? What happened exactly?"

"Well, sir," Mike began, clearing his throat. "A few weeks ago, Lieutenant Colonel John Taft attempted to rape Major Sybil Hansen at Achang Bay."

"That's a serious accusation," said the commander icily. He seemed to regard Mike suspiciously now, as though he had something to gain from the admission. "Why wasn't this reported by Maj. Hansen herself? And are you sure it was Lt. Colonel Taft?"

"Maj. Hansen is afraid to come forward, sir," answered Mike. "As for Taft, the records show he was the only one outside our group to travel there on the same day. Maj. Moon can confirm this fact."

Commander Stevens wrote a few more notes. When he was satisfied, he tossed the notebook onto his desk and sighed. He rubbed the stubble on his chin before he spoke.

"I'm glad you're approaching me with this, Major," he said finally. "I'm not sure why Maj. Hansen would stoop to spreading rumors about Lt.

Colonel Taft. Can you think of any reason she might have, Major Pike? Perhaps the two were dating?"

"Excuse me, sir?"

"It really is a shame when personal matters are dragged out like dirty laundry," he continued, shaking his head. "It's a private affair and should remain that way."

"But sir!" Mike exclaimed. He could hardly believe what he was hearing. "What if she's telling the truth? What if he did try to rape her?"

"Come now, Maj. Pike. You were all at the beach. Do you remember what she was wearing?"

"A standard bathing suit. But I don't see..."

"Exactly!" the Commander interrupted, slamming his hand on the desk. "So not only was she dressed revealingly, she put herself in a position alone with Lt. Colonel Taft. This is what we call in the service an 'occupational hazard.' The woman is responsible for her own conduct."

Mike's head was swimming. He felt nauseous. So Sybil and Flapjack had been right all along. They had virtually no protection from violence, mistreatment, and sexual abuse. She was considered responsible for her own rape! It was too much for him to process.

"So... so what now?" he asked nervously.

"Well, now we launch an inquiry into the matter. Talk to all those involved. After we ascertain the circumstances, a judgment will be made."

"And how long..."

"One month, Major Pike. We'll need to forward the information to headquarters and await an official decision. Thank you for your time."

Mike walked out of the office in a daze. He found the nearest bathroom and threw up in a stall. How could he have been so naïve, he thought, wiping the bile from his chin. Now he knew the truth. For the first time, he realized what it was like for a woman in the military.

Chapter 40

MIKE'S DAYS WERE NUMBERED in Tent City. His meeting with Commander Stevens had been the beginning of the end of his tenure on Guam. Word travels fast on a small island. It was only a matter of time before everyone heard the rumors. A hysterical woman was accusing an officer of rape. The man she claimed to be a witness refused to testify. In the court of public opinion, both the refugees and staff defended the accused man's honor. Sybil had become a pariah. The men avoided her. The women gossiped behind her back.

Mike found himself a target as well. He had become known as "the snitch" for his role in reporting the incident. His staff, colleagues, and even some patients considered him a traitor. Sybil was refusing to talk to him. Flapjack and Moon were now his only allies. Still, he knew even they could not protect him from the mounting threat to his safety.

In the end, it was Flapjack who saved the day. Her father, who sympathized with their predicament, managed to get both Mike and Sybil transferred to the states. The news came not a moment too soon. Conditions on Guam had deteriorated to crisis levels. Food, medicine, and shelter were all in short supply. It was into these squalid circumstances that the first Cambodian refugees began to arrive. Many were already more dead than alive. Their hollow, glassy eyes had seen firsthand the horrors of Pol Pot's reign.

* * *

The next time Mike saw Sybil, it was the day of their departure. Mike had said his goodbyes and packed his few possessions. Their transport, which was scheduled to depart early that morning, had been delayed. The two of them were left awkwardly waiting on the observation deck of the pier. Mike tried his best not to make eye-contact. He felt guilty enough over what had transpired. The last thing he wanted to do was make things worse.

Mike woke up suddenly. Had he fallen asleep? How long had he been napping? Mike was surprised to see Sybil standing over him. Her hand on his shoulder was ice cold.

"Sorry to wake you," she said sheepishly. "I figured you might like a coke from the vending machine."

"Oh… yeah. I mean…Thanks."

"Do you mind if I join you?" she added, not waiting for an answer. She sat beside him and took a large swig of her soda.

"Look, Sybil," Mike began, in his most penitent voice. "I'm really sorry about what happened. I just wanted to look out for you, is all. I just did what I thought was right. But I'm really sorry."

Sybil sighed and pulled her hand through her hair. She sounded tired and worn out. "I know. I know you've had it pretty bad yourself. No man can understand what it's like for us. They might think they do, but they don't."

"Hey, at least you're off that island. And headquarters might rule in your favor."

Sybil laughed sarcastically. She wiped a tear from her eye. "Oh, Mike. Oh man, you are a sweetheart, you know that?"

"They might! We just have to wait."

"I can tell you their decision right now. I've seen this before. The commander has complete control. Even if Taft is convicted, which he won't be, his commanding officer can just dismiss the charges."

"Are you serious," Mike gasped.

"Why do you think I didn't want it reported?" Sybil continued. "I've seen the process before. It's always the same. It's an 'occupational hazard.'" She punctuated the words with air-quotations.

Mike stared in disbelief. No matter how bad things got, he realized, he had still been holding out for a happy ending. This was the United States Military. Justice would prevail. It had to! As he listened to Sybil, a deep feeling of betrayal crept along his spine.

"I can't believe it. I just can't believe it." he repeated.

"You think I wouldn't get the bastard if I could?" she asked. "I feel so much rage in me. I feel violated. To be honest, I'd love to just cut off his dick with a butcher knife." Her voice was suffused with anger now. She crushed the empty can between her fists. "Chalk that up as an 'occupational hazard,' eh?"

Mike put his arm around Sybil. Tears were streaming down her eyes. "Hey Sybil?" he asked softly.

"Yeah?"

"Have you ever heard of Walt Kelly?"

"No, why?"

"For some reason, what you told me reminds me of an old Earth Day poster back in my Valkyrie office," he explained. "There was a quote on it that I never understood until now."

"What's that?"

"We have met the enemy and he is us."

* * *

Mike comforted Sybil until they were finally ushered aboard. The sun was still beginning to emerge on the horizon. He shivered in the dawn chill. It was an old, rickety transport ship, and flakes of paint fell when he gripped the railing. The water below was dark and choppy; turgid. The salt winds whipped at his face. What was it, Mike asked himself, that had compelled him to come forward? What had given him such a blind sense of conviction? In a flash, he remembered the source.

Mike had to rummage through his belongings to find it. It was hidden under layers of clothes, letters, and toiletries. Finally, he dug out his worn copy of *The Officers' Handbook*. The pages were dog-eared and yellow with age. He skimmed through until he found the "rule" he was looking for.

Ch. 2. Sec. B. Part I. An officer must report all cases of misconduct. He must defer to the chain of command.

So it was *his* duty, Mike thought to himself, not *hers*. The use of the masculine pronoun made sense now. There was no *her* in the eyes of the military. Only a man could hope to possess the full rights and privileges of an officer. The revelation made him sick to his stomach.

Mike returned to the railing and looked out on the vast expanse of the sea. He took one last look at the handbook before letting it fall from his hands. As he watched, it bobbed for a moment, before disappearing forever into the bubbling wake.

His eyes were open.

Part III:
The Promotion

Chapter 41

IT WAS THE LATE-AUTUMN of 1975. Mike gazed through the window at the fields beyond the highway. There was nothing but dead leaves and dirty ground as far as the eye could see. The skeletons of cottonwood trees stood, barren and alone, their bones exposed to the elements. He shivered. It can't be helped, he reminded himself. He had dreaded this day for a long time.

There had always been an excuse since his return from Guam. Always some menial task to occupy his concerns. It was at night, when he lay alone with his thoughts, that Mike's guilt plagued him. He had begun to have problems sleeping. As much as he dreaded this trip, it was a necessary ritual. A demon that had to be exorcised. The selfishness of his own thoughts struck him immediately. He was feeling sorry for himself, he knew it, and it made him sick to his stomach.

What a place for a mental hospital, Mike thought to himself. The drive from the city took an eternity. Far from the comfort of the urban lights, Mike felt painfully alone. It was though he was driving through purgatory itself. As a distraction, he focused on the rumbling of the car's engine. If he had come to depend on anyone, it was his trusty Volkswagen; that marvel of German engineering. The ancient beast still hacked and sputtered its way down the interstate. The familiar sound soothed his rattled nerves.

Mike's comfort was short-lived. As if on cue, the motor overheated with just over a mile left to go. He tried to revive the engine but it was no use. Smoke hung over the rusted rear hood. With a curse, Mike slammed the door. He wondered why he even bothered to lock it. Perhaps some benevolent thief would take it off his hands before he returned. He gritted his teeth with disgust. A long walk lay ahead of him. Into the heart of darkness.

*   *   *

It was a cold, grey afternoon, and Mike cursed himself for not bringing a jacket. The northern wind clung to the tips of his ears. His swollen sinuses gave him a throbbing headache. He was miserable. Even the site of the institution, in all its cold austerity, was a welcome sight. It loomed large before him, a monolith of steel and concrete against a barren landscape.

The hospital had seen better days. In years past, Mike remembered, its condition had not yet fallen into disrepair. Now, moss grew in patches on the outside walls. Vines crept along the pillars at the entrance; weeds sprung from cracks in the foundation. It was as though, Mike thought to himself, mankind had erected the place as a monument to compassion, nature was in the inexorable process of swallowing it whole—that and budget cuts.

The lobby was empty, save for an old security guard asleep at his post. The air was stale and smelled of mildew and urine. Even the elevator creaked ominously on the way up. The halls themselves were almost empty, and painted the same drab government green as his office at Valkyrie. After a few dead ends, Mike finally found the office he was looking for. "DR. FAROUK AHMED," read the placard on the door, "DIRECTOR, CHALLENGE PROGRAM".

The director greeted Mike with the congeniality of an old friend. After all, the two had known each other for over four years. Four and a half years, to be exact, since the day of the transfer from the previous hospital, a day of defeat for Mike. Dr. Ahmed, was a diminutive, but spry character, with white hair and a crooked nose. He was a personable man, almost too personal, and Mike awkwardly accepted the man's embrace. He was used to it by now. In some way, he even admired his gregarious nature. It was essential for a man in his line of work.

"Well, Michael! Long time no see, my friend! How wonderful."

"Um, yeah," Mike smiled, but cringed inwardly. It really had been too long. There was no excuse.

"Yes, yes," repeated the doctor, thumbing through a filing cabinet. Finally he came across the folder he was looking for. "Ah, Christine will be delighted, I am sure."

"So, she's doing better?"

"I'd say so. Yes! More active, you know. One day at a time."

"Will she ever be able to… you know…" Mike trailed off. In his heart, he already knew the answer. But he had to know for sure. Dr. Ahmed furrowed his brow. He scanned the documents before him briefly.

"Go home? Ah, if it were so easy," he sighed, stroking his beard. "I've told you some of the things I've seen working with traumatic brain injuries." He shook his head sadly. "Some of our patients have been here since the fifties. Christine has suffered the worst of the symptoms. Chronic dementia. Extreme psychosis. Wounds like those… never fully heal."

"But I know my wife," Mike protested weakly. "Christine is tough. She's always been a fighter. If anyone can recover from this…"

"It's not a matter of resilience," Dr. Ahmed interrupted. He rose, tucking the folder under his arm. He wiped his spectacles as he continued. "Your wife may show improvements, but… how to put this… she is not your wife. Not the woman you remember, I mean. The Christine you know died long ago."

"Died," said Mike softly. The word felt strange. He felt Dr. Ahmed's hand on his back. "It's hopeless then?"

"We prefer to be optimistic," exclaimed Dr. Ahmed, squeezing Mike's shoulder unnaturally hard. "It's a case of management and compassionate care, now. Of providing comfort for our clients-in-need." The alliteration seemed to roll off his tongue too easily, thought Mike. It was as though he were reciting from a script.

"Now, if you'll follow me," added the doctor, "let's take you to see your wife, shall we?"

Chapter 42

TRAVERSING THE WINDING, green hallways made Mike uneasy. Every so often, the occasional patient would drift past, their eyes glazed and vacant. The walls were paper thin and from each room he could hear the murmur of voices; the drone of television sets and old record players. Within this darkened labyrinth, he felt like a stranger, an alien from the outside. He was a traveler in a world which seemed to be floating.

Dr. Ahmed kept a brisk pace ahead of him. He seemed almost oblivious to the dull, oppressive atmosphere around him. After several twists and turns, Mike was ushered into a small, brightly-lit cell. The accommodations were as Spartan as he remembered them. The steel-framed bed and dresser were firmly bolted to the ground. A thick metal-grate protected the window. The air was thin and cold and the smell of ammonia almost made him gag. The smell of urine—always a sign of neglect.

There, on a mattress coated with thick plastic, lay Christine, her one good eye transfixed to the ceiling. She appeared to show no awareness of their arrival. Her mouth opened slowly, as if about to speak, only to close in silence. Saliva bubbled from the corner of her lips.

"Does she always stay in a locked room?"

"Only when she's not safe," said Dr. Ahmed. He tucked his large keychain in the pocket of his coat. "Not safe from others," he clarified, "but mostly from herself."

"And she's not safe now?"

"She couldn't sleep last night," answered Dr. Ahmed. A change seemed to creep into his tone as he spoke. To Mike, he sounded almost resentful. "We had another incident last night. She came out of her room and assaulted the staff. Urinated on the floor. Tried to choke an orderly. Her behavior has been a lot more aggressive lately."

"Aggressive?"

"Extremely paranoid. Belligerent. She's taken to stalking other patients and staff members. We never really know when she may become violent."

"She's at war," said Mike sadly. He walked to her bedside and stroked her hair. Her head lolled towards him in response, her jaw hung slack and unhinged. She groaned.

"I hadn't thought of it that way," mused the doctor, "but yes. She's in a war against her own mind." He thought for a minute and shook his head. "I can't say there'll ever be a winner."

"She's in a war with the kid who shot her. I know she must remember some of that," said Mike. Hot tears welled at the corners of his eyes. "But no, there never is a winner."

*   *   *

"There we go Christine, see, that was pretty good, huh?" said Mike, as he withdrew the spoon from her mouth. He could hear the patronizing tone in his voice. He felt angry and helpless. "Pretty nice digs you got here," he continued, wiping the stray pudding from her mouth. "I wish we were fed this well at the base," he smiled.

"You."

"Wait, what? What was that Chrissie?" gasped Mike. He almost dropped the spoon in his surprise.

"Youuu," she repeated in a slurred drawl. Her voice trailed off. Her eyes rolled wildly.

"Can you recognize me?" he asked desperately. He leaned over her head. "It's me, Mike! Your husband! Can you remember?"

"Youuu…"

"Goddamn it," Mike snapped. The tears returned to his eyes. "You have to remember me! I'm your husband! I love you."

Christine cocked her head suddenly. Suddenly, she seemed alert and aware. The light returned to her eye. For a moment, Mike felt elated. Even if it only lasted for a moment, even if it was in her compromised state, she at least showed a glimmer of the woman he knew.

"My husband," she croaked. She squinted at him, examining his features.

"Your husband, Mike."

"Well, how ya doin' Joe?" she giggled.

"It's not Joe," he repeated. "You know my name. It's Mike."

Christine's face contorted violently. Her mouth twisted into a grotesque parody of a frown. "I'm married to Joe, I tell you. I know my damn husband. You think I don't know?" Mike drew back from her gaze. He wiped the flecks of spittle off his face.

"You think I don't know?" Christine repeated, louder now, her voice poisoned with hate. "Joe isn't going to like this," she warned, gritting her teeth. "He's not gonna like this one bit."

"But... I'm your husband..." Mike protested meekly. He stumbled back from the bed. His eyes scanned the room for the call button.

"You better get out of here, you bastard!" Christine bellowed angrily. She lurched out of the bed towards him. "I fucking warned you. Joe's gonna come back here, and he's gonna be mad as hell!"

Mike watched in horror as Christine staggered forward. She collapsed, clutching at the air as she fell. Slowly, awkwardly, she crawled towards him. She was gnashing her teeth, and the sound of the molars grinding was like nails on a chalkboard. The creature moving towards him was not Christine. It did not even seem human. The face staring up at him was something wild and feral.

*   *   *

"I really must apologize, Mike," said Dr. Ahmed in dismay. He clicked his pen and began scribbling rapidly on his clipboard. "It's a good thing you got to the call button in time."

Mike sighed. He leaned back in Ahmed's plush leather chair. "It's okay, really," he assured him, "after all, I insisted on seeing her alone."

"Still," said Dr. Ahmed, as he continued his notes, "that sedative shouldn't have worn off for a few hours."

"Sedative?"

"Yes. To keep her docile. The last thing we wanted was for you to have to see her like that."

"Hey!" exclaimed Mike bitterly. "I'm a medical doctor. I don't come here to see some fantasy version of Christine. I don't want illusions. I want the truth!"

Dr. Ahmed looked up from his notes. Mike half-expected him to be angry, but instead a bemused smile formed on his face. His voice became soothing, his accent almost melodic. "Michael," he said, spreading his arms before him. "I understand, I do. You are her family, you deserve the truth."

"And what is the truth?"

"The truth is that your wife will not recover. We cannot say this with certainty. Nothing on earth is certain. But I will not string you along with false hope for a miracle. We have done everything we can."

"But what about ECT?" asked Mike. "I read they've made great strides in their research."

Dr. Ahmed shook his head. "Out of the question. ECT doesn't help with brain injuries and the psychosis that develops with it."

"Aren't there any new drugs coming out?"

"None that have been approved, and none that will be approved, either, for several more years."

"But surely there must be something," said Mike weakly. He knew he was grasping at straws. A knot began to form in the pit of his stomach.

Dr. Ahmed furrowed his brow. He adjusted his spectacles and leaned forward, his hands clasped on his desk. "I speak to you as a fellow professional," he began, "but also as a friend. With the truth must come acceptance. Only after acceptance can you consider the choices before you."

"What choices?" asked Mike curiously. "As far as I know my hands are tied."

"To the contrary, Michael. You are a rare case. Rarely have I seen a spouse willing to devote five years of their life in such a manner."

"Well she's my wife," he offered weakly. "I made a vow."

"On the one hand, you may now have a divorce. It is, I feel, the wisest course of action." He lifted his left hand in the air, palm-upward. His silver cufflink glittered in the light.

"And on the other hand?"

"On the other hand," he continued, raising his right, "on the other hand, you can remain committed to a woman with massive and incurable brain trauma which has left her psychotic—prone to delusions, mood swings, and dangerously violent fits of rage."

"But I made a vow…"

"To Christine, you made a vow, yes. But this is not Christine!" repeated the Doctor. His frustration was beginning to show. "Would Christine try to murder a nurse? Would she claim the voices in her head commanded her will?"

Mike hung his head. Dr. Ahmed was right. He had known it long before his visit. These were the words he had hidden from all these years. They hung in the air now. There was no escape from them.

"The way you put it, there's really not much of a choice," he replied finally.

"No, Michael," said the doctor sadly. He slid the papers back in the folder and snapped it shut. "There is always a choice. Even when both paths appear to lead into darkness. For Christine, however both of your paths lead to the same place. She will never recover."

Chapter 43

MIKE FELT HIS heart drop as he left. His mind wandered from one grim thought to another during the long walk to the car. In the distance was the sound of thunder. Then the rains came. By the time he reached his Volkswagen, he was soaked to the bone. He sat in the car for a few minutes shivering. So there was no hope for Christine, he thought to himself. The woman he had married was gone. In its place was a creature of instinct; a violent, paranoid being that saw him as a threat and nothing more. It all made Mike feel numb.

The ride back to Valkyrie was long and uneventful. The engine had cooled off, which afforded some small relief. The return trip seemed to take twice as long in the driving rain. It was during the latter half of the trip that the car began to gasp and sputter ominously. The car finally died just as Mike reached the gates. After a few desperate attempts, he finally managed to start the ignition, though the rattling, choking sounds from the hood warned of another imminent collapse.

By now, Mike had willed his mind out of entropy. For a moment his sorrows were forgotten. All that mattered was reaching the hospital. The tires screeched on wet pavement, as Mike cut through the visitor's parking lot. The shortcut would save him a minute or two, he reasoned, as opposed to his usual route through the base.

Suddenly, the sound of a horn blared behind him. Mike hit the brakes. Two blinding headlights pierced the rear window. He heard a car door slam behind him. Through the rear-view mirror, Mike watched as a hunched, dark figure staggered slowly towards him. It was an officer in full regalia. The medals on his breast clinked with each shambling step. He motioned for Mike to roll down his window.

"Hey. Hey!" the man yelled. "Whutha hell yer doin', huh?" He stopped directly in front of Mike and leered down at him scornfully. Mike could smell the alcohol on his breath. "You can't cut across a damn parkin' lot, punk!"

Mike had never seen the man before. Still, it was obvious he was a figure of importance. Even Colonel Creaser wore a less ornate uniform than the short, grey-haired, gremlin of a man before him. "My car is dying," Mike replied helplessly. "I just figured…"

"I betchu did, eh!" the officer slurred. "I don't care if yer wife is dyin'or even yer goddam dog, y'hear! It's against regulations. You gimme your name right now, soldier! You ain't even got a clean shave!"

Mike fished through his wallet. He reluctantly handed over his ID card, which the officer snatched from his hand. "Lessee here," he grunted, obviously struggling to read properly. "A doctor, huh!" he bellowed finally. "I figgered as much! Y'all doctors are all the same. Buncha damn commies if you ask me. Always causin' trouble. You think yer better than us? Huh?"

Mike couldn't believe what he was hearing. It seemed almost surreal. "I apologize, sir," he offered. Angry as he was, he just wanted the drunk to leave him alone.

"I bet you are!" the man continued to rail. He was gesturing violently with the card in his hand. "You come here from yer ivory tower, silver spoons in yer mouth. Dang commies. I oughta…"

In a flash, Mike snagged his card from the officer's grasp. He hit the gas. Filthy water splattered the man's uniform. As he turned to enter the emergency room entrance, he could still hear the old man yelling in the distance. Finally, as if on cue, his car shuddered to a halt and died.

* * *

"Excuse me, sir," Mike insisted. "But this is rather important." The man behind the desk nodded and smiled curtly. He continued his phone conversation.

"How can I help?" asked the air patrolman nearby. "Is it something about the noise I heard back there?"

Mike sighed in relief. "Pardon me, officer," he began, "but there's an intoxicated man in a powder-blue Lincoln out there. He was very belligerent and aggressive."

"Well, we can't have that," said the patrolman. He pulled a notepad from his breast pocket. "He shouldn't be drinking on the base at this hour, anyway. If you'd like to file a complaint, then I'll need a description."

"He was a short man," said Mike, as the officer clicked his pen and began to write. "About five-and-a-half feet tall, thin, silver-gray hair, balding." Mike thought to himself for a moment. "Oh! And he was dressed like a general, like Creaser, just... fancier."

As he spoke, the patrolman seemed to write slower and slower. There was a look of consternation on his face. "Fancier?"

"Yeah. Lots of medals and badges. Like he was headed to a ceremony."

The patrolman's face blanched. He looked towards the receptionist, who had hung up the phone. Mike could feel the tension in the room. It was unsettling.

"I'll... I'll be right back..." said the patrolman, his words trailing off absently. He donned a jacket and hurried out into the rain. Mike was left with the clerk, who now seemed extremely agitated and concerned.

"If that's who I think it is," the man said, in a thin, reedy voice, "then you'd better just head to the barracks and forget this happened."

Mike's face flushed angrily. He was tired of being the oblivious one. "No, I'm going to report it," he replied firmly.

"Not likely. Do you know who you just described?"

"Does it matter?"

"Does it matter!" echoed the man. "That drunk little leprechaun was General Snow. He's the second-in-command now."

"Him?" gasped Mike.

"Yes, him!" cried the clerk. "You're not the first person he's accosted either. He's always drunk. Everyone knows it."

"Then how does he get away with it?"

"How do you think?" groaned the man, rolling his eyes. "The chain-of-command protects him. He's got too many friends in high places. He's untouchable."

The conversation was interrupted as the patrolman rushed in from the cold. Like Mike had been, he was dripping from head-to-toe, and panting heavily. He slung his soggy coat on the back of his chair.

"That's him, all right," he said between breaths. "God damn it, I'll have to call for backup and escort him to his quarters." He turned to Mike. "I'm sorry for the trouble, Major," he offered sheepishly. "I'm sure he won't bother you again."

For a moment, Mike was speechless. "You guys aren't honestly afraid of him, are you?" he asked finally.

"He has a great potential for causing trouble," the patrolman replied. The receptionist shrugged and turned away. It was obvious that both men were eager to wash their hands of the situation. Mike balled his fists in his pocket. He was livid.

"Officer, I would like to file a report." From behind the desk, he heard the muffled laugh of the secretary. The patrolman just stared at him in disbelief.

"You can't be serious."

"I am," Mike announced. "I don't give a damn anymore. Fuck it. Let's see what happens."

The officer looked sick. He shook his head sadly. "If that's what you decide, Major," he said finally. "I guess it's your funeral."

Chapter 44

THAT NIGHT, FOR THE FIRST time in months, Mike slept like a baby. It was as though a burden had been lifted from his shoulders. He was neither surprised nor concerned when he was summoned to Creaser's office the next morning. The call was going to come eventually, he reasoned. Better to get it out of the way early. On his way there, Mike even felt a shiver of anticipation run through him. He was eager to discover what lay in store.

The colonel was a man of taste and distinction. Mike could tell from the lavish décor. On the wall hung great oil paintings in gilded frames. Antiques and books lined the shelves. In the center of an oriental rug sat a beautiful mahogany desk. The sunlight reflected off its lacquered surface.

"Ah, Major Pike! It's a pleasure to see you. Do sit down, do sit down!" the colonel was grinning from ear-to-ear. He looked Mike square in the eye and shook his hand. "So I hear we had a little incident last night, hm?"

"Yes, sir," Mike swallowed nervously.

"The base commander wants to know if we seriously want to do this," Creaser continued. He handed Mike the report he had filed. "The base commander wants to know if we—if you—seriously want to go through with this."

"Yes, sir. I do."

"Well, now, first things first," said the colonel. He leaned back, stroking his chin. "Why don't you tell me what happened?"

Creaser listened as Mike recounted the incident. Every so often, he would nod his head pensively, as if he were taking mental notes. He poured both Mike and himself a whisky. Just the smell made Mike sick to his stomach. It wasn't even noon.

The colonel took a sip of his drink and thought for a moment. "I see," he said finally, wiping his mouth with a handkerchief. "Tell me, did General Snow say anything else? Anything at all?"

"Not that I can think of," said Mike. "What really bothered me was what he said about the hospital and us doctors."

"Oh?"

"He said we're a bunch of Commies."

Creaser looked at Mike incredulously. Suddenly, to Mike's surprise, he blurts out laughing. "Oh that buffoon!" he said, wiping a tear from his eye. "Believe me, Major Pike, there are worse things in the world than being a damn Bolshevik!"

"Sir?"

"Things like having a cousin who's the biggest drunkard in the Air Force. He didn't always used to be that way," said Creaser, a touch of regret creeping into his voice. "Power is a funny thing, Major Pike. You either learn to master it, or it masters you. You can learn to play the system too well, and get caught in your own web of deception, corruption, and vanity."

There was a moment of silence between them. Once more, Creaser broke the austerity of the moment with a great peal of laughter. "Ah, but I am rambling, aren't I. My point is, report will be dismissed."

"Begging your pardon, sir," Mike protested, "but it won't."

"That's up to you, Major," remarked Creaser. He shrugged. "But you should know that General Snow is retiring in two months, and this complaint would hold him up."

"So?"

"So, my commander wants him gone as soon as possible."

"But... but what about what he said about us? About you?"

Creaser winced. "Well, he was drunk. But I do appreciate you defending our reputation. Believe me," he added, winking conspicuously, "we have ways of showing our appreciation. I've been watching you a long time, Mike."

"You have?"

"Yes, and I feel you have great potential. You're a natural leader,"

"Well... thank you, sir," Mike replied, "but I still feel it needs to be reported."

"Ah, a matter of conscience, yes," mused Creaser. "You are an officer and a gentleman, Mike. I'm sure the brass would agree. An officer and a gentleman."

"Sir?"

"Of course, if you do choose not to withdraw your complaint, I can't exactly protect you from their reaction. I can't exactly see an officer and a gentleman betraying the chain-of-command."

"But sir," he protested, "isn't it the right thing to do? We can't let General Snow get away with it!"

"I'll tell you what," said Creaser finally. He stood up from his desk and walked Mike to the door. "I'll give you some time to think it over, but remember," he said, looking down on Mike with a smile, "I'd hate to see an officer of your caliber go to waste."

Chapter 45

MIKE THOUGHT LONG and hard over the following days. Something had changed within him. Could it have been his visit with Christine, he wondered, or his run in with General Snow and Creaser, that had affected him so deeply? Or was it neither? Perhaps his time on Guam had opened his eyes. Whatever it was, Mike felt sick and tired of it all. He was tired of being a victim of circumstance. Tired of depending on karma's reward.

At the same time, Mike felt a great deal of nostalgia overwhelm him. He remembered his boyhood back in the fifties. Life was so much simpler back then. In that sleepy southern town, he had been taught to idealize the familiar institutions. His parents had faith in the government. He had been raised as a model student; a devoted boy scout. The difference between right and wrong had been firmly established. He missed those days.

Had he been blind all those years? Had he become naïve and complacent? As an adult, Mike had begun to see the cracks in the idyllic picture of his youth. He had worshipped his father. Until now, Mike had seen him as nothing less than a martyr. The man had tried valiantly to save his mother from the fire that killed her. Despite his disfiguring burns and crippling emphysema, he had raised Mike to be a man of faith and conviction. Never once had he questioned his fate. Tragedy, like all things in life, was a part of some divine plan. A man had no choice but to do his duty.

Mike's upbringing had been typical for his era. Tommie's parents had been even more strictly devout. The woman's place was in the house. The man's role was to provide. In war, his role was to fight and to die. Their pride forbade them from revealing the scars of battle. Instead, they drank heavily; they were strong and silent. What had it done for them? Only his father was left, an alcoholic who spent his days drinking alone in a dark room. Tommie's father was in prison. In a fit of rage, he had beaten his wife to a pulp. What good had karma done for them?

It was during one of those long, pensive afternoons that Mike came to a conclusion. For the first time, he decided, he would take control of his life. Dr. Ahmed was right. Flapjack was right. He had to choose his own path. Still, he knew the first step he had to take, and it would be the hardest. He picked up the receiver and swallowed.

*　*　*

Mike listened to the dial tone nervously. Perhaps they wouldn't be home. After all, Christine's parents traveled frequently. If he were lucky, he'd just have to explain to the machine.

"Hello?"

"Oh, hello," said Mike reluctantly. "Mrs. Ashford? This is Mike calling."

"Michael! Oh, how wonderful to hear from you! How have you been?"

"I'm all right. How about yourself? Mike felt his stomach turn. The voice on the line sounded so cheerful and melodic. It only made things harder.

"Oh, wonderful! Timothy and I just returned from Argentina. You simply must take Christine to South America, Michael. It would do wonders for her mood."

"That's, uh, what I wanted to talk to you about…" he said. He wished now that he had planned things further.

"A trip?"

"No, Christine,"

"Oh," squealed Mrs. Ashford. "How is my darling lately?"

"Not good," he replied gravely. "The doctor believes she'll never leave the hospital again."

There was a gasp on the other end of the line. "Oh dear," she replied. Her voice was softer now, and full of concern. "We knew it was bad. It's been so long since she's been able to come home. What should we do?"

"I think…" said Mike slowly. He took a deep breath. "I think we should establish a trust for her." The line went silent. He heard the sound of muffled voices on the other end. The next voice he heard was deep and severe. It was Christine's father.

"So, Mike, you think we should establish a trust for Christine?"

"Yes, sir. I've thought about it long and hard."

"Does this mean what I think it does?"

"Yes, sir. I believe that it does." Mike winced. He braced himself for the worst.

"Well, we had hoped it would not come to this," said Mr. Ashford finally. "But I suppose we can't blame you, Michael. Have you been seeing someone new?"

"Of course not," Mike cried, "but," he continued, "I would like to someday. I can have a life and still help you take care of Christine."

Mr. Ashford sighed. "I still can't help but say I'm very disappointed," he replied. "You're still family, Michael. We'll respect whatever decision you make."

"Thank you, sir," said Mike. He tried to hide the relief in his voice. Before he could say goodbye, he heard a click on the other end. The receiver went dead.

* * *

Mike's relief was short lived. The long, arduous battle had only begun, and the hardest part was yet to come. A barrage of calls came over the following month. Christine's parents, he learned, still lived in denial of their daughter's condition. They engaged in long discussions about the trust and how exactly it would be funded. The JAG office referred Mike to an attorney, who dictated the terms of a divorce based on his wife's severe dementia and secondary psychosis.

The entire process took almost three months. Christine's illness first had to be declared incurable by two doctors and a state hospital administrator. Dr. Ahmed had to prove that she had been institutionalized for at least five years. Even then, Mike was saddled with substantial debt. The lion's share of Christine's trust would come directly from his pockets. The Ashford's refused guardianship, and Christine became a ward of the state.

To his surprise, Mike dealt with the setbacks better than he expected. He had already grieved for his wife. She was well taken care of now. When he received confirmation in the mail, a bittersweet feeling washed over him. He was free.

Chapter 46

MIKE WENT ABOUT his work with a renewed sense of purpose. He had felt an incredible lightness of being since the divorce. His lack of guilt surprised and pleased him. The burden of the past had been lifted. The future lay before him like a glistening jewel. It was his for the taking.

At first, Flapjack enjoyed Mike's enthusiasm. She had never seen him so social and energetic. As time passed, however, she became increasingly unsettled. Something had changed in Mike. He seemed almost too carefree. His freedom had made him euphoric. He never spoke to her of his concerns or anxieties. Since her return from Guam, the two had been closer than ever. Now, as winter descended, they seemed to be drifting apart.

At one point, Flapjack even stormed off during lunch. When she brought up her concern for Colonel Tru—of whom she had still heard nothing—Mike chuckled derisively. The response shocked her. Even Moon seemed to show more regard for Tru's fate. Mike called that night, but his half-hearted apology only further disturbed her. He dismissed the colonel as a fool. A man whose own selfish conviction led thousands to slaughter. Someday, he would have a family of his own, he told Flapjack. He would not repeat the mistakes of the past.

* * *

"I wouldn't worry about it, man," said Moon with a smirk. He motioned the bartender for another round. "She's just worried about you, man, you know how she is."

Mike slugged a shot of whisky and grimaced. "God damn, that's powerful stuff!" He propped his elbow on the countertop and pulled his hair through his hands. "I don't know why she seems so uptight," he said, looking unsteadily at Moon. "Why can't she just be happy for me? I did this for her."

"You did this for you, man..." began Moon. He immediately thought better of it. "And I'm hip to that. Man's gotta do what a man's gotta do."

"Damn right."

"You've just been different lately," Moon continued. "I mean, the whole base was talkin' about General Snow, remember?"

"Yeah, I remember."

"And then it just stopped. Nothin' happened. Snow kept causin' problems, people kept their mouth shut, and he retires with distinction."

"And?"

"And didn't you file a formal complaint?" Moon persisted. "Flapjack says you must have withdrawn it. I think she was disappointed in you." He shrugged and laughed, patting Mike on the back. "But I know better," he added. "I tried to tell 'em. It's all politics. Complain all you want, them fat cats at the top won't do nothin'."

Mike raised his glass. Bourbon and soda water spilled from the sides. "To bureaucracy," he laughed sardonically. "May it protect our nation for a thousand years!" They clinked their glasses and drank.

Chapter 47

OVER THE NEXT FEW DAYS, Camp Valkyrie witnessed a spike in recruitment. There seemed to be new faces in the ward every day. Mike found this staff surplus more frustrating than helpful. Many of the new nurses and technicians were either incompetent or woefully under-qualified. The turnover rate skyrocketed. After all, as Mike discovered, the recruiters had promised them financial stability and an easy ride. Few were able to cope with the daily workload.

Mike was not alone in his frustrations. He could at least take comfort in that. Every day, as usual, he and his companions would commiserate with one another over lunch. Flapjack had to contend with a flood of new paperwork. Moon resented the hours he had to waste training wash-outs. If anything, Mike had thought to himself, the trials of dealing with an "all-volunteer" military had strengthened their bond of friendship. It was a target of mutual animosity.

It was on a Friday that this cafeteria ritual was interrupted. Mike was picking at a plate of spaghetti when he heard the dull, metallic clang of a tray slammed down. Drops of sauce splattered onto Mike's scrubs.

"Hey fellows, is this seat taken?" said a voice above him. Moon and Flapjack looked up. Before they could answer, the stranger had already slid onto the bench and tucked in. The thick smell of cologne almost made Mike gag. Cologne seemed to be an epidemic among new officers.

"The name's Major Real, George Real," he mumbled with his mouth full. He extended a thick, meaty paw. "But my friends call me George. Say, is this the kind of grub you guys eat every day?"

"Well, yeah," grumbled Moon. "Why?"

"Well, because it tastes like dog chow, that's why!" George guffawed loudly. He slapped Mike on the back. "Now I can see why they're payin' so much!"

Moon was already red and shaking. Even Flapjack looked visibly uncomfortable. Mike couldn't blame them. After all, the three of them had been more or less drafted into the service. These new recruits could dictate the terms of their contracts. A new major could earn a salary at least three-times higher than Mike's.

Flapjack smiled thinly. "So, George," she said, after a long, awkward pause, "How do you like the service so far?"

"That's a tough question," said George. He pondered for a moment, munching slowly on a roll like a cow chewing its cud. "It beats private practice, I suppose! The business of medicine is tough. All the paperwork, the insurance company bullshit, eh, it pays well, but I needed a break, you know?"

Mike looked at the major incredulously. "A break? That's what you see this as?"

"Well yeah," George shrugged. "I just have to wear the uniform and show up on time. Patients get better or worse. Either way, I get paid! You gotta love the government."

"Yeah, obviously," shot Moon venomously. He opened his mouth to speak, but Flapjack kicked him under the table. He turned to his meal grumbling.

"But you must care about your patients right?" Mike insisted. "I mean, we're treating people willing to sacrifice their lives out there."

George belched. "Hey, I got problems of my own," he responded. "Like these damn kids running all over the base."

"Kids?"

"Yeah," he continued. "Maybe you been here too long to notice, but there sure are a lot of hood rats and ghetto folk around here. Folk that don't know how to raise their own children." He winked at Flapjack. "And hey, I ain't racist!" he added, wiping his chin. "There's a good load of white trailer trash around these parts, too."

"Is that so," mused Flapjack. She was rubbing her temples in annoyance.

"Runnin' around, no supervision, vandalisin', listenin' to that disco and rock n' roll," the major slammed his fist on the table. "I tell you what, there's a good reason they call 'em 'army brats.'"

"That came from an old British term," Mike protested. "It's an acronym for 'British Regiment Attached Traveler,' not an insult like you seem to think." Flapjack was beaming across from him. Mike blushed. If arguing with Major Real earned him brownie points with Flapjack, well, maybe ol' George ain't so bad. The thought made him smile.

"Well, I'm not lettin' my kids around 'em." the major continued to grumble. "You guys are just like me, I bet. You'll be hightailin' it to the suburbs as fast as you can."

Chapter 48

THE MEAL SEEMED to drag on for hours. It had become painfully obvious that Major Real loved to hear himself talk. No one could get a word in edgewise. As George droned on about his family, his cars, and his golf game, Mike stared at his half-eaten tray of pasta. He had lost his appetite. At one point, he considered making a break for the exit. One look from Flapjack changed his mind. If he left her alone, and Moon lost his temper, Mike knew he would never hear the end of it. He felt himself begin to nod off.

As he made the long walk to the ward, Mike's thoughts began to trouble him. In some small way, he realized, some part of him had agreed with Major Real. It was a disturbing realization, but one he knew he had to face. Juvenile delinquency was on the rise. Domestic violence was at an all-time high. Children were being raised in a dysfunctional, hostile environment, and nothing was being done about it. It wasn't even acknowledged!

Mike racked his brains for an answer; for some kind of solution. He had seen too many battered wives, traumatized husbands, and frightened children in the past month alone. A seismic shift was occurring in the military, and it was tearing families apart. Still, despite the lack of support, enlistment was at an all time high. Unemployment and economic recession were the great motivators. He had even read that recruitment rose to 5% whenever the jobless rate neared 10%. These recruits had no idea what they were signing up for. There were just no other options.

There was a surprise waiting for Mike at home that night. He arrived at the barracks so tired that he hardly noticed the letter in his mailbox. It was stamped with Colonel Creaser's own seal. He nervously tore open the envelope and scanned its contents. The message was short. He was to be the guest of honor for dinner with the colonel and his wife. Even on official Air Force stationary, Creaser's florid penmanship gave the missive a personal touch. Mike was almost flattered. Still, he thought, as he collapsed into bed, the invitation came as a surprise. A sense of foreboding passed through him. What could the colonel possibly want? What was he being drawn into now?

* * *

Mike had no issue finding the place. As he suspected, the colonel owned one of the largest homes in Camp Valkyrie. It seemed almost like a small plantation, with its white porch and marble columns. It was intimidating, Mike thought to himself. A home befitting the stature of a colonel—a commander, no less.

The interior was decorated with the same lavish elegance as the colonel's study. Mike was ushered into the sitting room, where Mrs. Creaser sat reading by the fire. She seemed to light up when he entered the room. To his surprise, the colonel's wife crossed the bearskin rug and wrapped him in an embrace. Her bracelets dug into his side.

"Ah, welcome Michael, thank you for coming!" she giggled loudly, kissing her husband on the cheek. "We so rarely have guests. Edward must have really taken a liking to you!"

"Thank you, ma'am," gasped Mike. He sat down and adjusted his collar.

"Now don't get any ideas, Mike," laughed Creaser with a wink. "I know she's a looker, but I got her first!"

"Edward!" cried Mrs. Creaser in mock disbelief. She turned to Mike and smiled. "You see, this is why we don't have guests. Can I offer you anything before dinner?"

"We have wine if you're thirsty," the colonel added. "I think the roast needs just a minute or two longer to simmer, right Mary?"

Mrs. Creaser glanced at her watch. "Hmm, I suppose another minute or two wouldn't hurt. In the meantime, do talk to us. Eddie tells me you've been to Guam? How does it feel to be back?"

"Easy, dear," laughed Creaser. He began to pour wine from a crystal decanter. "Let the boy relax, after all," he continued, nodding at Mike, "we have much to discuss over dinner."

* * *

The evening went better than Mike could have hoped. The cabernet was strong. The ossobuco was tender and flavorful. In addition to being a good cook, Mrs. Creaser was a charming host, and it wasn't long before he felt at home in their presence. Her British accent seemed to melt off her tongue. When Mike noticed her hearing aids, she spoke fondly of her time as a professional musician. The couple had met in Great Britain when she was playing with the symphony.

"He came every night to my performances," she told Mike, between peals of laughter. "For the longest time, I thought it was because he loved Mozart, but he told me later he came to see me. I was so flattered!"

"You wouldn't have gone out with me if you didn't think I loved music," admonished the colonel. He winked at Mike once more. "She was quite the looker, Major, as you can see!"

The more Mike listened, the more he found himself re-evaluating his opinion of the colonel. Edward Creaser was more than an officer. He was a husband who comforted his beloved when her hearing died. He was the proud father of a daughter who had just won a full scholarship. "She takes after her mother," he said, as they enjoyed liquors in the sitting room. "She's one of the best violin players in North Carolina!" Mrs. Creaser nodded in agreement.

The three talked long into the evening. As the clock passed eleven, Mrs. Creaser placed her hand gently on her husband's leg. They smiled at one another and turned to Mike. "Well, we hope you had a lovely time with us Michael," said Mrs. Creaser softly. "We've enjoyed your company."

"I have!" said Mike. "I had never thought…"

"…that we'd be so friendly?" finished Colonel Creaser. He laughed at Mike's expression. "Oh, don't be shy," he chuckled. "I'm sure this invitation came as… something of a surprise to you?"

"To be honest, it did."

"Well, my boy, you did me and all of Camp Valkyrie a big favor. My cousin…"

"That drunk," corrected Pam.

"Yes, that drunk, General Snow, retired without issue. Believe me, we're all better off being rid of him. The last thing we wanted was a long, drawn-out review process."

Mike blushed and looked down. He had been trying to forget about the incident.

"Loyalty," the colonel continued, "is in short supply these days. I admire your loyalty, Mike. I'd like to talk to you about your future."

"My future?" Mike echoed curiously. He realized, to his surprise, that he hadn't thought that far ahead.

"We want you to stay, Mike," said the colonel gravely.

"What do you mean, sir?"

"To re-up. Make it a career. There's only three months left on your commitment. It's time to think about what lies ahead, son. I want you to go to flight surgeon school at Wright Patt."

"I appreciate the compliment," Mike stammered, "but I'm really not sure this is where I belong."

"Nonsense," announced the colonel. He swept his hand dismissively in the air. "Have you met our newly-minted major? Dr. Real? If you haven't, I tell you, you're in for a treat, all right. That's the bright future of our new 'volunteer' military!"

Mrs. Creaser gave her husband a stern look. "What Eddie is trying to say," she said softly, "is that they need men like you. Men who risk their lives for a patient in distress. Men who would care for their mentally-incapacitated wives, even when there was nothing more they could do. Those kind of men."

"B-b-but how…" sputtered Mike. "How did you…"

"A military base is worse than a small town," chuckled Mrs. Creaser. "There's no secret that can't be teased out with a silk tongue and a sharp ear."

"You handled yourself well in Guam, too," added the colonel. "CIA had glowing praise for your efforts to negotiate with Colonel Tru."

Mike groaned. He should have known. So much for confidentiality! Was there anything these two didn't know, he wondered. They were both looking at him expectantly now. He knew they were eager for his answer. It was all too much to take in at once. "I'll really need to take time to think it over," he said finally. The colonel's face fell.

"Of course, of course," Mrs. Creaser reassured him.

"Yes," Colonel Creaser agreed. "Take all the time you need."

"Of course," said Mike, his eyebrows raised, "there are a few things that might convince me to stay."

The Colonel grinned. "I'm all ears, Major Pike."

Chapter 49

"TELL ME IT ISN'T TRUE, Mike," groaned Moon. "You're siding with 'the man' now?"

"Oh, leave him alone," laughed Flapjack.

"You should have met them!" Mike insisted. He swallowed a mouthful of roast beef. "They're both really charming, good people! I was as surprised as you."

Moon rolled his eyes. "Yeah, right."

"No really! Creaser only joined the military in the first place because it was expected of him! His father and grandfather were both military surgeons, and besides," Mike continued, gesturing with his fork, "he stayed because there were so many chest wounds at the beginning of the war. He helped set up a system that saved hundreds of lives!" As he heard himself speak, Mike was surprised by the admiration in his voice. He felt respect for his superior for the first time in his career.

"So what did you say?" asked Flapjack. "Did you tell him you'd come back."

"I told him I'd think about it."

"Say it ain't so, Mike!" cried Moon. "I'm getting' the hell out of Dodge when my time here's up!"

Mike chuckled. "Hey, it's not like I'm just rolling over. I had certain conditions."

"Conditions?"

"I told him what I told you guys," Mike continued. "That there needs to be time and money dedicated to studying families. It's insane, the fact that it's the late-1970s and there's still nothing published about the difficulties they face. You'd think with all the alcoholism, domestic abuse, behavioral problems, and depression we see on a daily basis, that someone would do something about it."

Flapjack had paused from her lunch to listen. She nodded vigorously in agreement. "Yes! And you actually told him that?"

"I told him if I stayed, I'd need time and funding to do some research of my own. If no one else is going to help these people, I'm going to try."

"And what did he say?" asked Moon. Even he seemed curious at this point.

"He said he'd do what he could. He'd have to get approval first. He did sound optimistic."

Moon groaned once more. "Ugh, Mike, are you kidding me?" he said, tossing his fork aside. "He's stringing you along. Did he mention anything about giving us a raise? Huh? Or about why he's paying hacks like Major Real three-times our salary?"

"What's your point, Moon?" shot Flapjack.

"My point is, all the money from the Pentagon goes towards recruiting. That's all they're interested in right now." He gave Mike a patronizing smile. "You think he'll care about your research once he's locked you up with a generous contract? Think again."

* * *

Try as he might, Mike found it difficult to focus on his work. The decision that had once seemed so straightforward had changed. He felt torn in two directions. Could he trust Colonel Creaser to keep his word? Had he written-off the military too soon? For so long he had thought as Moon did. Every day that ticked off his commitment was a day closer to freedom. Now he wasn't so sure. With the right support, he felt, he could really make a difference here.

"Hey there, General Pike!" a voice called, as Mike left Two South after a long, harrying shift. He turned to see Flapjack approaching from behind him. She stopped to salute. "If you re-up and become a commander, will you give us a raise, sir?"

"If you give me a break," laughed Mike. "Hey, seriously though," he said, blushing, "if I get to work with great people like you, maybe I will."

"You should be so lucky! But listen," said Flapjack. She became suddenly serious. "I heard from my father. He sends his best, and," she added, leaning in closer, "he wants to talk with you."

Mike stopped in his tracks. He eyed Flapjack curiously. "He wants to talk? About what?"

"Well, he has a proposition," she said softly.

"A proposition?"

"Remember on Guam?" she asked. Her voice was hushed and urgent. "He wants to talk to you about... 'The Company.'"

"His company?"

Flapjack sighed. She began walking ahead. Mike jogged to keep up. "Look," she hissed, as they approached his quarters. "I can tell you more tonight, if you take me out to dinner."

"I dunno, Flapjack," said Mike warily. "I'm pretty tired out." He felt her hand grasp his forearm. Her grip was firm and insistent.

"Pick me up at eight," she said, looking Mike square in the eye. "You'll want to hear what I have to say, believe me."

Chapter 50

FOR THE FIRST few minutes they drove in silence. Flapjack gazed out the window, as Mike listened to the rattle of his Volkswagen on the old prairie road. He had finally cobbled up enough to have the jalopy patched up a few days ago. So far, so good, he thought to himself. Tonight would be a dreadful time for a breakdown.

"I think I owe you a bit of an apology, Mike," said Flapjack gently. She was looking down at her hands folded in her lap.

"How's that?"

"I've been kind of hard on you. I was back on Guam, too."

"It's all right."

"No," she continued, "it's not, really. I guess after what we've been through together... I hold you to a different standard than the others." She swept her bangs back from her forehead. "But how you stood up to Real, and your ultimatum to Creaser..."

"I wouldn't really call it an ultimatum," Mike interrupted sheepishly.

"Whatever it was, then. It showed me that you're still the old Mike. The guy I grew to respect and care for."

Mike felt himself blushing. He felt his heart skip in his chest. "I care about you, too, Flapjack," he said shyly. "But I don't get why your father is interested in me. I'm just an ordinary guy."

"You're less ordinary than you think," said Flapjack. She looked up with a coy smile. "Dad says you're related to the founding fathers. You've got the blood of Thomas Jefferson, to be exact."

Mike almost slammed on the brakes. He felt his fingers go numb as they gripped the wheel. Had he really heard right? How could he know? How could anyone know? He didn't even know, himself!

"H-how..."

"The Company looks into your background," she shrugged

"The Company?"

"The Agency, Mike. Did you think I meant General Motors?" said Flapjack, without a trace of humor. "And they learned you're related to Jefferson, among other things." She began to finger a few strands of hair nervously. "Look, if you think privacy is important, you shouldn't get involved. When you're under consideration, both sides of the Atlantic are checking you out."

"Do you work for the company?"

"My father would never allow it. He thinks they might try to harm me to get at him?"

"Who is 'they?'"

Flapjack sighed. "Whoever they happen to be dealing with at the moment. It could be the Russians, the Cubans, the North Koreans, the Mob…"

"As in the Mafia?"

"Yes. But there's a long list."

"Jesus Christ…" Mike muttered in disbelief. "And they want me?"

"Yep!" giggled Flapjack. Her cheerful, bubbly demeanor seemed to return as they pulled into the lot. "It'd be quite an opportunity, wouldn't you say?"

*   *   *

As soon as they sat down, the two were talking like old friends. There was something about Mrs. Lee's that brought out the child in Flapjack. The hard-working, professional demeanor she had at Valkyrie seemed to melt away as they tucked into barbecue spare ribs and mashed potatoes. Good ol' fashioned comfort food. Mike felt so relaxed, himself, that for a while he seemed not to have a care in the world. He was like a little boy again, and it was Sunday dinner at Grandma's.

"Dessert?" asked Mrs. Lee, the owner, in her rich, syrupy drawl. She draped a thick arm around Flapjack's shoulders. "I make a mean apple pie, y'all, and my bread pudding… you'd think you'd died and gone to heaven!"

"Gosh, Mrs. Lee, thanks!" said Mike. He leaned back and stifled a burp. "But I'm stuffed!"

"Dessert is on me," said Flapjack. "We'll have the apple pie a-la-mode, thanks."

"Oh god, Flapjack. I seriously couldn't handle another bite," moaned Mike. He watched as Mrs. Lee disappeared into the kitchen.

"Really, Mike, I appreciate you taking me to dinner like this," she reassured him. "And I hope you don't think I just asked you here to talk about work."

"I don't mind," said Mike. "It helps to have options. I didn't say it around Moon, but Creaser didn't seem too excited about my research interests." He wiped some sauce from his mouth with a napkin. "Most of the research goes through the Pentagon, or San Antonio. Even then, he told me it has to be approved for publication."

"I thought so," said Flapjack, shaking her head.

"Creaser did a study, himself, just a few years ago," Mike continued. "It took years to get through the committees. Anything that suggests a problem in the military gets scrubbed."

"So nothing gets done?"

"Nothing gets done."

"And what about the families?"

"He gave me the usual spiel," he answered sadly. "The commander's job is to support the mission. His fighting force has to be hardened and resilient. What matters is that they have the strength to handle their business at home and get the job done in the field."

"But what do they do with all the reports we file?" asked Flapjack. There were traces of anger in her voice now. She sounded almost hurt.

"There's a national registry. The Pentagon files away all complaints—child abuse, sexual assault, etc.—and they're only available upon request."

Flapjack picked at the pie in front of her. The ice cream was already beginning to melt. Warm rivers of caramel melted into pools on their plates. Mike gingerly took a bite of his. It was tart and sweet. "You should have some," he coaxed Flapjack. "After all, dessert is on you, remember?"

She pushed the plate away. "I'm not hungry anymore, to be honest."

*   *   *

Night had fallen on the prairie when they finally left. In the distance, Mike could see the lights of distant oil wells. The stars glistened above them. On the way home, Mike felt relaxed and content. The heavy meal made him drowsy. When he gazed over at Flapjack, he was struck by how beautiful she looked. He rarely saw her in anything other than a uniform. Tonight she wore a black dress and a necklace of pearls. She smiled at him fondly.

"There's something different about you."

"New contacts," she said, grinning. "See? No glasses."

"You look beautiful." Before he could stop himself, the words had already left his mouth. His jaw clamped shut. He stared at the road ahead.

"Wow… thank you!" she giggled.

"Y-you're welcome," he stammered. A wave of relief rushed over him. "I'm curious why you never wore contacts before."

"I guess it never occurred to me." She shrugged. "My sister was always the beautiful one in the family. I was the studious one. I guess my glasses always protected me, in a way."

"From what?"

"You know…"

"No really, what?"

"Well," she said hesitantly, "from stepping out of my comfort zone, I guess. I liked my sister being the pretty one. It let me focus on my studies. Kept away unwanted distractions, you know?"

"You never wanted a boyfriend?" asked Mike. His curiosity was piqued.

"Never needed one. I have my family, and they've always supported me. I've been very lucky."

"Oh I don't know about that," he responded. "I mean, I don't know how much luck has to do with it!

* * *

Mike and Flapjack talked long into the night. Even after they arrived back at Valkyrie, the two sat in a courtyard discussing their lives. Flapjack talked about her family summers in the Adirondacks and the holidays in New England. She had grown up surrounded by politicians, figureheads, and important officials. Compared to hers, Mike protested, his stories were boring at best. Still, Flapjack listened raptly to his boyhood memories. He told her about growing up with Tommy; how they almost won the state football championships. The nostalgia gave Mike a peculiar thrill.

It was midnight when their conversation reached the present. For the first time, Mike was able to talk about his experiences on Guam. Flapjack spoke affectionately about Colonel Tru and the people they had met. She talked sadly of Sybil's struggles since her return. A congressional appeal had led to nothing. She was transferring out of the service. For the time being,   Moon had placed her on sick leave. As long as she was on a military base, he had told her, she would never be safe. Her reputation was in tatters.

"The military is no place for a woman," Flapjack lamented. "Everyone tells me that, as if I didn't already know."

"It's not fair," agreed Mike. He gazed at the fireflies on the lawn.

"Sometimes I wish I could have been like Mrs. Lee," she continued. "Do the cooking and the housework while my husband managed the ranch. I could start my own little restaurant in a Victorian house on the prairie."

"She owns a ranch?"

"One of the largest cattle ranches in America. The people are the salt of the earth. You know, one time Mrs. Lee tried serving a lobster to the ranch hands?" Flapjack rocked with laughter. "They wouldn't touch the thing! Had no idea what it was!"

"Would you really want that kind of life?" Mike asked. "The work you're doing now, well, you're really helping people. You're good at what you do."

"I'd be a good cook, too, I bet," she said sadly, "if that's all I had to do all day."

* * *

It was long after midnight when Mike finally reached the barracks. Flapjack had fallen asleep on the way. For a few moments, Mike watched her lying peacefully in repose. Her head was leaned against the window and she was breathing softly. As he touched her arm, a smile spread across her face. Her eyes fluttered open.

"Are we here already?" she yawned.

"I thought I might drop you off first," said Mike, "then I'd head over to my quarters. It's getting pretty late."

"I want to thank you, Mike," said Flapjack. She had begun to blush. "I had a really nice time."

"Me t—" began Mike, but he was cut off in midsentence. Flapjack had taken him by the collar and pulled him towards her. The two kissed passionately. Mike's surprise turned to desire. He wrapped his arms around her. They both looked into each other's eyes before kissing once more.

"You know, Mike," said Flapjack coyly, "you can stay over at my place, if you want."

"Are you sure?"

"Yeah, I'm sure."

"I just wanted to make sure it wasn't too soon."

Flapjack giggled. "Oh Mike, I'm sure. I've been after you for months," she laughed. "I've been thinking about it since Guam. We've both been through enough already. Let's start living again."

Mike nodded. Flapjack's frankness never ceased to surprise him. But that was who she was, he reminded himself. Without pretense. Open and honest. He walked her to the apartment with his arm around her waist. It was time to start living.

Chapter 51

FLAPJACK DROVE MIKE to the office that morning. The two had slept in and had little time to prepare. Colonel Lowe had scheduled a mandatory meeting for all medical personnel that morning. As a result, Mike had to wear the clothes from the night before. He prayed no one would notice the stain on his lapel. Why did barbecue have to be so messy, he wondered sadly. Not that good anyway. He was more worried, of course, someone would notice he and Flapjack were 'different'.

They both managed to find seats just seconds before Lowe took the podium. Only Moon seemed to notice them come in together. It only took him a moment to put two and two together. He winked. Mike rolled his eyes in response.

Colonel Lowe looked harried and frustrated. He spoke loudly, dabbing at his face every few moments with a sweat-stained handkerchief. The midnight drug dealer had struck again, he told them. There was still no evidence to work with. Neither the staff nor the patients were willing to come forward. Mike was hardly surprised. As close as he felt to his patients, he had long since realized that they would never fully trust him. Many had been betrayed by the system more than once. Their alliance lay only among themselves.

It was obvious to everyone that Colonel Lowe was acting out of obligation. It had always been his policy to let sleeping dogs lie, and today was no different. News of the scandal had finally reached the Air Force headquarters. Colonel Creaser was facing pressure to resolve the situation. He had ordered Lowe to root out the culprit within a month's time. The countdown was on.

"We simply must apprehend this criminal. For the good of Camp Valkyrie—and our patients, of course," Lowe hollered. He smacked the podium for emphasis. A high-pitched scream crackled from the microphone.

"Some of the medical staff have even been customers of this guy," cried a voice from a nurse.

"They should step forward!" yelled an administrator,"or we're all in trouble."

"They should, absolutely," Lowe concurred. "It is what an officer and a gentleman would do, to be sure!"

Ricks shot up from his seat. "Are you kidding," he responded, his voice sharp with indignation. "You want to throw one of us under the bus to save your own jobs? I am saying to everyone here, don't do it."

A murmur of voices hummed through the audience. Ricks's outburst had provoked polarized responses among the doctors, nurses, and administrators. Lowe slammed his fist again like a makeshift gavel. A hush fell.

"You are out of order, Major Ricks, completely out of order," he chided, pointing a pudgy finger at the officer. "If anyone knows," he beseeched the audience, "they should tell at once. For the good of everyone here."

*   *   *

Complimentary coffee and donuts. Well, at least something good came from early-morning meetings, thought Mike, also thinking the word 'complimentary' didn't quite fit. Neither he, nor Flapjack and Moon, were eager to return to work just yet. A few others felt the same, it seemed. A small group gathered around the coffee machine.

"So did you hear about Major Real," said Moon, with a twinkle in his eye. Whenever he saw that look, Mike knew he had picked up on good gossip.

"I'll bite," said Flapjack, "what happened?"

"He hasn't reported in a week, that's what. He's not at home either."

"He's gone AWOL?"

"That's right!"

"Wow! I never liked the guy, but I didn't think…"

Mike listened and nodded in response. The news had surprised him, too, but he had much bigger concerns in mind. He had known who the culprit was since the meeting began. All the events from so many months ago came flooding back. The strange, unpleasant argument in the officer's barracks at night. The covert operation he had witnessed from the brush. Cochran was back. Mike's greatest anxiety had returned to haunt him.

"Are you okay?" asked Flapjack, rousing Mike from his thoughts. "You look a little pale and you've been awfully quiet."

"Yeah, I'm fine," he muttered unconvincingly.

"I bet I know what it is," said Moon. "He knows who the culprit is. I know who it is. Heck, half of the officers at the meeting know, aside from Lowe, of course."

"He's threatened me a few times," said Mike.

"Directly?"

"No, he's too clever for that, but he made it pretty obvious," he replied. "I just hate confrontations."

Moon grinned. "Are you serious?" he asked. "You're a foot taller than the little weasel. The guy is scrawny as a beanpole. Heck, with that squeaky voice, I bet he's still waiting for his balls to drop!"

Mike shook his head. "It's not about that," he responded. "It's just something from my past that I thought I left behind. It's not really about Cochran. Not really, at least. It's something I feel I have to confront."

"Well, you're in luck, bud," said Moon, as a wry smile spread across his face.

"Oh yeah?"

"Yeah, because I came up with an idea during the meeting. Lowe's offering a reward to whoever catches the guy, right? Well, I think I may have the solution, but," he continued, his voice lowering, "I'm going to need your help."

"My help?"

"Yeah, meet me at my place at twenty-hundred hours tonight."

Flapjack rolled her eyes. "I don't wanna know what kooky idea you came up with, but take my advice, Mike, it sounds like trouble. What kind of reward could Lowe offer anyway? An official US government pen?"

"Hey, that in itself is reason enough to not go to the trouble," said Mike.

"Hey, it takes trouble to catch a trouble maker," shot Moon. He winked at Flapjack broadly. "And trust me, sister, you're not gonna want to miss this one!"

Chapter 52

MIKE CHECKED HIS WATCH for what felt like the hundredth time. Moon was already a half-hour late. The lights were off in his quarters. Mike yawned and leaned against the door. The sun had set. The crickets were singing in the grass nearby. Finally, he saw a figure approach down the long row between the barracks. It was Moon, and he was carrying something bulky under one arm. As he came closer, Mike saw that it was a movie camera—a black and chrome Super-Eight.

"Where the hell have you been?"

"Would you check out this beauty," said Moon sheepishly. "I'm sorry I'm late, but it took longer than I thought to borrow this." He patted the black machine affectionately. "This baby is how we're gonna catch our man."

Almost as soon as he had stopped, Moon began walking again. He was heading for the parking lot. Mike hustled to keep up. "So how are we going to pull this off exactly?" he asked.

"You know Major Ricks of course?" said Moon.

"Yeah. He's also Cochran's supervisor."

"Well, he and I used to be drinking buddies." His smile evaporated as he spoke. "Before what happened with Sybil, of course," he added.

"And?"

"And lucky for us he's a talkative drunk. He tried to get me involved in this little operation Cochran is running. A fresh supply of prescription drugs comes in every Sunday night."

"Every single night?"

"Every Sunday night. Same time, like clockwork. The people these guys are working with," said Moon ominously, "well, they don't jack around. I'll leave it at that."

Mike knitted his brow. He was beginning to wonder if Moon's recklessness would put them in danger. There were stories about military personnel tied to organized crime. The last thing he wanted was a run in with the mob.

"Shouldn't we call the police?"

"Don't you want that reward?" asked Moon. His eyes were trained on the road as he drove near the outskirts of Camp Valkyrie. "Besides," he added, "If you think my word against his will work, I can tell you now that it won't. We both know this guy has protection. We'll be marked, for sure, and Cochran would just go quiet a few weeks. They'd change tactics and stay in business."

Suddenly, Moon swerved onto the shoulder of the road. "Yep, this should do nicely," he said, pulling the keys from the ignition. "We have to walk the rest of the way."

Mike had expected as much. Cochran and his cronies would recognize Moon's station wagon from a mile away. A million questions scrolled through his mind during their trek through the barracks neighborhoods. How long had Moon known without telling anyone? How long had this black market been running with impunity, even though half the base seemed aware of its existence? Mike would never have thought a military base could be a safe haven for criminals. Not, that is, until now.

*　*　*

Neither Mike nor Moon had ever set up a video camera. Their location in the brush only increased their difficulties. The two struggled comically with the tripod, before it was finally mounted, aimed, and ready to roll.

"Well, if we're court martialed for this, we can at least become news camera-men," said Mike sarcastically. He picked the burrs and nettles from his coat.

All that was left now was to wait. The two talked quietly amongst themselves for an hour or two. When they ran out of conversation, Moon offered a sandwich from his backpack. He had brought a canteen as well. Moon had come well-prepared, Mike realized, though he wished they had a pack of cards, at least. Something to pass the time. There was still an hour before the scheduled delivery. Already, Mike could feel his legs falling asleep. Mosquitoes began to circle them both.

After a long, uncomfortable wait, something finally caught his eye. The van was unmistakable. Black and unmarked. He signaled to Moon, who fumbled with the camera controls. It began rolling as the vehicle came to a stop.

"Come on, baby, come on," whispered Moon. He zoomed in as the doors shut. Two shadowy figures began approaching the building.

"Did you get 'em?" hissed Mike. He squinted through a pair of binoculars. It was Cochran, no doubt about it. Still, he could not quite make out his accomplice. As the man stepped into the path of the headlights, Mike recognized the other airman—also a tech from the hospital. He had suspected as much.

Moon seemed oblivious to Mike's voice. He was focused intently on the camera. After a moment, he turned to Mike and rubbed his hands gleefully. "Oh yeah, we got it. Here, see for yourself," he said, motioning for Mike to take the helm.

The view from the Super 8 movie camera was not nearly as clear as the binoculars. Still, from the light of the car, their identities were unmistakable. The doors to the back of the building opened, just as Mike had seen before, and one-by-one, the patients in blue scurried into the van. Each emerged with a small package in hand. The entire transaction took less than five minutes.

"You gotta hand it to the bastard," said Mike, flicking off the camera. They began the long process of dismantling. "The guy runs a tight ship. Everyone knows their part, everything runs on schedule. Clean and efficient."

Moon laughed. "It's kind of ironic, isn't it?"

"How so?"

"The criminals are the most competent group on the base!"

Chapter 53

THE TWO DEBATED whether to give the film to Lowe or Creaser. Mike trusted Colonel Creaser, but Moon reminded him that Lowe had offered the reward. If Creaser found out, he argued, he could overrule the colonel's offer. Big deal, thought Mike, but a coin was tossed. Lowe won.

The colonel was ecstatic about the news. The rotund officer turned so red that Mike felt as though he were shaking hands with a tomato. After congratulating them both, he warned them that neither of them could remain anonymous. The entire camp would know who turned in the culprit.

"You did the right thing, going through the chain-of-command," he told them. "I'll make sure the general gets a hold of this right away. Save you the trouble." Before they could respond, the colonel had already waddled out the door with the film. They were left to wait in the man's filthy office.

"Save us the trouble," sneered Moon.

Mike rolled his eyes. "We both know he wants his share of the credit," he replied. "I told you we should have gone to Creaser first."

A few minutes later there was a knock on the door. It was Creaser's secretary. They were to come to his office at once.

* * *

"Good morning, gentleman," said Creaser, after they had all taken a seat. "Colonel Lowe here was telling me about this film," he continued. The colonel beamed with pride. Creaser pressed a button on his desk. "I'm sending for a projector right now. Can you tell me what model you're using?"

"Super 8," said Moon, just as the door to the office opened.

"Sally, see if we have a Super 8," Creaser called to his secretary, chuckling about the camera. He turned towards Mike and smiled. "As we're waiting maybe you could tell me how you got this?"

"I had heard some rumors," said Moon with a trace of hesitation. "So I borrowed a camera from a friend and checked to see if they were true."

"And you both witnessed it?"

"Yes sir," they both said in unison.

At that moment, Sally wheeled in an old projector from the Dermatology Department. Mike was surprised by the quality of the film. The picture was crystal clear from start to finish. There could be no doubt what had transpired.

From the corner of his eye, Mike noticed a peculiar change come over Creaser. His face seemed to harden with each passing moment. The lines on his face were drawn tight. He looked grave and severe. As the film ended, Mike turned to the colonel. All the smug satisfaction had been wiped from his face. The fat man looked mortified. He was as pale as a cadaver and his nails were dug into the arm rests. A vein on his forehead throbbed violently.

"Well, I had my suspicions," said Creaser, as he let out a long, tired sigh.

"Colonel... this means... I had no idea!" blurted Colonel Lowe.

"Boys, do you know who that is?"

"Charlie Cochran, who else?" said Moon in annoyance. "Why?"

"Airman Cochran," continued Creaser, "is the son of Senator Cochran in North Carolina. You two are going to have to give a sworn statement about how you got this."

"Why'd it have to be him?" asked Lowe, shaking his head. "What are we going to do about this? We have to do something!"

"Pull it together, colonel!" Creaser barked. He stared at his desk blankly, stroking his chin in thought.

"How... should we handle it, sir?" asked Mike, after a brief, awkward pause.

"In a friendly manner," said Creaser. He pulled out a sheet of Air Force stationary and began to write with fervor. "Damn, what a bind," he muttered to himself. "Colonel Lowe!"

"Y-yes sir?"

"Colonel, I'm afraid this issue lies in your jurisdiction."

"But sir!" Lowe squealed, "I did what you asked! I found the guilty party!"

"These men found the guilty party," corrected Creaser. He signed the letter with a flourish and handed it towards Lowe. "You're responsible for the staff. I'll deal with the higher-ups."

"Y-yessir," said Lowe sullenly. He looked hurt, almost like a scolded child.

"See that you do it quickly, colonel," Creaser added. "I don't have to tell you our careers are in the balance."

Chapter 54

THE NEXT DAY, tragedy struck.

Mike found out early the next morning. There was a nervous tension in the air. Those he passed in the hall spoke in rapid whispers. Even the cafeteria staff seemed on edge. The food didn't taste right either, he realized, as he choked down a piece of burnt toast. Both he and Flapjack waited eagerly for Moon, who was late as usual. If anyone knew what was going on, it would be him.

"Tell me you heard what happened," panted Moon from behind him. He dropped his tray and began eating ravenously.

"I give up," said Flapjack.

"Mike, remember what happened yesterday? With Creaser and Lowe?"

"Yeah," said Mike, curiously. "He was supposed to handle the Cochran situation."

"Well, he handled it. Boy, did he handle it," continued Moon excitedly. "He had the man summoned to his office and tore him a new one."

Mike rolled his eyes. "Ugh, leave it to Lowe to make things worse."

"And how would you have handled it?" asked Flapjack.

"It's the son of a senator. A well-established senator on the Armed Services Committee."

"So?"

"So that needs to be handled delicately! Consider the circumstances. He's selling openly, so he obviously feels he has protection from authority. I would sit the guy down, get to know him. Find out what the senator knows and doesn't know. Creaser made a big mistake."

"Oh, really?" asked Flapjack, raising an eyebrow. She seemed genuinely surprised by Mike's answer.

"Yes, really. You don't let a bull loose in a china shop."

"If you two are quite finished," grunted Moon, "then I can tell you what actually happened." He waited until he had both their attention before beginning his narrative.

"Well, it happened like this, see," he began. "Cochran shows up a few hours late, and Lowe just blows a gasket. Some people could hear them yelling from the halls, so they call security. Next thing you know, the door swings open, just as the sergeant major arrives, see," Moon paused to take a long drink. He grinned. As much as he loved to tell a story, he loved to leave his audience squirming.

"So then what?" pressed Flapjack.

"Well, Cochran storms out in a huff. Before anyone can follow him, Lowe drops to his knees and starts convulsing. Starts turning red and blue all over."

Flapjack gasped. "Oh my god!"

"Tell me about it! So the sergeant major carries him to the emergency ward. He's unconscious and unresponsive when the cardiologist finally gets there. Turns out the poor guy had a heart attack."

"That's horrible," said Mike numbly. "Is he… well, you know?"

"Yep. Dead as Dillinger," Moon answered, his mouth stuffed with scrambled eggs.

"That's terrible."

"That's not all. So the sergeant major summons Cochran and really tears into the guy. Calls him every name in the book. He tells him what he did to the colonel. You know what Cochran does?" Moon looked from Mike to Flapjack, but neither answered. "The guy laughs. He actually laughs. A friend of mine who was there said he was cool as a cucumber. It didn't even seem to surprise him."

"He just… he just laughed?" asked Flapjack. A look of horror and morbid curiosity was painted on her face.

"Oh, come on," said Mike. "You can't be serious."

"Hey, brother, I may be a lot of things, but I ain't a liar," shot Moon defensively. "Anyway, the sergeant major loses control. Hits the asshole square in the jaw. Everyone heard the crack. But that just makes the guy laugh more. So the sergeant hits him again, breaks the guy's nose and lays him out. But Cochran just gets back up, still cackling like a banshee. There's blood all over the place."

Mike shook his head slowly. "I can't believe what I'm hearing. Please don't tell me there's more."

"Nah, show was over at that point. They managed to restrain the sergeant. Some medical personnel spirited Cochran away. No one's seen him since."

Mike pushed away his tray. Just the sight of his half-eaten breakfast made him nauseous. A part of him wanted to dismiss the story outright. After all, Moon was a natural storyteller, and was prone to exaggeration. But still, he reminded himself, a story like that needed no embroidering. In his heart, he knew it was true.

After the shock wore off, Mike found himself grappling with troubling emotions. He had never liked Colonel Lowe, but he felt sorrow for the man's family. The children would grow up without a father. A wife was now a widow. A righteous sense of anger passed through him. Anger at Cochran's cold-blooded contempt; anger at the needless loss of life.

Such feelings were familiar to him. He even took some comfort in still being able to feel. But now, in the wake of Lowe's passing, it was as if something had awoken within him; something dark and unfamiliar. It coursed through him like a sickly-sweet poison. Even as it gripped his heart, he felt light-headed, free. He felt hate for Christine's attacker who took her soul. The worst torture was too good for him. No more forgiveness. Pleasure from pain; sweet self-satisfaction. A bittersweet narcotic. If the enemy is a savage, what good is forgiveness and love, logic and reason. The Golden Rule! Well Cochran can kiss his other cheek, just the posterior one. Mike tackled his work with renewed vigor. For the first time in years, he slept like a baby.

Chapter 55

COLONEL CREASER was a disciplined man. Mike had learned that by now, even respected him for it. He received all news—good or bad—with the same stoicism; the same solemnity and gravitas. The colonel's death was no exception. All the same, Mike could tell it affected him. He could read the man's subtleties. The colonel's once-florid penmanship now seemed shaky and uncertain. There were traces of anxiety in his voice. This tall, broad-shouldered figure still commanded respect, but something was missing. For once, Mike thought, he actually looked his age; like a lion in winter.

"God damn," swore Creaser, tossing his pen aside. "Leave it to Colonel Lowe to go and die on me. Wasn't even tough enough to handle some two-bit drug peddler."

Mike swallowed. "I'm sorry, sir."

"What are you sorry for?" snapped Creaser. "You didn't force him not to exercise and stuff sausages down his fat throat for the last thirty years."

Almost as soon as he said the words, Mike could tell he regretted them. The colonel averted his gaze for a moment. There was a faraway look in his eyes.

"Well, now the high command is gonna have a field day. This is the kind of thing that makes or breaks a career you know." The colonel smirked sardonically. He drew a bottle from his desk and poured two drinks. "They have to find another patsy." He paused.

"A scapegoat, my dear major. A lamb for the slaughter."

"But maybe..."

"There is no 'maybe,' Mike. There is always a patsy. *Always*." Creaser raised his glass in a mock salute. He threw it back, and slammed the glass on his desk. "A patsy for every problem, Mike. If you don't learn that now, then that patsy is you. They'll lead you to the altar with smiles on their faces."

"I'll… remember that, sir." Mike shifted awkwardly in his chair. Creaser's confrontational manner always made him uncomfortable. The colonel was a domineering man; a natural leader. It was he who dictated the terms of discourse, no matter the conversation.

"Yes, a good lesson to learn," he said, nodding to himself. "One that should help you," he added, looking down on Mike, "if you are to serve as my new chief."

"Sir?"

"I'm promoting you, Major Pike. Someone will have to assume Lowe's position, at least in the interim. I believe that man should be you."

"Oh, wow, sir! I couldn't. I mean, I'm truly very flattered. But I couldn't…"

"Nonsense," interrupted Creaser. "This is no time for modesty, Major Pike. You have a big job ahead of you. Let's see if you're up to the task.

Chapter 56

MIKE SPUN IN HIS new chair. The large, empty office whirled around him. He put his hands behind his head and relaxed. There was very little unpacking to do, but for now, he would savor the moment. Gone were the drab olive walls, the faint smell of mold. For the first time, he had a window with a view, not to mention a desk with real drawers! He picked up the name placard from his desk. The long, triangular bar glistened in the like gold. On one side was engraved his name and title.

Major Michael Pike
Chief of Psychiatry

He read the words aloud, trying each syllable for size. They seemed to roll effortlessly off his tongue. It sounded natural, as if he were born for the position. He smiled and propped his feet on the desk.

A knock on the door startled him like a gunshot. Mike's body jerked instinctively. He swung his legs off the desktop. "Come in!" he replied, hastily smoothing the creases in his shirt. He was surprised to see a small, middle-aged woman in the doorway. Locks of brown hair flecked with silver flowed beneath her shawl.

"I hope you don't mind my stopping by," she said, peering hesitantly.

"Not at all. Come in, Miss…"

"Lowe. Margaret Lowe. We spoke on the phone."

"Ah, of course," said Mike. "I'm so sorry about your loss. We're all mourning the colonel's passing. He was a good man."

"Yes, a good man," she agreed, softly. As she approached, Mike was struck by her appearance. Mrs. Lowe was clad in black from head-to-toe. Only her pearls stood in stark relief. When she spoke, her voice was soft and distant; devoid of feeling.

"If there's anything I can do…"

"As a matter of fact, Major Pike. I think there may be." To Mike's surprise, she had begun to lean towards him. Twice she looked behind her, as if afraid of being watched. "I know who did this. I know who killed my husband. I want to hear it from you."

"Ma'am?"

"You! The man who took his place," she growled. The glazed look in her eyes disappeared. Her lips curled back in a smear. Cracks began to form in her mascara.

"I'm sorry, Mrs. Lowe," offered Mike, in both confusion and concern. "But really, I'm not sure what you mean. It was a heart attack."

"Please. You think I'm stupid?"

"Not at all!" he exclaimed. "I'm not sure what you heard," Mike continued, improvising an escape route in his mind. Whether or not grief had driven her to violence, he wasn't keen to find out. "There was an altercation that could have indirectly caused this tragedy, but really, I'm sure Colonel Creaser is doing all he can…"

Mrs. Lowe's fists struck the desk, killing his sentence in mid-stride. She stood up furiously. "How dare you!" she spat, her body quivering with rage. "How dare you invoke that man's name, like he's some kind of saint."

Mike wheeled his chair back slowly. "Colonel Creaser? Look, Mrs. Lowe, you're clearly upset, but I can't help you until you tell me what's going on," he said calmly and firmly. "Now, start from the beginning. Tell me what happened? Why are you angry with the colonel?"

"Like you don't know," she said, her voice shaking. She slumped back into her chair and began to cry. "I got the call from Major Ricks. He told me all about it. They're going to pin it all on that poor Cochran boy, I just know it. He knew as much. He knew Creaser had it out for my husband."

Mike's anxiety turned to confusion. Was it possible? Could the colonel have had a hand it this? Sure, it seemed far-fetched. This poor, grief-stricken woman seemed too emotional to trust. But really, he reminded himself, who could he trust anymore? Creaser's words echoed in his mind. For every problem a patsy.

"I still don't get it," said Mike, after a moment of thought. "Why Creaser? What motive could he have?"

"I don't know why you're doing this to me," whimpered Mrs. Lowe. Her voice was hoarse from sobbing. "You don't have to pretend. Everyone knows the story."

"The story?"

"Some scandals die out, but in the military they're never forgotten," she sighed. "You wouldn't believe it, but my husband was like you once. Young and handsome. A real charmer. He was married to some hussy, the daughter of a base commander."

"Creaser?"

"No, it was some other bastard. Same state, different location."

"Ah," Mike nodded. "Go on."

"We fell in love. Deeply in love. He divorced her, and the two of us eloped together. He didn't care what anyone thought. Neither did I."

"And that's when things got complicated?"

"Oh, they tried to make it look like he was incompetent. I knew better. Creaser had to take my husband as his Chief of Psychiatry. He owed that base commander some huge favor or other. Creaser had it in for him ever since!"

Mike thought for a moment. "But isn't that a bit extreme?" he asked, finally. "Why wouldn't he just transfer him again?"

"Oh, I bet my husband found out something. Some dark secret. He heard something he shouldn't have," she lamented. "That's how they handle this kind of thing. The military can't afford bad press. They run the risk of congressional inquiries, funding losses and sanctions. They're always looking to pin the blame on someone. If that's not possible, well…"

Mike swallowed. It still seemed too far-fetched to be true. Creaser may have been a cunning tactician and bureaucrat, but a murderer? He couldn't believe it. Mrs. Lowe smiled sardonically, as if she could read the doubt in his mind.

"You don't believe me, do you, Major Pike?" She stood up. "I suppose they'll give me a pension to shut me up. You'll take my husband's place. Life will go on as usual."

"I'm sorry, again, Mrs. Lowe. Thing is, life won't go on as usual for you — you'll always feel this — grief and betrayal. I wish there was something I could do," he offered. She laughed on her way from his office — a curious, hostile laugh.

"Don't bother. Your job is to kill the enemy, not help widows and orphans. If transgressions were ever brought to justice, well, you'd never be able to kill anybody!"

Chapter 57

THE NEXT MORNING, the conference room was filled to capacity. Mike had never seen it so crowded. Those who came late were forced to stand, and they jostled for positions along the wall. So far, he thought, everything had gone according to plan. There had never been an emergency meeting called on such short notice. It was a break in the daily routine, a disturbance in the dull, repetitive flow of events at Camp Valkyrie. The crowd was buzzing with curiosity. Everyone was eager to learn the truth of Lowe's death, and, more importantly, what it meant for their jobs.

Mike took a few deep breaths. He'd sat awake for hours that night rehearsing. It all had to seem natural. That was the key. Camp Valkyrie would learn the truth about the tragedy, that much was true, but they wouldn't learn it from him. Everything depended on strategy.

A hush fell over the crowd, as Mike ascended the podium. The room grew quiet in anticipation. Mike paused to adjust the microphone. To his surprise, all his usual nerves had left him. He savored the nervous tension in the room. He felt alive.

"I'm sure you all know why we're here today," Mike began, his voice echoing through the speakers. "We are sorry to announce the passing of Colonel Winston P. Lowe, our devoted Chief of Psychiatry." He paused for gravitas. There were a few murmurs in the crowd. A muffled cough. "Now, I know you are used to scheduled lectures," he continued, "but as new Chief of Psychiatry, I want to do things a bit differently. Think of this as a town hall, of sorts. I'll direct the discussion. If you have something to say, just raise your hand."

The staff took to the idea at once. Mike knew they would. These officers were eager for a chance to speak; eager for a chance to confirm the latest rumors and learn the juicy details. Through the Socratic Method, Mike reasoned, the staff would write their own version of events. He wouldn't have to divulge a thing.

"To start things off," Mike began, after answering a few initial questions, "I want to know what the rumors are around the base. What have you all heard about the tragedy?"

A number of arms shot up. Everyone had heard something. One of the techs heard he choked on a ham sandwich. Another claimed it was drunken brawl at the NCO Club. One officer had heard that Airman Cochran was involved. A voice from the back agreed.

"So, there are a few rumors," said Mike. "But was anyone actually there to witness what happened?"

As if on cue, the sergeant major took the floor. He furiously denied the lies and hearsay. Lowe had a heart attack. He had seen it himself. It was all the result of a conflict with Airman Cochran.

"But why?" asked Mike, feigning confusion. "Why would Airman Cochran, way over in forensics, be arguing with the Chief of Psychiatry? It didn't make sense!"

Once again, there was no shortage of theories. Cochran was a known entity; a polarizing figure. Some staffers were eager to confirm his notoriety, while others spoke passionately in his defense. As tensions rose, Mike was forced to restore order.

"More than one of you," he said, when the crowd became quiet, "have mentioned that Cochran was dealing drugs. Some of you claim that he wasn't." Mike kept his voice level and earnest. He was the voice of the administration. He had to appear neutral. "I'm glad the issue was raised. You see, a tape was anonymously provided to Colonel Creaser. A tape which implicates two unnamed suspects in an underground drug trafficking ring."

The room erupted in a cacophony of voices. Mike maintained his poker face. He had played his ace. As he rapped on the podium for order, he caught Moon's face in the back of the room. His eyes were wide with disbelief.

"Quiet, please! Quiet!" Mike barked, with an authority that surprised even him. "Now, my question is, could these two events have anything in common? An incriminating video tape. A drug scandal. The death of an officer. We need your help to put together the pieces."

"Isn't it obvious!" cried a nurse in the front row. "Colonel Lowe held that meeting. He wanted to catch that crook more than anyone! I bet he was the whistleblower! He made the video."

"He's a hero!" agreed another voice. "And those bastards cut him down!"

"Oh, come on," groaned an officer on the other side of the room. "We all know what a weasel Lowe was. I bet he was part of the whole scheme. He turned the others in and got what was coming to him!"

"But what about Cochran?" asked a nurse. "Is he being charged?"

"Now, let's not speculate," said Mike, cagily. "The suspects must remain anonymous until the Air Force decides to release them. Right now, no charges have been filed."

"I'll tell you why!" boomed a voice in the crowd. "It's because he has connections, that's why! I heard him brag about it himself. He's the son of some senator or governor. Someone high up."

"Now, now," said Mike, reasonably. "We can't hold the man's family ties against him. Airman Cochran can't help being the son of a North Carolina senator. The man is innocent until proven guilty."

"Bullshit" cried a voice from the crowd.

"No surprise," yelled another. "The whole system is corrupt!"

The crowd had become a cacophony of voices. Emotions appeared to have reached a boiling point. Hushed voices rose in anger, surprise, indignation, and disbelief, as the auditorium began to process the clues they were provided. Eager to not overplay his hand, Mike adjourned the meeting. The seeds had been planted. Now, all he could do was wait.

Chapter 58

"WHAT THE HELL, MIKE?" cried Moon.

Mike smiled. "Why, what do you mean, Major Moon?"

"You know what I mean. That little piece of theater up there!"

"I happen to think that was a rather productive little meeting," Mike shrugged. "Now it's out in the open. Everyone knows who Cochran was, now, and the privileges he's been exploiting."

"But… You lied…"

"I did you a favor," Mike answered. "Now you and I are in the clear. All the credit goes to Lowe, or the blame, for that matter. Did you really want Cochran's cronies on our tail?"

"But you still haven't handled the Cochran situation," Moon insisted.

"Oh, but I have," chuckled Mike, spinning idly in his chair. "I'd wager that there'll be a half-dozen calls to the office of Senator Cochran. These officers aren't dumb, they know better than to trust the chain-of-command. They'll go right over Creaser's head."

"And you expect Creaser to be okay with that?"

"I expect he'll be thrilled. He's out of the line of fire. Now he can plead innocence when the shit hits the fan."

Moon was silent. He turned to the window, stroking his chin in thought. "So when Air Force HQ and the senator come calling, Creaser can plead innocence and play Cochran's advocate. There's no blood on his hands."

"Good ol' Pontius Pilate."

"I gotta hand it to you, Mike," said Moon, with a grin. "I never thought you had it in you."

"Me neither!" Mike laughed. "I suppose I catch on fast."

*   *   *

The wheels were in motion, and the week passed in a whirlwind of activity for Mike. To his surprise, it was Mrs. Lowe who first received word from the staffers. She was demanding a congressional inquiry. Creaser was hardly concerned. She was a grief-stricken widow, he told Mike. No one would take her seriously.

The colonel had more pressing matters to attend to. Orders to arrest Cochran came all the way from the Pentagon. Word traveled fast, and it wasn't long before Creaser had a call from the North Carolina Republican Party. The senator's office, it appeared, was already in damage control mode. They found a willing ally in the colonel.

By the end of work on Friday, Mike was riding a cloud of euphoria. Everything seemed to be working as planned. The Cochran situation had been resolved. Mike was in the clear. He had earned the good will of Creaser, who had in turn won the gratitude of a U.S. Senator. Everything, it seemed, had been for the best.

It was not until the evening that things turned sour. Mike had taken Flapjack for dinner to celebrate, but her thoughts seemed elsewhere. She was not her usual upbeat self. Her responses were short and terse, and she seemed to shrink from his touch. Something was obviously wrong.

"Are you going to tell me what's bothering you?" Mike pressed, as they waited for their appetizers. Flapjack sighed.

"I don't know. I feel like something's changed about you."

"Changed?"

"Like at that assembly," she continued, "that wasn't you. It was, I don't know… it wasn't honest."

"I did what I was supposed to do. I don't see how I hurt anyone."

"And what happened to Cochran?" she asked, picking at the crust of a bread roll.

"He's out of the picture. We got lucky. The senator has service members in his liaison office. We just had him transferred there. Now daddy can keep an eye on him."

"You let him off the hook," said Flapjack softly. "Don't you feel ashamed?"

"Ashamed?"

"You're acting just like Creaser."

Mike recoiled. "And that's such a bad thing?" he shot back. "Colonel Creaser is a devoted husband and father. He knows how to separate is personal and professional life. Do you know how many lives he saved with his research? Do you?"

"Mike..."

"Countless. And he didn't accomplish that by being the nice guy. He understood the game and knew how things worked."

"And how, exactly, do things work?" asked Flapjack, rolling her eyes.

"If you want to get anything done—if you want to accomplish anything good—you have to get your hands dirty. You have to make compromises. The branch that doesn't bend breaks."

"Bend too much," said Flapjack softly, "and you're already broken."

Chapter 59

COLONEL CREASER knew how to negotiate. He had long since mastered the art of the transfer. A handful of phone calls to San Antonio, and Cochran was on a plane to North Carolina. As far as the Air Force was concerned, the issue was closed. All inquiries from the press, the police, and Congress were directed to Washington. There was a congressional inquiry, but it fizzled quickly. No one had any comment for the Congressman's investigator. Cochran left the service soon after with a spotless record.

* * *

Major Pike had no time to rest on his laurels. With Cochran gone, another foe had risen in his place. Fortunately for Mike, this new figure had neither the popularity nor the notoriety of his drug-dealing predecessor. Ever since his first disappearance, Major Real had become a pain in Mike's side. As a volunteer with a contract, the major made three-times the salary of his superior, a fact of which both he and Mike were aware. He received full benefits and free housing, as well. With perks like these, Mike could hardly blame the man for feeling untouchable.

During his first days as Chief of Psychiatry, Mike had been easy on his subordinates. He was determined to differentiate himself from the ornery, unpopular Colonel Lowe. It was a mistake the major was quick to exploit. At first, his actions seemed petty, but ultimately harmless. His staff complained that he was difficult to work with. His colleagues would report him for missing meetings. It was when he began to refuse emergency room duty and weekend call that Mike realized something had to be done. Real was testing his limits. He wanted to see how far he could go.

For the first time in his career, Mike sympathized with his predecessor. The burden of command must have weighed heavily on the deceased colonel. Mike's complaints to Creaser were rebuffed. It was the major's job to handle his men, he was informed. Responsibility for them lay squarely on his shoulders.

Still, Mike was hesitant to act. He had never been a confrontational person. When Major Real began to show up in civilian clothes, however, he realized he had to act fast. If Creaser caught wind of this—which he would, sooner or later—there would be hell to pay. Something had to be done, immediately.

Mike wracked his brains. There had to be some way to get to Real. If the man didn't respect the military, or the chain-of-command, then what did he respect? The answer came to him in a flash. His contract! Of course, Mike thought to himself; Real considered that piece of paper his golden ticket. Everyone around him knew the power it gave him. As far as Major Real was concerned, it made him untouchable. Well, we'll see about that, Mike thought to himself. Two could play at that game.

In typical military fashion, Mike's request to the JAG office took ages. For days, Mike waited on pins and needles. He did his best to ignore the major's behavior. If he wanted to beat the man, he realized, he had to beat him at his own game.

When the day came, and the parcel arrived, Mike was stunned by its thickness. It seemed more like a book than a contract. As he pored over the fine print on each page, he had to give Real credit. The administration jumped through hoops to win his signature. As a volunteer, the major had his choice of assignment and location. In addition to his salary and benefits, he would work only 35 hours per week, with time off for meetings, CMEs, TDYs, and Family Medical Leave. Mike could only dream of having it so good.

Finally, after a tedious hour and a headache, he found what he was looking for. He knew the clause was there. It had to be. The one rule on which he knew the military would stand firm. And there it was, buried in the middle of all the legal jargon. Mike sat back and smiled to himself. He had his trump card.

* * *

"This is an outrage!" cried Real. "An outrage!"

"I'm sorry, Major Real, but those are the rules." As hard as he tried, Mike couldn't help smiling. The look only made Real angrier.

"I volunteer my services—volunteer—and this is how I'm treated?"

"You are still subject to the direction of whatever supervisors or commanders you work under," said Mike, calmly. "And as it says in your contract, uniforms are to be worn at all times, by all military personnel. This simply is not negotiable."

"And if I refuse?"

Mike shrugged. "Failure to comply may result in disciplinary actions."

Major Real was breathing heavily now. His face was blanched. For once, there was nothing he could do, and Mike knew it. A copy of his contract was right in front of him.

"If you or Colonel Creaser are dissatisfied with my service," he huffed, "then why don't you fire me? I'm sure my work will be appreciated elsewhere."

"Oh, I could fire you, I suppose," said Mike. "But then I'd have to place you on paid leave while we waited for San Antonio to confirm your resignation. Then of course we'd have to compensate you, and you'd receive unemployment. And really, I don't think either of us want to put the military through all that red tape. Don't you agree?"

Real folded his arms. His face twisted in a grimace. "You think you're really smart, don't you, Major?" he said, sullenly. "You're just the last of the draft dodgers."

"Now, now," said Mike, raising his eyebrows. "Let's not resort to name-calling. After all, the military runs on favors. If you're assaulted by a patient—and it does happen—do you think anyone will run to your aid? If you're accused of malpractice, harassment, or discrimination, do you think anyone will be on your side? If you want to survive around here, well, you may want to play nice."

As Mike spoke, his tone dropped ominously. It was spiked with more than a hint of malice. Major Real's arms dropped. His lip quivered nervously.

"I'll quit," he whimpered.

"That's your call," nodded Mike. He tapped the contract with his pen. "But as you know, you must give 90 days' notice, in addition to forfeiting any bonus you may have. And a lot can happen in 90 days."

"Is... are you threatening me... Major Pike?"

Mike grinned. "Threatening? Not at all. In fact, I'm peaches-and-cream compared to some of the colleagues you've been mistreating. This is just a warning. Your only warning." He pulled a slip of paper and handed it to Real. "I just need you to sign here, as proof you've been counseled."

"I... um... I appreciate this, Major Pike," stuttered Real, hoarsely. He was already out of his chair and looking towards the door. "I'll... there won't be any problems."

"That's great to hear, Dr. Real," said Mike, his voice returning to normal. He walked him to the doorway and shook his hand. "Just play nice. Real nice," he added. "Your country appreciates your service."

Chapter 60

THE OFFICE WAS QUIET. Too quiet, Mike thought. He had never thought he would miss the ward. At least time passed quickly there. Now, as he sat dealing with tedious paperwork, the hours seemed to drag on interminably. Afternoons were the worst. By then, his caffeine buzz had worn off. The sunlight from the window made him drowsy and indolent. At a certain point, even the words on the documents seemed to bleed together. He fought off a yawn and waited.

Finally, his last appointment of the day arrived. Mike welcomed the interruption. One look told him all he needed to know. It was easy to tell the difference between a doctor and a soldier, and his visitor was obviously the latter. Still, Mike had rarely seen anyone in such peak physical condition. The man was built like a Marine; tall, muscular, with a scowl like a pit bull. His head was completely shaven.

"It's nice to meet you, Major…"

"Major Bell, sir, Eric Bell," said the man gruffly. He shook Mike's hand with a vice-like grip. "Reporting as instructed. Will this be in my record?"

"Oh, not at all," said Mike, who then offered him a seat. "This isn't a formal evaluation. Your commander is just concerned. He passed that concern on to Colonel Creaser, and the case was referred to me. They're just trying to help you."

Bell eyed Mike suspiciously. "Is this about my signing in under a different name? Because it only happened twice. I believe I explained."

"Yes," said Mike, scanning his file. "You told Commander Beltran you had a girl on your mind, correct."

"Yeah," said the man, pursing his lips. He looked away awkwardly. "I mean, yes sir. As I told the commander, it won't happen again, but me and this girl have been goin' steady, and, well, you know how it is?"

"How it is?"

"Yeah, just... how it is. You know."

"I'm afraid I don't."

"Aw, c'mon, Major," he groaned, shaking his head. He was blushing deeply. "I'm a red-blooded male just like you. Do I have to spell it out for you?"

Mike frowned. "I understand, I do, Major Bell. But this kind of infraction is very serious. You're a SAC pilot. They take everything seriously over there. Especially concerning security."

"Aw, come on," said Bell, his voice becoming more irritated. "You'd understand if you saw her, sir. She's a real looker. We just really dig each other is all."

"Well," said Mike, after a moment of thought, "Just don't let it happen again, okay? It's our duty to keep our private and personal lives separate." He snapped the folder shut.

"Is that all, sir?"

"That is all."

*   *   *

Mike looked on in bewilderment. He had rarely seen his friend laugh so hard. It took a while for Moon to regain his senses, and even then he would lapse into fits of giggles.

"Are you going to tell me what's so funny?" said Mike, beginning to feel annoyed.

"Hoo boy, are you serious," laughed Moon, wiping tears from his eyes. "You come a long way, baby, but you still got lots to learn."

"So spit it out."

"Come on. Pepper Arlington? Pepper Arlington?!"

"Yeah..."

"And that doesn't sound strange to you?"

"Well, I guess it's an odd name. So what?"

"Brother, you been had," laughed Moon. "That lady ain't a lady. It's a dude, dude."

Mike cocked his head. "Huh? You mean Major Bell is dating a man?"

"Mike. Pepper Arlington isn't dating Major Bell. Pepper Arlington is Major Bell. Well, Major Bell in stilettos, at any rate."

"You're kidding me!"

"Don't get me wrong," added Moon, becoming serious for a moment. "I'm not a fairy or nothin'. But there's a bar in the next town over. It's a well-known secret around here."

"So the other officers are…"

"More than a few."

"But how do you know Pep… Major Bell is involved?"

"I've heard names just like it," Moon chuckled, uneasily. "The ladyboys—the less creative ones, I guess—have a method for picking stage names. Take the name of your first pet, add the name of street you were born on, and voila! You're the belle-of-the-ball."

"So Pepper…"

"And Arlington. Could he have been more obvious? Heck, there's an Arlington Road a few blocks away!"

Mike swirled the ice in his drink. He still couldn't believe it. At the same time, he knew Moon was never one to lie. At least not when he had nothing to gain. Still, it didn't add up. Bell was one of the manliest recruits on Valkyrie. The man was built like a linebacker! There was not a trace of femininity about him.

"It's never the one's you suspect," said Moon, signaling for another round of drinks.

"Wow. So what do I do now?"

"You tell me," Moon laughed, slapping Mike heartily on the back. "You're the chief, after all."

* * *

"And you're sure about this? You're damn sure?!"

"A source on the base confirmed it, sir."

For a moment, Mike was taken aback. He had never seen the colonel so incensed. Creaser's tone was deadly serious. As he spoke in careful, measured tones, never once losing eye contact. When he finished, he poured himself a tumbler of whisky, and began to pace the room.

"It's a damn shame. A damn shame," the colonel repeated. Whether he was speaking to himself or not was unclear. "A young man like that, falling into deviance. It really is a shame."

"I didn't know it was such a big deal, sir," said Mike, hesitantly. "It's just a fantasy, after all."

Creaser slammed his glass on a nearby table. "We all have fantasies," he said, bitterly. "But we keep them in the bedroom where they belong. We don't bring them to work. Are you a Christian, Major?"

Mike bit his lip. "I was… raised Catholic, sir."

"Then perhaps you can understand. Or perhaps not. The world seems to be changing fast these days. First it was the long hair, then the music, I swear. Whatever happened to values in this country? Good, wholesome, family values? It's a travesty."

"But what about the pilot?" asked Mike, eager to change the subject. "What will happen to him?"

Creaser turned from the window. "Well, he'll lose his job, that much is for sure. He'll be discharged too. This is a matter of national security."

"Discharged?"

"What did you expect?"

"I don't know… I guess, I didn't think it was that big a deal." Mike felt as though he'd been punched in the stomach. Major Bell was about to lose everything, and it was his fault. He had turned him in. It was a sickening realization.

"You have to understand, Mike," explained Creaser. "It's a security issue. SAC pilots are entrusted with top secret information. Their lives are open books. A lie alone is enough for one to lose his clearance. But this… this is another level entirely!"

"Isn't there anything we can do," asked Mike, desperately.

"Now, don't beat yourself up for this, Mike. It's not your fault," Creaser reassured him. "The man should have known better. Now, anything else to report?"

Chapter 61

THE REST OF THE MEETING passed in a daze. Mike left the colonel's office feeling sick and disoriented. His first stop was the latrines, where he threw-up his lunch. He decided to take the rest of the day off. There was no way he could focus on work. Instead, he took a long walk to process his thoughts. It wasn't long until he had passed the administrative and residential districts of Camp Valkyrie. Beyond the gate, the pavement gave way to the rocky, tire-worn roads through the prairies. For hours he walked. Gradually, exhaustion began to distract him from his thoughts.

It was late that evening when Flapjack heard a knock at her door. She ignored it at first. After all, she wasn't expecting guests. The knocking persisted. "Who is it?" she asked, cursing her instinct to respond. Any single woman living alone on a military base would have known better. She had heard more than a few cautionary tales of unwelcome guests in the night.

"It's me, Mike."

"All right," she said, the tension melting from her body. "Give me a second, I'll get the lock."

Flapjack gasped. The man in the doorway was Mike, all right, but nothing like she'd seen him before. His thick, blonde hair was a mess, the bangs plastered to his forehead. His eyes were bleary; his lips dry and cracked. He looked as if he had just trekked through the desert.

"Jesus, Mike! What happened?"

"Give me some water, and I'll tell you," he croaked, weakly. "You're the only one who might understand."

* * *

Flapjack immediately helped Mike to her bed before pouring a drink. He fell asleep soon after. After weighing her options, she decided to wait before calling a medic. Besides, Mike often wandered alone when something was troubling him. Getting it off his chest would be the best medicine for now.

After a brief nap, Mike was awake and alert. He took another long drink and cleared his throat. "Thanks, Flapjack," he said, sitting up on the mattress. "I went for a walk, and I suppose I lost track of time."

She rolled her eyes. "Lost track of time? I swear Mike, sometimes I feel like I'm taking care of a puppy."

"At least I'm housetrained," he said, smiling weakly. Well, at least he hasn't lost his sense of humor, she thought to herself. That was a good sign.

"So what's on your mind, Mike? We haven't really talked much since that last dinner."

"Yeah." Mike rubbed the back of his neck sheepishly. It was sunburned, and beginning to peel. "I'm really sorry. I was a real asshole. I didn't even realize it until today."

"Something happened?"

"Yeah. Something bad. Something that cost a man his livelihood. And the worst part is, it's because of me."

Mike bowed his head as he spoke. His eyes remained downcast. Flapjack listened quietly, and sat beside him at the edge of the bed. She gently touched his shoulder.

"It's okay," she assured him. "I don't know what happened, and I know you've made mistakes, but I know you. You wouldn't do that to someone." She wrapped her arm around him, kissing his cheek. "You're just not that kind of person."

"I wish that were true," Mike sighed. He leaned back and reclined on the mattress. Flapjack fell beside him. The two of them stared at the ceiling. "But I can't fix that now. Now, I have to make a decision," he continued. "And I wanted to ask your advice."

Flapjack turned her head towards him. "I don't know, Mike." She pursed her lips. "You have to trust yourself to make these decisions."

"I do, but I trust your judgment, too."

"But why me?"

"Because," he said, looking her in the eye. "I care about you. You've always been there for me, and you've seen me at my worst. I trust you. Whatever the future holds, I want to experience it together."

Flapjack's eyes welled up. A tear rolled down her cheek. The next thing he knew, Mike found his mouth pressed against hers. She embraced him.

They kissed passionately, holding and caressing one another. She was such a strong woman, Mike thought, and yet she felt so delicate in his hands. His sweat and her perfume comingled in the air.

Just as he began to fumble with her bra-strap, Flapjack pushed herself away softly. He tried to pull her back towards him. "Not now!" she cooed playfully. She sat and brushed back her hair. "Did you forget what we were talking about?"

"Aw, we can talk about it later," groaned Mike.

"No, we can't I have to know now," she chuckled, rubbing his belly. "You can't leave me in suspense."

"Okay," said Mike. He cleared his throat. "I think I've decided something. I want to leave the Air Force."

Flapjack reclined on her elbow. She looked down at him skeptically. "Oh? And what would you do next?"

"I don't know. Maybe open a private practice. Work on my golf game. That kind of thing. Leave the military bullshit behind."

"You could do that," she nodded. "Or you could meet with my father. He's been asking about you a lot lately." She laughed. "It's kind of annoying, actually."

"Your father? At the Agency?!"

"That's the one."

Mike sat up and stretched. He let out a long, languid yawn. "Sure, sure." He reached out to stroke her hair. "What could he want? Don't they have enough recruits from the Ivies? I would think they have the pick-of-the-litter."

"Hey," said Flapjack, in mock indignation. She knocked his arm away playfully. "Are you callin' my father a snob?"

"Nah." Mike shook his head. "I'm just not a part of that world, is all."

"In any case you should at least talk to him. He says it's important."

"In any case, I'll have to confront Creaser sooner or later." He shivered at the thought.

"That old fossil?"

"He's my boss, after all. I should talk to him before making a decision."

"If you say so," she said, pulling him close to her. "Whatever you decide, you know I'll support you."

Chapter 62

"YOU WANT TO DO WHAT?" asked Creaser, more than a little surprised.

"Research. I just feel like I'm not cut out for all this administrative work."

"Then what are you cut out for, exactly?"

Mike shifted nervously in his chair. He had vowed not to let Creaser get the best of him this time. Still, listening to the authoritative, confident voice of his superior had already begun to erode his defenses. He steeled his reserve and continued. "I've thought about it a lot, actually. I've always wanted to study the lives of families in the military. Now that there's no longer a draft, we can't just focus on the soldier alone. We have to address the needs of others. The wives and the children, you know?"

Creaser raised an eyebrow. "It's an interesting thought, Major. But you won't find much support. The Pentagon doesn't have time for children. When it comes to the opposite sex, they're only interested in fighting the women's movement and attracting the wives of recruits. That's where the research money goes."

"That's the point!" exclaimed Mike. "It can't always be about discipline and control. These are human beings. The way the military treats women… it's not right!"

"You know as well as I do. It's not about right and wrong. It's about the mission."

"See, that's where you and I disagree, sir. I can't think that way anymore. Not after what happened to Sybil."

The colonel leaned back in his chair. His intense gaze became soft, almost thoughtful. He shook his head sadly. So he does care after all, Mike thought to himself. He had almost forgotten the man's sensitive side.

"That was a terrible thing, what happened to her," muttered Creaser, his voice dripping with contempt. "Off the record, and between you and me, I would have thrown the book at that filthy son-of-a-bitch. His commander too. The trauma they inflicted on that poor girl was terrible. What kind of a man, much less an officer, would do such a thing?"

"And there's nothing to be done?"

"Unfortunately not," Creaser continued. He leaned forward, folding his hands on his desk. "It's always been this way. Commanders rule their men with impunity. It's a savage rule, but it's effective, too. We can't be deployment-ready when we're bogged down in scandals and investigations."

"I just can't accept that," said Mike firmly. "It's just wrong."

"Like I said," responded Creaser, with a trace of agitation, "it's not about right and wrong. We don't have that luxury. In the military, an officer must have the power to command. He has to lead his men without hesitation. Ours is a higher calling. It's about the mission."

"And the women and children? The trauma of the survivors?"

"War is about sacrifice, Major Pike. There has always been collateral damage since warfare began. There always will be."

"Then maybe war isn't the answer. Maybe there are other ways."

The thought had struck Mike suddenly. He blurted it out without thinking, in the heat of the moment. The colonel laughed dismissively.

"You can't really be so naïve, Michael. Come on. I never took you for a peacenik."

"I'm serious!" Mike persisted. "Maybe you feel that violence is the answer, but I don't."

"It's human nature," argued Creaser. "We fight to survive. Mankind evolved through competition. History is written by the victors. The strong, the creative, and the innovative survive, and pass those genetics through generations."

"And that's really how you feel?"

"It's not how I feel. It's how things are. I hate war as much as the next man. But I'm no doe-eyed hippie. I live in the real world, dammit. And the real world is about survival."

Mike was taken aback. The colonel's logic was cold and calculated, but he defended it passionately. The emotion in his words was unmistakable. It's obvious, Mike realized, that Creaser must have felt as he did once. Behind the ruthless officer was an intelligent man; a scholar and a gentleman. There had to be some way to reason with him.

Suddenly, Mike had an epiphany. "So, you're a competitive man, Colonel Creaser?"

"I am."

"And you're disappointed with my decision to leave the Air Force?"

"I admit, I'd like to keep you on, Major," said Creaser. He eyed Mike suspiciously. "But what are you getting at, exactly."

"Well, I have a challenge then, a little wager, if you will. If you win, I'll renew my contract, and I'll focus on my administrative duties."

The lines on Creaser's face drew taut. He scowled thoughtfully. So this was the colonel's poker face, thought Mike nervously. The man regarded him with the predatory glower of a wolf.

"I'll consider it, depending on the conditions," he replied cagily. "But what if you win?"

Mike swallowed a lump in his throat. "If I win, you have to throw your support behind my research efforts, whether I decide to stay or not."

"I'll do you one better," said Creaser with a chuckle. "I'll even fund some of your work myself."

Mike extended his hand. The men shook on it. "Now," Mike began, "here's what I propose..."

Chapter 63

FLAPJACK'S EYES were as big as saucers. Her jaw dropped. "I can't believe it," she gasped, shaking her head. "And more than that... I can't believe he took you up on it!"

"Oh come on," Mike groaned. "I told you before. Colonel Creaser can be a tightwad, but he's a decent man."

"I'll believe it when I see it." Flapjack smirked and folded her menu. The candlelight bathed her face in a warm, angelic glow. "So tell me about this 'Operation Albert.'"

"It's pretty straightforward," he explained. "It's basically an unofficial study group. A forum. Creaser gets to pick two participants. I pick the other two. We meet five times to discuss the nature of war and its causes. After the fifth meeting, we have an anonymous vote. If the group decides that war is a natural element of human evolution, well, Creaser wins. If it's decided that war is antithetical to human nature, then I win."

"And that's all there is to it?"

"That's all there is to it."

"But you'll have six voters," said Flapjack, as she munched on a breadstick. "What if there's a tie."

Mike laughed. "We thought of that. There are actually seven people involved. Six people will be debating, and a neutral seventh individual will witness the arguments and add his vote to the total."

"A neutral participant? Is objectivity even possible?"

"We thought of that. Believe me, it took a while. But we finally agreed on a candidate. You remember Judith, my chief nurse? Well, she used to work under Creaser as well. We both trust her judgment. It seemed like a fair choice."

"And you really trust Creaser?"

"I do. He's an honorable man. He likes a challenge. I wouldn't have asked him if I thought otherwise."

"There's only one more thing I'm curious about," continued Flapjack. Why 'Operation Albert'? Where'd the name come from?"

"You like it?" Mike chuckled. "It was actually Colonel Creaser's idea. He wanted to give the group a codename, you know, just to keep the thing under wraps. Apparently, Albert Einstein was concerned with the nature of war, so that's the moniker he picked."

"But why keep it secret?"

"It seems harmless enough," he agreed. "But others could possibly report it as seditious. There could be serious repercussions from the Pentagon. Creaser could get demoted. Hell, he could even lose his career."

"No way!" Flapjack cried incredulously. "And you still got him to agree to this? Even with so much at stake?"

Mike winked. "Never underestimate the appeal of a good wager," he laughed. It was Creaser who taught him the art of manipulation. How fitting, he thought to himself, that the student should become the master.

*   *   *

Mike collapsed to the mattress. Beside him, Flapjack still panted heavily. The sweet ache of exhaustion washed over him. They both bathed in the after-glow. After a long nap, he was awoken by a gentle pressure on his mouth. He leaned into the kiss and opened his eyes. Flapjack had just finished a shower. Water still dripped from her curls. She smelled like lilacs.

"Mike, have you ever thought of maybe, I dunno, living together?" she asked, as she adjusted the towel snugly around her curves.

"I have, actually," said Mike. "It's a strange thought for me. I've become so used to living on my own! I'd have to get used to sharing my space."

"Well, I told my father about us." Mike looked up at her. She was focused on herself in the mirror, fixing the kinks in her hair.

"Oh? What did he say?"
"He said he could help find us a good home where he is. You know. Near the Agency."

"He really still wants me at the Agency, huh?"

Flapjack smiled. She lay back on the bed and giggled. "Yep. Leave it to my father to turn something into a recruitment opportunity!"

"I like the idea. I really do," said Mike. "But with that wager, and Colonel Creaser, I don't know. It all seems pretty complicated right now. It's tempting to just run away together and elope!"

"Out of the question!" cried Flapjack, in mock severity. "My father would find us within 24-hours. You'd be whisked to a military 'dark zone,' never to be heard from again!"

Mike smirked. "So is this how your dad checks out your boyfriends? Recruits 'em and then investigates their backgrounds? What happens after that?"

"Believe it or not, you're my first! So we'll just have to find out."

"And he disapproved?"

"You're asking a daughter who didn't even know what her father did for a living until just a few years ago. He's a complicated man. Some would even say dangerous," said Flapjack, a note of seriousness creeping into her tone. "But I know him," she added, cheerfully. "He trusts my judgment."

"So does he know… umm… you know…"

"Know what?"

"You know… everything…"

"Jesus, Mike. Just spit it out."

"Does he know we're sleeping together," he asked sheepishly. His cheeks burned. Flapjack burst into laughter.

"Of course he does, honey. He's got satellite cameras on us at all times!"

"Oh, ha ha ha."

"You think I'm kidding," she giggled. "But you never know!"

Chapter 64

NO SECRET WAS SAFE for long. Not in Camp Valkyrie. After two meetings behind closed doors, it became impossible to contain the staff's curiosity. A select few were allowed to sit in for the third conference. A larger room was chosen for the fourth, though Creaser would allow only officers to attend. The group's fifth and final meeting was scheduled in a small auditorium. Finally, Colonel Creaser succumbed to mounting pressure. The final arguments would be open for all to attend.

As Mike expected, the room was packed. It was an audience driven more by curiosity than genuine interest. The fact that Creaser—the man who ran Camp Valkyrie's hospital with an iron fist—would allow for debate seemed ludicrous. Until now, he had built a reputation as a hardliner; a career officer, whose devotion to the military was beyond reproach. For the first time, he seemed almost vulnerable. Almost mortal.

At the center of the table, Creaser adjusted his microphone. "I want to thank you all for attending," he addressed the crowd. "It is my pleasure to introduce our panelists. To my left, Major Lu; Major Kennedy; and the Chief-of-Nursing in Two South, Captain Judith Leonard." There was a brief pause. Some polite applause. "And to my right," Creaser continued, "Our new Chief-of-Psychiatry, Major Pike; Major Moon; and Major Fielder."

"Please," Flapjack added, "just call me Flapjack." There was a titter from the audience. A smatter of applause. Her popularity was obvious.

Creaser shrugged. "Flapjack it is. Now, let's begin."

* * *

Any audience members who had come for a spectacle were quickly disappointed. Creaser opened the discussion with a long, thorough disclaimer. Behind all his rhetoric, Mike knew, were a few essential points. First of all, this was the meeting of a study group, not some anti-war protest. It was neither endorsed nor officially sanctioned by the military. All resource materials were drawn from a list prepared by the War College and the Air Force Academy. He conveniently forgot to mention some 'approved' additions, thought Mike. Texts by Einstein, Freud, and other renowned theorists.

Opening arguments brought a refreshing change of pace. Before the debate, the panelists had drawn numbers from a hat. At the top of the order was Moon. Over the past few weeks, Mike's respect for his friend had grown. Moon was a joker, sure, but behind the levity was a cunning intellect; a natural orator. Creaser left the room frozen in silence, but Moon melted the tension away. The relief was palpable.

Over the course of the debates, Moon had emerged as the champion of psychoanalysis. He had spoken first about the 1933 correspondence between Einstein and Freud on the causes of war. Now, in his final address, he lectured on *Civilization and Its Discontents* (1930), Freud's postwar thesis on the innate savagery of man. It was a difficult text, but the major had a knack for explaining the most complex ideas in plain, everyday English. He had the crowd eating from his palm.

Mike cringed as he listened. More than once he had questioned adding Moon to the panel. Moon was a wildcard. No one knew that better than Mike. And now, over the course of the debates, the man had emerged as Creaser's staunchest ally. Even Creaser's pessimism paled in comparison to Moon's bleak assessment of human nature. He grimly proposed a "bottom-up" theory; the idea that man lived in a state of misery, and each individual longed to fulfill their own desires. Conflict derived from the selfishness of man. It was the "pleasure principle" that drove men to war; to destroy one another in the pursuit of glory and wealth. Only by learning to govern these aggressive and competitive impulses, Moon argued, could humanity ever be salvaged.

* * *

The argument was well-received. Colonel Creaser even rose during the applause, nodding sagely in agreement. His pleasure, however, would be short-lived. Mike smiled as Major Lu adjusted his microphone. Creaser's self-satisfaction evaporated into a scowl. He looked down on the short, hawkish young officer with disdain. Moon's opposition was a disappointment, Mike thought, but at least it wasn't wholly unexpected. Major Lu's betrayal, however, had blindsided poor Creaser. Lu was an ambitious young officer; a fresh-faced recent medical graduate with a quiet, bookish nature. He had a reputation as a staunch conservative. From the beginning, Creaser took his support for granted.

For the first two meetings, the colonel had Lu in his pocket. The major towed the party line. He supported the colonel so completely, that Mike began to wonder if he were reading from a script. There was neither passion nor conviction in his voice. It was during the third meeting that things began to change. Something seemed to awaken in Lu. He began to challenge his commander. From then on, his arguments became more independent; more personal. Even Creaser couldn't deny the man's insight.

Throughout the debates, Moon and Lu had become bitter rivals. Lu challenged Moon's 'bottom-up' argument with his own 'top-down' theory of social control. Unlike his emotional counterpart, Lu was a calculated, logical thinker. He relied on figures and statistics to support the 'Youth Bulge' theory; the idea that, throughout history, the population of adolescents in a region has always correlated with the occurrence of wars. The larger the population, the greater the risk of violence.

The idea fascinated Mike. It made sense, he thought. It was natural that overpopulation would create poverty, scarcity, and unemployment, which would then predictably lead to social unrest, war, and terrorism. It was these circumstances, Lu argued, and not some innate human bloodlust, that led to the devastation of war. In fact, war itself was a relatively recent invention. It was a phenomenon that coincided with the development of the first city-states some 10,000 years ago.

"He has a point," added Flapjack, before they adjourned for a break. "Plenty of anthropologists agree that, before then, people were fairly peaceful. There was relatively little intertribal warfare."

"You've got to be kidding!" argued Kennedy. "Do you follow the news? Have you seen what's happening in Africa and the Middle East?"

"What about them?"

"They're uneducated! Primitive! Those tribal folk are the perfect example of what happens when human instincts run wild. I hate dictators as much as anyone, but it looks to me like some folks aren't ready for good ol' American democracy!"

Mike and Creaser shared a look of concern. Even with Kennedy on his side, the man's bigotry made even the colonel wince. The last thing either of them wanted was for things to get personal, and, from the look of rage on Lu's face, it was already too late.

"I resent that, Major," he said, between his teeth. "My grandparents were North Korean defectors. Are you calling my people savages?"

There was a chorus of boos from the audience. Before Kennedy could retort, Creaser gestured for the mikes to be cut. His commanding address cut off their bickering.

"And with that, ladies and gentleman, we will adjourn for a break!"

Chapter 65

THE INTERMISSION CAME as a welcome relief. Only a few minutes were necessary for the crowd to regain its composure. When Creaser called the proceedings to order, the earlier conflict seemed a distant memory. Cooler heads prevailed.

Then came the moment Mike had been dreading. He knew the others on the panel felt similarly anxious, Creaser in particular. To their relief, Kennedy's talk passed almost entirely without incident. For a racist and a bigot, Mike thought, at least the major had the decency to be a disastrous lecturer. His speech was so absurd and convoluted that Mike had trouble following. The audience seemed confused as well. Kennedy began with an anti-Semitic tirade. From there, he transitioned into a long diatribe against Islamic fundamentalism. His point, he eventually argued, was that these groups showed the primitive side of human nature. It was America—the shining beacon of democracy—that had learned to discipline these savage instincts as a society. The conclusion drew some half-hearted applause for its patriotism.

Flapjack was scheduled next. Just the announcement of her name drew thunderous applause; a few cheers, even; a whistle. Mike was hardly surprised. Camp Valkyrie loved Flapjack as much as it feared Colonel Creaser. Her popularity alone had likely drawn a contingent of supporters. The unpleasantness of Major Kennedy was already forgotten.

For the first time that afternoon, the mood in the auditorium seemed warm; optimistic, even. Those before her spoke darkly of man's inclinations to war. Flapjack, on the other hand, took the opposite approach. Her talk focused instead on the prevention of violence. They had been asking the wrong question, she claimed. Instead, it was important to discuss peace, and how wars could be avoided through reason, understanding, and compassion.

To Flapjack, the answer was simple. The 'Golden Rule.' The practice of 'doing unto others what you would have done unto you' was more than   a

Sunday school lesson. It was a principle that applied to both individuals and societies; a way of life. The idea was familiar to Mike. He had been raised as a Catholic, and heard it a hundred times. The idea had actually developed into a kind of business strategy discussed in boardrooms around the country.

On the other side of the table, Creaser grunted. Lu even chuckled. Even though he applauded, Mike couldn't help sympathizing with his colleagues. It just seemed too simple; too idealistic. He was at least satisfied that he had Flapjack's vote. Even if they were a couple, her support was hardly a given. She was an independent thinker. Still, her argument seemed compatible with his perspective that it was not in man's nature to be warlike.

*   *   *

The speech was well-received. The polite applause grew louder, and more vociferous as the crowd began to understand it was not simply a platitude, but a powerful strategy. First one man rose; then another; and another. It was a standing ovation. Flapjack smiled. She waved appreciatively.

"Quiet! I will have Quiet! Stop this at once!" came from the back of the room.

The furious, belligerent drawl echoed across the auditorium. It had an almost poisonous effect. The room fell awkwardly quiet. Most staffers returned to their seats. Others stood nervously. They watched, as the heckler stumbled towards the podium.

"Treason! This is treason! Damn Commie bastards, the lot of you!" he continued drunkenly. Wielding an empty silver flask, he gestured towards the stage. "I'd expect this from them, damn peacenik hippie scum. But you, Colonel Creaser! You ought to be ashamed of yourself!" He stumbled for-ward and hiccupped.

Mike recognized the voice instantly. Even before he saw the gnarled countenance, he knew. It had only been a few months, but General Snow seemed to have aged a decade. The skin on his soot-stained face was weath-ered and cracked. A thrift store suit too large for him hung from his bones. Mike wondered how security could have missed him. The man looked like—and probably was—a homeless vagrant. Did they recognize him staggering around Valkyrie? Were they afraid to confront him? Mike had heard no one in his family would take him in because he was so damned mean and he "for damned sure wasn't going to any VA where they would steal his organs".

"General Snow! Contain yourself please," ordered Creaser. There was a mix of shock and horror in his voice.

"God damn you, Creaser," ranted Snow. He turned to the audience. "I told 'em. I told 'em all along. Look at all of ya; doctors, chaplains, nurses, the whole lot of ya, a pack of wolves. Talkin' about 'golden rules' n' singin' 'kumbaya.' Operation Albert, my ass. Get your hands offa me!"

Snow struggled, as two guards fought to restrain him. He flailed and clawed at them like a toothless cat. It was an almost comic scene, but those present knew better than to laugh. The audience recoiled in horror.

"We might as well hand over the White House," Snow continued, as he was dragged towards the door. "When folks is turnin' this camp into the Kremlin, god damn. Might as well hand the keys to Chairman Mao and be done with it!"

The door slammed shut. In the distance, Mike could still hear the man's ravings. He was still going on about how he would have them all hung; how they needed to attend the Officer's Christian Fellowship, and allow Jesus into their lives. Eventually, the sound faded into nothing. The room was silent.

"Well," said Creaser finally, "Mike, I believe you're up next."

Moon elbowed his friend playfully. "Good luck topping that one, bud," he whispered.

Chapter 66

COLONEL CREASER GAZED from his office window. He took a long, meditative sip from his drink, and smacked his lips.

"Well, that went about as well as expected."

Mike groaned. He picked up the decanter on the desk. "Mind if I...?"

"Please do. But savor it," said Creaser absently. "There's a place in hell for those who waste good scotch."

Mike choked down the amber liquid in one gulp. He grimaced. It burned his throat like fire. Still, he was eager for any distraction. Anything that took his mind off Operation Albert was a welcome relief.

"Well, we did cover a lot of ground, and our intentions were good."

"Oh yes. And we had got their attention too," replied Creaser. "I got a call from General 'Grasshopper' Van Hassel just before you arrived. I'm not sure what bothered him more; our little study group, or Snow's bad publicity. Either way, he's ordered the group liquidated at once."

"And the vote?"

"Canceled, I'm afraid. Lu, Moon, and even Judith have disavowed the group. Even if everyone were on board, I wouldn't let them. I couldn't put their careers in jeopardy. My days at Valkyrie may be numbered already."

"They don't think you're..."

"A Communist? No. They're not stupid. But others might. And that's even more dangerous. They'll want to nip this in the bud at once."

Mike sighed. He slumped back in his chair. "So there's nothing we can do?"

Creaser turned to face him. To Mike's surprise, a bemused expression played across his face. He seemed not the least bit mortified. "Major Pike, do you know why they call him 'Grasshopper' Van Hassel?"

"The General?" Mike shrugged. "I can't say that I do."

"That's because back in Vietnam, when Charlie shot down his helicopter, he survived for weeks in those jungles. He was a prisoner in the notorious

'Hanoi Hilton'. And do you know how he survived?" Mike looked at him blankly. He shook his head.

"While others starved, he lived on the insects that crawled into his cell. Grasshoppers mostly. But not only grasshoppers. Beetles. Rodents. Anything within arms' reach of the bars."

"But what does that…"

"What does that have to do with us?" hissed Creaser. "Everything. An officer is a survivor. He adapts to the circumstances and uses what he can. Lucky for us, we aren't dealing with the Viet Cong." He shuffled through a drawer and drew out a letter. "I called you here, Major Pike, because I need you to deliver a message."

"A message? To whom."

"To an old friend." Creaser smiled. "An old friend at the Pentagon."

Part IV:
The Rapture Cult

Chapter 67

IT WAS A COLD, grey afternoon when they arrived in D.C. Mike shivered as he stepped from the airport. Snowplows were busily clearing the runways and piling the snow in large dirty icy heaps along the edges. Now, even in his fur-lined coat, he was chilled to the bone.

Flapjack had recognized her family instantly. She had squealed as she rushed from the exit terminal, and into the arms of her father. David was much as Mike remembered him. He appeared much more at home here, than on the beaches of Guam, with his square jaw and chiseled features. As he gathered Flapjack in an embrace, he stared at Mike with frigid intensity. It was a gaze even more powerful than Creaser's, thought Mike; almost wolfish. Two marbles set in sculpted ice.

Beside David, with tears in her eyes, was Flapjack's mother, Anna. Mike recognized her from the pictures. She was smaller than he imagined, and older too, but she had the same kindly, gentle face. When they met, she clasped Mike's hand in her gloves and welcomed him, much to Flapjack's delight. As awkward as he felt, it warmed Mike's heart to see her so happy. Finally, Flapjack was home.

* * *

"Quite a collection, isn't it?" David spoke in slow, measured tones, as if he were considering each word that he spoke. Beside him, a fire crackled in the hearth. He poured another cup of tea.

"It really is!" said Mike in awe. "I've never seen such a collection. It's almost like a museum."

"But a little less musty, I hope." Anna chuckled. "I've been a collector since the war, you know. Since the two of us met in Paris. We were both studying at the Sorbonne. I try to keep each room in the house thematically consistent, you know. But this collection of 19th Century Russian abstracts, ah, it's a personal favorite."

Mike took a long, leisurely sip from the porcelain cup. The amber liquid was rich and herbal. As he sat back, and propped his feet on the ottoman, Mike could have melted into the warmth of the sofa. The Fielder's had a magnificent home; a baroque structure surrounded by hemlock trees and pines. The warmth of the fire and the sound of Mozart piping from the stereo made him drowsy. It had been a long journey.

"I would imagine you're tired," said David, still observing him carefully.

"I am, yes." Mike stifled a yawn. "That was an incredible dinner, Mrs. Fielder. I want to thank you both for welcoming me to your home."

"It's just Anna, dear," she replied, waving her hand modestly. "There's no need for such formalities. We're just so pleased to have you. Flapjack has said so very much, you know!"

"She speaks highly of you," added David. "Anyone who makes my little girl happy is welcome in my home."

"She means the world to me," said Mike, returning the man's gaze. He could still discern a hint of distrust in David's voice. As if his words were as much a warning as a welcome.

"I certainly hope so."

* * *

A loud knock on the door woke Mike from his slumber. He groaned and turned to the clock. It was six in the morning. Before he could respond, there was another, more insistent series of knocks.

"Michael, are you awake?" Mike grunted in response. "I'll need you ready in a half-hour," the voice continued. David's gruff tone was unmistakable. "We have sensitive business to conduct."

Mike shuffled reluctantly to the shower. He tried to will his mind out of entropy, with little success. Flapjack was sitting up in bed when he returned. There was a tired smile on her face.

"I'm sorry about father," she offered sympathetically. "I know how he seems."

"How he seems?!" Mike groaned. He collapsed on the bed. "I feel like I have to sleep with one eye open!"

She giggled. "You're not scared of him, are you?"

"I'd be stupid not to be," he replied, smiling weakly.

"Because he's at the Agency?"

"Because he's your father."

Flapjack sighed. She leaned over him and stroked his chest. "You're every bit as strong as he is," she reassured him. "You might not realize it, but he sees something in you. Something important. He just has a... different way of showing it."

"If you say so."

"Tell me, Mike, did you get a chance to see the backyard?"

Mike cocked his head. "No... why?"

"My father has a birdfeeder hanging from one of the hemlock trees. As long as I can remember, he always loved to watch the birds come in the evening. He loved their songs. He even gave them names."

"Your dad never seemed the sentimental type."

"He's learned to conceal his emotions," Flapjack continued. "But he loved those birds. Then the squirrels came. They attacked one at a time, scampering off with the seeds, chasing away the cardinals and wood thrushes. I was still a little girl, but I remember my father's war with those squirrels." Flapjack giggled. There was a faraway look in her eye.

"He used to lay out these elaborate plans. There were traps, poisons, exterminators. He used every strategy at his disposal. I thought it was all pretty silly. But dad was relentless."

Mike raised an eyebrow. "Is that story supposed to make me feel better?"

"It's supposed to give you an idea of who my father is. There are two kinds of people in his life. He has to decide for himself if you're a songbird or a squirrel. When he realizes I love you, you'll be part of the family."

"I hope you're right," said Mike. He shook his head. "I really do."

Chapter 68

"WE'RE HERE," DAVID announced, as he pulled his Mercedes into a dusty parking lot. As he examined his surroundings, Mike was more than slightly concerned. The drive had taken them far from the suburbs, and deep into the inner city, past vacant lots and abandoned homes. The place hardly seemed like prime real estate. But then, Mike thought to himself, what better place for a group like the CIA than here, the land that time forgot.

Mike followed behind, as David passed under the sign for the "Playboy Club," a garish neon display with a martini glass and a stiletto. The door jingled as it opened. To Mike, the interior seemed like any cheap dive on a Monday morning. A single, hung-over customer sat hunched over the bar. The bartender was busy scrubbing the countertops. It was dimly lit, and a jukebox in the corner rattled a familiar tune.

David snapped his fingers. He and the barkeep nodded to one another. To his unease, Mike noticed that the patron was squinting at him, as if trying to read his intentions. It was a relief when David finally led him to the back room of the establishment. The air in the small office was musty, but it was better than the acrid smell of smoke and cheap cologne in the bar. Finally, Mike could breathe easy.

It was cramped in the manager's office, and the presence of bookshelves and filing cabinets only made it more claustrophobic. The sound of their chairs scraping on concrete was like nails on a chalkboard. Both he and David sat across from two other men. Mike recognized the first from Guam. Mr. Colbert had a beard now, but his pinched features and lazy eye gave him away. The other man, however, was unfamiliar to Mike. Like Colbert, he wore a finely tailored suit, but he was at least a half a foot taller, with a receding hairline. He seemed to regard Mike with mild curiosity.

"Mr. Fielder, Major Pike, it's a pleasure to have you here," said Colbert. "You may remember me from Guam," he added, as he shook Mike's hand.

"My colleague here, well, he's here to observe. His identity is not of concern."
The stranger nodded slowly in agreement. He had already found a folder to
distract himself.

"Thanks!" said Mike amiably. "I'm mostly here on business from Camp
Valkyrie, but David—I mean, Mr. Fielder—said you wanted to talk to me."

"You were recently promoted, Major Pike, were you not?" asked Colbert,
his hands clasped on his desk.

"Well, sort of."

"Well, were you, or weren't you?"

"Well, I did take over after my former section chief had a heart attack,"
said Mike defensively. "But I'm just filling in for now on an interim basis.
My military contract is almost up."

"So, yes. You were promoted."

"I suppose so."

"Are you aware, Major Pike, that there was a full class ahead of you?"

"Well, yes…"

"But your commanding officer chose you. Why? It's proper custom to
award promotion based on seniority. I want to know why your CO broke
tradition. What's so special about you, Major Pike?"

Mike opened his mouth to argue. Before he could speak, he was surprised
to hear David rise to his defense.

"Now Sam, you know as well as I that seniority isn't that important when
active duty is two years. Anyone left from the draft just wants out. Wouldn't
it only make sense to promote the best candidate? Especially with so many
volunteer recruits to be trained."

Colbert bit his lip in thought. It was obvious, from his wide-eyed look,
that he considered David a man to be respected, even feared. "I suppose
you're right," he conceded. "You know you wouldn't be here, in this office,
if we didn't consider you an exceptional candidate," he continued, turning
to Mike. "From that suicide rescue to your work in Guam, your record has
been exceptional."

"But I don't understand," said Mike. He was beginning to grow frustrated.
"I'm here to meet with the Surgeon General. You're asking me if I want to
work for you?"

Before Colbert could answer, the man beside him dropped his folder on
the table. All eyes turned towards him in surprise. "Mike, can I call you
Mike?" he began, without waiting for an answer. "Good. Well, Mike, before

we go any further, I have to ask you a few questions. First, did you belong to any clubs or organizations in college?"

"I joined the Young Democrats. Phi Delta Theta in college. Phi Chi in med school."

"A Democrat," quipped David. "My wife will certainly like that."

"Did you ever protest the war?" the man continued. "Can you think of any reason that would disqualify you for a high security clearance?"

"Not that I know of…"

The man smiled benignly. "Good, good," he mused, nodding to himself. "Well, Mike, as you can probably imagine, this is only one of our haunts. The CIA has a number of offices throughout the D.C. area. This office is working on transitioning the U2 spy plane to new military programs."

"The U2 program?" Mike gasped. "I read about that in the news! I thought it was discontinued years ago, back when Gary Powers bailed over Russia and didn't take the cyanide pill."

"Fifteen years, to be precise," the man groaned. "But we made a lot of modifications and tightened security. Thanks to that, the U2 is still flying high. It's our greatest source of intel." He stabbed a finger towards Mike. "That, my friend, is where you come in."

"Me?"

"Mike, this program is critical to national security. The amount of data we process each day is immense. We can basically keep tabs on everything in the air, on the ground, and below sea level. What we don't have is a way of seeing into the future. That's what we need."

"What, like fortune tellers?"

"Precisely!" the man exclaimed, clapping his hands together. "But I want science, not magic. I want a man who can think two steps ahead of a Castro or a Khrushchev. Someone who can tell me what our enemies are thinking. A psychological weapon."

"And you picked me," Mike laughed aloud. He could no longer contain himself. "Are you crazy," he continued, as he regained composure. "Don't you have a psychoanalytic institute here in DC? Why not talk to them."

"Because you bring a commodity that can't be found at the institute."

"Trust," said David, before Mike could ask.

"Yes. Trust. It's a rare thing these days," the man agreed. "There's no one there we can be completely sure of. We need fresh ideas from a department outsider. And from what David tells us, that man is you."

"But I wasn't even the smartest guy in med school."

"No," snapped Colbert, with more than a trace of annoyance. "You finished 7th. And since two people ahead of you were caught cheating, that moves you to the top-5. Do you think we haven't done our homework? We know your life history. All your test scores, from preschool to med school. Your SAT scores were superlative. You aced the MCAT as well."

"What Sam is trying to say," said David, shooting Colbert an icy look, "is that we know what you're capable of. When it comes to national security, there's no room for modesty."

Chapter 69

MIKE SAT LISTLESSLY. He watched the bubbles floating in his beer. David still had some business with his CIA colleagues, and Mike felt more than a little like a child waiting for his parent. Earlier, it would have annoyed him, but at this point he just wanted to get things over with. Something about Colbert and his associate rubbed him the wrong way. There had been a patronizing tone to the entire interview. They spoke as if his fate had been decided for him; as if it were just a matter of briefing him on his duties. He couldn't wait to be rid of them.

"Hey there Mike! I bought another round. It's the least I could do."

David shuffled awkwardly into the booth. His body knocked the table, causing him to spill from both glasses. Drops of amber liquid splattered on Mike's jacket.

"Oof, sorry about that. I'm not as limber as I used to be!"

"That's okay," Mike reassured him. Flapjack's father seemed terribly out of place in a run-down strip club. Even in the ratty old booth, he still sat rigidly at attention, as if programmed to do so.

"How about that Colbert, eh?" he smiled awkwardly. "Trust me, Sam means well. He's been in the business a long time. That... well, that has its effects on a man."

Mike rolled his eyes. "You're telling me."

"I feel like we—like I—have been a bit too hard on you, Mike," said David. His voice seemed softer now, as though he were addressing family.

"Don't worry about it."

"No really. It takes a lot of courage. You've been good to my daughter, and it's obvious that she cares about you. I'm sure you must feel like a fish out of water here, so far from home, and surrounded by distrust and suspicion."

Mike chuckled nervously. He was already on his third beer, and it was just starting to take the edge off. "Now that you mention it, I do feel rather

out of place. I don't understand why they'd want me. I'm just not their...
type. You know?"

"We have a type?" David frowned. "The CIA doesn't have a type, Mike."

"You know," Mike persisted, awkwardly. "I always heard that the Agency
had their pick of the Ivies. I'm not from Yale or Harvard. I'm just a southern
boy; always have been."

David shuffled nervously. The movement was subtle; almost imperceptible. A rare moment of weakness that took Mike by surprise. For the first time
since his arrival, Mike wondered, had he finally found a chink in the armor?
Until now, David had seemed almost impenetrably detached.

David brushed the foam from his lip. He leaned in towards Mike, his
voice barely more than a whisper. "I'll be honest, Michael. I don't trust you,
not yet. Don't take it personally. But I feel I owe it to you — to my daughter —
to tell you what's going on."

"What's going on?"

"Keep your voice down!"

"Sorry."

"Yes, what's going on. I mean, an honest explanation."

"I don't understand," Mike whispered back. "I thought."

"Not here!" David hissed. "In the car. They can't hear us there."

* * *

Mike gasped. His first impulse had been to laugh out loud. It was too strange
to be true. One look at David, however, and Mike knew he was being serious.
There was no room for modesty in the CIA, and Mike had learned there was
no place for humor, either. All the same, it seemed too far-fetched to be real.

"You're kidding me?"

"Mike, do I strike you as a man who kids around?"

"But how did you..."

"DNA. Our scientists made a lot of progress in the seventies," David
explained. "In the eighties I imagine it'll revolutionize our society. You'd be
surprised."

"But how..."

"The blood sample from your Air Force physical. It was just a quick call
to the archives."

"...How is it even relevant, is what I was going to ask."

David let out a long sigh. "Michael, it's a long story. You know what you said about the CIA picking only the elite?"

"Yeah."

"Well, you were right, in a sense. But we don't just pick from the top schools. Back when the CIA began, it was more of a brotherhood. They chose men they believed to be true patriots. In those days, that meant anyone who could trace their lineage to the founding fathers."

"So if this is true, are you…"

"No, not me," David continued. "The agency expanded. The policy is a bit looser now. If you have the right credentials, it all comes down to who you know. I got in via referral."

"You're really serious about this?"

"Yep. Back then, if your ancestors weren't carried over on the Mayflower, you didn't have a chance. The pilgrim descendants and Congregationalists held the real power in New England. They only trusted their own."

Mike stared out the window as he listened. They had left the inner-city far behind them. Here, in the DC suburbs, each mansion seemed more elaborate than the last. It was a paradise of golf courses, country clubs, and manicured lawns. A world he found wholly unfamiliar.

"So, if this is true, I wasn't recruited for my abilities," said Mike. He was surprised to find that his pride was wounded. After all he had never wanted the job to begin with!

"Would that bother you?"

"Well, to be honest, yes. I would have hoped I'd have something of value to offer."

"Mike, you and Thomas Jefferson have the same DNA. We don't understand it yet, but you're somehow closely related." David exclaimed. "You're more valuable than you could possibly realize!"

Chapter 70

THE REMAINDER OF the ride was spent in silence. David turned on the radio, and the two of them listened to the local news. Despite his gratitude, Mike felt a gnawing sense of frustration. What did it all mean? How could he understand his purpose—his 'value'—if David wasn't willing to tell him? One look told him not to press the issue. From the grimness of the man's face, it seemed as if he had revealed too much already. The thought only fueled Mike's anxieties. A dark sense of foreboding overwhelmed him.

* * *

"Another glass of merlot?"

Mike snapped out of his reverie. He had been so mesmerized by the painting, he failed to hear Anna approaching. The red of her dress matched the lipstick of her smile.

"Oh! No, thank you. I probably shouldn't have had the one," he answered sheepishly. "Mr. Fiel... I mean, David and I had a few earlier."

Anna rolled her eyes. "At that awful club I'd imagine. I'm so glad you could attend this WPA show with us, Michael. At least you can see we have some culture in Washington!"

"Oh come now!" exclaimed David. He was escorting Flapjack on his arm. The other hand held a martini, and his cufflinks gleamed beneath the chandelier. "Anna, you and I both know the WPA was a project of Roosevelt's, and he was as down to earth as they come! I heard he may have even had a mistress, in fact."

"He's got you there, mom," giggled Flapjack. She winked at Mike. "This was all founded by a *real* man, not some fancy intellectual!"

Anna gasped in mock-surprise. "Why, Flapjack! You know as well as anyone he was a genius..."

"Oh Anna, she's just kidding," laughed David. He squeezed Flapjack affectionately. "She is her father's daughter after all!"

"Hmph, daddy's little girl!" said Anna, shaking her head. "You know I've always been a fan of his. I just think we shouldn't have gone to war when we did."

"Well you know what Churchill said," laughed Mike.

"What's that?"

"That 'Americans always do the right thing... They just try out all the alternatives first!"

The four of them shared a laugh. Anna clapped her hands together in delight. She wagged a bejeweled finger at Flapjack.

"Now see dear, it looks like you fell for one of those *intellectuals*," she quipped. "I heard about your so-called 'Operation Albert.' And I can't tell you how impressed I was with your literary argument!"

"We were both impressed." David nodded. "My wife in particular. She's a rabid pacifist. Myself, I'm a military man at heart. But any man who can appreciate Hemingway is a friend of mine."

"He loves his Hemingway," added Anna. "But even a manly-man like him loathed the horrors of war."

"Oh mom!"

"No, I'm serious! Personally, I liked your references to the post-WWI poets. 'Dulce et Decorum Est' is a personal favorite.

David snorted. "You can have your modernists, dear," he argued. He took the olive from his glass, popping it in his mouth. "I'll take the Victorians any day."

"Hush, dear," warned Anna, no longer in a joking mood. "You've had a bit to drink, and you're a bit loud!" Mike had to agree. He had never heard David speak so emotionally. The effect was unsettling.

"Nonsense," David announced, raising his glass. "A toast to the man who said it best! Lord Tennyson:

> Not tho' the soldier knew,
> Someone had blundered.

More than a few bystanders were watching. Flapjack looked at Mike helplessly. Even Anna was cringing. David seemed to revel in the attention.

Theirs not to make reply
Theirs not to reason why
Theirs both to do and die."

* * *

Mike leaned over the balcony. The cold granite felt like sandpaper on his forearms. Across the veranda, a small lake reflected the moonlight. The sky seemed darker here, he thought to himself. He could only see a fraction of the stars that glistened over the coast.

As he felt the cool, northern air against his cheeks, Mike tried to collect his thoughts. Things seemed to be happening too fast. David was right, he knew. He was a small fish in a big pond. There was no telling what predators lurked in its depths.

So what now? He asked himself. His first instincts were to run. To get as far away as possible. Even as he considered it, he knew it was impossible. This was the CIA. If they needed him, they would find him, no matter where he went. He thought of Flapjack. She seemed so happy here! All at once, his mind was made up. So long as he felt threatened, Mike reasoned, it was better to stay close to his allies. David could protect him, at least. Flapjack would have her home. They would look out for one another.

A gust of wind whipped through Mike's hair. If only he knew more, he thought to himself; then he wouldn't feel so helpless, so uncertain. His mind drifted back to David's drunken recital. Mike knew the poem well. He had memorized 'The Charge of the Light Brigade' in high school, for god's sake. Now, standing alone, the last stanza echoed ominously in his mind.

Boldly they rode and well
Into the jaws of death
Into the mouth of hell.

Chapter 71

MIKE EXAMINED HIMSELF in the mirror. Once more, he tightened his tie and adjusted his collar. There was still one last object, one final task before his return to Valkyrie. Creaser himself had sent Mike to meet with the Surgeon General on his behalf. The purpose of the meeting was anyone's guess. However, he could hardly expect to just waltz into the most guarded fortress in America!

Flapjack advised him to consult her father. After all, the Pentagon was just an hour from the house. She was not so naïve as to think her father didn't have regular business there. If anything, she told Mike, they'd likely given him his own office even if he was Agency! Mike shivered at the thought. An entire building of Fielder and Colbert look-alikes, marching through cold, dark hallways. What transpired behind those fortified walls? If anyone knew, Mike thought to himself, it was David.

Mike raised the issue over breakfast. David, who was shoveling through a bowl of cornflakes, hardly batted an eye. It was Anna who seemed to perk up at the mention of the Pentagon. She looked to Mike, and then turned warily to her husband. He continued to chew his cereal with military precision.

"More orange juice, Mike?" he asked, after swallowing a mouthful.

Mike turned to Flapjack. "Dad," she persisted, "did you hear what Mike was asking?"

"Dear, you know we don't discuss that business at the table," said Anna curtly. She dabbed her mouth with a handkerchief. "If your father has anything to discuss…"

"What is there to discuss?" interrupted David. "Mike needs to meet someone, I'm headed in that direction today. I'm sure I can talk to someone who can let him in."

"Just like that?" asked Mike in disbelief. He had expected more resistance, or at least a modicum of suspicion or curiosity. This was the most heavily guarded base in the country! And yet David seemed to treat it like a trip to the park.

"I'll be leaving in ten, Mike," announced David, as he brought his dish to the sink. "Please be ready by then."

*   *   *

The trip to the Pentagon was a long and complicated one. From David's efficiency, Mike could tell it had become a practiced ritual. First was the bus ride to the city, then a long, winding walk through the crowded downtown streets. Finally, David hailed a taxi, which would take them to the outskirts of the base. That was the closest any civilian was allowed to the Pentagon. A car was waiting beside the barbwire fence.

"I'm sorry I snapped," whispered David reluctantly, as the two sat in the waiting room. Behind the desk, a secretary with horn rimmed glasses and too much makeup regarded them carefully.

"It's fine."

"No really, I know you're new at this. But don't ever talk to anyone about what you're doing or where you're going, not when you're visiting a place like this."

"Is it because he was..."

"No, it's not because he was Muslim!" hissed David. "He could have been from outer space. My point is, when a cabbie asks about the Pentagon, you keep your mouth shut."

"Were we being watched?" asked Mike. He felt profoundly uncomfortable in the cold, metal chair.

"We're always being watched. Always. Never forget that, Michael."

Chapter 72

THE OFFICE OF the Surgeon General was hardly different than the lobby. It was a large, windowless room that smelled faintly of disinfectant. In one corner of the room was a great brass statue of a gold eagle, next to a display case of plaques, pictures, artifacts, and awards from a variety of foreign diplomats and politicians. Above the mahogany desk hung a large American flag; beneath it, in a gilded frame, was a portrait of the President. It was the man sitting below the picture, however, that took Mike aback. Instantly, he recognized the pinstripe suit, the receding red hair, even the scar over the left eye. It was Colbert's fellow interrogator, from back at the club. The mysterious stranger! He grinned.

"A pleasure to see you again, Major Pike."

"Likewise," mumbled Mike, shaking his hand.

David sat back in one of the black leather chairs. "Major Pike, allow me to introduce my esteemed colleague," he chuckled, tossing a mint in his mouth. "But you've already been acquainted with Dr. MacArthur."

"Oh do sit down," the man offered pleasantly. "It's a pleasure to meet you, Mike. May I call you Mike?"

"Well…"

"Fantastic! Well, Mike, Mr. Fielder prefers formality, but I'm not nearly so stuffy. My friends call me Benson. Everyone else calls me Dr. Surgeon General," He winked, sliding a bowl of mints towards him.

To Mike's surprise, David seemed at ease with the Surgeon General. He was leaning back in his chair, a bemused expression on his face. When he spoke, his tone was affable, even playful! As though the two were brothers or old friends.

"Stuffy, am I, Mac? I prefer to call it discipline."

"You're one to talk, Dave." Benson turned to Mike again. "I'm certain you saw him seducing poor Ms. Brooks at the front desk. That ol' Lothario is incorrigible."

Mike tried to hide his laughter. There was some truth behind Benson's retort. David loved his wife, but he possessed a magnetic charm around women, and he knew it. Flapjack and Anna joked about it themselves. Mike had begun to wonder if it were because David was everything he was not; muscular, rugged, stoic and chivalrous. Compared to Flapjack's father, he felt more like a boy than a man.

Mike began to giggle along with Benson's laughter. One look at David, however, and his smile evaporated.

"You think, that's funny, Michael?"

"Oh, no sir..." Mike sputtered.

"So you don't like the Surgeon General? He doesn't amuse you?"

The amusement on Benson's face fell. In an instant, he seemed deadly serious. There was a moment of silence.

"Oh, stop torturing the kid, Dave!" cried Benson, as he bellowed with laughter.

"It's too much fun, Mac. It's just too easy!"

Mike was bewildered for a moment. It was almost surreal, watching these powerful men laughing like schoolboys. A flood of relief washed over him. He hoped to never feel a moment of terror like that again. It was the instinctive, primal feeling of fear.

*   *   *

"But enough kidding around," said Benson, wiping a tear from his eye. "Let's get down to brass tacks, shall we? Do you understand why you're here, Mike?"

Mike swallowed. It took him a moment to find his tongue. "I have to admit, I'm confused Dr... I mean, Benson. I mean, I don't understand why you were at the interview? And I don't know why Colonel Creaser sent me in his stead."

"You have no idea why?" Benson frowned. He cocked an eyebrow at his friend. "How much did you tell him, David?"

Mike opened his mouth. Before he could speak, he felt the toe of David's shoe jab into his ankle. He fell silent.

"Nothing we didn't go over in the interview." David shrugged.

"Well, ol' Creaser and I go back a long ways," Benson explained. "I've been watching you for a while, Mike, ever since David brought you to my attention. So we made a bit of a deal. He transfers you to my DC office, and I make his little—well, his 'problem'—disappear."

"His problem?"

"A little debacle called 'Operation Albert,'" said David dryly. Mike winced internally.

"That was my fault. Not his."

"Hey, no one is here to point fingers," laughed Benson. "I ought to thank you actually. This couldn't have come at a better time. Judging from your composure during your interview, I have no doubts you're just the man for the job."

Mike regarded him warily. "And what job would that be?"

"The reason Creaser and I became acquainted was because of our work on the U2 program at Valkyrie," Benson explained. "To be frank—and this is sensitive information—there's been a breach of intel there. Quite a grievous breach, in fact. We have reason to believe that one of the pilots has been leaking information to his girlfriend. At least, he *claims* she's his girlfriend."

"That bastard knows better," snapped David. "To make things worse, we've confirmed that she's been passing information to a third party. We're not sure who."

"That's about the long and short of it, yes."

"But I still don't understand," said Mike. "What exactly is my roll in this? What do you want from me?"

Benson withdrew a pack of cigarettes from his trousers. "We have reason to believe the woman is a Soviet operative, or somehow connected to one, at least," he continued, as if oblivious to Mike's questions. "I don't know if she's being blackmailed or paid for her cooperation, and frankly, I don't care. The U2 program is one of the few valuable resources we can count on, and this problem needs to be fixed. Now."

The Surgeon General paused and exhaled. A thin cloud of blue-grey smoke hung in the air. There was a moment of quiet among them. Mike turned from David to Benson, but could read nothing in their cold, hard stares. The levity of just a few minutes earlier seemed already a distant memory.

"You seem perplexed, Mike. Let me explain," Benson continued. "They want to know more than just our activities. If they tap into our U2 program, they can access even more confidential material—info on our satellites, our missile defense system—they can interrupt air traffic control and naval communication. Pull one thread and the rest begins to unravel. Too much data in the wrong hands…"

"...could be disastrous," Mike finished.

"Exactly. So think of this as something of an audition, Mike. This should be a good test of your abilities."

"You still haven't told me what..."

"The pilot in question is scheduled for a routine psychiatric evaluation," Benson interrupted. "You will be conducting this interview at Camp Valkyrie. Find out what he knows and what he doesn't."

"Excuse me?"

"Get inside the man's mind, Mike. Figure out what makes him tick."

"But I don't understand," Mike objected. "What about patient confidentiality? My duty as a physician?"

"Issues of national security take precedence," answered Benson firmly. "As you're no doubt aware, all medical records—psychiatric evaluations included—are open to commanders."

Mike rubbed his chin thoughtfully. He needed time to think. On the one hand, he felt conflicted, but on the other, he was elated. Here, before him, was the Surgeon General of the United States, and he needed his help! The thought gave him a feeling of pride.

"Well, Mike? Do you have any concerns?"

"How do you feel about all this, David?" asked Mike. He turned beseechingly towards Flapjack's father. If anyone could offer guidance at a time like this, Mike thought, it had to be David. He had already begun to consider him a mentor.

David stared back. His gaze softened, as if registering Mike's uncertainty. "You don't have to do it," he said finally. "But if you don't want the mission, now's the time to say so."

"This doesn't feel right," said Mike. He let out a long sigh. "But I'll do it. For national security reasons. However, anything he doesn't say about the matter will be kept confidential."

"Wonderful!" exclaimed Benson. Elated, he rose from his chair, thrusting his hand towards Mike. "It's a pleasure to have you aboard and, by the way, you are to report to Wright –Pat before you return to Valkyrie."

Chapter 73

THE ROUTE LEAVING the Pentagon, as Mike was to learn, differed greatly from their initial journey. Two silent cab rides were followed by a long walk and a noisy few miles on the metro. David stopped by the Playboy Club on the drive home, which was as quiet and empty as usual. This time they were met by the squeal of a tall, leggy stripper, dolled up like a bunny.

"Oh my stars! If it ain't sweet D!" she cried, sidling up to David. "What brings you 'round these parts, soldier?"

"Now Rhonda, don't tempt me! You know I'm a married man!"

"And who's this sweet young thing? You want a dance, sugar?"

Mike smiled awkwardly. "Ah, no thanks, ma'am."

"Don't mind Rhonda," said David, when they were out of earshot. "She works for us. Everyone at the club works on our payroll."

"Everyone?"

"Everyone. Even the fellow in Chicago. It's all taken care of."

Mike watched David shuffle through the cabinets in the back room. "It seems like nothing is what it seems around here," he said uneasily.

"How do you mean?"

"Everyone is someone else, or has some hidden agenda."

David chuckled. "You learn that fast here in the capitol," he said, pulling the file he was looking for. "Keep on your toes and know who you can trust. We're all liars here."

* * *

"They've been to that awful Playboy Club again," said Anna coolly.

"Now Anna…"

"I can tell from the glitter on your sleeves, dear," she continued, sipping her wine. "You know I don't approve of that place."

Flapjack's jaw dropped. "Father!"

"Oh hush." David rolled his eyes. "Your mother knows as well as I that the club is a front. Heck, half of Eastern Europe probably knows by now."

"It's true," said Anna with a smirk. She winked at Mike. "They've usually packed up shop and moved by now."

"It'll be moved soon, dear."

"Oh David, you know I'm not a prude!" Anna laughed. "Gloria Steinem worked for the CIA in the 60s and dressed up as a dancer. I defer to her judgment."

"Well, I'm glad she approved of our business," chuckled David, with a mouthful of steak. "She's certainly done my marriage a great service."

"She's an amazing woman. You, my dear, have merely held my interest through the years."

Mike laughed along with the family. He wished he understood how they did it. How, he wondered, could David be the same intimidating man from the Agency? It was as if he changed emotions on a dime. From the outside, the Fielders appeared like any ordinary suburban family. At the dinner table, neither Anna, Flapjack, nor David seemed to have a care in the world.

"I have to ask a question."

The laughter died down. All eyes turned to him.

"I want to know how you manage all the secrets," he continued. "Flapjack and I have a trusting, loving relationship; there are no secrets between us. Now I'm talking to secret agents, and being placed in a situation where I need to worry about our safety."

"Oh, Mike," said Flapjack softly.

"I want to keep her safe. David, my word is my bond, but I need to know how you and Anna handle secrets."

David stared pensively at the tablecloth. "Well, let's see," he began, picking idly at his vegetables. "I took the oath and I have to take the polygraphs, not Anna, so I try to leave my work at the office."

"But when it affects your safety?"

He shrugged. "Most of it is pretty boring anyway. Stuff like the schematics of a Russian sub, or which aircraft use electronic flaps, you know? And besides," he added slyly, "you wouldn't share your patients' secrets, would you?"

"Not until now," Mike replied. "Now I'm told I have to, for national security reasons."

Flapjack gasped. "Is that true, Dad?"

"Now honey," said David, a trace of annoyance in his voice. "Even Mike has to admit, patient confidentiality goes out the window when it threatens the safety of others, and besides," he sighed, "it was more interesting during the Cold War, anyway. The Chinese are efficient, but damn if they just aren't as sexy as the Russians!"

Mike forced a polite chuckle. Anna excused herself to the kitchen. To Mike's surprise, she seemed almost as annoyed as her husband. He couldn't blame her. After all, she was the child of a different generation, no matter how independent a person she was. Domestic harmony came first.

"Really, Dad?" Flapjack persisted. "A joke about the Cold War crisis? Isn't that a bit tasteless?"

"You don't have to tell me, Flapjack, dear. I went through the worst of it," said David icily. "I've taken care of this family through good and bad times, and I'll continue to do so. I am still your father after all. There are some things you don't need to know."

"For my own good?" shot Flapjack.

"Yes. For your own good!"

A deathly pall fell over the table. All that could be heard was the clatter of utensils on crockery; the faint sound of Beethoven from the sitting room. Mike could have cut the tension in the room with a knife. He had never seen Flapjack stand up to her father.

"So..." he said uneasily. "Dessert smells lovely."

Chapter 74

FLAPJACK WENT WITH MIKE to the Flight Surgeon school at Wright-Patt to take a communications course herself. Creaser had kindly granted her the TDY. Mike was happy to have her in the quarters as he read up on the physiology of flight. His interest in it surprised him, but then he had to take a section on the mental stress of flight—being a psychiatrist, he was the only one in the class. It was rigorous, but he finished and got his wings. Flapjack looked at them. "Pretty," she said. "Your Caduceus has sprouted wings."

The return to Camp Valkyrie felt like a vacation. Mike felt a sense of relief the moment the plane touched down. Flapjack, on the other hand, was reluctant to leave the East. For much of the flight she stared forlornly at the clouds. As he watched her, Mike's conscience felt a twinge of guilt. After all, he had hardly been mistreated. David and Anna had been gracious hosts. The DC area itself was a vibrant cultural center with a thriving art scene. It was unlike anything he had experienced in the South. Still, try as he might, Mike couldn't help feeling painfully out of place. He was far from home; a stranger in a strange land. It was good to be back.

It was Mike's idea to move in together. They pooled their resources and leased an apartment in town. It was nothing fancy, but it was their first real home, just a half-hour from Camp Valkyrie. Their first few weeks together were a revelation to Mike. He had always been an introvert, ever since childhood. For the first time, he began to learn that a close, intimate relationship was possible. Flapjack was understanding and patient to a fault. She had a deeply empathic nature, and knew just how to handle his anxieties and concerns. Her calming influence did wonders for his peace of mind.

At first, Mike had worried about losing his privacy. Would they grow bored of one another, he wondered, after sharing a bed each night, and a bathroom each morning. He was relieved to find quite the opposite. Each day she seemed more beautiful than the last. She had a complex and challenging mind. When she took off her uniform and her coke-bottle glasses, she was the most beautiful woman he had ever seen. He had fallen in love.

Mike's conscience was divided. The longer they lived together, the guiltier he felt. There was nothing base or shallow about Flapjack. She was open and honest. More and more, the thought of keeping secrets from her—even for the sake of national security—became increasingly untenable. After a month on leave, Mike's mind was made up. He had decided against joining the CIA. Whatever threatened them, from Washington or elsewhere, they would face it together, the two of them.

*   *   *

"Well, well, if it isn't our ol' Chief of Psychiatry!" boomed Creaser, shaking Mike's hand. "I suppose you missed us, up there with your fancy new colleagues!"

"What can I say? Texas is my home," laughed Mike. "I even missed the humidity!"

"And how is the Surgeon General?"

"He's doing well! He was surprisingly warm and cordial,"

"Ah," said Creaser, nodding. "It's charisma like that that moves you up the ranks. And I heard you stayed with the Fielders? I remember David from a few years back and Colbert, I knew him in Vietnam."

"Yes sir."

"So you liked them? They didn't intimidate you or anything?"

"No sir, not really," Mike lied.

"Well they should, they're dangerous men. You don't get to their position without leaving a few skeletons in the closet."

Mike looked for traces of humor in Creaser's face. As usual, he found none. Then again, Mike thought, he was only being told what he already knew.

"I met Fielder back when the U2 program was in its infancy," the colonel continued. "I was a flight surgeon attached to that unit. He was a major back then, much like you are. Sharp as a tack. He went on to serve as our liaison with the CIA after they recruited him. So he told you about the program?"

"Yes sir, he did."

"It's still small, but it's of vital importance. Valkyrie serves as what's known as 'SAC', a 'Strategic Air Command' base, but we train two U-2 pilots a year, and the selection process is intense. This is the first problem we've had in five years of operation. I trust you were briefed in DC?"

"I was," answered Mike. "David gave me the man's personnel file."

"It won't be easy. You'll be interviewing one of our elite."

"I saw. Lieutenant Phillips was top of his class. A spotless record. What's still a mystery to me is this woman he's been seeing."

Creaser frowned. "We know little enough about her, which is rare in itself," he mused. "The Pentagon has been tracking the leak for almost a year. The evidence led to Phillips, who in turn led them to his partner. What we know is that she was in a two-year marriage with another military man. She was born in Boston. Lived there most of her life."

"Boston?"

"That's all we know."

"And the ex?"

"A former Captain. Discharged for undisclosed reasons. He's living in Germany."

"Could there be a link there?"

"We're not sure," said Creaser, after a moment's thought. "We really can't be sure where the rabbit hole will lead. These agencies aren't stupid. They know how to cover their tracks."

Mike pursed his lips. He skimmed over some papers Creaser had given him. It was nothing he didn't already know. "I'll do whatever I can, sir," he offered, as noncommittally as he could manage. He felt as though he were treading in uncharted waters. Time would only tell if he was in too deep.

"Good man, Major Pike. I'm sure we can count on you."

* * *

Mike listened to the dial tone. His mouth felt dry. He rehearsed the lines he had planned in his head. If only he had written them down! It was too late to turn back now. He knew better than to hope for the answering machine. David always answered his phone. It rarely got past the third ring.

"Hello. State your name and purpose of call, please."

"Hey David." He swallowed. "It's Mike, do you have a moment."

"What can I do for you," answered the cold voice in the receiver. There was nothing warm or familiar in his tone. It was expected, but still, Mike felt a touch disappointed. He had slept in the man's home and was living with his daughter. Surely a kind word was warranted.

"I met with Creaser."

"And?"

"And I'll be talking with Lieutenant Phillips tomorrow afternoon, thirteen-hundred hours."

"Very good. I'll contact you in the evening then. Will that be all?"

"Well sir," said Mike tentatively. "There was something else. Something personal."

"Go ahead."

Mike took a deep breath. He steeled his nerves before responding. "It's about Flapjack, sir. Our relationship together."

"Oh?"

"Well, I love her. Deeply. I've decided to ask her to marry me, and, well, I wanted to ask your blessing."

There was a pregnant pause. Mike cringed. He could imagine the look on David's face, hundreds of miles away. It was an unpleasant image.

"Michael. Am I hearing you right? You're asking for my daughter's hand?"

"Yes sir, I am."

"Congratulations." Another pause. "Yes, congratulations to you both. You're a good man, Michael."

Mike could hear the uncertainty in David's voice. The reaction came as a surprise. Mike had expected a variety of emotional responses—from anger, to concern, to resentment—but not this. He had never heard David so nervous, so shaken. For the first time since Mike had known him, he seemed genuinely uncertain, as though trapped in a corner.

"Mike..." he said hoarsely, his voice trailing off.

"David?"

"Mike, we need to talk. Immediately. As soon as possible."

"If there's something I said..."

"No, it's nothing like that!" David hissed, "but there are things we need to talk about. Things I should have told you before."

"What things?"

"Not over the phone! I'll... I'll take a plane to Valkyrie this weekend."

"I don't understand," said Mike, beginning to feel anxious himself. "Am I—are we—in danger?"

David hesitated again. Mike could tell the gears were working in his mind. He was trying to word things as carefully as possible. "No… no, just… meet with Phillips. And keep in close contact with Creaser. He's your strongest ally right now. He'll let you know when and where we're to meet."

"I really don't understand…"

"Oh, you will," said David urgently. "Very soon, it'll all be disturbingly clear."

Mike heard a loud click. The line went dead.

Chapter 75

LIEUTENANT SAMUEL PHILLIPS was punctual. Mike had to give him that. The pilot was a short young man, a few years Mike's junior, with a pale, moon-shaped face. He hardly resembled the rugged, battle-hardened airman Mike had expected. His manners were polite, almost finicky. Every few seconds he would straighten his tie, or adjust his lapels. Mike began to wonder if he were on speed. Considering the nature of his work, it wouldn't have surprised him.

"Is that a black lab?"

"I beg your pardon?"

"A black Labrador. The dog in the photo."

Mike followed the airman's gaze. It was focused on a picture at the corner of his desk.

"Oh! Yeah." Mike nodded. "That's the dog I grew up with. You like dogs?"

"They're beautiful dogs," continued the airman, in a dull monotone. "Black Labradors, I mean. They originated in Newfoundland. Or was it Portugal? I'm not sure." He paused. "Oh yes, I remember. They were bred by fishermen in Portugal."

"Excuse me?"

"Labradors! Hunting dogs are my favorite breed. I believe labs were introduced to England in the 19th Century. The Earl of Malmesbury devoted an entire kennel to them."

"Is that so?" said Mike, more concerned than curious. There was definitely something wrong with the man. That much was clear. There was a faraway look in his eyes, as though he were hypnotized. His voice was toneless and pedantic.

"Lieutenant Phillips?"

"Yes, Doctor?"

"Are you currently taking any prescribed medications?"

"None."

"Any type of drug or stimulant, recreational or otherwise?"

"Not that I'm aware of."

Mike opened the folder on his desk. He'd read it a few times already, but skimmed through it once more. "So correct me if I'm wrong, Lieutenant Phillips," he began, before reading off the page. "You were raised on a farm in Nebraska. Attended University of Nebraska on a football scholarship.

The airman perked up. "Yes! I was a running back. We almost qualified for a bowl game," he said, beaming. "Bob Devaney was coach. We finished the season 10-2. Finished 14th in the AP rankings. We only lost our first game, a 17-10 defeat against UCLA, and our fourth game, a 34-21 loss to Army."

He finished his recitation and turned to Mike, a satisfied smile on his face. Mike stared back. For a moment, he was lost for words.

"That's... that's all very interesting," he managed, rubbing his forehead. He could feel a headache coming on. "Perhaps we could change the subject? Discuss your part in the U2 program?"

"Finished flight school at the top of my class," he said proudly. "Then I flew Phantoms in Vietnam for 6 months, 14 days. As far as my statistics..."

"How about we discuss your personal life," Mike interrupted, not a moment too soon.

"What about it?"

"Have you been in any relationships?"

"That depends," answered the airman. He appeared flustered by the question. "What kind of relationships? I have family members, friendships, acquaintances..."

"How about romantic relationships? If it's all right with you."

"Well, let me see. I had a girlfriend back home. She broke it off when I left for Vietnam. If I recall, she married a plumber..."

"Yes, yes," Mike urged desperately, "but what about lately. Are you seeing someone currently."

"I am, yes. Is she in trouble?"

"Not that I know," said Mike, with a note of caution. He scrutinized the airman's face for some sign of emotion. It was as blank as a canvas.

"She is a good woman. Very kind. Very loyal."

"Can you tell me more about her? Her name?"

"Sasha," declared the airman. "She's a town girl from Moscow, Texas."

"Have you noticed anything... odd about her?" asked Mike, as delicately as possible.

"Odd?"

"Anything curious, I mean. Any little quirks or habits?"

The airman stared towards the ceiling. "Well let's see," he began, his eyes squinted in concentration. "She does have a unique accent. I've tried to place it. It's not southern. She says she grew up in Poland though."

"A Texas girl who grew up in Poland? What is she doing back here?"

"She doesn't like to talk about it." The airman shrugged. "Something about her ex-husband."

Mike sighed. He could already recognize the symptoms. There wasn't enough for a diagnosis, not from a single conversation, but there was hardly a doubt in his mind. Drugs were not the issue, but he almost wished they were. The solution would have been so much simpler. The patient before him—though clueless and naïve—was disturbingly sober.

"Lieutenant Phillips," began Mike, leaning forward. "Is it all right if I call you Sam?"

"I prefer Samuel."

"Okay. Samuel, then," he continued. "Samuel, I'm afraid I have some very bad news."

"Bad news?"

"This woman you've been seeing—'Sasha,' she calls herself—doesn't exist. At least, she doesn't *really* exist."

"Sir?"

"We've done the research, Samuel. This town—'Moscow, Texas'—she's not from there."

"No. No you don't understand," he interrupted. "It's a really, really small town."

"She's never been there." Mike insisted. "She certainly didn't grow up there."

"No. I don't think you're right. She's real. She works at an office downtown. I've been there."

"And you've been to her office? Met her co-workers?"

"We... met in the lobby..." said Samuel, his voice shaking as he spoke. It was clear from his face that the truth had set in.

"Did you ever get a last name?"

"No," said the airman, his eyes downcast. "She has betrayed me," he moaned, "just like the others?"

"The others?"

"And she was such a good listener. I would tell her all the countries I'd flown over, and the places I saw. She said she always wanted to travel overseas. It was her dream."

"I'm sorry, Samuel."

"But why?"

"I'm afraid she was only interested in picking up intel," Mike explained reluctantly. "We have videotape of her meeting with undercover agents. They got her voice on a wire."

Lieutenant Phillips sat silently for a moment. He ran his hand through his hair and moaned. "I can't believe it. I don't believe it," he repeated. He beat his forehead with his palm and groaned once more.

"And now it's all over isn't it?"

"What is?"

"My career. My life. Everything."

"I wouldn't say that," offered Mike. The words felt hollow, but he hoped in his heart they were true. "For now, get some rest. Leave everything else up to me."

Chapter 76

"SO, YOU FIGURED IT OUT?"

"I believe so," said Mike. "I've seen the symptoms before. Lieutenant Phillips has Asperger's Disorder."

"Asperger's?"

"He's a high-functioning autistic," Mike explained. "It's likely genetic. He's smart, when it comes to technical details, but oblivious to social cues. He can't read people at all."

"So this woman…"

"She's playing him like a grand piano."

"Selling the information, or feeding it to her husband."

Mike nodded. "Either way, Phillips is completely innocent."

Creaser thought for a moment, weighing the man's fate in his mind. "We'll give him a technical job, then," he said finally. "Something that doesn't involve sensitive information."

"And the woman?"

"The obvious solution would be to feed her faulty information," Creaser mused. "Her customers—whoever they are—won't like it, and that'll be the last we hear of her."

Mike gulped. The colonel's insinuation was a sinister one. "Why not just give her information selectively?" he countered. "Then you can have her in your pocket, so to speak. Use the situation to your advantage."

Creaser looked skeptical, but nodded. He must have had the thought himself, thought Mike. Years of experience had made the colonel cautious. "That's really up to the folks in DC," he said finally. "Meanwhile, you have another assignment already. David called me personally."

"He did?" asked Mike. "He mentioned something about wanting to speak."

Creaser smirked. "First, there's someone he'd like you to meet."

* * *

The trip to Midland, deep in the heart of Texas, was a long and quiet one. The two air police were poor company. Mike tried to keep himself occupied. There was not much to see from the window; nothing but miles of country-side, the occasional one-horse town. After a few hours, the armored vehicle turned down a side-street; a dusty, old path, worn by tractors and pick-up trucks. The wheels lurched over the potholes.

"We're here," said the driver, as they ground to a halt. Mike surveyed the surroundings. Besides the remains of a chicken-wire fence, there were no signs of human activity. They were in the middle of nowhere.

"We walk from here," the other patrolman announced gruffly. The three stepped out into the glaring sunlight. Mike shielded his eyes.

"Are you serious? For how long?"

The driver stared at him. "Until we get there." He motioned his companion. The two of them began down a narrow pathway. Mike hurried to keep up. After only a few minutes, his throat was parched. He could feel the skin burning on the back of his neck.

"We're here."

Mike looked up. They had reached an entrance, of sorts; the ancient remains of a gate. The doors were gone. Only the arch remained. A sign hung from the top.

DISCIPLES OF THE HOLY LIGHT

The letters were bold and clear, as though just painted on. The rest of the gate seemed weathered with age. Much of the gold paint had rusted off. Weeds had grown around the firmament.

"This is where we'll find him."

"Where we should find him." The policeman spat in the dirt. He rubbed it with the toe of his boot. "A-yep, this is the place."

The further into the compound they walked, the more people they saw. There were men on tractors, in dirt-stained overalls; women hanging wash beside makeshift shacks. They whispered or stared as he passed. Gradually, they came to the encampment. A group of men with long beards leered at them from a porch. Mike could hear singing in a nearby barn. He couldn't recognize the hymn.

One of the patrolmen, the driver, stopped the first woman in their path. Like the others, her hair was wrapped in a shawl, and she kept her eyes downcast as she walked.

"Ma'am," said the patrolman, in an official-sounding voice. "We're looking for Airman McKay."

"Who?"

"Airman Leonard McKay, Air Force. Where is he?" Mike scanned nervously. People were beginning to gather now. Some peered through windows, or cracks in the doors. He could feel the hostility in their gaze.

The woman shuffled nervously. She mumbled something indiscernible.

"Speak up, ma'am."

"No one by that name here."

"Ma'am, you understand that you are harboring a fugitive," warned the patrolman. The woman began to back away. He seized her arm. Mike watched in alarm, as the men rose from the patio. Armed though they were, Mike knew, they were easily outnumbered.

"All of you!" declared the other patrolman, addressing the gathering crowd. "All of you are harboring a fugitive from the United States Air Force! An Airman Leonard McKay!"

There was no response. The men, women, even the children stared sullenly, as if defying them to respond. Suddenly, there was a voice from the crowd.

"I am the one you seek."

The crowd began to part. A man, small in stature, with a shaved head approached them. He wore a white cloak, fringed with gold.

"Brother Jonathon," said a voice from the crowd.

"Brother Jonathon!" said another, more reverently.

"Brother Jonathon."

A murmur went through those assembled. The man raised a hand in acknowledgment. The patrolmen looked at one another, then at Mike in bewilderment. He entered the clearing.

"Both hands on your head! Now!" yelled a patrolman, as he let go of the woman. The man raised both hands in submission.

"On your head! Put 'em on your head! Now!" cried the other officer. The two approached cautiously. Mike would have laughed, had he not been in danger. Their target was obviously unarmed. He was docile as a lamb.

There was a gasp from the crowd. Airman McKay—or, Brother Jonathon, as he was called—dropped to his knees. "Airman Leonard McKay, you are under arrest." The clink of handcuffs. "You are accused of abandoning your post. Absence without leave."

The prisoner looked up. He stared directly at Mike. "As you say," he declared. "I shall fear no evil, for the Lord is with me."

There was a wail from the crowd. A whistle through the air. The sound of a stone impacting on a kevlar vest. Another flew past Mike's ear. He ducked.

"What the fuck!" cried one patrolman. He put his hand to his forehead. Blood seeped through the fingers. His friend rushed to his aid. More projectiles flew through the air. A clump of dirt struck Mike in the shoulder.

"You have to do something!" yelled Mike, as he crawled towards the prisoner. "This can't end well for anyone!"

The man nodded. He rose to his feet, hands still locked behind his back. "Brothers!" he yelled. "Sisters!"

The crowd fell silent. To Mike's relief, the hail of debris abated. A hush fell.

"These are sinners, but all has been ordained," he began. His eyes turned to the heavens. "Into the Lord's hands I commit my spirit," he continued. "For he alone shall judge the living and the dead."

Chapter 77

MIKE SPENT THE RIDE home nursing his shoulder. It was bruised, but not broken, and he tried not to move it too often. The patrolmen whisked the prisoner into Valkyrie. It wasn't until morning that Mike could evaluate him.

The stockade at Camp Valkyrie was in poor condition. It was infrequently used, except as a drunk tank. Serious offences were rare. Mike was ushered to the lone interrogation room, where the prisoner awaited him. His hands were folded in his lap, and he smiled serenely.

"I remember you."

"Major Pike," Mike introduced himself, "and I remember you…"

"Brother Jonathan, please," the man interrupted. "It was the name chosen for me."

"Chosen by whom?"

The airman leaned back in his chair. "I know why you're here," he said, folding his arms.

"Do you?"

"You're here to trick me into revealing information. You want to infiltrate our family." He chuckled to himself. "But you cannot. We are the chosen. The messengers of the Lord."

"We're not your enemy," countered Mike. "We want to help you. They took your life from you. Isolated you from your friends and family. Even emptied your bank accounts."

The airman snorted. "A sinner would not understand. We forsake this material realm. Ours is the Kingdom of Heaven."

"And you don't feel taken advantage of?"

"Taken advantage of?" the prisoners eyes were wide. "They have set me free! For first I was lost…"

"…but now am found."

The prisoner perked up. "You're one of us, brother? You've read the Holy Testament."

"Hard not to. I was raised Catholic."

"Ah," sighed the man sadly. He sunk back into his chair. "Worse yet. Better a non-believer than a heretic."

"And that bothers you?"

"Not me," said the airman. He grinned triumphantly. "I'm not the one going to Hell."

*   *   *

David arrived early, as usual. He had already finished his coffee. As soon as he walked in, Mike knew something was off. This was not the same man— the cool, confident agent—he had met in DC. The man before him looked much older, much paler. He sat, slouched down in the corner of the café, eyeing each patron with distrust.

"You're late," he admonished, when Mike had settled in.

"Couldn't find the place. How was the flight?"

David shrugged. "Red-eye from Chicago. I won't be staying long." He leaned towards Mike, whispering. "So is it true?"

"Is what true?"

"You know what I mean." There was urgency and irritation in his voice. David hated repeating things twice. "I can't tell you what I know unless I know you're serious."

"About Flapjack?" said Mike curiously. "Yes. Of course I'm serious."

"Creaser tells me you met our... person of interest."

"Airman McKay? I did." David glanced furtively through the window. "I don't know what you wanted to accomplish with that," Mike continued. "Whatever this weird cult is, I couldn't get anything out of him."

"The Disciples of the Holy Light."

"What?"

"The cult. That's what they call themselves. We know all about them."

Mike's jaw dropped. He gasped. "Then why..."

"A sect of Christian fundamentalists. Inhabited the ghost town of Moonshine Hill in 1968, just ten years ago. The land belongs to their parent organization. That was founded in 1965. At least, we think that's the year." David shrugged. "The dates can be a bit dodgy. That's how long we've been monitoring them, at least."

"What the *hell*, David?"

Mike's anger took the man aback. A few curious glances were cast in their direction.

"Watch it," David hissed. "I'm trying to help you here."

"Help me how?" Mike insisted. He fought to lower his voice. "I need to know what the hell is going on. Right now, David. What the hell is going on? And how does it concern Flapjack?"

David's eyes turned soft. He looked instantly contrite, even ashamed. "Mike, before I tell you this, I need you to know, I'm doing this because you're going to be family." He swallowed hard. "I would do anything to protect my family. My daughter."

"Tell me *what*?"

"You remember what I told you before? About your bloodline?"

"Something about my being related to Jefferson?"

"You have the same DNA markers, yes- as Thomas Jefferson."

"So?"

"What I didn't tell you," David began. He bit his lip, averting his gaze. "What I was told not to tell you, I mean, is that there's value in that information. The blood in your veins. That's what makes you important to the CIA. You're not an agent. You're..." he paused, searching for the right word. It never came.

"I'm... what?"

"You're an asset. A precious asset. And right now the stakes are greater than ever. For both sides."

Chapter 78

MOON WAS NOT OFTEN at a loss for words. Throughout the duration of Mike's tale, he sat in rapt attention. He didn't dare interrupt.

"That's how he put it. You're kidding." He managed a hollow chuckle. "I knew those cats were cold, but god damn."

"Tell me about it."

"And you really think you're in danger?"

"That's what David says," answered Mike, still surprised by the calm in his voice. Moon was staring at him in disbelief. "Apparently the science of DNA has been harnessed by those outside the military and the medical community," he continued. "Bad people. Really bad."

Moon shook his head. "I still don't get it. What would a bunch of fanatics want with that kind of science? I thought science was the death of religion."

"Apparently not. And these 'fanatics' are intent on bringing about the Rapture. They think they're God's instruments."

"But what would they want with you?"

"It goes way back in history," Mike explained. "These people believe the 'End Times' are before us. That the armies of God will battle the armies of evil. On the brink of defeat, the Savior is supposed to return, and open the gates of Heaven."

As he listened, Moon's jaw dropped. He put his hand on his head and groaned. "You're not telling me people believe that junk?"

"Most of them are based in the South. Texas in particular," Mike continued. "The Rapture is actually a lucrative business. These fringe cults are financed by a larger religious organization, who are in turn funded by politicians and special interests."

"And you fit into all this?"

"I was about to get to that," said Mike. He leaned back and finished his beer. "Anyway, they have this idea that the United States was founded as a

Christian nation. The 'chosen people,' so to speak. As a theocracy, it's our role to initiate the conflict in the Middle East, to act as the harbingers of the Apocalypse."

"But we're not a theocracy!" Moon erupted. "What about separation of church and state?"

Mike smiled. "Bingo. The brainchild of Thomas Jefferson. The strength of that clause stands on his reputation as a statesman. A *Christian* statesman." Mike paused, to let his statement sink in. "They argue that Jefferson would never have written that, as a God-fearing man. They claim that the idea of separating church and state was falsely attributed to him. To give it legitimacy, I think. They say what he really meant was to separate from state all religions except Christianity."

"They?"

"David was a bit vague," said Mike. He bit his lower lip in thought. "The head honcho is some guy named Pastor Roy. Runs a mega-church out in Waco. He's been tied to numerous far-right fringe movements."

"But what about you?" asked Moon. "Surely they don't think you can prove otherwise."

Mike shook his head. "No, not me. But the blood inside me can."

"Huh?"

"DNA. Like I said. With my genetic material they've been able to track my ancestry through generations."

"And...?"

"And it proves Jefferson wasn't a Christian." Mike paused to correct himself. "Well, not completely. The Agency believes he actually descended from Jewish ancestors in Europe. That alone is enough to legitimize claims that he used the Hebrew nation as a model for developing the Declaration, the Constitution, and any number of founding documents."

"And if word of that were to go public..."

"The results could cause a lot of damage," finished Moon. "To the movement as a whole."

"Exactly, the US has to be a pure Christian country for the Rapture to come off properly."

Moon chugged the rest of his beer, and slammed the glass on the table. He motioned for another round. "Look Mike," he said, more than a little dazed, "This is all too much to process. It's like some pulp novel. Just listening makes me want to drink, and drink."

"Tell me about it."

"But what I don't get," he persisted, "is why they still need you. They have your sample right? The damage is done."

Mike sighed. "It beats me. That's all David could tell me. That my existence makes me a threat. People don't understand science. They need to put a face on it. He says that word has leaked out about my existence."

"David." Moon sneered. He smacked the table. "I'd kill that motherfucker."

"Honestly, he didn't even have to tell me that much. The higher-ups didn't trust me with the information, I guess."

"And David did? And you trust him now?"

"I have to," said Mike helplessly. "He's going to be family, after I marry Flapjack."

"No way." Moon leered at Mike, looking for signs of humor. "No fuckin' way."

Mike laughed drunkenly. "Would I lie to you, man? You're like, the one man I can trust right now. The best man!"

Moon lurched to his feet. The stool tumbled to the ground. With a laugh, he slung an arm around Mike's shoulder. He smelled of sweat and cheap liquor.

"Congratulations, kemosabe!" he declared. "Things are lookin' up already!

Chapter 79

FLAPJACK FROZE, her mouth agape. For a moment she was lost for words. It took a moment for the news to sink in, but when it did, she crushed Mike in a bear hug.

"You really mean it! Oh Mike, this is really wonderful. Really."

"You are welcome!" Mike wheezed, gasping for air.

Flapjack squealed. She let herself fall back on the couch, elated. "What a week. First you ask me to marry you, then you tell me this… it's almost too good to be true!"

"And that's not all," Mike chuckled. "Your father says they'll be paying me nearly twice what I made here at Valkyrie! Plus benefits and bonuses."

"We can start a family," cooed Flapjack dreamily, gazing at the ceiling. "Have our own little place in the suburbs." She sat up, adjusting her hair. "I have to say, dear, that I told you so."

"Told me what?"

"That dad may seem tough, but in the end, he came to a decision."

"Oh?"

"That you're a squirrel," laughed Flapjack, "and not a songbird."

Mike grinned ruefully. "Maybe," he replied, "but your father is a tough nut to crack!"

* * *

Moon picked idly at his food. Mike turned to Flapjack in concern. They could both tell he was sulking. He would balance the peas on his fork, then let them drop, one-by-one, onto the plate, like a petulant child. For once, Mike actually found the behavior endearing. The frigid stoicism of men like David and Creaser made him weary. It was a relief to be in the company of a friend, one who wore his heart on his sleeve like a banner.

"Hey, chin up! We came back just for you!" offered Mike.

Moon shrugged. "Yeah. For a day."

Flapjack rolled her eyes. "Oh don't be such a baby, Moon. Come on."

"I know, I know. I'm sorry you guys," said Moon, looking up sadly. "But you guys have been up in DC all the last two or three months. I always kind of hoped you'd stay here, you know. Have a kid. I could be Uncle Moon…"

Mike laughed. "Well, we had two months of leave. We had a lot of stuff to work on before the move."

"I would imagine," teased Moon. "Romantic trips to galleries, picking your wedding cake, hobnobbing with the Washington elite."

"Oh my, Moon." Flapjack laughed, slapping him on the back. "Do I hear a little jealousy?"

Moon snorted. "Hardly! I guess it's the glamour that comes with working for the Surgeon General."

"Actually," countered Mike, lowering his voice, "to be honest, we haven't done any of that stuff. I mean, we probably should have. But we didn't?"

"Huh?" Moon cocked his head. "Then what…"

"Keep this quiet," whispered Flapjack excitedly. "Dad did more than just offer Mike a job."

"Is that so?"

"He also gave him a research stipend. And access to the Agency's and the Pentagon's archives."

"*Some* of their archives," Mike corrected. "We spent almost every day researching together."

"Together?"

"Yes, together!" shot Flapjack playfully. She folded her arms. "What? You thought I wouldn't be interested? That because I'm a woman, I only have time for kittens and soap operas."

"Hey, hey!" said Moon, lifting his hands in surrender. "I just thought those big words would hurt you're pretty little head, sweetheart."

"I couldn't have done it without her," claimed Mike. "I mean it. She seriously broadened my horizons. I initially just wanted to study the effect of post-traumatic stress on military families. Our findings on the military's deceptive recruiting techniques, and the mistreatment of women in the service, all of that was her."

"So let me get this straight," said Moon. "You spent the first month of your engagement doing archival research?"

"Golly, he makes it sound so glamorous," laughed Flapjack. She placed a hand on Mike's arm, and looked him gently in the eyes.

"It's true," Mike agreed. "He left out the cold, dusty halls and florescent lights!"

Moon groaned. "Oh hardy har. Y'all are a bunch of squares if you ask me."

"Maybe," hinted Flapjack coyly. "But by the end of the day, we may   be published squares."

Moon shoveled a forkful of flan into his mouth. "I must concede," he managed, with both cheeks still full. "That certainly would make ya'll more hip!"

Chapter 80

"ABSOLUTELY NOT!" bellowed Creaser, pounding a fist on his desk. "Absolutely not! Are you out of your mind?"

Mike swallowed. "But sir, we've made so much progress. And you won't be implicated," he added, with a note of conciliation. "Major Moon is out of the service in a month's time. He's offered to publish under his name. He understands the risks."

"You think I give a damn what that punk thinks?" continued Creaser. "You don't know these people like I do. They'll take him in, they'll find out you're involved, and that'll lead them to me. I can't let that happen."

"Are you serious?" cried Flapjack. "Do you have any idea how incriminating this information is?" She dropped a folder on his desk, with a dull thud. It was almost an inch thick. "Ever since the end of the draft, the Pentagon has used all its marketing tools to lure families into the military. The amount of money they put into their 'Spousal Combat Readiness' program is staggering. An entire program dedicated to 'shaping' women into 'model' army wives!"

"It's true. And that's just the tip of the iceberg," added Mike. He nodded towards the folder. "We've got enough on the Pentagon's 'secret' war on feminism to fill volumes."

Creaser waved dismissively. "Come on, Mike," he muttered. "No offense to your fiancé. She does good work. I know her father well. But I'm shocked you would recruit her for your witch hunt." He turned to Flapjack. "I apologize, ma'am. It's only natural such stories would make you a tad... emotional."

Mike eyed Flapjack nervously. There was a smoldering look in her eyes. She had dug her nails deep into the armrest, in an effort to control herself. "No apology necessary, sir," she spat, with a thin smile. "In fact, I'm glad Mike *asked* for my help. See, I had an idea in my tiny little female mind that violence against women in the military was through the roof; that millions were being spent to discredit the women's movement. And now I know I was right."

Mike shivered. Flapjack's icy tone seemed to drop the room's temperature. She sat back and crossed her arms, a satisfied smile on her face. It dropped, as Creaser slid the folder towards her, and off the edge of his desk. The papers spilled in all directions. No one made a move to retrieve them.

"Major Pike," Creaser hissed, deliberately ignoring Flapjack. "This little project has gone on long enough. I have no idea how you managed to gain access to the Pentagon's archives, but they're not going to let this public. You and I both know you signed a non-disclosure agreement."

"But sir..."

"That means no publishing. Not under a pseudonym, and not through a proxy. They're smarter than that. You wanted the truth. Well, now you know."

"This is bullshit!" Flapjack cried. She rose to her feet, fists clenched.

"Miss Fielder, if you would..."

"Straight bullshit. You think you can muzzle us like this? I'll be informing my father of what's going on. We'll see what Mr. Fielder has to say about this!" She stormed out of the room. Creaser's secretary peered in through the open door, her eyes wide with surprise.

"She's just upset, sir," offered Mike, but Creaser's attention was elsewhere. He was still staring daggers towards his office entrance, as if anticipating her return. His face was flushed with anger. The artery on his temple throbbed dangerously.

"Major Pike," he said finally, never turning his focus from the doorway, "perhaps you should learn to control your fiancé. She seems hysterical."

Mike dropped to one knee. He began gathering the papers together. "What can I say," he answered, from below the desk. "She's as passionate about this cause as I am."

"I know women have it rough in the military. I'm not daft. It's a shame, really. But it's not all as bad as it sounds. We're not running a tea party. They should know what they signed up for." He paused. "Did something I say amuse you?"

Mike had retaken his seat. He realized, too late, that the flicker of a smirk had surfaced on his face. Creaser had seen it immediately. "Well sir, if you really want to know..."

"Spit it out."

"Do you think Sybil knew what she was signing up for? Do you think what was done to her was fair? She was violated, shamed, and abandoned by the Air Force."

Creaser sighed. He leaned back in his chair. "Mike. If only you knew. This is the reason I'm concerned. I'm not protecting the damn military. I'm trying to protect you."

"You mean, you're trying to protect yourself."

"Yes," he admitted. "Self-preservation is an instinct I possess. But believe it or not, I am trying to help you, and your fiancé. If you keep pulling threads, the whole sweater will unravel, and they're not going to let that happen. The ones in charge, well, they have a way of handling... undesirables."

"Oh really, and what's the worst they could do? Censure me? Discredit me? I have nothing to hide. It's in their own best interests to avoid a scandal."

"You have a rather high opinion of your value." Creaser was gnawing on the edge of a pencil. It was the first time Mike had seen the man so distressed. His earlier fury seemed to have seeped from his pores. He was sweating. "I admire confidence. But at some point, any person can go too far."

"And then?"

"And then that person could have an 'accident.' A fall from a helicopter, perhaps. Have you seen a body after a thousand-foot drop?" He winced visibly. "Well I have. It's not pretty. If you're lucky, you're gone on impact. If you're not lucky..."

Mike raised his brow. "Oh come on. I doubt they'd ever go that far."

"You'd be surprised. You remember Deputy Commander Taft? Sybil's... attacker?"

"Yeah, but..."

"If it can happen to him," he said, pointing grimly across the desk. "It can happen to you."

Chapter 81

FLAPJACK WAS IN a sour mood when Mike got home. He could tell from the sounds in the kitchen. She had a habit of cooking when she was upset—a way to distract herself, she had told him—and the smell of lasagna was less than comforting.

"How can you let him walk all over you?" Flapjack was stirring a large bowl of batter. She didn't even turn as he entered. "After all the hours we put into that research, I figured you'd at least put up a fight.

"He's just doing his job. We're not the only ones involved in this." He wrapped his arms around her from behind, kissing her neck. She shook her head.

"I'm serious, Mike. Did you even tell him what you discovered about their cover-up regarding PTSD research? The British learned thirty-years ago that shell-shock and battle fatigue results from the length of exposure to combat. Thirty-years ago!"

"I know. You don't have to tell me."

"And when NATO supported those findings, and adopted the policy from the British 'Harmony Guidelines' that limited deployments to six-months, what did the Americans do? Did they listen?"

Mike groaned. "They didn't. We both know that."

"Damn right they didn't. We're the one nation that still deploys troops for twice that long. For years even, with back-to-back tours!"

She was right. Mike couldn't argue with that. He was the one who had dug up the documents, and it angered him as much as it did her. As he sat at the kitchen table, listening to the anger in Flapjack's tone, he was troubled by his own complacency. Try as he might, he could not accept that the Pentagon would ignore such vital information. Would the military really conceal this occupational hazard, all for the purpose of recruitment? His own experience only confirmed the possibility. Many of the injured soldiers during the war had been issued 'Stop Loss' orders, which only extended their time on the front.

"And what about the families?" continued Flapjack. "The fact that post-traumatic stress isn't limited to the soldier alone. It can pass to his family—his wife and children—who can in turn pass it to their children. Generations of military trauma!"

"You think I don't know that?!" Mike snapped. Flapjack stopped in mid-stir. She turned to face him. Rarely had she heard him so bitter. "I know," he added, gritting his teeth, "I compared our files to the civilian clinics. I know that reports of behavioral disorders are far higher in military children than in civilians! You think I don't know?"

As he talked, he watched Flapjack's expression change from anger, to sympathy, and then to confusion. She untied her apron, and tossed it on the counter. "So you're as passionate about this as me. Then why didn't you say something? Why didn't you fight for this?"

Mike sighed. "You may want to sit down for this." He nudged a chair towards her with his foot. "You remember Lieutenant Colonel Taft, from Guam," he began, when she settled down beside him.

"How could I forget. Our would-be rapist."

"And you remember how nothing happened, when he was reported."

"The fucker got off Scott-free," she fumed. "He's one of the reasons I collaborated with your research. Someone needs to give a voice to us women in the service."

Mike paused. "What if," he began, biting his lower lip. "What if he didn't get away with it, after all?"

"Huh?"

"Some might say he had a tragic accident, a fall from a helicopter, for instance. Others might say he was pushed…"

"You mean…"

"Creaser told me himself. The high command has methods for disposing of, well, 'undesirables,' as he calls them."

The lines on Flapjack"s face grew tight. She didn't look afraid, to Mike's surprise. It was something different; concern, perhaps, or uncertainty. "Well," she concluded, "I don't doubt it. You know better than I do what these men are capable of." She thought for a moment. "The way I see it, there's only one thing left to do."

"Oh?"

"Talk to my father."

"Are you kidding me?"

"You have to talk to Father," Flapjack insisted. "We can trust him. I know we can. He can help us."

Mike shook his head. "No. Not yet, anyway."

"Ugh," she groaned. "Then how are we supposed to publish?"

"You'd be surprised to find," said Mike, with a sly smirk, "that my powers of persuasion may be a bit more effective than yours!"

Flapjack brightened. "You mean, you convinced him? You got his approval to publish?"

"I did one better. I got us a new reader. Someone to personally consider our report."

Her face fell. "A single reader?" she asked, skeptically.

Mike smiled. "Right now, he's the only one we need."

Chapter 82

DR. BENSON MACARTHUR drew a long, slender Toro from a gilded cigar box. With careful precision, he cut the end and flicked his lighter, turning the cigar so as to light it evenly. As a thin stream of blue-white smoke hung in the air, he savored the rich, pungent aroma.

"I don't suppose I can offer you one."

"You suppose correctly," chuckled David. He popped a mint in his mouth.

Benson chomped down on the end, inhaling deeply. He blew a ring that dissipated in the air. "Suit yourself," he shrugged. "Those Cubans may be a pack of communist bastards, but they make a mean cigar. That's for damn sure."

David shifted uneasily in his chair. "Benson, good as it is to see you again, I can assume you had a matter of some importance to discuss?"

"Oh yes!" Benson sat up, propping his cigar in a marble ash tray. He shuffled through a mountain of folders, before finding the right one. "I received this yesterday morning," he began, handing the report to David. "An expose on our inner workings, apparently. The treatment of women and military wives, our recruiting tactics, and some interesting thoughts on our handling of Post-Traumatic Stress Disorder." Benson smiled sardonically. "Quite an engaging read, really. Who doesn't love a good scandal."

David blanched as he skimmed the report. His hands began to feel clammy. "This... this is career suicide. I didn't... I mean..."

Benson waved his hand in the air. "Oh relax, David. You're one of the old boys here. I know you didn't authorize this piece of treason."

"Then who..."

"Creaser, that old softie," chuckled Benson. "He didn't sign it. It's an anonymous report. Your boy must have really done a number on him. Appealed to his early work on chest injuries, or something." He took another puff of his cigar. "Creaser always had that humanitarian streak in him. It just takes the right tune to tease it out."

"These are pretty disturbing facts," muttered David, "You're telling me recruiters are trained to 'cloak' all occupational hazards when advertising? That nothing's been done to combat the problems of violence, sexual assault, child abuse, PTSD, suicide and depression?"

"I didn't call you here to discuss the finer points of this hippie manifesto," said Benson, gesturing with his cigar. "I called you here because we both know who wrote this. You need to keep a leash on your boy, Fielder."

David threw up his hands. "What did you want me to do?" he asked angrily. "What was it you told me? Get the boy involved *by any means necessary*? He wouldn't join up unless he had access to our archives."

"And what did you think would happen?"

"I don't know! I figured it was only for a month. We have decades-worth of documents. It couldn't hurt."

Benson shook his head. "I could expect this from a young pup, but not from you Fielder. I must say, you disappoint me."

David chuckled nervously. He could feel the tension in the air. Of all the powerful people, he thought to himself, the last one to cross was the surgeon general. The man was a sadist. A ruthless social climber. "Just toss it, then," he suggested. "It's all misinformation anyway right? Who is gonna believe some rogue conspiracy theory?"

"You and I both know the position we're in," said Benson coldly. "I know it. You know it. Hell, even Reagan knows it. The Commies have Cuba, Nicaragua, they're turning the central Caribbean into a Soviet lake. You think we can afford dissent in our own borders? Do you want to see Washington turn into Red Square, comrade?"

"How dare you!" David practically leapt from his chair. He gripped the edge of the desk, fighting to keep his composure. "You've known me for how long, MacArthur? We were in the academy together, for God sakes."

The outburst took Benson aback. It took only a second for him to regain his usual poker-face, but the damage was done, and David knew it. For a brief moment, Dr. MacArthur was afraid.

"Then for the love of God, Fielder, keep your boy on a leash. I know he's your future son-in-law, and his value makes him feel untouchable." He paused, grinding the butt of his cigar against the cold, green marble tray.

"But after the Founding Father's operation, even you can't save him."

*   *   *

It was not until he was miles from the Pentagon that David allowed himself to tremble. He knew how to stay calm under pressure, it was part of the job. Now, alone at last, he let the sweat flow freely. He could not remember the last time he had felt so agitated. Not since Vietnam. Not even since Korea. To make things worse, it was his fault, and he knew it. He had done the one thing he thought he'd never do. He had trusted someone outside the family. Now, if they got to Mike, they got to Flapjack. And David couldn't let that happen.

After steadying his breathing after a few minutes, David finally allowed himself a chance to think. He tried to organize the mess of concerns that flooded his brain. One-by-one, he would address each in turn, and weigh his options carefully. Above all, David trusted his faculty of reason. It had kept him alive more times than he could count.

What he found surprised him. As much as he wanted to hate Mike, as much as he wanted to distance his daughter from the danger ahead, David couldn't help but respect him. He knew as well as Benson that Mike's report was accurate. How many friends had he lost to PTSD, he wondered; how many families had he seen torn apart by sexual violence and child abuse? Mike's claim that PTSD raised the risk of suicide by four-times, with the presence of firearms raising it a further 60%, didn't surprise him in the least. He could remember each of the funerals he attended in turn. Each time he had felt the same helplessness, the same frustrated grief.

David's thoughts turned to Flapjack. How many times had she told him about the thousands of sexual assaults reported each year? He had never allowed himself to believe it. Her claims that these cases were rarely prosecuted—that it was the victims who suffered –seemed preposterous. He had dismissed it all as feminist propaganda. Of course these women couldn't collect disability! They had the burden of proof, after all. They should have known the dangers when they signed up. Now, after having these words echoed in the report—by a man, no less—David felt his conviction dissolve. Had he been wrong all along? The thought made him feel hollow. Was he a man without a country?

And what about this Founding Father's thing? Could he go through with it?

For the first time in a long and storied career, David began to question his orders.

Chapter 83

MIKE HATED WEARING SUITS. They never seemed to fit right. He always felt more at home in his scrubs, or even a plain shirt and tie. Here, in the lobby of the Washington Hilton, he felt as though he were in someone else's clothes. The starched shirt was too stiff, and the pants too tight. He took a sip of his second gin-and-tonic. At least the drinks were free. He would need more than a few to get through the afternoon.

In a couch on the other side of the table sat David and Benson. Both wore their tailored suits as though they'd been born in them. The Surgeon General was taking a nap, or meditating, Mike couldn't tell which. The man's patent leather shoes were propped on the table, his hands crossed behind his coiffed red hair. He seemed perfectly at ease. To Mike's surprise, however, David seemed curiously agitated. Had it been their first meeting, Mike would have never noticed, but now, over time, he had come to recognize David's 'tells.' The man repeated the same actions whenever he was anxious, be it checking his watch, or re-adjusting his tie.

And lately, David had been growing increasingly anxious. But what was the cause, wondered Mike. What was going on?

"Hi! Hey! Hello! Sorry I'm just a touch late!" came a voice from behind him. "Hank Stapp. Washington Post."

A small, diminutive man, with glasses thicker than Flapjacks, shook each of their hands in rapid succession. To Mike, he almost resembled a chipmunk with his quick, frenetic movements. It took only a moment for him to whip out a pen and a notebook, and take stock of his surroundings. His gaze flitted from one subject to the next.

"Alright, gentleman. So what's the story here?"

So much for the pleasantries, thought Mike. Oh well. Best to get this over and done with.

"Have we got a story for you!" exclaimed Benson, with the energy of a salesman. He gestured towards Mike. "The man you're looking at, right here, is the last living descendant of Thomas Jefferson!"

"It's true," added David. "The DNA confirms it."

The journalist began scribbling madly, only to stop. He clicked his pen once, then twice. "And you call me here for this?" he asked. He eyed Mike dismissively. "When you said 'front-page material,' Dr. MacArthur, I didn't think you meant some local puff-piece."

So the reporter was disappointed. Good, thought Mike. Let him be disappointed. He was only doing this as a favor for David, anyway. The compensation for a month's access to the Pentagon's archives. That, and a consulting job with the Pentagon, which paid twice as much for half the work. The deal was more than fair.

Still, he wondered, what was this all about anyway? What was the point?

Benson laughed.

"Easy, Hank. There's a lot more to this. I know you've been looking for an angle into this business with the Rapturists. The network of doomsday cults across America. Imagine if you could follow the money trail. There are politicians involved. Big names."

"You know as well as we do," added David, "that this is Pulitzer material."

Easy on the hard sell, thought Mike. The reporter had perked up at the word 'Rapturist.' By the time he heard 'Pulitzer,' he was practically salivating.

"But what about you," asked Hank, stabbing a pen towards Mike. "What's your role in this?"

Mike began to open his mouth.

"He's a big piece of the puzzle," cried Benson. "Our trump card! Our ace-in-the-hole!"

"Go on," urged the reporter. His pen was moving a mile-a-minute.

"You've heard the political debates regarding the separation of church and state," Benson continued, "well, a lot of money is coming from grass-roots, right-wing movements. The Rapturists. The Tea Party. More than a few conservatives are getting a fat paycheck for towing the line on this."

"And?"

"And the whole argument is founded on the idea that Jefferson never wrote that clause. That it was a misrepresentation of his ideas. That, as a God-Fearing member of the Founding Fathers, he would have abhorred the idea."

"And they're wrong."

"Major Pike is living proof," said David. He gestured towards Mike. "The DNA confirms Jefferson's Jewish ancestry. His family was a part of the tribe for generations."

Hank looked up from his notebook. "But that doesn't prove Jefferson himself didn't have Christian ideals," he said skeptically. "And anyway, even if it's true, and they believe you—which they won't—you already have a sample of his DNA. What more use does he have to either side?"

Yeah, thought Mike, go ahead, keep talking like I'm some guinea pig. See what happens.

"You'd be surprised, Hank," explained David. "It's 1983. DNA is considered legal evidence now. And don't underestimate Mike," he added, nodding in his direction. "He's got Jefferson's resolve. The passion behind the science. We need him to spread the word, as our representative."

Mike unclenched his fist. David was eyeing him warily. So he noticed the anger, thought Mike, and came to his defense. It was a nod of confidence, a reminder that they were allies. It strengthened his resolve.

"We're organizing a 'Founding Father's Tour'," said Benson proudly. "That's where Mike comes in. We need to put a face on the science; to humanize it, so to speak. He's agreed to speak about his family's political and religious history. About how Jefferson and Adams both admired the Hebrew people. He and his compatriots modeled the Declaration of Independence, the Constitution, and other documents on the principles of the Hebrew nation."

Mike was stunned. He couldn't believe what he was hearing. A Founding Father's Tour? He had never agreed to participate. No one had even mentioned it in the first place!

"That's just the tip of the iceberg," Benson continued. "Jefferson, Adams, Madison, all of them were Masons. That secret society studied a prolific number of religious and philosophical texts. As a member of the most prestigious Masonic order, Mike's agreed to share the secrets concerning just how our great nation was founded."

Hank listened intently. "Secrets?"

"Secrets about just how secular our nation really is."

Mike looked desperately at David. He wanted to say something; to get up, to run. Some force kept him glued to the couch. Why didn't you tell me, Mike wondered. Was all the support just a lie? How could you betray my trust?

For the first time since the two had met, David averted his son-in-law's gaze.

Chapter 84

THE WINTER OF 1983 was a cold one, the coldest Mike had ever experienced. He had seen heavy snow before, on a family trip Colorado, but that was only a week. Now, he struggled to acclimate to the frigid D.C. climate. The tedium of shoveling snow and staying indoors was beginning to wear on him. He found some warmth, however, in the arms of his wife. Flapjack had never been happier. She hardly seemed to feel the cold, save for the rosiness on her cheeks and ears. He envied her.

Mike's relationship with David—with all involved—had been frosty, to say the least. At first, he held out. He refused to participate in the tour. It was Flapjack who convinced him to put his foot down. When the article hit newsstands, her fury eclipsed even his own. Mike couldn't help feeling a pang of guilt, having to listen to David's muffled arguments with his daughter. The walls in their temporary apartment, which the government had provided, were paper thin. Mike was almost certain it was bugged.

It was now, in midwinter, that Mike's resolve began to waver. Say what you will about David's chicanery, the man delivered on his promises. His findings with Flapjack were published after all, with Moon as the author, and the government response had been swift. Benson MacArthur resigned his post. The new Surgeon General established a congressional mandate to investigate cases of PTSD in Vietnam veterans. In less than a month, they had verified the dose-response relationship. Early reports suggested that over 830,000 veterans have been functionally-impaired by PTSD. The vast majority received no VA assistance.

It was a victory, Mike knew, but a small one. To identify a problem was one thing, but to solve it was quite another. For all their concern, neither the government nor the military had proposed any solutions. There would be no financial aid. The system would remain more-or-less intact, unaltered. Besides, the bulk of the government's findings would not be released until

1989. Maybe the politicians can wait six years, thought Mike, but our home-less veterans can't. Time was not a luxury they could afford.

It was a start, at least, and the departure of Benson helped melt the ice between Mike and his father-in-law. David, as if obligated by guilt, had stretched his influence to the breaking point on Mike's behalf. He risked his career to ensure Benson's resignation. Money was no option when it came to supporting his daughter and her husband. It took a while, but day-by-day he began to build back his trust. He even went so far as to put the tour on hold. Never once did he challenge Mike's refusal. To Mike, it was a huge relief. He even promised to reconsider.

To Mike's surprise, it was only Moon who seemed to benefit from his groundbreaking publication. He had taken a risk, challenging the military, and it seemed to pay off almost instantly. The University of Virginia called the day after his contract expired. There was a cushy position awaiting him in the Psychatry Department. The news made Mike chuckle. Never, in a million years, would he have associated Moon with academia. Still, he was relieved at his friend's good luck. If some misfortune had befallen his friend, Mike never would have forgiven himself, but then, to Mike's dismay, Moon disappeared.

November turned to December, and Mike enjoyed his first Christmas with the Fielders. It was a relief, Mike felt, to put all the intrigue of the past few months behind him; to begin a new year with his family beside him. He and David had begun spending more time together, too, and Mike found that they had more in common than he realized. They were both men who were driven. Men with ideals. Men who lived with the regrets of the past. For the first time, Mike saw just how vulnerable this man of power was.

It was a new year. But Moon was gone and, as Mike was soon to learn, he had not yet exorcised the ghosts of the past. They haunted him in the shadows; biding their time. It was not long before they would strike.

Chapter 85

IT BEGAN WITH a powder-blue Cadillac. David was the first to notice. To anyone else, it was just a random car on the side of the road. To a seasoned agent, it was a textbook maneuver. David, himself, had done it countless times. Routine intel work. He laughed about it over dinner. Flapjack and Mike had nothing to worry about, he assured them. It wasn't the first time he was under surveillance. It was the Russians, or maybe the Chinese, just trying to flex their muscles; to show they meant business. No agency would dare touch a senior at the Agency. To do so meant a fate worse than death.

It wasn't until Mike began to notice the same powder-blue Cadillac that he began to worry. At least twice a day it passed by his apartment window. So David wasn't the target after all, he told Flapjack. It was them. There was nothing Mike could do, David told them on the phone. Not until they made the first move.

He didn't have to wait long.

* * *

It came when Mike least expected it. It was a typical DC morning in January, the air was frigid, and sunlight made the icicles glitter in the cold, quiet dawn. He was midway through his morning jog, when he heard a sound from behind. The creeping of wheels on the road to his right. Mike quickened his pace. Whoever it was, they had picked the perfect moment, and were in no hurry to accost him. The driver made no attempt to conceal his purpose. There were no other vehicles in sight. No pedestrians. Mike's only avenue of escape was the field to his left. He was too far from home.

The car crept closer.

Mike fought to control his breathing. He tried to focus on the sound of his boots on the frozen grass. He had to stay calm. He couldn't panic.

"Hey!"

Mike slowly wandered further from the sidewalk, beyond the glare of the headlights. He fought the urge to respond.

"Hey! Mike! You gonna just run off, man?"

Mike turned. It was just what he expected. The telltale blue Cadillac. A head, hidden beneath a wool balaclava, popped out the driver side window.

"Because if you just gonna run off, we can meet at your place."

Mike stopped in his tracks. He grit his teeth in frustration. Sooner or later, he would have to deal with this. Best to just get it over with, far from the apartment and Flapjack.

"Why don't you get in the car?" said the stranger, motioning Mike forward. "I'll give you a ride home. How about it?"

Mike swallowed. Each footstep felt heavy, as he approached the rumbling vehicle.

Time to get this over with.

*   *   *

"Do you know who I am?"

The man had removed his cap. Mike looked him over again. If they had met before, he thought to himself, he probably would have remembered. He was a thick, stocky man, with a nasty scar running across his face. His presence was hardly comforting.

"I'm afraid I don't. Who the hell are you?"

"We went to the same high school, friend. I was a senior on the football team back when you were a freshman. Remember those years?"

Mike thought for a moment. "Back when Bum Philips was still around?"

"One heckuva' coach, huh?"

"Yes, but I don't remember you," said Mike. "And you're a long way from home. Why are you in D.C.?"

"My old man's in the oil business, you know. Got me this job with a congressman and he has a message for you. That's why I'm here."

"Much as I'd like to talk about the good old days," began Mike, with a note of apprehension, "next time, could you do it without stalking my wife and me? And what's the message?"

The driver became silent. He pulled into the nearest parking lot, and turned to Mike with a frown. "Seeing as we're school pals and all, let's just say this is a courtesy call."

"A courtesy call?"

"See, my employer hears you got this gig, some kind of fancy government show. You're gonna be telling folks that America ain't a Christian nation. My employer, he'd rather you didn't do that."

"And who's your employer?"

"He prefers to remain anonymous."

"And he's paying you well for that discretion, I hope?"

"Don't be a wise ass," the driver snarled. "You seem like a good kid. I'm tryin' to do you a favor."

Mike knew he should hold his tongue. It was the smart thing to do. Just let this tough guy deliver his message, and he might get home in one piece. Still, he could feel a well of anger bubbling within him. He had felt it before. The old, familiar feeling of indignation and resistance.

"And what if I refuse your employer?"

The man shook his head, sadly. "You don't want to do that, kid. Trust me. This goes deeper than you know. Let's just say, a lot of people are proud of this being a good, God-fearing nation of Christians. People with power. And they're not gonna let you get away with this."

"Is that a threat?" asked Mike. "Because I don't respond well to intimidation."

"Hey, hey, who said anything about intimidatin' anyone!" chuckled the driver, raising his meaty paws. "My employers are reasonable folks. They hear you're related to Jefferson. Well, how'd you like to get acquainted with Ben Franklin, eh."

As he spoke, the man reached into his leather jacket. He pulled out a thick stack of bills.

Mike flushed with anger. "You can't be serious. I can't accept that!"

"It's a gift, that's all."

"It's a bribe."

"I advise you to take it. There's an old code my employers live by. In the words of Pablo Escobar, it's *plato y plomo*, silver or lead. You take care of business, or our business takes care of you."

*   *   *

David sighed. He looked at Mike sadly. "Did you tell Flapjack?"

"I figured it best not to, for now. I didn't want to upset her."

"We'll have to, eventually," David reasoned. He shook his head. "This was my fault. I should have taken this more seriously. I should never have involved you two in the first place."

"Well, I suppose it's too late now."

"And you're sure about this decision?"

Mike smiled grimly. "The way I think about it, there's no other decision to make. This is something I have to do. It's the right thing."

"Then we better get started," announced David, after a moment of thought. "Because when our enemy finds out the Founding Fathers Tour of '84 is underway, they'll hit back, and hit back hard."

"And," answered Mike, "we'll be ready."

Chapter 86

GENERAL LORDE'S FIRST WEEK in office was hell. The rest of the month wasn't much easier. As the new Surgeon General, his first order of business had been to clean up after his predecessor's mess. Dr. MacArthur was a shrewd bureaucrat, and his whole network of corruption collapsed with his absence. It was up to the new boss to pick up the pieces. The whole system had to be rebuilt from scratch.

The ring of the telephone interrupted his work.

"General Lorde? Congressman Peterson here for his meeting."

"Send him in."

Lorde groaned. This was the worst part of the job. The constant parade of businessmen, politicians, and lobbyists, all circling in for their piece of the pie. Suddenly, every beltway insider had a favor to ask, or a service to offer. Everyone wanted something.

And he knew what the congressman from Texas wanted. It was obvious before he burst through the door.

* * *

"Well howdy there, General!"

"Congressman Peterson. Welcome to Washington."

"Well thank you kindly!"

Lorde smiled at the portly congressman. It wasn't that long a walk to his office, and the man was already huffing and puffing. The man's attendant, however, gave some cause for concern. Did Peterson really need a body-guard? Security must be getting lax, he thought to himself, to let a tattooed gang-banger like this into the Pentagon. What was the congressman thinking?

"Now General, I'm a straight-shooter," began Peterson, when he finally regained his breath. "And I'm gonna tell it to you straight."

"By all means."

"Now, my constituents are good, hard-workin' people. Salt of the earth. They're a God-fearin' people too. When they got a concern, well, I reckon I'm the one to set things right."

Lorde fought the urge to roll his eyes. Sure, he thought to himself, you're a real hero. Get to the point.

"Well General, this here's the land of opportunity. Take Patricio here," the congressman continued, gesturing towards his guard. "Hell, even the colored folk can make something of themselves, they ain't all hoodlums and criminals."

Lorde pursed his lips. "You are aware, Congressman, that I happen to be one of those 'colored' folks you were referring to."

Peterson's face flushed. His eyes widened. "But... but you're..."

"White?" finished Lorde. "That would be my mother's side. If you did your homework, you'd know I'm half Latino. And proud of it."

"And... and right you oughta be," blustered the congressman. He dabbed at his face with a handkerchief. "You know some of my best friends..."

"Peterson," Lorde interrupted. "If there's nothing I can do for you, I'm a very busy man."

"Well it's like this," began Peterson, eager to start anew. "Some folks— cornerstones of the community, really—well they think that liberty is under attack. Word is, some Jews in the government got an idea to take control. Push some consarned notion that our founding fathers were hook-nosed members of the tribe."

"Is that so?"

"Well you tell me, General," added the congressman. "So these folks, they started up a petition, and they want the truth. Are the Jews taking control? Are you harborin' their leader?"

"Their leader?"

"Some boy claims he got ol' Jefferson as his grandpappy. Well, great-grandpappy."

"Oh!" exclaimed Lorde. "You mean our keynote speaker. You're mistaken if you think he's some kind of revolutionary or politician. He's as patriotic an American as you or I." He smirked at the congressman's look of dread. "And so what if Jefferson was Jewish? People of all faiths and philosophies helped found our great nation. There were Christians, Jews, Muslims..."

"Muslims!"

"Oh yes, some of the first slaves kidnapped from Africa were Muslim, after all."

"And they didn't convert?"

Lorde shrugged. "They couldn't. Their white masters thought conversion would lead to emancipation." He paused to relish the look of horror on the congressman's face. Lorde couldn't help himself. It was just too easy. "In fact, they passed a law to outlaw the freedom of converted slaves."

"Well, uh, you and I know that!" stammered Peterson, in an attempt to conceal his distaste. "But, well, you know how it is. We got a lot of concerned Christians in West Texas. Some are real overzealous. And from yer tone, I take it you plan to take this show on the road."

"That would be correct."

"Well, sir, I must ask you to kindly reconsider."

"We'll take that into consideration," said Lorde, already returning to his paperwork. "Now if that is all..."

"That ain't all. Not by a long shot," Peterson interjected. There was fear in his voice. The man made no attempt to disguise it. "Because it ain't me askin', and the man who is, well, he don't ask twice."

"And what man is that?"

The congressman rose. "You know who, General. If you fellas do your job here like you boast, well, you oughta know him real well."

Lorde watched the man depart, with his bodyguard close behind. As the door clicked shut, a bead of sweat ran down the side of Lorde's face. The congressman was right, he thought. They both knew who pulled the strings. He picked up the phone, his hand shaking, and dialed a number.

"David? It's Lorde. It's worse than we thought. Far worse."

Chapter 87

"**DO YOU KNOW** what I found on my desk this morning?"

Congressman Peterson's lip trembled. He was sweating, heavily, and he could feel the receiver slip down his meaty paw. His heart beat in his chest like a hammer. "No, sir, but I been wearin' down these Washington fatcats like a rented mule. I... I think we're makin' real progress."

"I'll tell you what I found on my desk." The disembodied voice was cold and emotionless.

"Sir?"

"I found a red-white-and-blue pamphlet. All stars and stripes. Do you know what it said?"

"Pastor Roy, I..."

"It said I was the guest of honor at this 'Founding Fathers Tour.' They're making their first stop in Amarillo, too. Isn't that thoughtful?"

On the other end of the line, Roy spoke through clenched teeth. His blood was boiling. It was his Southern temper, he told his parishioners. His passion. His greatest asset, too. It inspired fear, and fear inspired loyalty. Fear got things done.

"Congressman, need I remind you who your largest donor is."

"Now sir..."

"Who put you in that cushy capitol office for, what, two-terms now? Who pays the rent on that summer house on the Gulf Coast?"

"You do, sir"

"Wrong!" bellowed Roy. "Western Glory Baptist Church keeps you in business. Our board of directors, the men who control our commercial and industrial assets. You didn't get a nickel from me."

"I understand sir. But Washington don't work like that. There's... there's complications."

"Do you understand?" pressed Roy. "Then tell me, what happens when this tax-payer sponsored 'tour' hits schools and colleges across the country? What happens when the masses are spoon-fed some cock-n-bull story about our Jewish masters?"

"But sir, we have faith in the lord..."

"I'll tell you what happens," Roy continued. "Democracy collapses. Secularism spreads like a plague. It's the road to communism! How does that sound, comrade?"

Silence. The awkward sound of static. Of course you don't know, thought Roy with disgust. Take away the fancy suit and you're just one more country bumpkin. He must be, if he really thinks 'faith' gets anything done. Peterson was a hack, a simpleton. To explain to him how an entire empire relied on his own carefully-molded 'doomsday theology,' how it could all come crumbling down, would be a lost cause. No, thought Roy, God helps those who help themselves.

"I apologize Congressman," sighed Roy. He laced his voice with milk and honey now. It was an asset that had served him well, the ability to slip between emotions at will. The congressman would be putty in his hands.

"Oh, sir, pastor, no apology necessary," babbled Peterson. The relief in his voice was palpable.

"But you're right. We must pray over this. In the meantime, you must act as God's vessel, and do his holy work. Pray tonight. The lord will not forsake you."

"I'll press harder, sir. I'm sure we can get through to them somehow."

"I'm counting on you." Roy smirked. "Stop this tour. By any means necessary."

Chapter 88

IT WAS A BEAUTIFUL DAY in March. The first day in a long time that Mike's breath didn't freeze before his face. Flapjack was right, he thought, it was a perfect time to shop for real estate. While Mike was busy at the Pentagon, Flapjack had taken it upon herself to research the best condos, town homes, and neighborhoods in the DC area. Now that life seemed back to normal, they agreed the time was right to start a family of their own. The thought alone suffused Mike with happiness.

Their search was a short one. It was still early that Saturday morning when Mike knew they found the perfect home. It wasn't far away from the Fielders, in nearby Bethesda. It was a respectable area too, with a good school system and a low crime rate. Flapjack agreed, it was perfect. Their agent was pleased as punch.

They didn't see Congressman Peterson until it was too late to avoid him.

At first, when they entered the parking lot of the complex, Mike was confused by the sight. A short, overweight, bald man in a suit, huffing and puffing to catch up with the couple. Neither he nor Flapjack felt the urge to avoid him. The sight was just too comic. It was as if they were being chased by the Mayor of Munchkinland, straight from the Kingdom of Oz. The fellow seemed harmless enough. Between belabored breaths, he introduced himself as Congressman Tucker Peterson, from the Texas Panhandle.

"Just like you, big hoss." He laughed, his spittle just missing Mike's sleeve. "A bonafide fellow Texan, here in Yankee Country!"

Mike forced a smile. Is that supposed to make us buddies, he wondered. He knew who the man was now. David had warned Flapjack as well. The Western Glory Church had the Amarillo Congressman in its pocket. Still, Mike had been on the lookout for tattoo-inscribed toughs and sicarios. It seemed almost absurd to imagine the politician getting his hands dirty. Yet here he was.

"It's... nice to meet you, Congressman," offered Mike awkwardly. "Rather early in the morning for such a random coincidence like this, eh?"

"I'll say! And to meet a fellow southern boy, and a soon-to-be celebrity, too! The descendant of Jefferson, in the flesh! Well, I'll be."

Flapjack stepped forward. She always was the decisive one, Mike thought. She was sick of the games. "We're very busy, Mr. Congressman," she replied coolly. "If you'll excuse us, we have a very busy day planned."

"Oh come now, darlin'," cooed the Congressman. "I think you wanna hear what I have to say. It's important."

"As I said, we're *very* busy."

"Coffee, then. Ten minutes. And you won't see me again."

"Ten minutes, then. Then we really have to get going."

Flapjack glared daggers at Mike. For a second, he regretted interrupting. It wasn't his intention to overrule her. Still, the congressman didn't pose any threat, and besides, perhaps it was best just to hear him out. The more they knew, the easier it would be to protect themselves.

"Ten minutes," hissed Flapjack.

"I promise," he reassured them. "And believe me, it'll be worth yer while."

* * *

"Ah," sighed the congressman, reclining on the sofa. He spread his arms, as if to encompass the whole of the café. "Now this is more like it. I always did feel better outside the board rooms. Hell, I'm a man of the people. Good, wholesome Americans like you two. I suppose I've always been a country boy at heart!"

Mike sipped his latte and nodded politely. Being raised in Texas, he was no stranger to the congressman's manner. It was not until he established some rapport between them, until he was assured of their confidence, that he would make his move. Like any good Southern politician, he was blessed with a silver tongue.

"Is that so?"

"Hell, I reckon I should have come to you first, man-to-man." He looked at Flapjack and smiled. "And to you as well, ma'am," he added. "None of these empty suits up here in the capitol really understand what the people want."

"And what would that be?" asked Flapjack. Her arms were folded against her chest. She hadn't even touched her scone.

The congressman sighed. "Well, I'll tell it to you straight. My constituents back home—good, tax-paying, family men and women—they're concerned. What, with the government pushing this secular agenda, and using you as their pawn, I can't blame 'em either."

Mike cocked his head. "You mean the Founding Father's Tour?"

"It's downright unAmerican!"

"Are you kidding!" exclaimed Flapjack. "What could be more American than that?"

"With all due respect, ma'am, I've been around a long time. I remember back when the government started catering to civil rights. We started seeing mixed-marriages on our own military bases, and I haven't seen my constituents in such a frenzy since those days. It was a real mess."

"You can't be serious!"

"Just imagine how dangerous it could be," the congressman continued. "Mixing religions together. It's just asking for trouble."

Flapjack turned to Mike. Her eyes were wide with disbelief. She was speechless.

"So tell me, congressman," he asked. "What can I do for you?"

"Michael, have you ever heard about the Western Glory Church?"

Mike nodded.

"Well, they're even bigger than you might think. There are several million congregants. Then there are the hardliners, too, the fringe groups with their own compounds in Alabama, Texas, and Mississippi."

"We've heard of them," snapped Flapjack. "What's your point?"

"My point is, I know what they're capable of. They aren't afraid to act. You, you're good people, I feel like you understand what I'm saying. It's up to you to do the right thing. Refuse to speak. Cancel the tour. You owe it to your country."

"Owe it to our country?" cried Flapjack incredulously. "What about what you owe to your own constituency? You're supposed to work for the people, not for the special interests of some religious fanatics!"

The congressman looked pleadingly towards Mike. "The lady is clearly emotional, I understand. She doesn't know how this works, where the money comes from. You're the man, here, Michael." He pointed a pudgy finger in his direction. "You know what the right thing to do is. I'm tryin' to help you folks out."

Mike clenched his fists under the table. He was livid, but fought to contain his anger. Already, some patrons were starting to stare. "You'll find I have quite the same opinion as my wife on the matter," he answered, between his teeth. "The tour will go on as scheduled, with the first stop in Amarillo. Your own backyard."

The congressman blanched. He jumped from his seat, knocking the table with his belly. He violently rearranged his shirt and adjusted his trousers. "Well, I guess there's no use tryin' to reason with Jews. I've done my Christian duty to try to help. But I suppose all you folk understand is the swift justice of the Lord."

"Are you threatening us, Congressman?" asked Flapjack. Her tone made Mike shiver.

"You take it however you want, ma'am," he hollered. "But if you knew what I knew, you'd already know. That tour will never happen!"

Mike and Flapjack watched the man waddle indignantly towards the entrance. They turned to one another. Flapjack struggled to withhold her laughter. "Well," she chuckled finally, "I guess we'll have to keep looking. They'll know to look for us at the apartment."

Mike laughed hollowly. He wished he were as strong as Flapjack. Below his calm façade, however, his anxieties were mounting. The implications of his actions were clear. Was he doing the right thing?

Chapter 89

"OF COURSE IT HAS to be Texas!" David was staring, wide-eyed at Mike, as if he'd asked the most obvious question in history.

"It just seems a bit much. Like we're trying to poke an angry rattle snake."

Flapjack looked up from her notebook. Surrounding her on the couch cushions were stacks of paper, half-open books, and file folders. Her coke-bottle glasses had drooped to the bottom of her nose. "Well, that's the idea Mike," she said sleepily. "We're baiting him. Everything hinges on this debut." She rubbed the sleep from her eyes. "You let us worry about the bad guys, you just focus on your speech."

Mike gave her a half-hearted smile. He knew she hadn't slept a wink that night. It was as if the Founding Fathers Tour had given her a new purpose, and she had dedicated herself to it completely. Watching how well she worked with David, and her ferocious intensity, Mike realized more than ever that she was her father's daughter.

"It just seems like a lot of pressure to apply. Especially with the new article."

"Seriously Mike?" groaned Flapjack. "Are you just going through the motions, or do you want to make a difference?"

The irritation in her voice bothered him. Of course he wanted to make a difference! Still, this newest scoop, leaked to the same journalist, was turning this whole operation into an attack on their right-wing detractors.

"Look me in the eyes, Mike," she continued. "Tell me that the public doesn't need this story."

He couldn't do it. She knew it, too.

David had struck gold through his contacts. The Pentagon and the Agency had new evidence on Pastor Roy, or rather, the entire Western Glory organization. It had taken some digging, but they had unearthed records linking Pastor Hefflin — Roy's predecessor — to the then-emerging Nazi Party in Germany. The church had sent substantial contributions to the National

Socialists throughout the 1930s. To the shock of Mike and the Pentagon, however, those donations were sent to *protect* the Jews, rather than ensure their eradication. Regardless, the news only added to Flapjack and David's momentum.

"It's a win-win either way," David had explained. "We tell the national press he contributed to the Nazis. We tell the local press in Texas that he's a Jewish sympathizer. We can't lose."

Mike, however, wasn't so sure. Was it right to act, without knowing all the facts? At what point, he wondered, did putting a 'spin' on a story turn into deception. In a way, he didn't like this side of Flapjack. For the first time, he saw how ruthless she could be, in pursuit of her prey. Her drive narrowed her perspective; gave her tunnel vision.

Ultimately, Mike resigned himself to their judgment. He was under enough pressure already. The tour was just a few weeks away, and with it, a trip into the belly of the beast. Still, for all his concerns, he slept with a clear conscience. He had a chance to do some real good, especially in a state that was pushing to remove the 'separation of church and state' clause from history textbooks. If there was one thing, Mike hated, it was ignorance, and he was happy to be fighting towards its destruction.

He only prayed it wouldn't make him a martyr. The death threats were increasing by the day.

* * *

Special Agent Colbert spread the silk napkin over his lap. He tried to remember the proper order for the silverware. Best to start with the small fork for salad, he decided, and work his way up with each course. That was one of the perks of being trained by the service. One had to know proper etiquette for any situation. Still, he had never dined at so lavish an establishment.

From across the table, Pastor Roy smiled warmly. He motioned a waiter with the flick of his wrist.

"We'll have a bottle of your finest champagne." He looked at Colbert. "Shall we have the next course? You've barely touched the appetizer!"

Colbert looked at the two prawns on his plate. They were decorated with a splash of golden glaze, with local herbs adding color to the presentation. It was almost too elegant to eat.

"We'll have a few minutes more, garcon."

Roy smiled. "So what do you think, Sam? I hope the food is to your liking."

"It's excellent," he replied. "I just had a rather heavy lunch."

"Well, I hope you have room for the main course. You know, I have it on authority that Tom Hartwell loves the Beef Wellington here. Pitcher for the Rangers. You like baseball, Sam?"

Colbert nodded. "Sure, I like baseball."

"I have to come here to enjoy it," Roy grumbled. You won't catch any Major League action in Amarillo. You want to experience the best, you go to Dallas, or Houston. You go to the city."

Colbert nodded. The rich texture of the dish seemed to melt in his mouth. Pastor Roy spent almost all of his time away from his base in the panhandle. Still, the money streamed in, and Roy had more than enough to afford life's luxuries. Certainly enough to assure Colbert's loyalty, for the time being. It was strictly business.

"You'll have to stay in Dallas a few days longer," he replied, dabbing the corner of his mouth with the napkin. "I've set up a meeting with some of the biggest names in the Republican Party right now. Cheney. Rumsfeld. The Bush brothers." He took a long sip from his champagne flute. "And they have serious concerns regarding their association with your… organization. Serious reservations."

"Just say it," groaned Roy. "I'm a big boy. I read the news."

"Well, some in the party would rather not be associated with—and you'll excuse me for saying—a history of Nazi collaboration."

Roy scowled. "Heck, I wasn't even born back them. Times were different."

"It doesn't matter. The Republican mainstream picks up on this, and they won't touch you with a ten-foot pole."

"Hell, Sam, how does this even get out? What do I pay you for at the Pentagon, anyway?"

"I can't be everywhere at once." Colbert shrugged. "Besides, without me, you wouldn't have any idea what's going on. I think I've earned my keep."

"Well, we gotta do something," urged Roy. "Contributions are down. People don't seem to get it. Hell, we sent all those dollars to convince Hitler *not* to attack the Jews. It wasn't the time. We needed them alive, for the final holy days of Revelations. They have to wage a final battle against the Arabs and the forces of darkness!"

Colbert raised his eyebrows. "Oh come on Roy, you don't honestly believe…"

"It doesn't matter what I believe! What matters is what my congregation believes. What matters is keeping a unified front, under the Rapture theology. Otherwise, a business so big it could register on the NASDAQ goes belly-up."

There was a moment of silence, as Colbert considered the gravity of Roy's claims. It would be unfortunate, he thought, to lose a client who paid so well. He did always prefer the working for religious organizations. It was less bloody, at least. But still, he would survive. He always did. Roy, on the other hand, was up Shit Creek without a paddle.

"The way I see it," he offered finally, as he chewed a particularly tender chunk of beef, "it's a catch-22."

"A catch-22?"

"You can stay out, let the media define the narrative, in which case this all spins out of control. You can play the 'hero,' as a savior of the Jews."

"In which case, I lose my core support from fundamentalist Christians."

"That, or you reveal the real reason behind those contributions," finished Colbert. "And you become—at best—the laughing stock of the political establishment."

"And at worst?" squeaked Roy.

"At worst, you're branded as a neo-Nazi hate group by the Southern Poverty Law Center. Just try campaigning for funds after that kind of publicity."

"Dessert, sir?"

The voice behind him made Roy jump. Up to that moment, he had been lost in thought, the wheels in his head were turning like mad. There had to be something he could do. Something to nip this in the bud, to manage the media, before it was too late.

"Ah! N-no, thank you. I'm fine."

"I'll have the chocolate lava cake," said Colbert. He handed both their menus to the maitre'd.

"How the hell can you be so calm," Roy hissed, when he was sure they were out of earshot. "If I go down, you know I'll have no reason to protect you. I'll sing like a canary about your involvement with us."

Colbert laughed. "Relax! I think I have an idea that just might solve our problems. But it involves leaking information to an enemy of the state. A group that wants the Jewish people discredited as much as you guys, in fact."

"I think I know just who you mean," said Roy, who had brightened considerably. "But just know, Sam, that when this goes down, the Western Glory

Church will condemn it. We'll be horrified by the acts of those terrorists responsible."

"Of course. You'll be vital in our push for military intervention abroad."

Colbert grinned, as the warm smell of molten cocoa wafted from his plate. Sure, they weren't as violent as the criminal underworld, he thought to himself. But when their interests were at stake, these holy men weren't afraid to get their hands a bit dirty.

Chapter 90

CONGRESSMAN PETERSON was late. When he finally burst through the door, panting and sweating more than usual, both Roy and Colbert were in mid-discussion.

"My apologies gentlemen," huffed the congressman. "The security, you know. Always checkin' and pokin' around for god-knows-what."

"Sit your ass down."

"I... I beg your pardon?"

"You heard me fat boy. I said sit your ass down. Being late is the least of your worries right now."

Peterson recoiled. He had never been spoken to like that before—particularly by a stranger—but he dared not disobey. The man's voice had a cold authority, but it was the eyes that scared him the most; the grey emptiness behind his gaze. Peterson had seen that look before. It was unmistakable. Placid and emotionless. The look of a contract killer.

"Congressman Talmadge Peterson, meet Agent Randall Colbert."

"And we wouldn't be having this meeting," snarled Colbert, "if you had just done your job in the first place. Now we're down to the wire. We're out of options. That's why you're here. You can't solve this problem. But you know someone who can?"

"What about what we talked about before?" asked Roy. "I thought we had a solution in place. With... you know..."

"With the Muslims?" barked Colbert. "We might have. Before the press ran wild on you. Now the word is out. Hell, they're even calling your ministry a Zionist front, for fuck sake!"

"You called them?"

"Yes I called them! The Popular Front for the Liberation of Palestine. The Afghani Taliban. I even called some contacts close to Saddam in Iraq. They almost laughed me off the phone."

"You'd think," said Roy, shaking his head, "that those ragheads would want to do something to stop a Hebrew plot!"

"Not for us they don't. Not when they think we're in on some joint U.S.-Israel operation. I don't blame them. It looks too much like a trap."

The congressman listened in silence. He was already having trouble following the discussion. After all, he always billed himself as the common man; a corn-fed, good ol' boy. He rarely followed up on current affairs. Leave that to the other scoundrels and snake-oil salesmen, he thought. They're the ones running Washington anyway. As long as he towed the line, and the checks still cleared, Talmadge Q. Peterson was content.

"Now," announced Colbert, turning to glare down at Peterson, "Congressman, it's time for you to earn your keep. You're our man on the southwest border. If Pastor Roy's done his job, you should have a few *compadres* in the Cartel, *si?*"

"Uh, si... I mean, yes! I... Yes," grunted Peterson, practically choking on his own words. He motioned weakly towards the door. "The guard. My personal bodyguard, Patricio. He's our liaison with the Gulf Cartel. It's how we scrub the money, you know?"

There was a moment of deathly silence. Pastor Roy took a deep breath.

"The Gulf Cartel... you mean..."

"*El Caballo?*" Colbert grinned. "Say what you will about his methods. His sicarios get the job done. And it's time we called in a favor."

After another awkward silence, Roy clapped his hands. "Well then, it's settled! The cartel will get their smuggling routes, why they even want to use UPS at the border—an easy thing to do—we'll snuff out this Founding Fathers operation, and things return to normal." He clapped Peterson on the shoulders. "Think you can handle it, Congressman?"

"There better be no fucking question," snapped Colbert, stabbing a finger towards the cowering figure. "Be a professional. Take care of your business. Or the business will take care of you."

Chapter 91

PATRICIO WAS LIKE a shadow. Wherever the congressman went, Patricio Hidalgo was never far behind. Always silent. Always somber. Congressman Peterson never could understand the boy. If only he could have hired a young black kid or African-American or whatever, he thought to himself; some rowdy lad to keep him company, to talk sports with. Instead, he had Patricio. A sullen teenage specter, haunting his footsteps like a ghost.

It was a necessary arrangement. After all, this was no ordinary boy. Patricio Hidalgo was not the son of some illegal orange picker or poppy farmer. No, this was the nephew of the most powerful man in Mexico. *El Caballo. El Patron.* The same blood ran through those veins. If the man wanted to connect a better life for his kin, the congressman didn't dare refuse. He had seen what happened to those who challenged the cartel. So Patricio worked in the office of a politician, and Congressman Peterson and his head remained attached. The agreement was mutually beneficial.

The congressman stared out the window and sighed. It was a dirty business. He knew that much, at least. For men like Roy and Colbert, the situation was delicate and complex. In Peterson's eyes, it was simple. The whole ruse hung in a perilous balance. A balance that had to be maintained, no matter what the cost. Shift too much aid towards Zionists, and the Jews would gain momentum. Leak too much to Hamas, and they could wipe Israel off the map. If either side broke the stalemate, Pastor Roy's "Rapture theology" fell apart. The two armies had to remain at war. As long as the forces of God warred with the Antichrist, well, Pastor Roy remained the Prophet of Revelations.

And donations flowed like milk and honey. He even thought up 'food baskets' for the end times which had brisk sales.

Congressman Peterson let out another audible sigh. "Patricio?" he wheezed. "Patricio? Dadgum, son. Where you hidin' at?"

The door opened slowly. A pair of soft brown eyes, from below a curly patch of dark hair, stared at the congressman expectantly. Slowly, quietly, Patricio shuffled towards his desk. His head bowed in submission.

"Si? Senor Peterson?"

"I'm gonna need a l'il favor, son. It's time to become a man."

* * *

Patricio was homesick.

He tried to repress such emotions. They made him feel guilty. Any young man, Tio had told him, would kill for his position. He was in America, and America was the land of opportunity. He knew he should be proud. The possibilities for advancement were limitless.

Still, Patricio hated the work. He hated the dull, stuffy government halls and offices. He hated working for such a pompous oaf, who always treated him with condescension. Part of him hoped some sniper would take out the bloated weasel. Then he could return to his home in Sinaloa, to the fresh mountain air of the Sierra Madre, far away from the Congressman Peterson and his lackeys. He missed his mother, his sisters, his friends in Culiacan. Now, after his briefing with the congressman, he shuffled sadly through a collection of old photographs. They were all he had left.

The memories gave him strength. Strength to do what was necessary.

He had to follow orders. Not only for himself, but for his loved ones. They depended on him. Still, he hated himself for it. This wasn't the first favor the congressman had asked of him. It wouldn't be the last, either, after he pulled this off. *If* he pulled this off. And that was a big "if," Patricio thought to himself. He had never done anything like this. It made him sick just thinking about it.

Patricio agonized over the decision. The congressman always had under-estimated him—equating his silence with weakness—and Patricio had always used it to his advantage. Even now, he knew the real reason he had been roped into this mission. Congressman Peterson was afraid. Afraid of *El Caballo*. Too frightened even to ask his assistance. Instead, he had passed the buck to this naïve foreign boy. Patricio could read the man like a cheap paperback. He knew the congressman assumed he would follow the orders of a white man without question.

Well, thought Patricio, he assumed incorrectly.

* * *

El Caballo had a hobby. It was no ordinary hobby, but then, the lord of the Gulf Cartel was no ordinary man. *El Caballo* collected dolls. More specifically, he collected their heads.

It was his way of remembering the dead. A tribute to *Santa Muerte,* like the ancient Aztecs had racks of skulls. For each man he killed—from the lowliest drug mule to the deadliest rival—he would add another head. Over the years, he had accumulated an impressive collection, which he proudly showed off to his guests. Tales of that ghastly menagerie had only added to his notoriety. The mariachis sang about it in their *nacrocorridos.* Death did not release those who crossed *El Caballo.* Their spirits remained trapped on his mantle, the gruesome trophies of his reign.

El Caballo spent a great deal of time with the dead. They were his only companions, now. The only ones he could trust. He was admiring them in his study when the call arrived.

"*El Patron?*"

"Patricio, my boy! You must call me Tio! We are family."

"Ah, Tio," continued the voice, "I am afraid I have a problem. The congressman, Señor Peterson... He has asked a terrible thing. A thing I fear I cannot do."

As *El Caballo* listened, the anger began to boil within him. If there was any love in his heart, it belonged to his children. He doted on his sons and daughters; his nephews and nieces. Patricio was among his favorites. Now, the congressman had crossed his bounds, that much was clear. Still, he mused, perhaps this was an opportunity for Patricio. A chance to get his feet wet in the family business. He made his decision.

"So, the congressman wishes for you to kidnap a man and a woman? To threaten them into silence and intimidate them? *Dios mio,* the man is such a fool."

"But what must I do?" urged Patricio. "I can't dare disobey the man. He is a man of power."

El Caballo smiled. "Calm yourself, *mijo,*" he reassured him. "I shall send a trained sicario. We will do what the gringo cannot do himself. It cannot be a kidnapping. It must be a hit."

"Murder?"

"It is business," he continued. "It is the only way to bring things to a conclusion. Something swift and final. Something professional."

"Ah," moaned Patricio. "It is a shame. But I respect your will, Tio."

"As for you," finished *El Caballo*, as he rearranged a line of heads, "you shall go along as support. But you shall stay in the car, where it is safe. It is time, now, for you to see how things are in this world. How business is transacted in blood."

In that alone, he thought, the congressman was right. The time of innocence had passed. The boy must become a man.

Chapter 92

IT WASN'T HOW Lorenzo preferred to work. He could take care of business himself. Experience had taught him, time and again, never to work with a partner. A partner is a liability. And now, here he was, planning a double-hit and babysitting the boss's kid. If *El Caballo* had one weakness, it was the *muchachos*. Lorenzo never could understand the Mexicans. They could torture, behead, and massacre all day, and then play with their kids after work. That was just how things were, south of the border.

Lorenzo Moreland considered himself lucky. As the son of an American lawyer and a Mexican nurse, he had the luxury of being educated and raised in the States, while still enjoying the perks of dual-citizenship. It had been a relatively carefree life in the suburbs of Miami. He spent most of his days surfing and lounging on the beach. Every so often, he and a group of friends would cross the Gulf to party in Cancun.

That all changed when he met *El Caballo*.

At first, it had started as a cheap thrill. A way to break the boredom. He met a few friends in the cartel, and began smuggling small amounts of marijuana, cocaine, and heroin across the border. It was easy money. The border agents saw his nice car and white skin, and waved him through. No questions asked. As time passed, he began to forge relationships with cartel insiders.

Then came the killing.

He had been drinking with friends, when *El Caballo*—then only a young lieutenant—swaggered into the bar. Lorenzo felt instant envy. They were the same age, yet he seemed to have it all; gold chains, diamond watches, his own entourage, and a beautiful woman on each arm. The man walked into the joint like he owned it. When he recognized Lorenzo, he picked up everyone's' tab, and sent a bottle of champagne to the table.

It was that night that Lorenzo made his decision. He had seen the tedious, 9-to-5 grind of his father's job, and held it in contempt. Now he knew what he was meant for. And the cartel embraced him with open arms.

Now, almost a decade later, his career had taken him from coast-to-coast. From the Gulf Coast to the Baja Peninsula. For a *sicario*—especially a trained killer like Lorenzo—the 49th Parallel offered a wealth of opportunities. There were always scores to be settled. Critics to be silenced. People who had seen or heard too much. Their bodies were rarely recovered. Cartels ruled the border towns with an iron-fist. For them, law enforcement was never an issue.

They *owned* the law enforcement.

* * *

As far as jobs go, Lorenzo thought, this was a routine operation. It was only a shrink and his wife, after all, and two bodies meant double the profit. And now, *El Caballo* had thrown a wrench in his plans. If anything happened to the boss's nephew, he figured, he would eat the barrel of his revolver. There was no way he'd be the next head on the mantle.

"Are we almost there?"

Lornezo grit his teeth. "We might have been, if you hadn't told me the wrong address. Twice."

"I dunno. Those were the apartments. The guy said they moved there."

"Well, they aren't there."

"I dunno."

In the front seat, Patricio gave a vacant, doe-eyed stare. He sucked noisily from his straw, again, for what seemed like the hundredth time. The sound was like nails on a chalkboard.

"Can you knock that off, kid?"

"Sorry."

"Don't be sorry. Just don't do it."

For a few minutes, Lorenzo enjoyed the silence—the blessed silence—while the boy fidgeted nervously in his seat. He knew it couldn't last. Sure enough, the boy turned on the radio, and began whistling with the music. Lorenzo switched it off.

"Hey. I was listening to that." Patricio pouted.

"Just sit still a little longer," Lorenzo snapped. "I just need to survey this neighborhood before we head back."

"But why?" whimpered Patricio. "We're not gonna find 'em."

"Because I said so." Lorenzo sighed. "Because we might get lucky and spot them. It's a long shot, yeah, but it's our best option."

Our best option, Lorenzo thought. Like finding a needle in a haystack. First the kid gives me an address forty-minutes away. Then he remembers the address, but the couple apparently don't live there. Exasperated, Lorenzo was cruising the nearby area, hoping to stumble across a sign of either target. It was a futile endeavor. He knew they were grasping at straws. Still, it beat reporting empty-handed. *El Caballo* was not one to take disappointment lightly.

"Hey! I think that's their car."

Lorenzo snapped to attention. A surge of adrenaline shot through him. It was the same thrill he'd felt a hundred times. The thrill of the hunt.

"Yeah. I remember that car from the picture," said Patricio. He pointed towards a lime-green Mercedes—an older model—parked just outside an art gallery.

Lorenzo slammed on the breaks. He grabbed the boy by the collar. "Listen kid," he hissed. "It's been a long day. If you're messing around…"

"I swear!" squeaked Patricio. "I swear to god! That was the car!"

As he backed up slowly, Lorenzo caught a glimpse of Patricio's face. It was drained of all color. So the boy is afraid, he thought to himself. Good. Fear makes one alert. Fear keeps a man alive. He parked the car a safe, but manageable distance away.

"Now," he said grimly, "we wait."

Patricio nodded.

"Sit there, shut up, and let me do my job," he added, as he trained his eyes on the building's entrance. "This should all be over soon."

Chapter 93

IT HAD BEEN a long day at the gallery.

Right now, all Anna wanted was to get home and rest. Her feet were aching. Her back was killing her. She hadn't even taken a lunch break. A long bath was in order, she decided, and a nice dinner out. David never took her out, after all. Well, tonight she was putting her foot down! But where to go?

Lost as she was in thought, Anna never noticed the strange man approaching from her right. By the time she saw him, it was too late to turn back. Anna braced herself. The last thing she needed right now was a discussion with a stranger. Still, she thought to herself, it could be worse. The man was well dressed, with a pencil-thin mustache and a swashbuckling grin. Was he a salesman, she wondered? Or was he a scam artist? Either way, he made her uneasy.

"¡*Hola Senora*!" She kept walking, as though she hadn't heard. He waved towards her. "Hello there, ma'am!"

"Umm… hello?" Anna forced a thin smile. The man was at least a foot taller than her.

She tried to recall where she kept her mace.

"May I speak to you a moment, ma'am?"

"I'm sorry, I'm really not interested." She shook her head. Her steps began to quicken, now. Just a little further to the safety of the car.

"Oh no, ma'am! You mistake me," laughed the man, now trailing behind her. "It is just, I believe I remember you from somewhere."

"I don't think so."

"Is your name Flapjack?"

Anna froze. She swung around, a look of suspicion on her face. "Who are you?" she asked tentatively. "What is it you want?"

"Ah, Senora Flapjack," said the man, his arms outstretched. "I am simply here on business. I simply must have an interview with you and your husband. Perhaps, if you would be so kind," he continued, gesturing towards his truck, "you could come with us, and we could all talk together."

Anna turned. "I'm afraid I'm not who you think I am," she replied, resuming her pace. "Flapjack is my daughter. And if you'd like an interview with her and Mike, well, you'll have to consult with the Surgeon Gen…"

Her voice trailed off. Something cold and hard was pressed against her back. She dropped her keys to the asphalt.

"I'm afraid, ma'am, that I was not asking."   Anna remained silent and motionless. The man's breath was hot on her neck. "Do you know what this is?"

She nodded. "I can hazard a guess."

"It's .38 snub-nosed revolver."

"Young man," said Anna, as she fought to remain calm. "Whatever you're trying to do, I assure you, it's not worth it."

The man shoved the barrel hard against her spine. "Turn," he commanded gruffly. "Turn and start walking."

Slowly, carefully, the two of them began walking towards the dark shadow of the truck.

*　*　*

On the outside, Lorenzo was a professional. He was cold as ice. On the inside, however, his anxieties mounted. This wasn't how the job was supposed to go. Not at all. A kidnapping would only make things messier. Still, it couldn't be helped. First, he had to verify if this was, in fact, one of the targets. Civilians were off-limits. After confirmation, she'd have to lead him to her husband. If all went to plan, he'd have the job wrapped-up before sunset.

But things weren't going to plan.

To make things worse, the lady was hardly an agreeable captive. Still, he had to admit, this was one tough broad. Being held at gunpoint hadn't fazed her for long. First, she tried to reason with him. When that failed, she turned to insults and threats. For the entire walk, she hardly seemed to stop for breath. It was beginning to give him a headache.

"You're crazy and simple-minded!" snapped Anna, as they approached his large Chevy. "Do you realize you're kidnapping me here? That you could go to prison?!"

"Dios mio," Lorenzo groaned. He opened the back door. From the front seat, Patricio stared at him, his mouth agape.

"Hey!" barked Lorenzo. "Don't just sit there! Pass me the rope."

"I don't see it!"

"Look under the seat!"

Patricio's head popped up. He shrugged dumbly. "I don't see it."

"¡Hijo de puta!" swore Lorenzo. He released his grip on the hostage for a moment. "Then check the compartments! Check the-AUGH!!"

A moment was all it took. One small distraction. The last thing he saw, as he yelled out his orders, was a blur in front of his face. Then the burn. It seared his nostrils. His eyes burned like hot coals. It was as though a hot iron had been pressed against his face. Lorenzo dropped the gun and doubled over. Through the hot tears, he could see only blurry shapes and objects. One of them was moving quickly towards the building.

"¡Mierda!"

Chapter 94

ANNA WAS BREATHING HARD. The last few seconds seemed to pass in a blur. It was as though she had been on autopilot. Now, as she came to her senses, she realized she was breathing heavily. In her hand, she still clutched the small can of pepper spray. It took less than a second for her memory to recover.

She was alive.

She was still in danger, she knew, but at least she was alive. Her assailant had been close behind. He was kicking at the oaken doors to the gallery. They held firm. Even from her office, she could hear him cursing in a fluid mix of English and Spanish.

Then she heard a blast. Then another. The sound of glass shattering.

Anna screamed.

Helplessly, she watched through the glass doors of her office. There was a scuffling sound against the walls. Oh God, she realized. He was climbing up the window. How long until he reached the opening? All she could do was wait. Wait, and pray that the cavalry was coming.

The she heard it. The sound—faint at first, but growing louder—of sirens.

The scuffling outside stopped.

Moments later, she heard a motor revving up, it's tires squealing on the pavement. Then the sound of yelling. A man on a megaphone.

Gunshots.

Then only the wail of the squad car.

Exhausted, Anna collapsed in her chair. It was finally over. Then she realized, with a sickening feeling, that perhaps this wasn't the end. Perhaps, for her daughter and Mike, the danger had just begun.

* * *

At first, the voice on the receiver was indiscernible. All the congressman could hear was the sound of sobbing. There was an engine in the background. Besides that, the words were muffled and confused.

"Breathe deep now, y'here?" grumbled the congressman. "I can't make out a dadgum thing. Calm down."

There was a pause. Now he could hear the sirens.

"Congressman Peterson?"

"Patricio? Dear God, Patricio, is that you?"

"Congressman, sir," whined the terrified voice. "This is all wrong. I cannot do this."

"Patricio, what in tarnation?!"

"Got Lorenzo! They got him! I saw it! They're after me!" he whimpered between gasps. "You must help me!"

Congressman Peterson shot from his sofa. "Well, Jesus Christ, Patricio! Don't you come over here!" he bellowed. "Don't you even think about it, now!"

There was a click. The receiver went dead. For a few moments, the air was deathly quiet. Congressman Peterson could feel his heart pounding like a hammer. His mouth hung open in horror. This could not be happening. Would Patricio really lead them right to his door?

The sound in the distance confirmed it.

The sound of a truck. The wail of one siren. Then another.

Before long, his driveway was bathed in the red and blue lights. The sounds of struggle. But by then, Congressman Peterson heard nothing. He had already passed out.

Chapter 95

FLAPJACK AND MIKE had been busy all day. For hours, they remained unaware of Anna's ordeal. In fact, they themselves were halfway across the city, when their would-be assassins struck. It was nightfall by the time David reached them.

The news left them speechless.

Shots had been fired. Three men were under arrest. One of them was Congressman Talmadge Peterson himself. Anna—to their overwhelming relief—had emerged unscathed. Her assailant had taken a bullet to the shoulder. He was in stable condition.

By the time they reached the gallery, the investigation was almost wrapped up. There were still police at the scene. One suspicious officer stopped them as they attempted to cross the yellow tape, but backed off when David called them over. He ushered them into the office.

"There you two are! Apparently I still look as young as my daughter!"

Wrapped in a blanket, Anna smiled up from the sofa chair. She raised her cup of tea to them. Flapjack began to cry.

"Oh Mom!" she sobbed, as she embraced her in a bear hug. "If something had happened to you..."

"Oh nonsense," Anna chuckled. "It would take more than a hooligan and a pipsqueak like that to bring me down." She patted her daughter on the back tenderly.

Flapjack smiled through the tears. At least her mother hadn't lost her toughness. Even after all she had been through, she was the one who consoled them. It was another reminder of their love for each other.

David and Mike walked through the gallery together. When they reached the second floor, David motioned a short distance ahead.

"Right over there."

The floor was littered with glass and plaster. The window was shattered.

"That's where the bullets hit," he added, gesturing towards the wall. There were two bullet holes in the paintings. One had torn through a Thomas Hart Benton piece, the other through an expensive Howard Cook.

"Oh no."

"Yep." David shook his head. "This really hit Anna hard. I told her we could restore them, but she's still devastated."

Mike couldn't help a small smile. "She's quite a woman," he said sheepishly. "Anyone else would still be traumatized from the attack."

"And she's more concerned with her art," David finished. He smirked. "No one messes with her art."

"God help them," Mike agreed. Then the thought struck him. "Who are *they* anyway?" he asked. "Who would do something like this? It doesn't make sense."

The smile evaporated from David's face. "We need to talk about that. Let's just say, someone *really* wants to stop this tour."

* * *

Everything seemed surreal to Patricio. He had never been incarcerated before. It was only a holding cell, but it made the world seem dark and small. At least he was handling it better than his cellmate. Congressman Peterson was almost unrecognizable in a standard orange jumpsuit. Patricio had only seen the large man in tailored suits. Yet here he was, this once great man, who was cowering in the corner of their cell. He was still sniveling with self-pity, even hours later. The scene filled Patricio with disgust.

"¡Que putada! Be a man."

Huddled in the corner, the congressman groaned.

"At least stop whining," Patricio snapped. "It's giving me a headache."

"This is your fault," his ex-boss replied. "What is wrong with you anyway? Do you realize what you've done?"

"You told me it was time to be a man."

The congressman spat on the floor. "You think the police are going to believe you?" he growled. "I'll be out as soon as I post bail. You Mexicans are savages. Shooting up art galleries and kidnapping old ladies! You should be ashamed."

"Ah, but *Señor* Peterson, that is the justice of the gang."

The door to the bloc creaked open. Even from across the hall, the man's voice was unmistakable. He twirled the keys on his finger and whistled.

"You protect your brothers, and get revenge on your enemies," *El Caballo* continued. He unlocked the door. "You should know, *Señor* Peterson. Patricio has one boss. *El Jeffe*. The father who takes care of him."

Congressman Peterson fought to respond. His tongue turned to ash in his mouth. Silently, he watched as *El Caballo* crooked a finger towards his nephew. Patricio trudged from the cell with his eyes downcast. He was as docile as a puppy.

"I… I don't understand," the congressman stammered. "I'm not in a gang! I'm a member of Congress!"

"Oh but you are," laughed *El Caballo*. "In my country, it is the cartel. In America, you call them Republicans. Who is more criminal? Your gang steals from the poor and gives to the rich. They spill blood for their oil."

"Now just a minute…"

"Let us see, Señor Peterson, if your gringo *patron* will take care of you."

The door clanged shut. The key clicked in the lock. In a moment, the footsteps disappeared. Congressman Peterson was alone. Miserable, cold, and alone.

Chapter 96

AGENT ANGELO FALCONE admired the paintings. He had never been a man of the arts, but he did admire the vivid colors and characters. As he waited, Anna had come to offer tea and company. It was remarkable, he thought, how full of life she seemed. It was only a day after the ordeal! As they talked, he wondered if she understood the gravity of the situation. She was only a woman, after all. He offered his sympathies.

"Ah, Agent Fielder!"

"Angelo, please sit," urged David, as Falcone began to rise. "And call me David. We're not at the office, after all."

Anna smiled. "Well, I'm sure you boys have some business to catch up on." She stood, and gave her guest a polite nod.

David waited until they were both alone. "You must accept my apologies," he said finally. "I hate to keep you waiting. I hope my wife wasn't a bother."

Falcone shook his head, as David refilled their tea. "Not at all! It was a pleasure! It's rare to meet a woman so..." he paused, in search of a word.

"Clever?"

"Exactly!"

"She's a rare one, especially after what she's been through," David agreed. "I'm a very lucky man."

* * *

It took a long time for the conversation to reach business. It was just how things were between agents, the code of brotherhood. Theirs was an elite fraternity. Honor and chivalry was to be maintained. And so, as the tea grew cold, David endured the tedious nonsense.

Still, as Angelo droned on, David couldn't help realizing the absurdity of it all. Neither man trusted the other, and they both knew it. The danger of betrayal was a constant threat. It was like the Mafia, he thought darkly. Your killer comes with a smile and a handshake.

"So Angelo," said David, when he felt enough time had elapsed. "I know your investigation is private, but I must ask. Have you had a chance to question the congressman?"

Angelo laughed. "Question him? The fat man sang like a canary. He couldn't wait to try and butter us up."

"And?"

"And it was what we suspected. He gave up contacts linked to Pastor Alvin Roy, who's holed up in the panhandle. From there we followed up on papers, telephone records, and cancelled checks. There's even a money transfer to Palestine." Angelo grinned. "And this is the best part. We found Peterson's journal in his office."

"Jesus Christ. He kept records?"

"Yep. The man took notes on a whole criminal conspiracy. Not the sharpest tool in the shed."

"Congratulations," offered David. "What I'm really concerned about is, are they still out there? Is there still a danger to Mike and Flapjack."

Angelo smiled. "That's the other good news. We no longer require the use of your daughter or her husband. I believe we have all the evidence we need."

"And the tour?"

"What tour?"

"The Founding Fathers Tour. It's still to proceed as scheduled?"

Angelo peered at him curiously. Then he laughed. "Oh please, David," he said, slapping his thigh. "You're kidding right? You didn't actually think there was a tour, did you? That we need that kind of publicity."

David stood up violently. His empty cup and saucer fell to the floor. "But Angelo! I gave him my word? How could we deceive him like this? How do you expect him to trust me? To trust the government for that matter."

"Then don't tell him." Angelo sipped his tea calmly. "You know it's not personal. It's just the nature of the business."

The words never reached David. He had already stormed from the room.

*   *   *

"There is a fine exhibition of 19th century German bisque dolls at the Smithsonian," said *El Caballo*, reading from the Post article.

"*Que es esto?*" asked Patricio, "this 'bisque'. Do you eat them?"

"No, at least not these," said *El Caballo*. "I have come to prefer a symbol for my trophies. It is more civilized. I take off their heads and still put them on the *Azteca*. My children are no longer afraid, which is good, no?"

Patricio forced a smile, but felt crazy. Everything in his life was crazy. There was no moral compass, no compass at all, in fact, and he began to realize he would never know when or where or how he would die.

Chapter 97

THE EIGHTIES PASSED slowly with an Administration in denial of everything. Not even the effects of agent orange on Vietnam veterans was enough of a wake-up call. Mike was astonished when the White House shut down the CDC's research on dioxin toxicity since the sixties, back when they found it was a contaminant in herbicide.

Mike went the extra mile to educate Congress about the carcinogenic effects of dioxin. Still, his warnings fell on deaf ears. A member of the Texas delegation even made land near the San Jacinto river a dumping ground for dioxin. Years later, the area would report one of the highest rates of cancer in the country.

The decade began with a deep recession, to which almost the whole world responded by loosening controls on business and industry. Reagan dismantled the progressive income tax and Alan Greenspan convinced him to pay for it by borrowing billions from the Social Security trust fund. Wealth began to drift into the hands of a smaller and smaller group of people as the middle-class began to disappear. Eisenhower's belief that redistribution of wealth into the hands of a few made fascism possible was lost on the Neo-cons.

The trend toward a global economy was aided by the computer revolution—with names like the 'IBM 5150', 'Eniac', Unix', Univac'—and the machines became commonplace in the Pentagon and other government facilities. Reagan began the military build-up to compete with the Soviets, all the while calling for "open communication."

The Vietnamese continued to fight with the Khmer Rouge. Le Duan died in the latter part of the decade, which caused the country to transition to a free market economy. John Lennon was killed in 1980. Reagan was shot in 1981, and Anwar Sadat was killed later that year. Revolutions occurred in Africa, South America, Yugoslavia, Fiji, the Philippines and other small countries. China crushed its student rebellion. Iraq and Iran battled for almost the whole decade. Afghanistan depleted Russia, and, following the Chernobyl incident in 1986, the Soviet Union fell apart. Reagan's tenure in the White House was disastrous. Under his watch, Central America became another killing field, as children watched their innocent parents mowed down by U.S.-funded butchers.

The Agency was busy. George H.W. Bush, the previous director, chose to stay under the radar after conservatives accused him of attempting to assassinate Reagan. The vacuum he left behind was quickly filled with greed and political infighting. Chaos reigned in the government.

Despite the efforts of the far-right, Bush managed to become President. He immediately focused his attention on the middle-east. Already, Saddam Hussein's reign of terror had surged over the border into Kuwait. Saddam's days as an ally of the Reagan administration were at an end. Now, Bush's Generals began to push him back towards Baghdad. Bush seemed to sense that Saddam was the key to controlling disputes between the Shia and Sunni, however, and ultimately left him in power.

Clinton defeated Bush in the next election, and went on to build a surplus the next Bush would squander on his "new militarism." During the Clinton administration, the Branch Davidians in Waco, Texas were attacked by the FBI, and the Oklahoma City bombing of the federal building in 1995 was allegedly perpetrated in revenge.

*   *   *

When Moon left the Air Force, he managed to publish Mike's research as planned. The Pentagon was livid. Almost immediately, it released a barrage of criticism against the report. It quickly commissioned new studies, all claiming that families were "happy" and "resilient." Moon had to deal with harassment both personally and professionally. He eventually joined Doctors Without Borders and disappeared off the grid. Try as he might, Mike couldn't find a trace of him.

"Damn, Flapjack," said Mike one night, after a long and fruitless search. "I feel bad about this. Maybe he shouldn't have published it."

Flapjack frowned sadly. "I know what you mean. Still, he knew what might happen, and he knows where we are. I think he's protecting us by disappearing."

"I just hope he's all right."

"Me too."

Chapter 98

THE FOLLOWING MONTHS felt surreal.

Everything seemed to happen at once. Suddenly, Mike and Flapjack were under constant surveillance. Neither could leave the house without armed protection. The Founding Fathers Tour was suddenly and abruptly cancelled. David never talked of it, nor answered his questions. It was as though it never existed in the first place. Meanwhile, Mike found himself working long hours in the Pentagon. He was safe from an assassin's bullet, but still, the tedium of the routine was wearing on him. It was a relief when he and Flapjack were finally taken off twenty-four-hour guard. For now, it appeared, the danger had waned. David and Anna took them for dinner to celebrate.

Anna, as usual, was in high spirits. Her good mood always seemed to rub off on her husband. Her kindness and generosity made Mike feel increasingly guilty. After all, she had almost taken a bullet for him. He often shuddered to think how he would have handled the situation in her place. And yet, ever since the incident, he had never heard her speak a word of complaint.

"I have to ask," said Mike, as they shared desserts. "How did you do it, Anna? How did you stay so calm? Weren't you afraid?"

Anna peered at him curiously. "Afraid of what?"

"Of your kidnappers!"

"Oh, that!" she laughed. "I'm not sure. I suppose instinct kicks in? Something just clicked inside me when he mentioned my daughter." She smiled affectionately at Flapjack. "No one harms my daughter."

"Aw, mom!" Flapjack's eyes began to water. "I love you so much."

"What I want to know," said Anna, pointing a fork towards David, "is whether she and Mike are finally safe."

David paused. He wiped the crumbs from his mouth carefully. "I believe so," he announced. "The congressman helped us the most. His journal helped us put Pastor Roy and some of his high-ranking staffers behind bars. From there, the money order receipts at the Western Glory headquarters told the stories. Turns out they were funding a dizzying number of conflicting interest groups. Roy was in bed with the Palestine Liberation Front *and* the Jewish Defense League."

Flapjack gasped. "Jesus Christ."

"No kidding," added David, with a mouthful of crème brulee. "Not only that, he's on the hook for tax fraud, polygamy, and money laundering. The good pastor has built quite a rap sheet."

Mike listened in rapt attention. The details made his head spin. All this had been going on, and all the while he had lived in the darkness, never knowing the danger he was in. He realized, suddenly, that something was missing. A major player in the story.

"And what about El Caballo?" he asked. "Wasn't the Gulf Cartel involved."

David shrugged. "Honestly? I have no idea."

"No idea?"

"He just vanished. Into thin air." David shrugged. "He's a survivor. Who knows when he'll show up again. What matters is, we should be safe. At least for now."

So they were safe? Mike wanted to believe it. Not too long ago, he knew, he would have accepted David's words without question. He would have trusted the powers that be. Now he was unconvinced. He wondered if he would ever be sure of anything again.

*   *   *

Late after dinner, when both Anna and Flapjack were fast asleep, Mike still felt awake and restless. He sat by the hearth, watching the fire and drinking coffee with David. From the look on his face, Mike knew the man bore a great weight on his shoulders.

"Mike," said David, after a long period of silence, "I have something I need to talk to you about. Something I couldn't discuss in front of the girls."

"Oh?"

"It's these goddamn cults. It's like attacking a hydra. Cut off one head, and three more grow in its place."

Mike sipped from his mug as he listened. It seemed unnecessary, he thought, to avoid serious discussion around the women. Flapjack would be particularly interested in the subject. Still, David was from an older era, and there was no changing his ways.

"But the Western Glory…"

"Yes, we stopped them, and that just opened a power vacuum," David continued. "There's already a power struggle between rival evangelicals. These groups, they just grow and mutate like a virus."

"It can't be worse than the Rapturists, can it?"

"You'd be surprised. There are bigger fish out there. One "elite" group in Washington believe they are God's 'chosen people.' That they are the ones to implement a 'Seven Seas Strategy' for world domination."

Mike listened, in rapt attention, as David spoke at length about the threat. The group had already recruited a congressman into its ranks, he found, and planned to control America by transforming the military. There was documented evidence that the group had infiltrated large service academies. Its leaders had been emboldened by Reagan's election, and pressured the Military Construction Committee to build chapel complexes that would serve as their bases of operation.

As Mike listened, he realized that nothing seemed too outlandish or far-fetched anymore. The idea that congressmen could be mobilized to form voting blocs on such issues as abortion and climate change seemed entirely plausible. He was no longer under any illusions. Power in America rested less with the people and more with the special interests of corporations and fundamentalists.

"How would you like some of these fanatics, like the Rapturists, to be stationed at our missile silos?" David asked finally. "These are people that want a holy war in the middle-east!"

"I get it," said Mike, "believe me, I do. But what can I do about it? I've been a pawn in this game the whole time."

David shook his head. "You underestimate yourself, son," he responded gravely. "You're still in an important position, in a place where you can make a difference. That's the only reason I can share all this information with you."

"I want to do what I can."

"Well, that's what I wanted to talk about," said David, looking Mike square in the eye. "I have another job for you. One that I'm not asking you to do for me, or for the agency, but for the well being of our country."

Mike stroked his chin. He took a moment to think before responding. "I don't know, David. Honestly, I don't feel I can trust anyone anymore." He paused. "Except, that is for Flapjack."

"Ah, yes. You can trust my daughter."

"Good," added Mike, "because I won't take the job without her on board.

David winced. He sat back in his chair and sighed. "Very well. I don't agree, but I'll allow her to join you. But I hold you responsible for her well-being."

"You won't have to worry," Mike assured him. "She's more than capable of thinking and acting for herself."

David sighed once more; a long, tired sigh.

"I certainly hope so. Because you're about to enter the world of a very depraved and twisted individual. An extremely dangerous man."

Chapter 99

MIKE KNEW HIS WIFE was up to the task, and she didn't disappoint. Within a week, she had scoured every resource at their disposal, and they had more data than they knew what to do with. As Flapjack continued to search for leads, Mike was hard at work mining the documents and putting the pieces together. What began to emerge was the portrait of a profoundly disturbed figure. A tyrant controlled by his own narcissism and megalomania. Just as David had suggested, Saddam Hussein was a dangerous man. Already his influence had spread like a weed across the middle-east.

Mike was particularly fascinated, however, by Saddam's rise to power. After all, he had emerged from relatively humble origins. As Mike researched, the story gradually unfolded. Born in the tribal regions of Tikrit in 1937, Saddam spent much of his youth in Baghdad, where his Uncle Talfah instilled in him a deep belief in Arab Nationalism. As a young revolutionary, he would later join the Ba'athist Party and collaborate in an assassination plot against the President of Iraq, who favored the Communists over the Arab Union.

When the plot failed, Saddam fled to Egypt, where he attended law school. He returned to Iraq in 1963, after the Ramadan Revolution, but was imprisoned until his 1966 escape. When the new President took office, however, the balance of power changed. Saddam was appointed as his deputy in 1968. It was from there that he began his bloody rise to power.

When Saddam Hussein eventually took over, he would rule his people with an iron fist. Any opposition or resistance to his regime was crushed. His rivals were executed. His paranoia about ethnic uprising in Iran would lead to all-out war against the Shi'ites. During that time, he tortured and murdered with impunity. Entire villages and towns were annihilated in his attempted genocide of the Kurdish people. The dead were buried in mass graves. Perhaps unsurprisingly, he was influenced by the regime of Stalin.

The realization that such a dictatorship could still exist shook Mike to his core. He was stunned. Outraged. Why wasn't anything being done? Could anything stop the carnage? And what would happen when Saddam turned his eye overseas? It was a thought that made him shudder.

* * *

"What I can't believe," Flapjack told him, over dinner one night, "is the guy still had a chance to have a personal life."

"Come again?"

"You know! A personal life. Didn't you read over the dossier?"

Mike poured himself a drink. He cocked an eyebrow at Flapjack. "I'd hardly call that much of a personal life. More like, well, more like a bad soap opera."

"Two wives and five kids," she continued. "And each one raised to be as brutal as their father."

"And don't forget what happened when he married his second wife, Samira, without getting a divorce from Sajida," added Mike. "She gets her son Uday to murder Kamel, the man who introduced Saddam to Samira, and he does it at a party for Mubarak's wife, no less!"

"Yep. And Kamel was Saddam's friend and food taster, too. I read he was so mad that he banished Uday to Switzerland."

Flapjack smirked grimly. "So much for Saddam's family values." She pulled a worn notebook from her purse, and handed it to Mike. "So if you take a look at the checklist, we have grandiosity. We have lack of empathy. Ruthlessness. Not to mention revenge, mass-murder, adultery, torture, and narcissism. What on earth could produce such a monster?"

Mike frowned. "Does it matter? Understanding behavior is sometimes mistaken for excusing it, and there is no excuse for this. What I want to know is how monsters like Stalin, Hitler, and Saddam get these positions of power in the first place."

"They murder the opposition," replied Flapjack. "They build an army to bully, torture, and threaten everyone else into traumatized submission. It's like Stockholm Syndrome. The victims identify with their aggressor and completely submit."

"And you think that's the case with Saddam?"

"Probably."

"If I were a psychoanalyst, I'd say he exhibits a form of pathological narcissism," said Mike thoughtfully. "The result of his mother's depression and abandonment. And of course, there was the abuse at the hands of his stepfather."

Flapjack nodded. "And that would cause him to lack empathy," she added, "to lose himself in his own egomania. It enables him to brutalize his enemies without guilt. All that matters to him is the acquisition of power and his own self-aggrandizement. The suffering of others is only the means to an end. He exploits the religious and political ideals of his people for his own gain."

"Does that sound familiar to you?" asked Mike sadly.

"Pastor Roy?"

"Yep. Pastor Roy all over again."

"And we know he won't be stopped—not by wealth or power or family. He may come to the notion of starting a war—none of his generals will oppose him and he's not one to negotiate."

"Perhaps Uday's loyalty should be explored," said Flapjack.

* * *

After developing a comprehensive profile, Mike and Flapjack passed their ideas to David, who in turn discussed them with the director of the Agency. For the next few days, Mike thought little about the assignment. David had assured him that the response to the threat would be swift and effective. It finally seemed that the proper measures would be taken. It was all the more shocking, however, when David told them the news.

"Nothing is to be done."

"Nothing?!"

"That's right. The powers-that-be have decided to leave the situation alone." Mike was stunned. Had they even read the report?

"But... why?" asked Flapjack, who sounded as confused as Mike felt.

David shook his head sadly. "The director thinks differently," he replied. "He believes any man or woman can be redeemed, if they repent and live a religious life."

"But the man is a psychopath!" argued Mike. "He's beyond rehabilitation!"

"Tell that to the director. To him, no one is beyond redemption."

Mike left the meeting in a daze. He couldn't comprehend the ignorance of the people in charge. He felt the old familiar feelings well within him. Frustration. Frustration and helplessness.

Chapter 100

IT WASN'T UNTIL the early years of the '90s that Mike began to feel optimistic. Finally, Reagan was out of the White House, and the tide began to turn against Saddam. President George H.W. Bush had no love for the Iraqi tyrant. When Saddam's forces began to spill into Kuwait, the combined might of the U.S. armed forces would push him back to Baghdad. Still, Bush seemed hesitant to take decisive action. Saddam Hussein was a necessary evil, a way to control disputes between the Shia and Sunni peoples. It wasn't until the election of Clinton that Mike thought the threat might be finally dealt with.

The best news, by far, came the same year as the election. A new administration meant a new Surgeon General, a changing of the guard, and Mike couldn't believe who earned the promotion.

"General Creaser!" blurted Mike, as he entered the office.

"That's Surgeon General Creaser to you, son!"

Mike laughed. He shook Creaser's hand firmly. It was good to see his old boss again. It had been a long time, after all. Too long.

"I can't believe it!" said Mike, before correcting himself. "I mean, I can believe, I just didn't expect it! How does Mrs. Creaser feel about all this?"

Creaser grinned from ear-to-ear. "She's in heaven. The move is perfect for her, what with the symphony and all. She asked me to invite you and Flapjack to dinner."

"We'd be delighted!"

"And you'll never guess who recommended my promotion."

"Who?"

"Senator Cochran!" laughed Creaser, as though it were the punchline for a joke. "I'm sure you remember Senator Cochran and his boy."

"Oh God, how could I forget?"

"Well, it turns out he thinks I did him a huge favor. Having his son back has had a lot of advantages. After all, the kid figured out all sorts of ways to smuggle Cuban cigars, earn campaign money on the sly, and even do special favors for certain constituents."

Mike chuckled. "Sounds like the apple doesn't fall far from the tree."

"Nope. The boy's a natural politician. Just like his old man!"

* * *

Mike had a long talk with Flapjack that night. Creaser's promotion had changed everything. Until then, the couple had felt increasingly discontent with their work at the Pentagon. They're work on the Saddam assignment had been thorough—too thorough, it seemed—and they had been relegated to the role of glorified paper-pushers. Both of them had agreed to resign at the end of the year. Now, even with Creaser in charge, Flapjack was skeptical things would be different.

In the end, Mike persuaded her to stay a while longer. She was particularly impressed by Creaser's interest in helping military families and veterans with PTSD. As long as the two of them were given meaningful work—work that would actually make a difference—she wanted to stay.

The next few years would be some of the most rewarding in Mike's career. Life was good in Washington. The work was exhausting, but endlessly stimulating. It was during this time that he and Flapjack began a family, too, with the birth of their first child. Anna and David, for their part, were loving grandparents, who spoiled the child with attention. Still, David always seemed reserved around Mike. Always distant and aloof. It was not until years later that Mike would learn the reason why.

* * *

At the Pentagon, Mike was able to accomplish more than he ever thought possible. He could hardly remember a time before the use of computers. The machines fascinated him, with their ability to synthesize data and study complex human interactions. One of his first studies discovered that the addition of daycare centers on military bases could dramatically reduce the rate of child abuse. True to his word, Creaser presented Mike's report to Congress, who then provided the funding and resources necessary. As a result, the rate of domestic abuse dropped nationwide.

Creaser was a skilled bureaucrat, and he knew how to get things done. Nothing could be accomplished through military channels. Congress, he knew, was the only hope for military families and traumatized veterans. For the rest of the Pentagon, ignorance was bliss.

Mike and Flapjack's work did not go unnoticed. Gradually, the office of the Surgeon General began to gain a reputation. It earned the notoriety of being the "progressive department" of the Pentagon; the "Congressional Wing." Through it all, Mike had to give Creaser credit. It was obvious that he faced a mountain of pressure to narrow his focus. Still, the Surgeon General held firm. He remained steadfast in his efforts to improve the lives of military families.

For all their opposition, however, the Surgeon General's office received some high profile support. Creaser's stance made him something of a national hero, in a time when the public had begun to sympathize with the plight of military wives, children, and veterans. Invitations came for him to speak before family and child advocacy groups, conferences, and universities. At one point, he was even invited to the White House by the First Lady. It was during these absences that Mike, Flapjack, and a handful of associates would act as his deputies.

Mike hardly envied Creaser's new found fame. The last thing he wanted was the invasive attention of the press. He was simply content to work with his wife on issues that were important to him. It came as a surprise, therefore, when an invitation came not for Creaser, but for him! Try as he might, he could not figure why someone would single him out. Neither he nor Flapjack knew anyone at the University of Virginia, and yet here was an invitation, on official letterhead, from the Department of Psychiatry. Who was it, he wondered, that wanted to recognize his achievements? The answer came as a shock.

Part V:
The Confession

Chapter 101

MIKE HAD LITTLE TIME to ponder his mysterious invitation. For the first time in a long while, the pressure seemed to be getting to Creaser. Their meetings were longer and more frequent now. The days of the Clinton administration were almost at an end. To Creaser, the polling data drew a bleak picture of his future in the department. He had, after all, been a vocal critique of the emerging neo-conservative movement, a movement that seemed poised to seize control of the White House.

"I can't believe we're on the verge of another Bush presidency," he lamented to Mike and Flapjack. "He's only the puppet. The ones I'm afraid of are Rumsfeld and Rove and Cheney. The ones pulling the strings."

"There's still the election," offered Mike weakly.

Creaser stared him straight in the eye. There was a wild, almost feral look in his eyes.

"You!" he announced, pointing towards Mike. "You of all people should be alarmed! You know there are rumors that a lot of our work for military families is about to be undone?"

Mike looked helplessly to Flapjack for support. She shook her head sadly.

"He's said he's in favor of increasing American influence abroad," she added. "That means more troops abroad, and longer deployment times. He's already pushed for "Stop-Loss" maneuvers to keep troops in the field for 15-months at a time. And you know what happens when it hits that threshold."

"The rate of PTSD skyrockets," finished Mike. "Up to 40%." He had to admit, she had a point. The consequences could be disastrous.

"It's bad enough I can't even work through my colleagues at the Pentagon," continued Creaser angrily. "Things only get done through Congress. And most of them are in the pockets of the lobbyists."

"And lobbyists are having them build more churches than clinics," said Flapjack, as if on cue. "I've heard the academy at Colorado Springs is like a Christian Mecca."

"Exactly!" declared Creaser. He turned his attention to her now, as he continued. "And that reminds me! We've had a lot of complaints coming all the time from parents of cadets. Worrisome complaints. There's a culture of hazing that still exists, and it needs to be investigated."

"I'd like to volunteer for that post, sir."

The words took the wind from Mike's sails. He had just begun to open his mouth, when Flapjack took the initiative.

"I think that's a good idea," Creaser mused. "After all you seem to have the best handle on the situation."

"I'll do my best sir."

The words cut Mike to the bone. As he flinched, he was surprised to feel a new, unfamiliar emotion course through him. Was he jealous, he wondered, of his own wife? The idea would have seemed absurd. But by volunteering, it felt as though she had violated some unspoken rule between them. Until now, they had always talked things over first. Usually, the assignments had fallen to him, but he had assumed Flapjack wanted it that way. Could he have been wrong the whole time?

More importantly, Mike wondered, did he have some of the prejudice he so disliked in David? Was he unconsciously afraid of a woman in authority? The thought was a humbling one. He dismissed it offhand.

Chapter 102

AS THE DAY OF THE SPEECH drew closer, things went from bad to worse. Creaser's worst suspicions were confirmed. After a long, contentious battle over recounted ballots, the conservative-right was in control. To the surprise of everyone, Creaser maintained his post as Surgeon General. The more Mike thought about it, however, the more it all made sense. With no source of funding and few allies, Creaser was hardly the threat he once seemed to the Bush administration. Keeping him in office at least propped up the illusion of bipartisanship.

It was a clever move, thought Mike. Too clever for a man like Bush. Every day, the influence of Karl Rove and Dick Cheney and Donald Rumsfeld seemed more obvious and transparent than ever.

In the midst of the seismic power shift, Mike tried to take comfort in small blessings. He still had a job, after all, and he was excited about his trip to Virginia. As he drove through the countryside near Charlottesville, all his anxieties seemed to melt away. The wide-open fields were a welcome relief from the concrete austerity of the District. The low-lying green hills were turning orange with the changing of the season.

And Charlottesville!

To Mike, it was the most beautiful town in America. Monticello, Montpelier, Ash Lawn-Highland, he loved it all. The Founding Fathers had loved it too, as he'd learned from his readings. A strange chill ran through Mike as they passed the old slave quarter ruins. He recalled a patient he had seen many years ago, a young girl who hated the color of her skin. No words of reassurance had done any good. He remembered the day she brought a book for him to read her. It had been about the early plantation owners and how they procured their labor. First they tried Scottish prisoners, but they escaped and mixed with the other settlers. Then the planters tried using Indian captives, who also escaped. The girl laughed as he described the poor aristocrats in tears. Finally, they reached the part when the Portuguese arrived with a boatload of Africans from the Barbary Coast.

In the end, he read to her about how the aristocrats reluctantly tried African labor, after their failed attempts to subjugate the Scots and Indians. They only succeeded now because Africans could not mix with the settlers or escape into the heartland. A simple, unfortunate evolutionary advantage left them vulnerable to exploitation. It was not intelligence or inferiority that led to enslavement, after all. Just the misfortune of living as strangers in a strange new world.

"Your skin could have been golden and it wouldn't have mattered to them," he had told her. "All that mattered was that your skin was different than theirs."

"So color doesn't matter?"

"Nope. You could be violet, indigo, blue, green, yellow, even orange!"

Mike could still remember her peals of laughter at the thought. For some reason, the memory gave him great comfort as he neared the city lights.

Chapter 103

IT TOOK MIKE AWHILE to find the Department of Psychiatry. The UVA campus felt like a maze. It was impossible to consult any of the students or faculty for help. Everyone seemed to turn away the moment they saw his uniform. Mike could hardly blame them. The only military personnel on campus were recruiters, after all. Still, he hated feeling like a pariah, and a lost one at that.

By the time Mike reached the building, he was sweating profusely. His knees ached. This had better be worth it, he thought. Who could have invited him anyway? He had no contacts in Virginia, or at least none that he knew. Creaser wasn't much help either. The Surgeon General had been working sixteen-hour days, so Mike could excuse the lack of an explanation. Whoever had invited him, he would find out soon enough.

Mike had little trouble finding the office. He was frustrated, however, when his knocking went unanswered. Then he noticed the nameplate, just below the number. What it read gave him a shock. Was it possible? Could it really be?

"Moon!"

"You callin' my name, brother?"

Mike whirled around, to find a large and familiar figure approaching down the hall. The years had certainly changed him, thought Mike, as he noticed the beard and tailored jacket. His friend seemed like a different man, a more mature, refined individual. Still, he had the same swagger as before, and he greeted Mike with a cockeyed grin.

"My God, Moon," Mike exclaimed, his eyes wide as saucers. "Where've you been? We were trying to find you for years! I'd practically given up!"

Moon laughed. "Hello to you too, Colonel!" he replied, pointing to the insignia on his friend's hat. "I've never seen the ol' 'farts-and-darts' look better on an officer!"

"So you invited me here!" said Mike, as the two embraced.

"Yes indeed! And I appreciate you coming from your fancy headquarters to join us in the slums!"

Now it was Mike's turn to laugh. "Charlottesville!?" he exclaimed, in earnest protest. "Are you kidding me? This is hardly a wasteland!" he smiled. "In fact, you seem pretty comfortable here in your ivory tower!"

Moon groaned. "I wish," he said ruefully. "It sure feels like a prison sometimes. All anyone talks about is 'tenure'-this and 'tenure'-that. Publish or perish, you know."

"I suppose we've both been busy," agreed Mike. "But still, I wish I could have invited you to my wedding." He paused, as the realization dawned on him. "Wait, you know I married Flapjack right? You remember Flapjack?"

A curious change seemed to come over Moon. It was almost as though hearing her name had triggered something inside him. His face sunk, he seemed to show his age now, and the weight he had accumulated over the years. Still, if he were disappointed, he hid his feelings well. He laughed once more, slapping Mike on the back.

"You and my girl, eh? You sly dog, you! You better be treating her right!"

Mike felt the blood rush to his face. He winced inwardly. "I'm sorry I brought it up," he apologized. "I remember you two used to be lovers, all those years ago."

Another change came over Moon, but this time he wore a different expression. He seemed confused, perhaps suspicious even. Of what, Mike could hardly guess. Then, even more curiously, his jaw dropped, as though an epiphany had struck him. A moment later, he was doubled-over with laughter.

"Why don't you come into my office, old friend," he wheezed, wiping a tear from his eye. He threw an arm around Mike's shoulder. "We have a *lot* to catch up on!"

* * *

Even after they had settled, Moon was still chuckling softly to himself. If there was some joke, thought Mike, it was lost on him. He was relieved that there were no hard feelings, at least. Whatever Moon was feeling, it obviously wasn't jealousy. The man's confusion and delight seemed like that of a child watching a magic trick. There was not a trace of resentment in his manner.

"I'm not sure why I didn't tell you before, brother," said Moon finally. "I guess I was just used to hiding it. But I'll be honest. Flapjack and I were not lovers."

"You weren't?"

"No," he continued, with a heavy sigh. "Our relationship was much different. And the things she did for me, well, it takes a rare person to play the role she played. A rare friend. And she played it to perfection."

Mike cocked his head. "I don't understand," he began tentatively. "She was…"

"She was my beard."

"Your what?"

"My beard," Moon repeated. "My double-agent, of sorts. We were never lovers. God no. But she was one of the few who knew my secret. She understood me. She looked out for me. She played the doting girlfriend at military functions, at family reunions, hell, even among friends. All the while it was an act."

There was a pause. Mike tried to process the information. He knew Moon was watching him, just waiting for the realization to dawn on him. Still, he was clueless.

"Your beard?" he asked, feeling embarrassed.

Moon leaned back in his chair and groaned. "God, Mike, are you really still so innocent?" he laughed, shaking his head. "I'm gay! She covered for me."

"No way!" gasped Mike, as he struggled for words. "But… but you were the ladies man back at Valkyrie! Women loved you!"

"Loved my company," Moon corrected. "Call it overcompensation, I guess? A lot of the girls knew back then, actually. I suppose they felt safe around me. The one man who wasn't a potential predator!"

"And now?"

"Now everyone knows." Moon laughed. He spread his arms and shrugged. "Times are a lot different than they were in our day. I tell the kids today, but I know they don't understand. No one who experienced it ever could."

"Tell me about it," Mike found himself adding. "I remember all the homophobic jokes and slurs. Even in polite company, even with my parents, it was understood as a disease. A sort of perversion."

"Don't ask, don't tell." Moon nodded. There was a look of sadness in his eyes. "Don't ask, don't tell." Then, in a moment, he regained his enthusiasm, and the old, familiar grin returned. "But enough of that," he said dismissively, "I'm overjoyed to hear about you and Flapjack. I can't imagine a better man for such an amazing woman!"

"That means a lot, coming from you," said Mike. The words touched him deeply.

"Besides, there are a lot more things to talk about," Moon continued. "I traveled a lot after the Air Force. Spent a month in the Himalayas."

"After we published that paper?"

"I guess I was waiting for the smoke to clear." He rolled his eyes. "Pretty naïve, eh? Of course, it never did. Publishing that paper put a bull's-eye on my back. So I stayed off the radar."

Mike cringed. He felt a wave of guilt pass over him. All that had happened to his friend, he was responsible for all of it. All just to cover his tracks. It was a debt Mike knew he could never repay.

Moon seemed to read the regret in Mike's eyes. "Don't you blame yourself," he admonished. "It was my decision to make. And I don't regret it. I've had some amazing experiences as a result. But I'm sure you heard enough about me!"

"Not at all," urged Mike. "I'm dying to know!"

"Well, after my time in seclusion, I met a fellow in Nepal who introduced me to Doctors Without Borders. I must have been nuts to join up. The gig paid something like nine-hundred a month, and man, you experience some weird, wild shit."

Mike smirked. "Probably safer than some of the streets in DC!"

"Nah, man," continued Moon. "It was really violent. Constant danger. Most of the places didn't even have streets. Just mud paths between the huts. We were working on infant-mortality in different African republics. You know, trying to provide prenatal care for the mothers and diagnose birth complications."

"Complications?"

"Yeah, like breech or twins," he answered. "But a local warlord got pissed when we admitted another woman before his wife. It didn't matter that the patient needed an emergency c-section. His militia shot the place up and burned it to the ground."

"Jesus Christ."

"Tell me about it. We're lucky we got out of there alive." Moon paused solemnly. Then burst out laughing. "Oh god, enough about me! I'm sure you've got some stories yourself! And I want to hear all of them."

Mike gulped. "You know Thomas Jefferson? Well.."

Chapter 104

MIKE SWALLOWED THE LUMP in his throat. The lights on the podium were glaring hot, and the sweat was trickling down his neck. He had spoken a handful of times in his life, sure, but never at a venue like this. The crowd swelled before him like a black mass, occasionally lit by the flash of a photographer. The echo of his own voice was deafening.

"I'll take another question?" he announced tentatively. It was almost over now. He had stumbled through his speech, so the hard part was over. Now just a few more audience queries.

"I've got one!" barked a lady, as she snatched the microphone from an usher. "You spoke against fascists earlier, correct?"

"That's correct."

"Well, isn't that a bit hypocritical? Don't you work for the Pentagon?"

A murmur of voices swept through the crowd. Flash bulbs snapped. Moon leapt from his seat on the stage.

"I'll have you know Colonel Pike is no fascist!" he snapped, hijacking the microphone from Mike. "This man is a gentleman. A man who's dedicated his life to the cause of others!"

The woman seemed to brush off the rebuke. "Well!" she continued, "I heard the academies were turning cadets into missionaries for the religious right. Are you going to deny any part in that?"

"I... I really can't answer that!" Mike stammered helplessly.

"They're trying to create an official state religion!" cried another voice. "Not only that, they're setting up gulags, and spying on citizens with the NSA, TSA, and Homeland Security! An individual can be held indefinitely, tortured, brainwashed... shall I go on?"

"It's the super wealthy in the country who are buying out the politicians," added the woman angrily. "You know, people are beginning to say   we've lost our democracy! Hell, Eisenhower himself said it was income inequality that led to fascism!"

"That's quite enough!" roared Moon. He waved Mike back and took command of the podium. He was shaking with rage.

"Let the colonel answer the questions!" demanded the man in the crowd. "He won't admit it! Won't admit that the damn Aristocrats are bunch of conniving idiots! They can't tell shit from shinola!"

There was a harsh bump of static. A metallic squeal cut through the air. From his position, Mike could see that the man was being led out by security. They'd finally confiscated his mike. A chorus of boos echoed through the chamber.

"You can't censor us!" cried the woman, as she saw the security close in. "People need to know the truth! The Government is planning a military invasion in 2003! And it's all for the sake of oil!"

Finally the woman was escorted from the auditorium. There was a smattering of awkward applause from the spectators.

"This is absolutely unacceptable!" barked Moon. "Absolutely unacceptable. If these protestors had even been listening to my former colleague," he continued, gesturing towards Mike, "they would have realized that he's been fighting the corruption of folks like Pastor Roy and Congressman Peterson! And as for his time in the Pentagon…"

Moon turned as he felt Mike's hand on his shoulder. He stepped aside.

"As for my time in the Pentagon," began Mike, after clearing his throat, "I can't say I speak for the whole organization, but I can say that there are good people there. Not just in the Office of the Surgeon General either! My own father-in-law consults there, and I can personally vouch for his character."

From behind him, Moon began to clap. As if on cue, a wave of applause swept through the audience. They were relieved it was over, Mike felt, and he couldn't blame them. He was glad it was over himself! He made a mental note to decline future speaking invitations.

"Now, if there are no more questions…"

"I have one," interrupted a voice from the front. Even from a distance, Mike could tell it was neither a reporter nor a student. The man spoke with the calm authority of an officer. Still, it was a tired voice. Both world-weary and wise.

Moon re-adjusted the microphone. He waved an usher towards the man in the crowd. "Ah yes," he announced quickly, a hint of surprise in his voice.

"Of course we can make exception for our esteemed Department Chair. Do proceed, Dr. Lawson."

A hush fell on the assembly. Now Mike knew this was a man of some renown. Even Moon spoke his name with reverence.

"Colonel Pike," the professor addressed him. "I did indeed hear a great deal about this case myself. The one involving your curious lineage with our Founding Father." He paused, as a coughing fit overtook him. "Is it true," he continued, "that this Pastor Roy was paying the PLO?"

"Sir?"

"To set off bombs in Israel."

"Ah!" spoke Mike, as he tried to recall. "Yes. That was the evidence, at least."

"And tell me, what did your colleagues plan to do about this?"

Mike thought for a moment. "They were hoping to discredit him with his church," he answered finally. "You know, cut off his revenue flow."

"And you wouldn't be bullshittin' me, Colonel?"

"I'm sorry, sir?"

The elderly man turned to address the crowd. "I had been informed by a trusted source from the agency that there were different plans. Assassination plans. He was a national security threat, and they were going to take him out—at this "Founding Fathers tour" you mentioned—with a trained sniper. Now what do you say to that?"

Mike stood frozen. He was speechless for a moment. Another hush of whispers swept through the audience. Even a few scattered claps.

"N-nothing…!" Mike finally managed. "I don't know a thing about it!"

But he did know, he thought to himself, as Moon took over the microphone. A whole new understanding of the events had begun to form in his mind. He had his doubts before, but now everything seemed brutally clear. Once again, he had played the patsy. How could he have been so naïve? All along, he had been putting both Flapjack and himself in mortal danger.

At the reception, Moon clapped Mike on the shoulder. "Well, that went rather well, all things considered!" he laughed. "Now you can relax, buddy. You look like you've seen a ghost!"

"I think I just did," said Mike hollowly. "And I think it was me."

Chapter 105

THE TURN OF THE CENTURY was not kind to the Surgeon General's office. After all, as Creaser often said, the armed forces were a machine that ran on "testosterone and alcohol, not milk and cookies." For his part, Mike was baffled by the government's resistance to reform. It was not so long ago that the Secretary of Defense had overruled the generals, and allowed married men and women into the service. With Rumsfeld in control, those days seemed a distant memory.

As the new Secretary of Defense, Donald Rumsfeld clashed immediately with the Surgeon General. The new administration focused all its energy on recruitment. Any studies of family stress, PTSD, TBIs, or depression were denied funding. Creaser was told, in no uncertain terms, that he would not interfere with the primary objective. Something big was coming. An event that would alter the course of history forever.

* * *

Agent David Fielder was among the first to see the ominous signs on the horizon. Intelligence reports were becoming increasingly alarming. In early-August, 2001, David knew he could hesitate no longer. He called the White House to warn of an impending terrorist attack. Several reputable sources had confirmed that Al-Quaeda planned to hit a major target in the U.S., an attack that could result in massive civilian casualties. Actions had to be taken. And fast.

The response he received left him horrified.

They had already been informed.

In fact, as he learned from his colleagues, other agencies had been trying to warn the President and his Secretary of State that an attack was imminent.

Still, President Bush and Condoleezza Rice did nothing. The response from the White House was static.

What frustrated David most, was that he didn't know who he could blame. This wasn't the ignorance of a single administration. Clinton had been aware of the threat since 1998. Osama Bin Laden made no secret of his hatred for America. He had been broadcasting his intentions to strike. The FBI had evidence of terrorist training camps, and that suspected terrorists had attended flight schools. Still, even now, the government did nothing. Bush spent the next months fishing at his ranch in Texas. He was on vacation, and the CIA was just an annoyance.

Then, on September 11th, all hell broke loose.

Chapter 106

MIKE AND FLAPJACK heard the news before the Pentagon was hit. A plane had crashed into the World Trade Center. It was the news that saved their lives. When the attack came, they were safe in the northeast wing, still gathering information on the events in New York.

Others weren't so fortunate.

The offices of the Army and Navy were hit hardest. There were 125 killed, besides the 54 passengers and 5 hijackers on Flight 77. The point of contact had been demolished. It would take military pathologists over two months to identify the DNA of the victims.

The sound of the crash was deafening. Before he knew it, Mike found himself lying dazed on the floor, a loud ringing in his ears. People were running and screaming, but he could hear none of it. There was a dull ache at the back of his head, and he felt the wound instinctively. It was wet with blood.

Mike pulled himself to his feet. He had to find Flapjack! To his relief, she was alright, and had already jumped into action. Creaser had gathered with a few colleagues in a group, and they fought valiantly to maintain order amidst chaos. No one knew what had happened. It was hours later that they learned the tragic details. The entire Pentagon was consumed with grief. Daily operations came to a near stand-still.

Meanwhile, a nation began to mourn the fallen. Their lives had been changed forever.

*   *   *

While Mike's injury healed, his anger increased with each passing day. He couldn't believe the things he was hearing. In the aftermath of the carnage, all the Secretary of Defense could talk about was the two-trillion dollars missing from the night before. His lack of empathy seemed as callous as it was absurd.

Flapjack had no doubt who was responsible. She argued vocally with David that the government was to blame. The ineptitude of an administration had led to disaster. Worse, she was exasperated by her father's continued faith in the White House. He knew better. He was too smart to believe otherwise, and Flapjack knew it. Still, he clung to his patriotic ideals, and denounced her views as "downright unAmerican!"

It took a few months for David to come around. Eventually, the actions of conservatives stretched his faith to the breaking point. He was dumbfounded when, rather than attacking Bin Laden in Afghanistan, Bush instead painted the target on Iraq. Try as he might, David couldn't make any sense of the logic. Saddam Hussein had nothing to do with 9/11. The man was an enemy, true, but he wasn't responsible.

David knew there could be only one reason Iraq was the focus. Oil. Natural resources. The country was a veritable goldmine. And it was right there for the taking. The thought made David sick. Just who were the good guys, anyway, he wondered. What side was he on?

*   *   *

General Creaser was in the middle of a meeting when the door burst open. Without waiting for an invitation, a hawkish, headstrong young bureaucrat swaggered into his office. Creaser groaned inwardly. He would have recognized Deputy Schular anywhere. So Rumsfeld had sent a lackey to do his dirty work. Wonderful.

"I'm sorry sir," came an exasperated voice from behind. Creaser's secretary, Ms. Gibson, brushed past the deputy, blocking his path. "He just burst in," she panted. "I'm afraid I couldn't stop him!"

"Just need to talk to you for a minute, Sir," whined Schular insistently, scanning for a way past his obstacle. Creaser chuckled inwardly. The young man was harmless, even if his slick blond hair and square jaw make him look like a Hitler Youth. At least, that was how Creaser pictured him. The personality fit the bill.

Creaser smiled. "That's quite all right, Miss Gibson," he declared, motioning Schular forward. "Please, take a seat. I was just in a meeting with General Harrison here. Harrison, have you met Deputy Schular?"

"I can't say I've had the pleasure," answered the elderly commander. He offered a respectful nod.

Deputy Schular acknowledged the man with an icy grimace.

"Yes. I don't have time for pleasantries," he answered dismissively, his sights still firmly trained on the Surgeon General. The disrespect made Creaser wince.

"You can't keep us waiting, you know!" insisted Schular in his high-pitched, nasal tone. Harrison began to rise, but Creaser motioned for him to stay. He wasn't going to be bullied. Certainly not in his own office!

"Have I kept you waiting?" he answered coolly.

"You can't keep us waiting," the deputy repeated, his voice wavering slightly. "The President wants your answer now!"

"I believe he already has my answer."

"So you haven't changed your mind?"

"My answer is still *no*. We've had this discussion a hundred times."

"Sir, you're being unreasonable!" snapped Schular, growing visibly more agitated. "He already has the support of the hawks in Congress! He needs the Joint Chiefs of Staff to support him. Your country needs you to support him!"

"Well, we're not changing our minds," Creaser reiterated. "To try to effect a regime change in Iran is just insane. It's *wrong*."

"It's just as the President said," shot the deputy. "You're either with us, or you're against us. We can't let the terrorists win."

"I hope," stated General Harrison, who had been listening intently, "that you are not calling the Surgeon General of the United States a coward."

The room went deathly silent. Both Creaser and Schular were staring at Harrison now, as if waiting for the man to pass judgment. The old general stroked his chin thoughtfully. Slowly, he turned towards Schular.

"I asked you a question, deputy. Are you calling the Surgeon General a terrorist?"

Schular swallowed the lump in his throat. "N-no, sir," he croaked. "I...I mean, you misunderstand me! You must realize we're at war."

"And you must realize, deputy, that the Surgeon General has given his answer."

"But we're doing God's work!" insisted Schular desperately. "Iran has Weapons of Mass Destruction! He's harboring our enemies! We don't even need a large scale operation. Secretary Rumsfeld has proven that a small, lethal force, dedicated to twenty-month deployments..."

"Twenty months!" gasped Creaser. "Are you insane?"

"Deputy Schular," added Harrison, "I've seen the National Intelligence estimates. Any conflict would take over a decade to resolve. If there ever *is* resolution. I work in diplomacy, as well, so I know that no other nation supports this plan."

Schular leapt from his chair. "I can't believe you people!" he declared violently. "I never thought I'd hear this kind of treason in the Pentagon! We're doing God's work!"

"Let me put it this way," replied Creaser. "I believe I speak for myself, General Harrison, and all the Joint Chiefs when I say this plan is absolutely insane."

"It will happen! With or without your support."

"Then you can expect our resignation. Good day, Deputy Schular."

The red-faced deputy threw up his hands in despair. He turned and stomped out of the office. Creaser waited for the door to slam before rolling his eyes and groaning.

"Dear God," sighed Harrison, "I'm no theologian, myself, but these people are damned confused about their own religion."

Creaser shrugged. "You can't get through to people like that. That moron doesn't know his ass from a hole in the ground."

"He does realize we're *losing* the war in Iraq?" asked Harrison. "From the reports you're showing me, our PTSD rates are projected to break the 40% mark. The Brits are still only 5%. That's unbelievable."

"It's believable as long as Rumsfeld is issuing stop-loss orders and extending deployment times."

"So what do we do now?"

"There's only one thing we can do," Creaser lamented. "We're going to ask for his resignation."

Harrison shook his head. "Are you serious? It won't work."

"Well, do you have a better idea?"

Chapter 107

IT WAS A PARTICULARLY cold winter. Even by Washington standards, Flapjack had to admit. It was mid-December, 2003, and the days seemed to crawl like molasses. She and Mike had already fallen into a dull routine. Long nights were spent working at the kitchen table and discussing their bleak prospects. The economy was in decline. Their research budget had been slashed to the bone. They still had their jobs—by some small miracle—but it was only a matter of time. The Pentagon would no longer tolerate dissent.

The news in the papers read like cheap science fiction. Headlines announced how the President was on a mission from God. How he met with the leaders of fundamentalist sects, even those as far-right as the Rapturists, and praised their "holy" work. Some emboldened politicians and members of Congress began to talk about the approach of the "end times." And these were the elected leaders of the people! It hurt Flapjack's brain just thinking about it.

But what could they do? Mike and Flapjack had spent hours mulling their options. There was the thought of moving to Canada, but it was dead on arrival. Neither of them wanted to leave family behind. They could resign. After all, Creaser talked about the idea *ad nauseum*, and they were probably on the chopping block anyway. But then what? They had neither the time nor energy to pursue their research. Things seemed to grow increasingly hopeless, until that evening, in mid-December, 2003.

Flapjack was reading through a stack of papers when a memo caught her eye. At first, she couldn't believe what it contained. The message didn't sink in until a third or fourth reading. She turned towards Mike, who had dozed watching television. A tray of Chinese take-out lay open on his chest. "Hon! Psst! Hey, hon!" hissed Flapjack urgently. Mike grunted and sat up slowly. He let out a loud yawn.

"Ugh," he groaned, scratching his belly lazily and wiping his mouth. "Did you really have to wake me up?"

"Have you read this?"

"Read what?"

"This, Mike! This memo!" Flapjack held up a sheet of stationary, tapping it with her pen. "You have to see this! They must have been trying to bury it in the paperwork!"

Mike was wide awake now, and fully alert. It had been a long time since he'd last felt truly challenged or inspired. For years now, he had felt his mind begin to atrophy, as he dealt with one stack of paperwork after another. He had to hand it to the neo-con brain trust. They spared no expense to make his life—and the lives of all Creaser's allies—as tedious as possible.

From a distance, it looked like a hundred other memos. Official letterhead, a few paragraphs of terse, official-sounding prose, and a signature. But as Mike read its contents, his jaw dropped. He stared at Flapjack, his mouth still agape, then turned back to the paper.

"You can't be serious."

"I know! I'm as stunned as you. This is insane!"

"This is criminal," corrected Mike, his voice beginning to rise.

"I *know*!"

"Do you realize what this means?" he continued. "It means they've infiltrated our ranks. I don't even know why I'm surprised, to be honest. I think a part of me always knew."

"And now they've trained their sights on you. This is a direct attempt to undermine all our work on behalf of veterans and their families!" Flapjack's voice cracked with anger.

"We'll see what Creaser says about this," declared Mike angrily. "If those assholes want a fight, well, they've got one!"

* * *

Creaser peered carefully through the gold rims of his spectacles. As he read, the lines on his face drew tight, as though he were aging before their very eyes. He tossed the file down in disgust.

"It's definitely Elwood, that new Undersecretary of Defense," he confirmed grimly. "That son of a bitch."

"So let me get this straight," began Mike. "In the past three years, the rate of disability claims at the VA have more than doubled, correct."

"Correct."

"In the meantime, there's a six-month wait period before a claim can even *begin* to be resolved. The VA has only approved around 19,000 of the over 52,000 PTSD claims alone."

"Also correct."

"And somehow they're able to authorize pay raises and bonuses for aides?! Even with a backlog that massive?"

"What really gets me, though," added Flapjack, "is the obvious religious bias behind it all. Can you believe they want to call post-traumatic stress a 'faith deficit disorder'? It would be hilarious if it weren't so depressing."

Mike groaned. "So what now? They're pushing some kind of resilience training program? Something they think will help cure what they call cowardice?"

"I wish it were otherwise," answered Creaser. "They've been selling their programs everywhere lately. Just last week the Undersecretary gave one of those groups permission to shoot a fundraising video in the Pentagon. Gave them high-level clearance and everything!" He paused for a moment, as if waiting for a response. There was only silence. "Members of the Pentagon are appearing on the video to voice their support for the project," he continued.

"And there's nothing we can do?"

"As long as they wield that kind of influence, there's little that we can do."

So this is it, thought Mike darkly. The evangelicals had penetrated the military, the Pentagon, Congress, and the White House. And it was all to push their agenda. To earn a profit for their investors. It was all for the welfare of Big Oil.

And there was nothing he could do to stop them.

*　*　*

Flapjack shifted uncomfortably. She shouldn't feel guilty, she reminded herself. Mike met with Creaser dozens of times without her knowledge. Still, it felt as if she were going behind his back. What could the Surgeon General have to tell her that was so private? Whatever it was, Mike wasn't to be notified. At least not yet.

"Ah, my apologies," said Creaser finally, as he finished the last of his breakfast. He brushed the last of the crumbs from his desk. "I do appreciate you meeting me like this, Flapjack."

"It's my pleasure, sir."

"I'm sure you're wondering why I only asked you here."

Flapjack smiled awkwardly. "The question had occurred to me."

"I'm afraid we'll have to tell Mike sooner or later," continued Creaser. "For now, at least, I want to see if something can be done to overrule the Undersecretary's order."

"His order?"

"All facilities are to diagnose patients with personality disorders instead of PTSD."

"You can't be serious!" stammered Flapjack. "But why?"

"The bastards think too much money is going into disability payments and treatment for post-traumatic stress," Creaser explained. "If personality disorder is used as a diagnosis instead, then the VA is off the hook. The soldier is discharged without benefits. It's to juke the stats too, I'd imagine. They want to hide the fact that they could've prevented the rising number of cases. It's a 'win-win' in their opinion."

"But a lose for us," snapped Flapjack. "Mike has to be told. He's devoted so much of his career advocating the prevention and treatment of PTSD!"

Creaser bit his lip. "Don't think I don't agree," he assured her. "But we both know he'd be crushed. And right now, we need him at his best."

"But what can I do?" Flapjack protested. "Why are you telling me all this?"

"Because I need your help to fight this. For Mike. For all our wounded veterans," he answered fiercely. "And because you know the one person who could help."

Chapter 108

THE YEAR HAD NOT been kind to David Fielder. He had already spent most of the winter in a hospital bed, as doctors worked to treat the problems with his heart. David hated doctors. Hated feeling vulnerable and powerless over his condition. At least, as he often reminded himself, he had his family to comfort him. Even if Mike had to be a damn physician!

Of all his visitors, his daughter had been the most frequent visitor. Only Anna spent as much time by his bedside. Unlike her mother, who was constantly fretting over him, Flapjack offered him a chance to relax. She never troubled him with questions about his treatment. Instead, the two spent hours laughing and sharing old stories. His habit of flirting with the nursing staff had become a running joke between them, and she always admonished him playfully. When she visited, at least for a brief time, he felt like his old self again.

On this particular day, however, something was different. Something was not quite right. He had felt it when she walked in the room that morning. It was written all over her face.

"So are you going to tell me?"

"Tell you what?"

"What's troubling you."

Flapjack averted her gaze. "What makes you think something's wrong?" she asked defensively. "Is it really that obvious?"

"I'm your father, honey," he assured her. He reached towards her, taking her hand in his. "I know you better than anyone. I can tell when you're troubled."

Flapjack sighed. She never had been able to hide her feelings. Least of all from her parents.

"Well, there's trouble at work. General Creaser wanted me to ask for your help on a pressing matter."

"Me?"

"He said you would know what to do."

"The Air Force has always bugged the CIA for help," chuckled David. "So what is it this time?"

"We've had a directive. It's 'unofficial' for now, but it's only a matter of time," Flapjack explained. "The administration has decided that veterans are receiving too much compensation. They've always suppressed the number of cases, but now doctors have been instructed to stop diagnosing PTSD."

David propped himself up in bed. He furrowed his brows in concern.

"But isn't that fraud? Why would they do that?"

"Because veterans with PTSD get VA treatment and disability compensation."

"And veterans with personality disorder?"

"They get nothing," continued Flapjack grimly. "Several doctors are already complying with the order. And the Undersecretary has slashed the approval of PTSD claims by over 60%."

David frowned. "They're covering their behinds. Is this directly from the Secretary of Defense?"

"All we know is that it came from his office and the VA."

"I've heard troubling things about that man," David mused. "Has the press gotten word? I know there are generals calling for Rumsfeld's resignation. They would have a field day with this!"

"Not yet," answered Flapjack. "We only received the directive a few days ago. Mike doesn't even know yet."

"I don't suppose you can ignore it?"

"We'll be implicated if we do. But giving false diagnoses is malpractice and fraud. We can take a stand, I suppose, and see if they fire us with a gag order." Flapjack sighed. "Other than that, we're out of ideas."

David ran through the options in his head. "My best suggestion is to alert the press," he said finally. "Leak the story anonymously. It'll at least take you out of the crossfire, and the public will be informed. Hopefully that could put some heat on the bastards. Force them to reconsider."

Flapjack nodded in agreement. Creaser was right, David always did seem to have the right answer. She leaned back in her chair and forced a smile.

"You know, I wish I could tell Mike about this," she replied.

"Why haven't you!" cried David. "For God's sake, dear! After all he's done, the man has a right to know!"

The outburst took Flapjack off guard. "Really, Dad?" she asked, her eyes wide with surprise. "I mean, no offence, but the two of you have never been… well, chummy."

"That's not the point!"

"It's not up to me," she added defensively. "Creaser didn't want to upset him, or provoke him into acting rashly, I guess."

"Creaser, eh?"

"If it were up to me I would have told him myself!"

David sunk back into the mattress. His face fell. The sudden change made Flapjack fear for his health. She began to reach for the call button, but felt a firm grip on her wrist.

"Don't make the same mistake I did," said David weakly. "It's not worth it, in the long run. You'll regret it."

"You're scaring me, Dad," said Flapjack anxiously. She was surprised how easily she escaped his grip. Never before had he seemed so frail.

David lay back. His eyes turned to the ceiling. "Just trust me," he muttered softly. "It's not worth it."

Chapter 109

THE TRIP CAME as a relief for Flapjack. Any vacation from her personal and professional troubles was a welcome one. Even if it was on business. Besides, the prospect of investigating the Air Force Academy was intriguing. She'd never been to Colorado Springs, nor explored a military campus. Still, she felt confident in her abilities. Creaser had chosen her, after all. It was a mission of some importance.

Over the journey, Flapjack passed the time reading and examining Creaser's files. There was no shortage of material. The Air Force Academy had a long history of scandal and corruption. It would have taken weeks to pour through every interview, case file, and report. The number of sanctions alone could fill volumes.

The Surgeon General had kept her briefing mercifully short. He had described how lobbyists had been using the Trojan Horse of religion to gain economic and political power. One senator—the chairman of the science committee, no less—had begun to advocate curriculum reform in public school. "Intelligent Design" was to be taught alongside evolution. "Separation of Church and State" was to be removed from textbooks. Support for such ideas had been gaining momentum.

In essence, intrusion into the government and the military was becoming a national security issue. Flapjack's mission was to quietly investigate the allegations of parents and cadets that techniques were being used to "brainwash" the student body. There had been several complaints that the academy was "literally overrun" with evangelical "fanatics." Over two-dozen even feared for their safety! In all, there had been over 350 complaints of harassment, the majority claiming that threats and intimidation were used to gain converts.

On the long drive to the academy, Flapjack's suspicions were confirmed. She began to observe a number of strange buildings within the campus vicinity. Some were ornately constructed churches. Others were no bigger than shacks. They all bore Christian iconography. From her reading, Flapjack had learned that Colorado Springs was home to at least 81 religious groups. Did all of them surround the academy?

Somehow, deep down, she knew the worst was yet to come. She was an outsider now. A stranger in a very strange land.

Chapter 110

MIKE SHIFTED UNCOMFORTABLY. He had arrived only moments ago, but already things felt awkward. David was a husk of his former self. His face seemed sallow and haunted. Worst of all, the light in his eyes—that burning gaze—had died out. His stare had turned bleary and unfocused, as if clouded by ash. He nodded weakly towards Mike.

"They don't know what they're doing," he laughed weakly. His voice was strained and faraway. His breathing ragged. "Talk about fraud. They're telling me I'm dizzy because a carotid artery is blocked."

"Did they do the tests?"

"They did."

"And did they tell you it could cause a stroke?"

David groaned. "They want to bore it out. Endartasectory, or something."

"Endarterectomy," Mike corrected. "What do you call it?"

"A whole heap of trouble to go through, for an old man like me."

Mike frowned. "You're going to do it though, right?"

"Anna says I am," he answered, rolling his eyes. "But it's not her body is it? Not her brain either."

"What would happen, David," pressed Mike, "if you had a stroke?"

"I'd want 'em to kill me."

"You'd be paralyzed."

"Then I better remind 'em to pull the plug," hissed David. Mike knew he was annoyed, but too weak to protest. Even now, David was as stubborn as ever, as if he could live or die through the sheer force of his will. His resistance gave Mike hope.

"You know that's against the law," he argued. "Besides, this isn't an option. Think of your family. Your wife and daughter would be heartbroken. I'd be pretty devastated myself."

To Mike's surprise, David begin to laugh. It was a dark, cynical laughter, however, without a trace of mirth. It echoed hollowly through the room.

"You'll excuse me," David offered, as fatigue overtook him. "But you wouldn't say that if you knew the truth."

"The truth?"

"The reason I called you here today."

David reached out towards Mike. His touch was cold and clammy, but his grip was firm.

"There's something I need to tell you," he moaned weakly. "While there's... still time..."

David's voice trailed off in midsentence. His eyes rolled back, and his hold on Mike slackened. He had passed out cold.

Chapter 111

FLAPJACK HAD NEVER felt so paranoid. Not even in the refugee camps of Guam. Everywhere on campus, she could feel their eyes on her. Watching her. Keeping tabs on her every move. Her student escorts were friendly, but *too* friendly, and their banter seemed painfully rehearsed. For her part, Flapjack tried to focus on her objective. Reminded herself to stay patient and congenial. In time, she believed, the cracks in the foundation would reveal themselves.

She just had to stay patient.

It was not until she met the deputy commander that her confidence began to waver. Colonel Allen Paul was a giant of a man, towering over Flapjack by at least a foot. The students fondly referred to him as "Tall Paul," her guide had told her, but only because he "stood tall for Jesus." Maybe, thought Flapjack ruefully, but the man was built like a modern Goliath. A large, gilded Bible sat prominently on his desk.

"What can I possibly do for the Surgeon General," he had boomed, looking down on her with a wolfish grin. "And might I say, *she's* never looked better!"

The compliment only reminded her to double her guard. This was hostile territory. Anything could happen. She decided to cut to the point.

"I'll be frank, Colonel. We've been receiving complaints at the Pentagon. A lot of complaints. Most of them regarding the abuse of cadets."

"Is that so?"

"Apparently, methods are being used by the more... evangelical among you," she continued carefully. "Methods to convert others by force."

"I wouldn't say that!" argued the colonel, with a degree of indignation. He folded his arms defensively.

"Oh?"

"These students are model Christians. Warriors for Christ. I can't fault them for trying to spread the Good News!"

"The Good News?"

"That Christ is our savior, who died for our sins. We're saving souls here!"

Flapjack nodded politely. "I suppose that's one way to look at it."

"It's the only way! The one true path to salvation!"

"Still," she continued, "I'm here on official government business, and I'll need to conduct confidential interviews with the students and faculty. I trust that won't be an issue?"

The colonel initially tried to resist. "Out of the question!" he declared violently. "I mean, I wish I could allow it," he added, softening his rhetoric, "but it's a distraction, wouldn't you agree? Besides, their lives are an open book."

"Even so, I'll need to conduct interviews." Flapjack insisted. "Now, if you'd like me to contact my superior…"

*　*　*

Just the memory of "Tall Paul" gave Flapjack chills. She hadn't escaped a moment too soon, she thought, recalling his invitation to "pray together." It had been a pretext, of course. An excuse to move close enough to stroke her thigh. Just the memory made her feel nauseous. Such predatory behavior—from a devout Christian, no less—filled her with revulsion. She admonished herself for letting her guard down, if only for a moment. It was a mistake she could not make twice.

Still, she reminded herself, she had got what she came for. For all his sound and fury, the colonel folded like a house of cards. The confidential interviews were arranged. Days were spent interviewing students, faculty, and even the football coach, who referred to his squad as "Team Jesus." The entire process was exhausting. The results, however, were worth it.

Several students, who spoke under the condition of anonymity, stood out in Flapjack's memory. She felt for the young Catholic girl who was told she would "burn in hell" for her beliefs. Others supported her claim that men referred to the women as "sheep," over whom they were the "shepherds." More than once she was told how the faculty delivered lectures as though they were sermons, with enough flailing and dancing to make a televangelist blush. A Jewish student spoke emotionally about being labeled a "Christ Killer." By her count, Flapjack had met with 23 students—13 of them Christian—who lived in constant fear of harm. Another 20% reported being converted through threats and intimidation.

As a whole, the results of the investigation were shocking. Even Flapjack could not have predicted the graphic details she would hear. On the other hand, a number of students earned her respect and admiration. It was a testament to their character that they had endured such hardships. She vowed to fight on their behalf.

* * *

"So what did you find, little lady?"

Flapjack winced inwardly. She fought to hide her anger. It was their last meeting after all. She just had to report her findings and pay her respects. In a few minutes, she would be on a plane bound for Washington. "Tall Paul" would be no more than an unpleasant memory.

"Well," she replied curtly, "I'm sure you'll find out in my report."

"Oh, don't be so coy," teased the colonel. "There's no need for bad blood. How about you and me make up over dinner tonight."

"Are you serious?!"

"It's my treat."

Finally, Flapjack could bear it no longer. "With all due respect, Deputy Commander," she snapped, "You have more pressing issues to be concerned with. I was troubled to find serious First Amendment violations being conducted on campus."

The colonel's charm evaporated. He looked hurt, then angry, his lip twisted in a snarl.

"Is that so?"

"And what's more," she added, "I'll be recommending a full scale investigation. Now if you'll excuse me, I have a flight to catch."

Chapter 112

IT HAD TAKEN a few hours for David to recover. Mike had considered letting him rest overnight, but couldn't bring himself to leave. Whether it was his sense of loyalty or his curiosity, he felt compelled to stay. After all, with his schedule the way it was, the opportunity for visits would be rare. He had wanted to forge a connection with his father-in-law for a long time. David always seemed so distant, so aloof. Now, for the first time, he had something meaningful to share with him. Mike was aching to hear him out.

Mike entered to find David sitting up in bed. Some of the life seemed to have returned to his body. Still, it was not the man's usual energy that seemed to animate him. It was something different. He seemed somehow anxious and unsure of himself. His eyes shifted around the room, as if in search of a hiding place.

"Have a seat, Mike," he said, his voice trembling. "There's something I need to tell you. As I said before, I don't know if I'll have another opportunity."

"Don't talk like that!" said Mike. He forced a smile. "I'm sure everything will be fine!"

"Nevertheless, this needs to be said." David took a long drink of water before he began. He cleared his throat.

"Back in the day, we had a technique in our dark-ops division. In some operations, we would need to cover our tracks. A "patsy" was essential. Someone would be groomed to take the fall."

Mike's throat ran dry. The accusations he had heard in Virginia echoed in his mind. He knew what was about to come next.

"I… I'll just say it," David continued sadly. "It was Colbert's idea. But I was the one who agreed with it. You seemed to fit our criteria; you were naïve, trusting, with a strong sense of duty and loyalty." He sighed. "But then my daughter became closer to you. I got to know you better. I tried, I really tried hard to shelve the original plan. Colbert even tried to have me reassigned."

Mike sat for a moment in stunned silence. David averted his gaze. Tears began to form in the old man's eyes.

"You're saying the whole thing was a lie? The Jefferson connection? The Founding Fathers tour?"

"I don't know for certain," answered David weakly. "The genetic testing was a separate program. Colbert had the idea when it came across his desk."

"And General Creaser?"

"He had nothing to do with this. The man was always your biggest advocate. He was too loyal?"

"Too loyal."

"He saw you as a son." A tear rolled down David's cheek. "A son," he repeated, "and that's how I should have seen you."

Mike slumped in his chair. Somehow, he had already known. Even before his speech in Virginia. It did little to soften the blow, however. The weight of David's confession hit him like a sledgehammer.

"B-but how… I mean… What was the plan?"

"We were going to take him out. We just needed to wait until he donated to the PLO."

"Take him out? As in, kill him? I would have taken the fall?"

"It would have been easy," croaked David hollowly. "You had already been a suspect in your wife's shooting. You would have been positioned in range of the target. We had the paid witnesses, the DNA planted, and it would have been an open-shut case."

Mike listened in stunned silence. He could feel the bile at the base of throat. It took him a moment to fight back his nausea.

"So that's why you chose me," he groaned. "I just don't understand. You never did think I was good enough, did you? Not for my job. Not for your daughter." His voice rose, as his shock turned to bitterness. "I see how it is. I wasn't born with a silver spoon. I didn't attend some New England school. I was just some empty-headed southern boy. Someone you could use and discard."

David looked up towards Mike. His eyes were red and brimming with tears. His body wracked with sobs. Try as he might, Mike could feel nothing but pity for the old man.

"You must understand," David pleaded. "We really have little choice in these matters. There are powers beyond the President and Congress. Powers that buy politicians and put them in office. Republican, Democrats, all puppets dangling on golden strings. The designs of a master puppeteer.

"Then you took a great risk in stopping it," Mike conceded. "But David, I trusted you. Why didn't you tell me then?"

David shook his head sadly. He lay back, staring towards the ceiling.

"It's hard to say. You have the same orders drilled in your head so many times. Your feelings become compartmentalized. You begin to justify acts, even horrifying ones, in the name of sacrifice. For the greater good. It's like being caught in a spider's web. The venom of corruption numbs you."

He turned to Mike and took his hand.

"Take what you've learned, and raise your child well," he said softly. "Don't be taken in like me. Don't be drawn in by the darkness."

Chapter 113

MIKE LEFT THE HOSPITAL feeling forever changed. In the days following David's confession, life seemed to improve for the better. David put
Flapjack in contact with a reporter, whose story on the Undersecretary's
corruption was picked up by CNN. A congressional inquiry was made. The
Secretary of Defense himself was even called in for testimony. Everyone in
the Pentagon was eager to pin the blame elsewhere. The first evidence to
materialize was a letter, from a colonel in Texas, which explained the new
policies to military doctors. From there, the blame shifted to an intern with
the Secretary of Defense, a man named Garcia who had been caught on tape.
As it later turned out, there was no intern named Garcia—there had never
been one—and yet there was a recording that seemed to state otherwise.
Both Mike and Flapjack agreed it was a curious case. The more the thread
was pulled, the more the fabric seemed to unravel.

So who was this "Garcia?" The press clamored for an answer. Pentagon
lawyers fought a losing battle to censor the tape. Ultimately, the congressional committee decided to consider it as evidence. As Creaser, Flapjack, and
Mike listened, they looked at one another knowingly. They could all tell
who it was.

Then, almost as quickly as it began, the investigation stalled. Neither
Mike nor his colleagues could make sense of it. Press interest evaporated.
The committee issued a statement discontinuing their inquiry. In a poof
of smoke, the issue had disappeared completely. In its place came public
endorsements from high profile congressmen. In their words, Secretary
Rumsfeld was a paragon of virtue. He and the Pentagon cared deeply about
disabled veterans, they claimed. The alleged policy changes were excused as
a product of miscommunication.

Mike, for his part, remained skeptical. He had long since learned that
money was the great problem solver in a bureaucracy. Money and   power.

And the neo-cons had them in spades. The VA would go on to approve only a third of PTSD claims over the following months. One base in Colorado was even found using a "forensics team" to reduce or deny benefits. The team would review cases for complaints which, they claimed, "might have been exaggerated by the soldier." In such cases, the patients were diagnosed with "Personality Disorder," rather than PTSD. The practice not only reduced costs, it protected the doctors from being charged individually.

Even after the forensic teams were disbanded, however, rates of PTSD continued to skyrocket. Soldiers were still deployed often and for extended tours in combat areas. The more things changed, thought Mike, the more things stayed the same.

Even these setbacks, however, could not entirely dampen Mike's mood. David had recovered after a successful endarterectomy. Anna and Flapjack had never seemed happier. Finally, Mike felt like a part of the *whole* family now, with David included. Meanwhile, the media exposure brought him new allies and research grants. For the first time, Mike no longer felt like he and Flapjack were alone in their fight. There were good, ethical men and women who wanted to support veterans' rights. Many officers and physicians were horrified by the military's efforts to conceal its widespread corruption.

For the first time, Mike began to think, perhaps the tide would finally turn. Perhaps this was their moment.

Chapter 114

"I'M SURE YOU'RE wondering why I've called you here today."

Mike smirked. He must have heard the words a thousand times. Creaser was a creature of habit. His opening phrase hadn't changed in a decade.

"Good news, I hope."

"Why Michael," he gasped, cocking an eyebrow, "why on earth wouldn't it be."

Mike chuckled. "Gosh, where do I start?"

"At the beginning."

"Well, let's see. We've heard rumors from the directorate that there'll be new attempts to change the diagnoses of PTSD victims. Flapjack mentioned it this morning. They're calling it PTI, 'Post-Traumatic Injury,' or something similar. Apparently that would suggest a likely recovery and thus disqualify them for benefits and disability. And don't get me started on their ridiculous plan to study "biomarkers" in the blood that supposedly predict the likelihood of PTSD. Shall I go on?"

Creaser laughed. He raised his arms in mock surrender. "All right, all right! You've made your point. But believe it or not, I come today bearing *good* news."

"Is that so."

"I've chosen my successor."

"Your successor?"

"The next surgeon general."

Mike peered at him curiously. Then the realization dawned on him. "Oh God, please," he begged. "Please don't let this mean what I think it means."

Creaser doubled-over laughing. "I knew it, I just knew you'd say that," he said, as he fought to regain composure. "And that's exactly why you're the man for the job. The only man I trust."

"I appreciate it. Believe me, I do," blustered Mike. "I just don't think I'm the kind of man for the job. I'm a researcher, not a negotiator, and it just seems that everything we were assigned is irrelevant at best, or part the administration's agenda at worst." Mike sighed. "I get what the Secretary is doing is *probably* not illegal, but still, they refuse to follow operational policies and procedures. It's almost as if they make up the rules as they go along."

"Your point being?"

"How am I supposed to work with people like that?"

It was true, Mike thought to himself. If anything, he had understated his case. The religious-right was more emboldened now than they were under Reagan. The Bush administration had invested millions towards the development of "Resilience Programs," designed to handle such problems as "cowardice" or "faith-deficit disorder." Even the Psychology Association had jumped into bed with the neo-cons, defending their methods against allegations by the CIA that they were "useless and cruel." The rejection of these programs by the Rand Corporation had little effect. If they couldn't make a difference, Mike wondered, then how could he?

"You surprise me, Mike," said Creaser, a bemused expression on his face. "You really do. I thought you'd see this as a chance to make a difference."

"With all due respect," Mike answered, "I've always been the researcher. I've never been able to act as proactively as you."

"How so?"

Mike thought for a moment. "Well," he began, "I remember when Bush won the presidency, and we suddenly had to fight tooth and nail to get the necessary providers for optimal care. You almost immediately developed a computer model to calculate how the department's needs changed over time. It was a program that could accurately gauge the staffing needs for injuries in chemical, biological, and nuclear warfare. Every type of injury was covered, too, from massive burns to radiation exposure."

Creaser smirked. "Ah, I remember that," he recalled. "That program could transfer staff from base-to-base, too, depending on need. All while saving the government money."

"Exactly."

"But what you're forgetting," added Creaser, "is that my models were discarded without even a second thought. They didn't even look at them. No one wanted to 'waste their time' learning a new system, even if it meant saving lives and billions of dollars annually." Creaser slumped into his chair sadly. "So you see, I'm no more able to force others to change than you, Flapjack, or anyone else."

"But why now," asked Mike. "Why all of a sudden."

"Because," began Creaser, looking crestfallen and beaten. "You and I both know I've had heart complications in the past. Well, I received some test results from the Sibley Hospital yesterday. Three of my arteries are closing up."

Mike gasped. He had known Creaser was having chest pains, sure, but he never would have guessed the severity. As far as he knew, it was just a bad case of acid reflux.

"I'll need emergency bypass surgery," Creaser continued grimly. "I'll be frank. There is always the possibility of complications. I'm hoping for the best, of course, but regardless, I'm getting my affairs in order."

"Don't talk that way!" cried Mike. "I'm sure you'll be all right! You can beat this."

"I've already decided," Creaser insisted. "We cannot risk the work we've been doing. If I don't come back, I know they'll replace me with one of their cronies, someone they can use to shut down our efforts permanently."

Mike swallowed the lump in his throat. His head was swimming. It was all so much to take in, at once.

"How can I help?" he offered.

"I'm naming you Acting Director," Creaser announced firmly. "If I don't make it back, my nomination for you to become surgeon general will be put forward."

"And if they resist?"

Creaser furrowed his brow. "You may have a fight on your hands," he conceded. "But I have a trump card up my sleeve." He winked. "I'll tell you, but it's not to be revealed to anyone. Not even your wife."

"I understand."

"The Secretary of Defense is resigning," said Creaser excitedly. He leaned over his desk, as though under surveillance. "The man replacing him is a personal friend of mine. His methods are a bit unorthodox. He likes to be called 'The Boss.'"

"I've heard of him," said Mike. "But I've never met him."

"Yes, Robert Gates." Creaser chuckled. "He's a good man. Worked with Air Force intelligence for several years. Has decades of experience under his belt. I expect you'll work well together."

The rest of the meeting passed in a blur. Only the concrete details stood out in Mike's mind. The Secretary would resign within three weeks. Over the next few months, "The Boss" would need Mike's support in building his directorate. The new Secretary would likely bring in staff from the CIA, and Mike was to tell no one of his prior work with "The Agency." He would have to play his cards close to his chest.

"And for the love of God," Creaser had warned him, "don't say anything bad about the current Secretary of Defense! You never know who might be listening."

Chapter 115

MIKE'S PROMOTION MADE him feel deeply uncomfortable. It was almost as though he'd been tricked into the role, he thought, as if the choice was never his to begin with. Still, he couldn't fault Creaser for his actions. The general had been proactive as usual, even with his own mortality on the line. Mike, on the other hand, felt awkward and unsure of himself. Aside from his time on Guam, he had never felt like part of the Air Force. Doctors like him were seen only as "assets." They were not a link in the chain-of-command. They didn't give orders. Their purpose was to act as caretakers for the broken and the defective. The job description was clear, either fix the patient or send him packing. There was no room for ambiguity. No time for reflection.

Now here I am, Mike thought to himself; on the verge of becoming the Chief Surgeon of the USAF. It would be his responsibility to oversee the operations in all Air Force hospitals. He would be the one lobbying Congress for legislation. The well-being of veterans and their families would fall on his shoulders. Just the thought of it all felt overwhelming.

"You shouldn't be so hard on yourself," Flapjack had admonished him, after a long first day at his post.

"How can I not?" he lamented. "How can I even begin to address what our folks in Iraq and Afghanistan need? I've never even been there. Hell, I've never even been in a fire fight."

"And thank God for that!"

Mike groaned. "The sooner Creaser recovers the better," he continued, cracking open another beer on the couch.

"Oh come on, Mike."

"I'm serious! The first few times someone called me 'General,' I didn't even respond. I just looked behind me, like I was expecting to see someone older; someone wiser than me."

Flapjack laughed. "Well, get used to it, General Pike," she joked. "You've worked as hard as anyone to earn that title. You deserve it."

"I sure hope so," said Mike, as he stared at the ceiling above him. "Because I have 43,000 medical personnel taking care of 2.5 million people globally. How do I even begin to know how and where to distribute those resources?"

Flapjack shrugged. "I dunno. But you could start by asking."

*   *   *

The next morning, Mike called his first team meeting. He had to hand it to his staff. Everyone was settled and ready in the conference room in under five minutes. Well, here goes nothing, he thought to himself.

Overall, the meeting was more painless than he expected. The staff all seemed comfortable with his promotion. Everyone was relieved to hear that Creaser's condition was improving. His wife must be a miracle worker, Mike thought to himself. She was the perfect nurse and caretaker. After the initial announcements, Mike cut right to the point. He needed comprehensive information on their worldwide operations. There were five young captains, each of whom managed a section of the department, and they agreed to produce an integrated report. Their weekly meetings would continue as scheduled.

The meeting did raise a few concerns, however. One captain, the man in charge of the stateside operation, had reported being overwhelmed by the demand for psychiatric treatment of children. The volume of requests was already eleven-times higher than average. Meanwhile, the department sorely lacked the necessary manpower. Under Creaser, Mike was told, they had already begun contracting out to private providers. Insurance companies would usually manage patients or refer them to providers at a discount. It was little comfort to Mike that they weren't alone in their concern. Both the Army and Navy had reported the same issue.

It troubled Mike that children were being sent to pediatric clinics to be medicated. There were simply no therapy services available. Many wives of service members, too, were requesting treatment for anxiety and depression, the result of long-term deployments. The divorce rate was increasing exponentially. With reports like that, it was perhaps not surprising that bases were reporting high suicide rates. For many, the combination of depression, PTSD, alcohol, drugs, and divorce had made life intolerable. Easy access to guns offered a final escape.

As he met each captain in his office, Mike's concerns only deepened. One of the men described how servicemen were leaving the military in record numbers. The VA, for its part, was already stretched beyond capacity, and unable to handle the number of traumatic brain injuries, dismemberment victims, and spinal injuries arriving daily. The numbers were stunning. The sheer cost of these wars—in both blood and money—made Mike sick. It was clear the Secretary's office had never been forthcoming with the statistics. Had the President even bothered to read them?

Acting as surgeon general was every bit as hard as Mike expected. The weight of responsibility weighed heavy on his shoulders. No longer could he leave his work at the office. At night, he would lie awake in the dark. The faces of the fallen haunted him. In his dreams, he would wander a barren wasteland, a desert expanse littered with corpses. The sands were stained with the blood of 1.2 million Iraqi civilians. Among the fathers, wives, and children, were the bodies of the soldiers. There were over 9,000 of them now. Some were still in the early throes of rigor mortis. On others, the tatters of their uniform still clung to bleached bones. Their eyes were hollow and sightless.

Often he would awake in a cold sweat.

How did they sleep, Mike often wondered. How could they look in the mirror, those politicians and businessmen who found opportunity in the tragedy of others? It was obvious now that this was not a war fought for freedom. Nor was it for the betterment of the people of Iraq. Oil companies and corporations had carved the country up amongst themselves. It was the wealthiest conservative donors who won the biggest slice of the pie. Many, Mike knew, were heavily involved with the Christian groups that had infiltrated the government and the Pentagon. Congress had made some effort to curb privatization, but it would prove woefully ineffective. Over 80% of Iraq's oil was now exported to the west, while over 25% of the country continued to starve.

Such were the complex webs of deception that controlled America. Mike often wondered if so many lives had been sacrificed in vain. They had been led to slaughter on the altar of the American oligarchy. And now, even as Surgeon General, there seemed little he could do.

Chapter 116

AFTER MIKE'S FIRST WEEK at his new post, he finally found time to pay Creaser a visit. Even now, with his symptoms abating, his wife Mary continued to fret over him. The general, for his part, was in high spirits that weekend. His nights had been restful for the first time in ages. He was still on a soft diet, but had begun spending more time on his feet each day. If not for the old pajamas, Mike thought, his old boss seemed as bright and alert as usual.

Mike was hesitant initially to discuss work at the Pentagon. It seemed like that last thing a man recovering from surgery should worry about. Still, Creaser was headstrong as ever, and demanded at least a brief report. Against his better judgment—and a look of reproach from Mary—Mike described how he was reviewing their global operations. He was still trying to learn all the ropes. Whatever the trick was, he lamented, he had not learned it yet. He was beginning to doubt he ever would.

"My boy," Creaser laughed, "There is no trick. Believe me. I used to dread going to work each day. The constant reports of injury and death. I was having nightmares long before my surgery."

"I've been having them too," Mike nodded.

"In fact, I was anticipating a heart attack long before I felt the symptoms."

"Oh, come now!" cried Mary. She turned to Mike anxiously. "He's just saying that because of the pain medications."

"Nonsense! In fact, I think it would have been a relief!"

"Edward!"

Mary stormed from the room in a huff. Creaser snorted.

"Eh, she does that all the time these days," he explained to Mike nonchalantly. "The whole ordeal has made her quite emotional." Creaser paused. He smiled sheepishly.

"I suppose I shouldn't say what I've been meaning to tell you, Michael."

"And why's that?"

"Because you might storm out as well!" Creaser chuckled weakly. "Ah, but I suppose it has to come out some time. I'm afraid your tenure as Surgeon General may be longer than expected."

"*Acting* Surgeon General," Mike quickly corrected. "And I'm sorry to hear that," he added. "The staff misses you a great deal. How much longer will you need me to run the show?"

"Well..." Creaser began, averting his eyes. "Indefinitely, it would seem."

Mike sat up in concern. "Indefinitely?" he echoed. "Are you alright, sir? Is something wrong with your recovery."

"Not at all!" declared Creaser. "In fact, I feel healthier than I have in a long time. And I'd like to keep it that way."

"So you're saying..."

"I'm saying I'm not coming back, Michael. I'm retiring."

"You're retiring?!" cried Mike, his eyes wide as saucers.

"That's right," answered Creaser. He smiled nervously and extended his hand. "Congratulations, Surgeon General Pike."

* * *

Mike left Creaser's room feeling more overwhelmed than before. The house was quiet, save for the ticking of a grandfather clock. Outside, the wind was howling fiercely. It had begun to rain.

"Would you like some cocoa?"

Mike paused. Mary's voice filtered melodically from the sitting room. He had already tied his boots and pulled on his jacket.

"That's all right, Mrs. Creaser," he apologized. "I don't mean to be an imposition."

"Oh, nonsense," Mary replied sternly. "I won't have you running around out there. Not in weather like this."

"If you insist!"

A warm, steaming mug of hot chocolate was awaiting Mike on the coffee table. It was next to a plate of homemade cookies. From her chair by the fire, Mary smiled at him softly.

"I really appreciate this, Mrs. Creaser," offered Mike, with a mouthful of chocolate chip cookie. He brought a napkin to his mouth in embarrassment.

"Oh, it's nothing really," reassured Mary. Her eyes never left her knitting. "To be honest, I'm the appreciative one. I haven't had someone to talk to in ages. No one besides Edward, at least, and he hasn't been himself since the operation."

Mike nodded. "I would imagine so," he agreed. "It's been hard on everyone, these days. He's had to deal with a lot."

"All he talks about now is the war," she continued sadly. "The illegality of it all. How Saddam had allowed U.N. inspections and posed no real threat. How Iraq wasn't recognized as a 'rogue state.' And it's all true, I know." She paused to wipe a tear from her eye. "But the anger and bitterness of it all... it's like it's consumed him."

Mike tried to find words to comfort her. He wanted to tell her that it would be okay. That Creaser would return to his old self. That everything would work out for the best. He wanted to believe it himself.

Try as he might, the words never came.

Chapter 117

OVER THE NEXT few weeks, Mike felt like a drowning man. Every day was a fight to stay afloat. It was not until three months later that he was thrown a life-preserver. Finally, Robert Gates became Secretary of Defense, and Mike saw him as nothing less than a savior.

Just as Creaser predicted, "The Boss" assumed his new role with confidence and conviction. The changes were immediate. High-ranking generals were replaced. A new mandate was established to bring troops home. New strategies were implemented. Once again, research was encouraged and financed. Nuclear war with Iran was to be avoided at all cost. One step at a time, the new secretary reigned in the influence of the military-industrial complex. Anxiety and paranoia decreased in the Pentagon for the first time in years.

The fact that "The Boss" was supportive was a breath of fresh air for Mike. To his surprise, the Secretary approved of his work in office, and immediately advanced him as the next surgeon general. Mike's attempts to resist fell on deaf ears. Creaser had recovered, but he remained steadfast in his determination to retire. The more time they spent together, the more Mike realized what Mary had been talking about. The old general wasn't the same anymore. He was constantly moody and sensitive now. For the most part, Mike left him in peace. The man had already dealt with enough.

Finally, the day came when Mike formally took office. He was the new Surgeon General. Secretary Gates came in person to congratulate him.

"I know you're a man of character," he had said, as he shook Mike's hand. "And I know you're very service oriented, and want to improve the lives of military families."

Mike flushed. He wished his palms weren't so sweaty. "Well, I'm ready to work, sir," he affirmed. "I want to do what's best for our veterans and their wives and children."

"Well, we're cutting back on our instruments of war," Gates continued. "I want you to play an integral role in our operations. If you can put together a proposal, I'd be willing to put more resources at your command. Is something wrong, General Pike?"

Mike stared in disbelief. Then vigorously shook his head. "No sir!" he exclaimed. "It's just, I never thought I'd hear those words. We've always had to fight for every inch we could get!"

Gates laughed. "Well then, I trust you'll be ready tomorrow."

"Tomorrow?"

"Your proposal! In your office, 0800 hours." Gates continued to chuckle as he walked to the door. "And don't forget," he added, "this is your big chance. So make it count!"

*   *   *

Flapjack knew he had good news when he walked in the door. She could read Mike like a book by now. Even then, it was obvious to anyone from the grin on his face. His eyes brightened and he told her the news with breathless excitement. It was a side of her husband Flapjack had not seen in a long, long time. The sense of curiosity and enthusiasm had awoken, and he seemed like a kid again. The two threw themselves into their work.

After a long night with little sleep, Mike arrived at his office. He had taken special care that morning to arrive at work early. Now he had enough time to caffeinate himself and rehearse his proposal. Everything had to be perfect. He and Flapjack had spent hours sifting through years of statistics and reports. Finding the best material wasn't easy, as a flood of articles had followed Moon's original publication. It was hard to believe, Mike thought, that when he and Flapjack began their research, so little had been written on military families. Back in the Vietnam era, the military family as an institution had been a novel concept!

Mike tried to keep his mind occupied. As the minutes ticked by, he could feel himself shaking with anticipation. The Secretary arrived right on schedule.

"All right," he began, his arms folded from across the desk. "You have one hour of my undivided attention, General. Begin."

Mike cleared his throat. "Mr. Secretary," he began, "our troops have been exposed to the same hazards they were during WWII.   .

Safeguards have been developed to protect them, but for decades we have failed to utilize them. In the meantime, these hazards have continued to cause severe handicaps in personal and vocational functioning. The rates of early dementia, depression, divorce, domestic abuse, addiction, and even suicide continue to rise exponentially. You may be familiar with the Holocaust lawsuit based on intergenerational PTSD. Well, I would say these current wars will only lead to more bloodshed, all because of the intergenerational PTSD they are causing."

Mike paused for a drink. He had begun tentatively, but the more he spoke, the more sure of himself he became. Now it was a matter of letting it all sink in.

"These wars have overwhelmed our VA services," he continued passionately. "They put a tremendous financial burden on taxpayers for treatment and disability funding. And still, it's never enough. I'm sure you're aware of how the previous administration has fought to block our efforts. We attempted to deal with these hazards, and were met with resistance, denial, and rejection. The efforts of the Bush administration were focused on hiding these problems from troops, their families, and the public at-large.

The Secretary raised his hand. "I appreciate what you're saying," he interrupted brusquely. "But let's talk solutions. What plans did you have in mind."

Mike grinned. "Good question," he answered, as he passed the secretary a folder. "You'll find all the details in my report. First, I believe there needs to be a mechanism by which these hazards are identified and corrected. A mechanism preferably developed in the office of the Surgeon General, protected from outside interference."

The Secretary nodded thoughtfully as he turned over the pages. "It's an interesting idea," he conceded. "Go on."

"We also need to establish a 'best practices' rule. Right now, our deployments can last 15 months or longer, and troops can be deployed frequently with little relief. Hell, our troops have been taking psychiatric medication *in the field!* We need to adopt NATO's recommendations. Deployment times must be reduced. A period of rest between deployments must be mandated."

"Is that so?"

"And we have to somehow do away with 'Stop-Loss' orders, which extend the length of deployments," Mike added. "They are extremely demoralizing and contribute to the incidence of PTSD."

406 D o n   M i c h a e l   l a G r o n e ,   M D

"And you really think the problem is that substantial?" asked the Secretary. The tone in his voice had turned from skeptical to concerned. Mike knew he had hit a nerve.

"There's no question these lengthy and multiple deployments are a problem for families," he answered. "Anxiety disorders are already a third higher than civilian rates. If a soldier returns with PTSD, he can pass that disorder on to his spouse and children. Incidences of anxiety, depression, and post-traumatic stress are high in these families. The cost of providing treatment for all these cases can run into the billions. And who do you think foots the bill?"

"The Boss" listened thoughtfully to Mike's appeal. Every so often he would nod in agreement, or jot something down in his notebook. "If what you're saying is true," he said finally, "then we need to act, and act fast. Otherwise we'll have one hell of a legal problem on our hands. There's bound to be proof that generations have been hurt by our leadership."

"I can't argue with that."

"What we need now is a massive overhaul. There needs to be a focused effort—a 'surge,' if you will—to identify and treat those affected."

"That makes sense," Mike agreed. "That ought to help us in the long-run. Eventually we'll have to inform the public. When they learn what we know now, at least they can see we've made substantial progress. That ought to soften the backlash."

Gates smirked. "It'll still be a feeding frenzy," he replied, rubbing his chin ruefully. "It'll be just like the Agent Orange issue after Vietnam. Only worse, because spouses and children are involved."

The Secretary had a point, and Mike knew it. There was no sugarcoating it. When the news broke, they would have a huge liability on their hands. All they could do now was minimize the damage. If the public saw the government take responsibility, then maybe, just maybe, they could begin to heal old wounds. Lost trust could be rebuilt. Mike knew he was being idealistic, but he couldn't help it. There was still hope for the future.

"I'll expect an update on this 'treatment surge,'" the Secretary announced as he left. "One week from today. Same time, same place. Be ready!"

Chapter 118

FLAPJACK'S INITIAL EXCITEMENT turned to shock and dismay.

"You're kidding me," she gasped, as Mike told her the news.

"Nope. We have one week and all the resources at our disposal!"

"But that's insane," she sputtered. "Don't get me wrong, I'm happy about the news, but it's not enough time!"

"Well, we have to at least try!" Mike countered. "The tools are there, all we need to do is build it."

"And hope that it works!"

"That too."

*   *   *

Mike called another meeting the next morning. After a few hours of brainstorming, the team had developed the rough outline for the task ahead. First, all the relevant literature had to be reviewed, to gauge of scope of their "surge." As he returned to work, Mike could sense the anticipation in the air. Even the younger and more headstrong officers seemed daunted by the project. He couldn't blame them. His office would have to identify and care for thousands—if not millions—of patients, all suffering from the trauma of war. With a staff as small as theirs, the odds were against them.

At the next meeting, an important consensus was reached. All five captains agreed that every branch of the military was understaffed by at least 50%. The Army, Navy, and Air Force would each require an additional 200 to 600 psychiatrists, psychologists, social workers, nurse practitioners, and physician's assistants. The cost could range anywhere from 4 to 6 billion, and was necessary immediately to meet the current demand. To accommodate those families affected before the 21st Century would be almost impossible. But the word "impossible," Mike reminded them, was not in the Secretary's vocabulary.

It still amazed Mike that the system had devolved so severely. Things hadn't always been this way. He had read how the mental health movement was born and flourished under President Kennedy. Under the old MHMR system—which stood for "mental health and mental retardation"—clinics were established throughout the country. There were enough caseworkers to help those with chronic disabilities. Quality care could be ensured. It was a time when psychiatrists and social workers worked closely with families in need. Housing and group homes were even available, so patients weren't confined in state schools and hospital rooms. It had been a different time. An era of progress.

Then the train fell off the rails.

It didn't happen suddenly. Changes were slow and imperceptible. Gradually, as years passed, the system began to erode. Cracks formed in the foundations. Conservatives cut funding to the bone. Staffers were laid off and clinics were shut down. The number of homeless veterans increased dramatically. If they weren't struggling in the gutters, they were rotting in the prisons, as incarceration rates reached record highs.

From there, the system turned from bad to worse. Privatized prisons were built and filled to capacity. Corruption was rife, as judges took kickbacks from wealthy contractors. It was only a matter of time before there were more people in prison than in the military. By then, it seemed like the government was waging a war against the poor, the disenfranchised, and the mentally ill.

And now, here I am, thought Mike. Tasked with cleaning up the mess in a week.

*   *   *

Finally, the week came and went, and Mike was back in his office on pins and needles. This time, "The Boss" wasn't alone when he arrived. He had brought two of his senior staff members along, and they trailed behind him like obedient puppies.

Mike was surprised to feel his nerves disappear. Presenting to Gates felt more familiar now. It was no mystery where he stood with the Secretary. The man spoke his mind, and was always open to ideas.

"You have forty-five minutes of my time, General Pike."

"First," Mike began, "we've developed a program of primary prevention. Now, occupational hazards can be identified and eliminated."

"And the issue with deployments?"

"We have workable plans from the British and NATO. Both have reduced their PTSD rates substantially. Using those, we've put together a plan that could reduce veteran and family-related cases of PTSD by 75%"

Secretary Gates perked up at the mention of statistics. It was the response Mike had hoped for. All the altruism in the world meant nothing without concrete results.

"Occupational hazards should be addressed in all aspects of resiliency training," he continued. "Shifting from a draft to volunteer force was no excuse for deceptive recruiting practices. 'Informed Consent' must be established as a written regulation, as it is in Britain. We must do away with the practice of issuing 'Stop-Loss' orders to extend tours of duty."

"But sir," interrupted one of the Secretary's aids. "What about our current resiliency program?"

"It's probably illegal," Mike countered. "Not only does it violate the Nuremberg Rules, but there's no evidence that it's in any way effective. It's been denounced by the Rand Corporation."

"And proposals to search for genetic markers of PTSD?"

Mike shook his head. "A ruse. A ruse, and a waste of funds."

The Secretary began to stand as Mike finished. He extended his hand forward. "Well, I appreciate the report," he declared. "I do have a few questions about treatment effectiveness and liability, however. And I'll need to meet with the other Surgeons General."

"There's one more thing," Mike added. "And this is from the research of Major Fielder."

Gates smirked. "Flapjack, eh?" He checked his watch. "All right, but make it quick."

"We need to address the rising rates of sexual assault and harassment on military bases," Mike insisted. "These rates are higher than ever before, and are linked to the incidence of PTSD."

"And what do you suggest, general?"

"At the moment, the major has been working with a congresswoman on a bill that would remove such cases from the chain-of-command. We feel we cannot offer a comprehensive plan without including this measure, as it has been neglected by previous administrations."

"It's certainly an interesting idea," agreed the Secretary. "You'll receive my response very soon."

Chapter 119

MIKE DID NOT have long to wait. The good news came almost immediately. Most of their requests had been approved for funding. A part of the budget was to be set aside to implement the program and recruit mental health providers. The use of "Stop-Loss" orders would be severely reduced.

The other Surgeons General may not have been psychiatrists, but even they seemed aware of the flaws in the system. Mike was also pleased to learn that Flapjack's work had been approved. "The Boss" not only supported, but encouraged her work with the congresswoman on the issue of rape.

Of course, these rewards came with a steep price. Mike and Flapjack found themselves working long hours to implement the planned "surge." Over the next few months, their time together became limited. Gradually, however, the new recruitment and development plans began to come together. New rules for troop deployment were adopted along NATO guidelines. Finally, at long last, the military was taking care of its members. There was change on the horizon.

*   *   *

Finally, after all their hard work, it was time for a break. It was on Creaser's insistence. The last thing he wanted, he told Mike, was for him to wear himself out. After all, it was stress and overwork that put him in the hospital in the first place. The Secretary of Defense agreed. He had full confidence in Mike's staff. They would be able to function without him for a few days, at least.

Mike and Flapjack began their break with a dinner at the Creaser's. Mary had planned an elaborate banquet. Creaser himself surprised them with a bottle of vintage champagne. He popped the cork, and filled each glass with bubbling wine.

"General Creaser, this first toast is for you," declared Mike, raising his glass. "When I first met you, I had no idea what it meant to be an officer. You were my mentor. Throughout your career, you have fought for the health and well-being of our soldiers and their families. I have watched you self-lessly work hundreds of hours to make the Air Force a safer place."

The old general blushed, but clinked his glass with the rest of them. "Hear, here!" agreed Flapjack. "You worked with us on our research even when it was against your best interests. I may not have been on this journey as long as you and Mike have, but it's been one hell of a trip, for sure!"

Creaser smiled politely. He graciously accepted their praise. Still, he seemed subdued, as if there were something on his mind. He took little part in the conversation, and barely touched his food.

"Why Edward," Mary finally asked, "is something wrong? You look troubled."

Creaser sighed. "I suppose," he said with a shrug. "Don't get me wrong, I'm overjoyed with our success. It's just… it's just that those idiots have caused so much damage already. I wonder how much we can do."

"The surge in Iraq seems to be going well, too," Flapjack offered helpfully. "So the war should be over soon!"

"The war that shouldn't have been," shot Creaser.

"Edward!"

"Well, it's true."

"Please excuse him," Mary apologized. "It's all been hard for him. We've decided to move back to North Carolina next month. Our daughter lives there, and I think she can cheer him up."

The conversation quickly shifted to personal matters. Edward and Mary spoke proudly of their daughter and her family. She had two children of her own now, and was considering retirement when her girls finished college. The general considered it a ridiculous plan. How could she support herself, he asked, with a husband that only talked about teeth? Mike laughed along with the others. For the first time in a long time, he felt himself relax.

* * *

After a long and hearty meal, the evening began to wind down. Flapjack and Mary were in the sitting room now, looking through a photo album. Mike began to work on the dishes. For a long while, Edward sat pensively at the table. Finally, he began to speak, his voice soft by serious.

"Mike."

"Hm?"

"Mike," he repeated. "Come close. Have a seat for a moment."

Mike paused. He dropped the sponge in the sink and approached curiously. "Is something wrong?" he asked. "I mean, is everything all right."

"No," Creaser lamented. "No, to be honest, Mike, I'm disturbed with what I've been hearing. You and I have only scratched the surface of the Bush Administration. Concealing occupational hazards is only one in a long list of abuses they committed. Now there are accusations coming from abroad that the CIA was ordered to lose people."

"To lose people?"

"To make them disappear," he clarified. "It was hidden from the Red Cross, too. They're still trying to find those missing individuals. In fact, the Red Cross has publicly recommended the prosecution of Bush and Cheney. Ramsey Clark's campaign to impeach them has been developing steam. The Spanish courts have considered trying them for war crimes."

"That could be interesting," Mike mused. "Considering they finally convicted Pinochet."

"There's a law professor in Illinois, a Dr. Boyle," Creaser continued. "He's been articulating this very well, and has called for the Hague to get involved."

"On what grounds?"

"He's found a legal basis for prosecution in this torture nightmare they've carried out. It violates the Geneva Convention, the Nuremberg Charter, Article Two of the Constitution, the Army Field Manual, and several statutes in the U.N. Charter."

"'Who's been telling you all this?"

"I have my sources," snapped Creaser, his voice beginning to rise. "And that's not all. They are saying the administration is wanting to target both Iran and Pakistan. Conservatives have been carrying out a campaign against Muslims that resembles Truman's treatment of the Japanese in WWII. Bush and his cronies have committed conspiracy in their effort to hide evidence, promote torture, and fabricate reasons for war. There's a tribunal in Malaysia that might take up the issue."

"But these aren't international courts," Mike protested. "Wouldn't it have to be tried at the Hague to really matter?"

Creaser pursed his lips thoughtfully. "They can at least influence the Hague to take the case," he rationalized. "They can publicize the crimes internationally. The thing is, I'm concerned about the senior officers in the military. I know several of them personally, and I truly believe they were kept in the dark through all this."

"Are they at risk of being charged?"

"We're always at risk, Mike."

Mike frowned. "But why was the administration so generous with our budget and our plan to extend the medical corps?"

"That's 'The Boss' pushing back. It's damage control now. He and others know they could be accused of war crimes. Taking care of soldiers now is just a PR strategy. They can always change it back when the heat dies down."

"I know." Mike sighed. "I suppose I knew from the start. The thing is, I don't even blame them. Not anymore. I'm just happy to have their support, for now, and I just hope we can finish what we started."

"I must say, Mike," Creaser lamented, "as old as I am, I still wonder how men and women can be so evil. I figured one day, when I was wiser, I would figure it all out. Now I suppose I'll never know."

The two sat in silence for a moment. A thought struck Mike, and he rummaged through his pockets. The paper he fished out was crumpled and frayed at the edges. It was almost falling apart after being folded and re-folded so often. He carefully opened it.

"You know General," he said, as he smoothed out the creases, "David is often fond of quoting Robert Frost. He gave me this poem once. I suppose I've kept it with me ever since."

"A poem?"

"It's called 'Design'," said Mike, handing the page to Creaser. "It comes the closest to answering your question, I think."

Creaser was intrigued. He read over the lines carefully, reciting them softly.

> *I found a dimpled spider, fat and white,*
> *on a white heal-all, holding up a moth*
> *like a piece of rigid satin cloth-*
> *assorted characters of death and blight*
> *mixed ready to begin the morning right,*
> *like the ingredients in a witches' broth-*
> *a snow drop spider, a flower like a froth,*
> *and dead wings carried like a paper kite.*

Creaser looked up in bewilderment. "What the hell does this even mean?" he asked. Mike motioned for him to continue.

> *What had that flower to do with being white,*
> *the wayside blue and innocent heal—all?*
> *What brought the kindred spider to that height*
> *then steered the white moth thither in the night?*
> *What but designs of darkness to appall?-*
> *If design govern in a thing so small.*

"David told me once that he took a class with Frost at Dartmouth," Mike explained. "The poet was writing a lot about death back then. There was a particular passage in the Old Testament that inspired him. The one from Solomon, which said that God did not create death. I suppose the simple truth of that intrigued him."

"I'm still a bit confused," Creaser admitted. "But go on."

"Death was a fascinating topic to Frost. He wanted to understand where it came from; why it existed. He conceived the idea of the 'designs of darkness," where darkness is not only the absence of light, but the absence of what is good and righteous."

"The places where vast webs of deceit and corruption are woven," mused Creaser.

"Exactly. Death and destruction reign there. There is no protection for the innocent."

Creaser slumped back in his chair. There was a faraway look in his eye. "We get used to killing and righteousness is forgotten," he continued sadly. "It's a vicious cycle. We kill, then traumatize our children, who themselves become killers. Mercy and compassion are sacrificed on the altar of self-interest."

"But it's not too late," Mike argued. "We can still make a difference now."

"My God," Creaser muttered hollowly. "I still have all the images in my mind. All those boys from Vietnam. They came with missing limbs; with gaping holes in their chests. The blood was everywhere." He paused for a moment. His eyes grew wide, as if he saw the vision before him. "Once, when I was at Quang Tri, they brought me a young lieutenant to pronounce him dead. The kid was all blown to hell. Nothing was left but fragments of bone, chunks of flesh, and the scorched remains of a uniform.

The NVA had found his helmet. They paraded it around like a trophy—like the moth in your poem—until the rangers got it back."

Mike listened in horrified silence. The details Creaser described were so vivid. He could almost hear the cries and smell the napalm in the air. Tears were streaming from the general's eyes now. He let them fall as he continued.

"I can never forget the boy's name. Tommy. The same as my brother's son. He could have been my son, had I been lucky enough to have one of my own." He choked back a sob, and looked to Mike with bloodshot   eyes. "Will it ever end?"

"I don't know," whispered Mike. He was in shock. It was as though the voice he heard was not his own. Here he was, in the warmth and comfort of this home, and Tommy was dead. A tide of grief washed over him.

"I wish I knew."

Chapter 120

GENERAL CREASER HAD been right. It was only a matter of time. The day came when Gates arrived at Mike's office with the inevitable news. This wasn't his idea, he repeated several times. If it were up to "The Boss," then work would continue as planned. But alas, his hands were tied. Congress had rejected the plan to reduce the frequency and length of deployments. They had turned down his proposal for a treatment "surge," along with the plan to recruit more professionals.

"It's just a setback, is all," Gates had offered apologetically. "We can still go full steam ahead. We just have to work with what we have. I'm sure they'll come around."

Sure, thought Mike. Just like they always do. It was the same old story. Visiting the iniquity of the fathers upon the children, for generations to come.

A story with no ending. Ripples passing through our DNA.

Epilogue

General Pike's Journal

THE FOLLOWING selections have been reproduced from the journal of General Michael Pike in their entirety. Spelling and grammar have been edited for clarity. Entries are not presented in sequence.

United States Air Force Medical Service
Office of the Surgeon General
Washington, DC

12 December, 2013
The Creasers left for North Carolina soon after he left the hospital. I still talk with him from time to time. Since he installed me in my current spot, he expects a periodic report for his approval—or not! He still has medically-induced depression, which is common after cardiac bypass. Mrs. Creaser has been doing all she can while getting acquainted with her grandchildren. She tells she's teaching them violin. One of them played for the general and he smiled for the first time in months!

David and Anna still live in Bethesda. David is still doing four crossword puzzles a day. He's always eager to spend time with his grandchild. He likes to talk, sometimes hours, about his time in World War II and the CIA. All in all, he seems like a new man now. I never thought I'd call him a friend!

25 December, 2013
Our child, who is now 20 years old, insisted upon going to one of the service academies. Needless to say, we have our concerns about a military career which neither of us ever wanted for ourselves. Yet here we are. We are all celebrating Christmas today.

5 August, 2012

Sybil went to work for Planned Parenthood after she left the service. She was arrested for hitting a protester with his own sign at an anti-abortion rally. It even made the news! After that, she was a hero for the women's movement, and eventually won a congressional seat. She's still in office to this day, fighting for the rights of women everywhere.

2 June, 2012

The Rand group has determined the military's resilience training programs have little or no effect on prevention of PTSD.

18 March, 2009

The Boss issued instructions for commanders to cut the numbers of "Stop-Loss" orders, which extend the service time of soldiers. The practices should be phased out by 2011.

14 May, 2009

A letter from Cassie came. She finished law school a few years ago, and worked for the State Department until Bush was elected. She now runs a foster home in Virginia for abused children. She never reconciled with her father.

2 June, 2006

With help from General Creaser, I was able to have Christine transferred to the best residential treatment facility in the country. She lived five years before dying peacefully in her sleep. God rest her soul.

Because of equipment improvements, more soldiers have managed to survive with TBIs. It is estimated that two-thirds of our soldiers have TBIs of varying degrees. Over 10% percent are severe. About 50% die within in the first three months. Those who survive six months are still three-times more likely to die than in other developed nations. After going through a rehabilitation program, 80% of surviving veterans are sent home.

10 May, 2008

General Creaser was outraged at the numbers of orphans and widows the Vietnam War created. I'm surprised he didn't learn until now! He and his wife are working with Methodist and Catholic Charities to provide them shelter.

Creaser was particularly dismayed at the casualty numbers in the Iraqi war. Just recently he petitioned Congress for aid. Along with other retired generals, he called for the director's departure, and he joined with the Red Cross to condemn the administration's use of torture and confinement.

5 May, 2011
The Texas Board of Education, mostly Republicans, voted last year to exclude Thomas Jefferson from school textbooks. After reaction from educators and others, the decision was reversed. They also voted to omit the idea of separation of church and state.

1 April, 2006
Work Notes:
The attempted "conditioning" of wives failed after the initial trials. After the second and third attempts, the divorce rate had reached obscene heights. The whole project, which they've poured money into for two decades now, was finally declared a waste of time and resources. Worse, it's an egregious violation of civil rights! Yet another violation of the Nuremberg Code.

3 April, 2007
Corporations:

> "Hope we shall crush in its
> birth the aristocracy of our
> monied corporations which
> dare already to challenge
> our government to a trial
> by strength, and bid
> defiance to the laws of our country."
> —Thomas Jefferson

The Boss said you couldn't talk about national security unless you included the influence of corporations. He knew his military history. The idea of "war" had been invented by the first kings. Perhaps the cycle of war and PTSD started then? Gates tells me corporations have been with America from the start. Our titans of industry are just modern versions of tyrants of old. The Oil Kings, like Texaco, who sponsored the Nazis. The

Chariot King, Henry Ford, who sold trucks to the Nazis. The Cannon King, Alfred Krupp, who armed the Nazis. The Wall Street Kings. Those and the many others who thrived on the profits of war.

It's still a surprise to me that an elite Wall Street society, Kappa Beta Phi, remains a secret after all these years. They started back in 1929, on the eve of the Great Depression, and their members have always been the nation's wealthiest. They still meet annually at the St. Regis hotel in New York City, for a night of bacchanalian revelry. Their motto is, *Dum Vivamus Edimus et Biberimus*—"As long as we live, we will be eating and drinking," an old phrase of the Roman nobility. Some things never change.

4 April, 2007

Had another interesting talk with The Boss. The continuation of yesterday's subject. He argues that aristocrats have governed the poor since the 16th century. Back then, the Elizabethans said it was poverty that made people productive. Laws were passed to make the poor even poorer. The wealthy even built workhouses where the poor labored in deplorable conditions.

These ideas have not changed over the centuries. They are the basis of our new private prisons, where many young black males are sent to manufacture furniture for corporate owners. The U.S. has more people in prison the rest of the world combined. The dark truth is that almost no one escapes poverty. The rich have a constant supply of people to exploit. This has been the organizing principle of our culture.

Jefferson hated corporations, but even he couldn't stop them. So how can I? It all feels quite futile.

11 April, 2007

The corporate algorithm is designed to destroy the middle class entirely and reestablish the disparity between rich and poor. These corporations have no restraint. They're run by sociopaths.

Take Saddam Hussein, for instance. Extreme cases of malignant narcissism. His ego was ruthless. There was no reforming a man like that. No hope for salvation. He had to be destroyed.

We have studies now, too. Computer researchers at Texas A&M ran a series of character simulations. Psychopathic traits are essential in the business world. The most pathological in society thrive. More 'Designs'.

15 April, 2007
Pastor Roy was released today. He served only three years of his thirty-year sentence. I'm surprised he even wanted to leave. The facility they held him in was like a minimum-security Hilton. He practically owned the place. Apparently he won a lot of converts as well. They were collecting money from the guards, their families and all the local churches. He even had a television ministry from his cell. The warden let him go with the governor's blessing. The pastor's collaboration with terrorists was blamed on Patricio who was arrested again. He's still rotting in an overpopulated hellhole.

7 February, 2012
There are 260,000 homeless veterans in a given year. Of these, 45% have mental illnesses like PTSD.

After 2003, the suicide rate began to climb from 15 to 21 per 100,000.

After 2007, the suicide rate among veterans went from 18 to 22 per month.

There were over 320,000 servicemen with TBIs by 2010.

There are now almost 300,000 veterans with PTSD and depression. Troops with PTSD have a twofold risk of developing dementia.

Veterans of WWII and Korea continue to have a PTSD prevalence rate of 12%, 45 years after combat. From Vietnam, it is 30%.

The VA, as of 2010, has 650,000 patients. It takes 180 days to process a new claim for medical care, and there are now 550,000 disability claims. Instead of making known how overwhelmed they are, many VA hospitals are concealing their actual wait times for medical care.

As of September, 2012, there were still 271,000 Vietnam vets with PTSD. One third of those also had depression.

This is our legacy…

21 August, 2014
General Martin Dempsey, of the Joint Chiefs, said today that new Jihadists — the offspring of Al Quaeda — have emerged. ISIS poses an imminent threat to our homeland. They are trying to implement an "Armageddon strategy".

Speaking of the Armageddon, Rep. Bachmann has been claiming that Obama's policies are leading us to the apocalypse. She must have poor long-term memory. During Bush's term, the numbers of Christian fundamentalists grew within the government. The ones preaching about the "coming rapture." Among the general public, the number of Episcopalians and Presbyterians fell dramatically.

The fanatics seem to think Jesus will be returning as some "Warrior King," who kills with vengeance. Many Biblical scholars see this belief as a literal, concrete interpretation of scripture, and point to the ancient wars through the millennia.

Meanwhile, we have this problem of savagery in the Middle-East, where war has become injected into the generations to come. Perhaps it's a problem larger than Hell itself. If I were to ascribe to the fundamentalist view, this would only be resolved with the spear of Jesus thrust through the black heart of the Antichrist.

However, if Galileo was right, and there is a God who expects us to use the minds and hearts he gave us, I rather doubt this outcome. I prefer to think the Prince of Peace would have us solve our own problems. He might remind us of one of Solomon's songs, one that inspired Robert Frost.

> *Because God made not Death,*
> *neither delighteth he when the living perish.*
> *For He created all things that they might have their being.*
> *And the generative powers of the Earth are healthsome*
> *and there is no poison of destruction within them.*
> *Nor hath Hades royal dominion upon the Earth,*
> *for righteousness is immortal.*